Our greatest misfortunes come
to us from ourselves.

Rousseau

MIKE GAYLE

SEEING OTHER PEOPLE

Complete and Unabridged

CHARNWOOD
Leicester

First published in Great Britain in 2014 by
Hodder & Stoughton Ltd
London

First Charnwood Edition
published 2015
by arrangement with
Hodder & Stoughton Ltd
An Hachette UK company
London

A catalogue record for this book is available
from the British Library.

ISBN 978–1–4448–2560–2

Published by
F. A. Thorpe (Publishing)
Anstey, Leicestershire

Set by Words & Graphics Ltd.
Anstey, Leicestershire
Printed and bound in Great Britain by
T. J. International Ltd., Padstow, Cornwall

This book is printed on acid-free paper

A loud noise.

Like a door slamming followed by the scent of a heavy, sweet-smelling perfume. I opened my eyes but the darkness was impenetrable. Trying to make sense of it all I reached up with my right hand to the back of my head, clenching my teeth together in readiness for the moment my neurones would signal the full extent of my injuries. But there was nothing. No matter how hard I rubbed my scalp I couldn't find so much as a spot of tenderness, let alone the blood and bruising that I was expecting. I had been hit hadn't I? I'd been hit from behind. A blunt object. A stick or a club or something similar. So where was the damage?

I went over the little that I could remember. I'd been in East London. For the Divorced Dads' Club shoot. I'd had a drink with Carl the art editor and his assistant. I'd been using my new phone. Bella had texted me. I'd texted Bella. A young kid had approached me dressed as if auditioning for a part on a gritty TV drama as 'council estate youth #1'. He'd wanted a light for his cigarette. But he'd been wearing a Zippo around his neck. And then I'd been hit. Cigarette Boy must have been some kind of decoy, distracting me while his mate came up from behind. They must have been after my phone, laughing at me as I lay on the pavement.

1

The pavement.

I arched my back slightly. Whatever was underneath me was clearly not regulation paving stone. It felt soft. Like a bed. I fumbled around in the darkness. I had a duvet over me. I was in a bed, not lying on the pavement where I'd fallen. Who'd found me? Who'd picked me up? Was I in hospital? Nothing was making sense. Gingerly I touched my scalp again. Still no cuts or bruises. What was going on? Ridiculous thought: I'm not dead am I? I pinched my arm hard. The pain was very real. I attempted to collect my thoughts once more. I'd been mugged but I had no cuts. I'd been mugged but I was no longer on the street. I'd been mugged but someone had put me to bed. I touched my chest. I had no shirt on. I moved my hand downwards. I had no trousers or underwear on either. I was completely naked.

Now I really was panicked. An urban myth sprang to mind: the one about students getting drunk on a night out in Sheffield and then waking up in a Chinese hospital minus one of their kidneys. It couldn't be true, could it? Disconcerted by this theory I reached across to feel the wall behind me. Maybe there was a light somewhere. My hands knocked against a glass object. I ran my fingers over it. It felt like a lamp. I traced a line down the base to the cord and then along to the switch. Click. And then there was light. The bulb was quite dim, barely bright enough to read a book by. I looked around the room. I wasn't in hospital but I wasn't at home either. It was a medium-sized bedroom. On the wall nearest to me was a chest of drawers with a star-shaped mirror on top. Draped across some of the star's points were a number of necklaces and below that, lying flat on its side, a hairdryer. Against the far wall was an open clothes rail. The clothes were feminine, dresses, blouses and the like. There might even have been a fur coat on the end but it was hard to tell in the feeble light. On the wall partially obscured by the clothes rail was a Rothko print in a clip frame. I knew the print because Penny and I had bought one from the Museum of Modern Art on a trip to New York. It used to hang in the hallway of the last flat we rented before we bought our current house.

As I concluded that the regular inhabitant of this room was most likely a young woman I heard a gentle sigh emanating from the opposite side of the bed. I was not alone. I picked up the lamp and lifted it in the air a little so that I could get a better look. I almost dropped the lamp in shock. It was Bella. The intern. She was the person lying in the bed next to me. I carefully set the lamp back down on the bedside table and collated this new information together with what I already knew. I was naked in bed with a woman who was not my wife. The news hit me like a punch in the stomach. How could this have happened? The last thing I remembered was getting hit across the back of the head and now I was in bed with Bella. Was I dreaming? Was this part of some elaborate ruse? Maybe I'd just got the wrong end of the stick. I gently lifted the duvet up and took a peek underneath. She was naked too. I took a moment to digest this news. I

3

was naked in bed with a naked intern who I'd met for the first time less than a week ago. My stomach lurched uncontrollably as again I tried to recall the night before. I'd been out for a drink after the shoot and had been heading home. Bella had texted me. She'd wanted me to meet her. I'd told her I couldn't. She'd persisted and though sorely tempted I'd just about managed to say no. She'd promised me that I wouldn't regret it then . . . what exactly? I hadn't said yes to meeting her, I was sure of that, and yet here I was. And if I had said yes to meeting her then why couldn't I remember anything — not even the taxi ride over to Soho — about my evening with Bella, let alone how we'd ended up in bed? There had to be some kind of rational explanation for what had happened. There just had to be. And whatever the explanation I was absolutely sure that it wouldn't involve me having cheated on Penny.

I thought hard. Maybe I'd met up with Bella and we'd started drinking and had ended up so drunk that she'd taken me home and put me to bed. That made sense, surely? And maybe I didn't have any clothes on because . . . I don't know, maybe I'd been sick over myself and she'd put them in the machine to be ready for the morning. That sounded plausible. I never could hold my drink. Relieved to have conjured up a life-saving narrative I concluded the best thing I could do was grab my clothes and get out of there.

Easing aside the duvet I edged my legs out of the bed and stood up. The laminated floor beneath my feet felt cool but there was something rough stuck to the underside of my right heel. I reached down and plucked the offending object from my foot and studied it in the light of the lamp. It was an empty condom wrapper.

I felt sick.

I couldn't have, could I?

I looked over at Bella's sleeping form.

If I'd slept with Bella surely I'd remember it. I'd been faithful to Penny our entire relationship. Twenty whole years! If I'd cheated surely it would have made some sort of impact? This made no sense at all. I had to get out of here.

I scanned the floor and lying at my feet as though they had been abandoned in the heat of the moment were my clothes. I put them on as quickly as I could: underwear, socks, jeans, shirt and then my jacket which felt oddly weighted as though there was something in one of the pockets. I put my hand in the inside pocket and pulled out the object. It was my phone. But how could that be? What kind of attacker mugs someone but doesn't steal a phone when there's one there? I took it out and checked the screen. It was five twenty-five. This too confused me as I knew for a fact that Jack had been waking early all week because it was too light in his bedroom. I walked over to the window and pulled back a corner of the curtain to see a blackout blind beneath. I tugged that too and sure enough it was getting light outside. At least that was one mystery solved.

I wondered if my phone might be able to shed

5

any light on my activities the night before but after checking it I was left even more confused. The last text I remembered making was at 21.18 and read: *Really I can't* in response to Bella's promise not to keep me out too late. But then at 21.24 I'd apparently sent one saying: *I'm just looking for a taxi. I'll be there as soon as I can.* At 23.55 I'd sent a text to Penny: *Had a bit too much to drink. Will crash at Carl's place so as not to wake you+kids. Will call in morning. J xxx.* My brain throbbed under the weight of this revelation as I finally joined all the dots together. The mugging had been a dream. I'd obviously sent the texts, met up with Bella and having most likely dulled my conscience beyond all recognition had reached a point where I'd agreed to go home with Bella, covering my tracks with a text to Penny. With the exception of my lack of a hangover — how could I have drunk so much that I'd forgotten the whole night and yet didn't have so much as a headache? — it all made sense. After the best part of twenty years of faithfulness I'd done the one thing I'd never dreamed I'd do: I'd cheated on my wife.

I started to panic. All I wanted was to go back in time and erase the last twelve hours of my life; maybe even the last twenty-four so I could undo ever meeting up with Bella. Why had I made such a fool of myself that I'd had to take her out for coffee to apologise? Why had I acknowledged her texts instead of ignoring them and going home to my wife? Penny would never forgive me if she found out. Her dad had cheated on her mum half a dozen times before he finally ran off to Canada with one of her mum's best friends when Penny was fifteen and so she knew first hand how much destruction cheating caused. 'I'd never forgive you if you did that to me,' she'd said to me on the night she told me about her dad back when we were students. 'If you ever cheated that would be it.' And even now after kids and the whole of our adult lives together I had my doubts whether her opinion had changed. As emotional as Penny was sometimes there was a steely pragmatism about her — a legacy of her teenage years — that made me seriously wonder whether in fact she might be capable of calling quits on us if she thought that there might be any chance of history repeating itself.

This was all too much. My head was spinning. I needed to get out of there, to put distance between me and the scene of the crime. I checked the room one last time to make sure I hadn't forgotten anything and realised that my watch was missing. I must have taken it off at some point but it was nowhere to be seen. It had been a thirtieth birthday present from Penny and losing it would take some explaining; still, I knew I'd have no choice but to mark it down as a casualty of war. Watches could be replaced; the kind of scorn I'd receive for getting caught in the process of sneaking out of Bella's bedroom would not be easily forgotten. After all other than sleeping with someone who wasn't my wife, leaving Bella like this was the worst thing I'd done to date in my career as a human being. Aside from her obvious lack of judgement when

7

it came to men, from the little I knew of her she seemed like a decent person and certainly didn't deserve being made to feel cheap. She'd hate me forever. But given the damage I'd wreaked in less than twenty-four hours she'd be better off hating me than having anything more to do with me ever again.

★ ★ ★

At the front door I caught my reflection in the mirror. I looked old, drawn and haggard. Just as I was about to look away out of the corner of my eye I could have sworn for a moment that I saw Fiona Briggs standing behind me. Not the adult Fiona whose photo had been displayed in the church vestibule on the day of her funeral but rather the eighteen-year-old one complete with the spiral perm she thought made her look like eighties teen pop sensation Debbie Gibson. She was wearing a snow-washed denim jacket covered in pin badges, white T-shirt featuring the cover of The Cure's *Boys Don't Cry* album, black leggings and brown monkey boots, the exact outfit that she'd been wearing on the day in the student union when I'd told her I was with Penny. I rubbed my temples and blinked hard. The image was gone. All I could see was my own reflection. I hurried out of the door, closing it quietly behind me. This was ridiculous. I was so tired and my mind was undergoing so much turmoil that now on top of everything else I was seeing images of my dead ex-girlfriend. I needed sleep. Preferably in my own bed in my own home so that I could forget that this day had ever happened. I couldn't do that of course, not without Penny wondering why I was coming home at six in the morning and taking the day off work just because of a hangover. No, if I wasn't going to raise alarm bells unnecessarily there was only one option: I'd have to find out where I was, wait for the tube to start up again and then wander the streets until it was late enough for me to roll into work for the day. My heart sank. I had meetings to attend, features to write and a working lunch with a high-profile PR. How would I manage to get through any of that when I'd be thinking about what I'd done to Penny and the kids? I'd blown my life into smithereens for something that I couldn't even remember doing and I hadn't a clue how I was ever going to begin to put it back together. How on earth had I got here?

One week earlier

1

I suppose in a way it all started with the news of Fiona Briggs's death.

My wife Penny, a senior social worker, had just arrived home from work. A problem had come up at the last minute which was why, once again, she was late.

'Bad day?' I asked as she came into the living room and slumped down into the armchair without taking off her coat.

'The worst,' she replied, kicking off her shoes. 'Everything that could go wrong did go wrong. I got shouted at by Martin, learned that I have got half a dozen staff reviews to do before the end of the month, and then a case that I thought would need an hour to close ended up taking all afternoon. To top it all the new junior had a meltdown and it took me two hours to calm her down and persuade her not to leave.' She rubbed her feet. 'Everything OK here?'

I thought about filling her in on my day as that had been no walk in the park. I worked as deputy editor of *The Weekend*, the Saturday magazine supplement of the *Correspondent*, a mix of culture, fashion, celebrity interviews and lifestyle features, and today it had been announced that due to budget cuts we'd all have to reapply for our own jobs.

'Everything's good, nothing to report. Haven't heard a thing out of the kids since they went up at eight. Do you want me to heat up your tea in the microwave? I made my signature rice and chilli.'

'Thanks, that sounds lovely, but do you mind if I give it a miss? It was Mary's last day at work today and I've done nothing but pick at cake all afternoon. I think I'll just get off to bed if that's OK.'

'Yeah that's fine,' I replied even though it wasn't. Since she'd gone back to work after a seven-year career break to bring up our kids Rosie, aged ten, and Jack, aged six, things had been tough. It was the need for money that had forced her back to work rather than a desire to fulfil herself through her career. The truth was we'd eaten through every last bit of our savings making sure she could be there for the kids when they were very young and now the money had run out.

Back when it had been just the two of us we could easily cope with the stresses and strains of a household where two people worked but now with two primary-school-aged kids added into the mix it was a struggle to keep all the balls in the air. Every day required military-style planning: who was dropping off at school, who was picking up, who was cooking tea, who was helping with homework, and it only took one thing — like Penny being called into an impromptu meeting five minutes before she was due to collect the kids — for all of our lives to be thrown into disarray. And as much as I tried to pick up the slack, with a sprawling seemingly never-ending job like mine it was virtually impossible. The truth was that the pressure was all on Penny, and while she never forgot anything to do with the kids — the lunches, the homework, the parties and playdates — she occasionally forgot us as a couple. And while I understood everything, from her missing specially prepared meals because of late-running meetings through to the evenings I spent alone on the sofa while she caught up with paperwork at the kitchen table, it was hard not to feel just a little bit neglected. I couldn't say anything though because it wasn't her fault. She was working really hard for all of us and I was a big boy, I could handle it, besides which I had a plan. A month earlier I'd applied for the editorship of *Sunday*, the *Correspondent on Sunday*'s magazine supplement, and in terms of pay and prestige it was about as good it could possibly get for someone like me. If I got the job it would be the answer to all my and Penny's problems: I'd get a rise and we could afford for her to go part-time or even give up work altogether.

⋆ ⋆ ⋆

Penny stood up and kissed me goodnight and was about to leave the room when the phone rang. We exchanged wary glances. Good news never comes via a late-night phone call.

'It's your mum,' said Penny, handing me the receiver.

'Hey Mum, everything OK?'

'I've got some bad news,' she replied. 'I've just

had a call from the uncle of that girl you used to go out with when you were young, you know the one, Fiona Briggs. Well, she died apparently, some sort of accident while playing tennis.'

'Tennis? What kind of accident can you have playing tennis that can kill you?'

According to my mother Fiona had been playing tennis at her local club and was struck on her temple by a ball which briefly knocked her unconscious. She insisted that she was all right and determined to play on and eventually won the game but fainted an hour later in the tennis club showers hitting her head on the corner of a tiled bench. She was in a coma for a week but never regained consciousness. They couldn't make any funeral arrangements until after the coroner's verdict but that came in yesterday — death by misadventure — and the funeral was at St Thomas's next Tuesday. According to Fiona's uncle my name was down on a list of people she wanted to be there. My mother paused. 'Is that something people do these days? Make lists of who they want at their funeral like it's a birthday party?'

'No, Mum,' I replied, 'but it is a very Fiona thing to do. She was a control freak of the highest order.'

My mum sighed, as though I was speaking gibberish. 'Well, I don't know about that but he said that if you wanted to pay your respects you'd be more than welcome.'

★ ★ ★

16

Fiona Briggs.

Dead.

By tennis ball.

There should be a name for it when the first person you ever slept with dies. There should be a word that communicates the fact that a little part of your history is gone forever. That she was a complete and utter nightmare of a girlfriend and that my buttocks clenched at the very thought of her was neither here nor there. She might have been one of the most obnoxious and controlling human beings I had ever had the misfortune to encounter but she was my first, and I was hers, and as such we would always be inextricably linked.

I was never quite sure how I started going out with Fiona. Looking back it was almost as if one moment I was a carefree sixteen-year-old enjoying a lazy summer of messing around in the park with my mates and then out of nowhere Fiona appeared with her big hair and fashionable clothes reeking of the designer perfume Poison by Dior. In no time at all I was coupled with Fiona with no means of escape. Nothing I did was good enough for her, she hated my friends and wasn't all that keen on my family either. During the eighteen months we were together — in which time I endured daily bullying, belittling and deriding at her hands — I attempted to split up with her on at least a dozen separate occasions but it never seemed to stick. Every time I raised the topic of ending the relationship Fiona would invariably dangle the prospect of my gaining access to her underwear

17

to dissolve my resolve and because I was seventeen and shallow it worked every time. Finally however, a fortnight before we were due to go to university at opposite ends of the country I received a handwritten note pushed through my parents' letter box:

Dear Joe,
This is the most difficult thing I have ever had to do but I do it all the same because deep down I know you will understand. Of late I have been giving great consideration to my future. Although I care for you deeply I feel we have been growing apart for some time now, and therefore think it's best that we end our relationship sooner rather than later. Please always think fondly of me.
Yours faithfully,
Fiona xxx
PS. Please do not try to change my mind.

It was all lies of course. Two days later my friend Tony saw her in WHSmith in Swindon town centre hanging off the arm of Ian Mallander, who was five years older than her and worked at the local B&Q. By rights, I should have been hurt by the deceit she'd employed to get rid of me but I was too busy celebrating to give it a second thought. Finally I was a free man, one who was about to go to university to study English Literature with hundreds if not thousands of members of the opposite sex some of whom I was pretty sure would have sufficiently low standards to actually consider sleeping with

18

me. And I wasn't going to be satisfied with sleeping with one girl with no standards: no, I was going to sleep with as many girls with no standards as would allow me into their beds and only when I had reached double figures would I even contemplate becoming embroiled in another relationship.

At least that was the plan. Two days into my university career I was attempting to inveigle my way into a group of female modern language students at the freshers' night disco when I'd felt a tap on my shoulder. I turned to see Fiona's best friend, Sara, accompanied by a pretty, dark-haired girl wearing a vintage floral tea dress and lace-up ankle boots. I couldn't tear my eyes from this girl. Something about her was so warm, inviting and strangely familiar that all I wanted to do was get to know her.

'Sara,' I said, forcing myself to sound pleased to see her even though I loathed her as much as she had patently loathed me. 'How funny to see you here.'

'It's not that funny,' she said sharply. 'You knew I was coming to Sheffield because I told you and where else would a first-year student be on freshers' night?'

'Good point,' I replied, hoping that Sara's friend hadn't taken me for a complete idiot. I flashed a hesitant smile in her direction and got an equally hesitant one back. 'Hi, I'm Joe, I didn't quite catch your name.'

'That's because I didn't introduce you,' Sara butted in. 'I only came over to tell you that Fiona has changed her mind. She wants to go back out

19

with you. She'll be up the weekend after next to stay with me so if you know what's good for you, you'll meet her outside my halls first thing on the Saturday morning.'

This was all too much. I wanted to cry. To shed actual man tears that would express the level of desperation I felt. Fiona was like the serial killer in a horror film who just wouldn't die and stay dead.

'But I — '

'But you what?' demanded Sara. 'You want me to pass on some message to Fiona that we *both* know will make her angry? No, if you have something to say to Fiona, say it to her face when she gets here.'

Fizzing with frustration at the thought of falling into my ex's clutches once more I nursed bottle after bottle of Newcastle Brown in an effort to build up a head of steam sufficient to propel me to call Fiona's parents in the hope of obtaining her number in Southampton. I was going to stop this madness — which I was pretty sure it would be — before it started if it was the last thing I did, but as I reached the wall of payphones that lined the lobby of the union I noticed Sara's friend standing next to one. She seemed upset.

'Hi, you're Sara's friend aren't you? Are you OK? Anything I can do?'

'I'm fine,' she said. 'Just leave me alone.'

The tears. The telephone. It could only be one thing.

'Boyfriend trouble?'

She nodded. 'Am I that obviously pathetic?'

20

'Not at all, it's just . . . look, are you really OK?'

'It's silly, really. We were finishing the call and I told him that I missed him and he didn't say it back, and when he finally did say it I knew he'd only said it because I'd made him say it.'

I winced. 'The insincere 'miss you' is the worst kind. What you really want is someone saying: 'All days are nights till I see thee, And nights bright days when dreams do show thee me.''

The girl looked at me in awe like I'd just grown a foot in height right in front of her. 'That's beautiful,' she said. 'What's it from?'

'One of the sonnets, I forget which,' I lied. 'For some reason those lines always stuck in my head.'

The girl grinned. 'I'm Penny, Penny Morrison.'

'Nice to meet you, Penny Morrison, I'm Joe.'

We stayed up all night, Penny and I, listening to music in her room and talking about what we hoped to do with our lives. Penny told me that she wanted to change the world and work for a campaigner like Greenpeace while in turn I told her that I wanted to be a writer and move people with my words. When we finally kissed at dawn watching the sun rise over the self-catering accommodation block and I told her that even if I lived to be a hundred I would never forget this moment she smiled and told me she felt the same.

★   ★   ★

21

By the time Fiona arrived on campus a fortnight later Penny and I were practically living together. Although Fiona's friend Sara was well aware of this fact she clearly hadn't wanted to be the bearer of bad news and I'd been so wrapped up in Penny that I hadn't given Fiona a second thought, which was why I was so surprised when I came face to face with her in the union bar while waiting for Penny to come back from the toilet.

'Fiona, what are you doing here?' There was genuine fear in my voice at the thought of how this whole situation might play out.

'Looking for you,' she replied tersely as she coolly played with the zip of her snow-washed denim jacket. 'Didn't you get my message? You were meant to meet me this morning. Why didn't you call me instead of making me track you down round this dump? I don't know what gets into you sometimes. You obviously need me to organise you. Anyway, we're out of here, so get your things. Sara knows a good place in town that's doing cheap shots until ten.'

'No,' I said firmly and Fiona stepped back in surprise. I'd never used that word to her before.

Her eyes widened. 'What do you mean, no?'

'I mean, I'm not going out with you tonight, I'm not going out with you at all. I've moved on. I've got a new girlfriend.'

Fiona took a menacing step forward and jabbed me in the chest with her index finger. 'You don't get to dump me. I'll be the one who does the dumping around here so consider yourself dumped. But just remember this, Joe

Clarke: I was the best thing that ever happened to you and one day you're going to look back at this moment and regret how you've treated me.' With that she was gone and it was the last I ever saw of her.

2

I felt distinctly odd as a week later I walked up the front steps of St Thomas's Church in Swindon dressed in a dark-blue suit and black tie. I had been in two minds about the virtue of attending Fiona's funeral — I just couldn't begin to imagine how exactly any good could come of it — but Penny was firm on the matter. 'You have to go,' she said. 'As odd as it is that she put your name down on her special list we have to believe it was because she wanted you to be there.' I'd tried to explain that it was probably part of some evil practical joke from beyond the grave but Penny wouldn't budge. She even offered to take the day off work to come with me but I couldn't see any point given the logistical conundrum of arranging childcare.

In the porch of the church resting against an easel was a large framed photograph of Fiona. It was hard to connect the Fiona in the picture with the girl I had known. In the picture she looked grown-up, calm, confident and self-assured like a newsreader or a politician. She had remained attractive but in the same hard and unyielding manner as when I knew her, only with much less eyeliner.

Breaking away from the photograph's unsettling gaze, I made my way inside the church and took a seat on one of the pews at the back, partly because I wanted to be able to make a quick escape once it was all over but mostly because I was afraid that it might be an open casket affair: I wouldn't put anything past Fiona.

The service kicked off with a couple of stirring hymns followed by a reading and then the eulogies. The first came from Fiona's elder brother Frank who had an unfortunate tone of voice, which made him sound bored even though he was obviously devastated. He was followed by Fiona's boss who used the opportunity to recite some incredibly bad poetry that he'd written over the weekend (lots of stuff about her being 'a shining star' and heaven having 'one more angel'; it was mortifying). He was followed — rather oddly I thought — by the head of the tennis club committee where apparently Fiona spent a lot of her spare time and was 'admired' by all who came across her and finally, because Fiona had been resolutely single for many years, the last speaker wasn't her partner but rather her dad, Peter Briggs, who was just as tall and world-weary as I remembered back when Fiona and I had been together. Mr Briggs barely uttered three words before he was crying. It was awful stuff to watch. Terrible. I felt guilty for even daring to think a bad thought about his daughter. Maybe she'd changed in the course of the last twenty years. Maybe she'd learned her lesson and become a decent human being somewhere along the way. It wasn't impossible was it? People changed all the time. Mr Briggs concluded his eulogy with a story about how the week before Fiona died he'd noticed how tired she was and had asked her why she didn't slow down a bit. Apparently she'd laughed and said, 'You have to make every day count because you only live once.' To some degree it was a pretty tactless thing to say because you could argue that if Fiona had been just a little less 'seize the day' she might have gone for a lie-down after getting hit in the head rather than soldiering on with the game for the sole purpose of thrashing her opponent three sets to two. I don't know whether it was just because I was having a bad day or simply because funerals always make you think about your own mortality but somehow this stupid, cheesy, piece of homespun wisdom moved me more than I ever could have imagined. So much so that when I accidentally brushed a hand against my cheek as we stood up to sing Fiona's favourite hymn, 'All Things Bright and Beautiful', I noticed it was wet from tears.

That night, lying in bed next to Penny, my mind was plagued with so many thoughts about Fiona, mortality, and the search for life's meaning that I barely got any sleep at all. I couldn't seem to let go of this idea that I was drifting through life like a ghost barely registering with anyone. Penny was absorbed in a demanding job, the kids were busy missing their mum, and I was just going through the motions in a job where no one really appreciated me. I felt like I was sleepwalking through life and crossing my fingers in the hope that somehow it would magically get better all by itself. If Fiona was right, if you really did only get one life, surely this was no way to live it.

Fiona's death was the last thing on my mind however as I entered the lobby of the *Correspondent* on the following Monday morning. It couldn't be. I had too much to do, chiefly making last-minute preparations for the photo-shoot that was happening that day for *The Weekend*'s alternative Father's Day issue.

As feature ideas went it was hardly the most original: corral a selection of photogenic, professional, recently separated fathers together into a photographic studio along with their adorable kids, get in a decent snapper, make-up artist and stylist to transform them into eye candy for the female readers and then once the shoot was in the bag, interview them making sure to gather plenty of background colour and tear-jerking anecdotes about their internal emotional states as they approached this, their first Father's Day as single parents. The title of the piece (which had come to me in a flash as I'd pitched the idea at the weekly features meeting) was 'The Divorced Dads' Club', and my boss, Camilla, had loved it so much she decided on the spot that it would be the cover story. To be honest I'd been more than a little surprised she'd gone for it in such a big way, but after the meeting she'd explained in her own inimitable way. 'Truth is Joe, our readers never get tired of seeing good-looking guys who have made a mess of their lives.'

At the time it had sounded like the easiest brief in the world. As a journalist working in the high-pressure environment of a national newspaper I knew a lot of guys who had made messes of their lives — in fact if I had closed my eyes and thrown a stick across the office it couldn't have failed to hit a divorcee, recovering alcoholic or budding gambling addict — and some of them were actually not bad-looking. Yet while these guys were ruled out of my search by dint of working on the paper I'd felt sure that they'd all have enough good-looking but emotionally damaged friends of their own to make the feature a slam dunk. But the more I began to investigate the clearer it became that none of the potential interviewees I dug up quite fitted the bill. I could find good-looking guys who had separated from their partners in the last few months but had no kids; I could find good-looking single dads who had separated from their partners years ago and remarried; and of the three guys who fulfilled the first two criteria, one had a bitter ex-wife who wouldn't let their kids appear in the feature, the second couldn't make the day of the shoot because of work commitments and the third turned out to be living in Seville and it simply wasn't worth the expense of booking flights and hotels just to make up the numbers. And so with the clock ticking I had resorted to the tactics of the truly desperate hack: social networking sites. The message read as follows: *Journalist for national newspaper requires recently separated fathers and their children for feature (must be free for shoot on Friday morning). Reasonable expenses will be paid.*

I just needed them all to be up to scratch.

★ ★ ★

As the lift doors opened I nodded to the receptionists and was about to head over to Carl Smith, *The Weekend*'s art editor, who was co-ordinating the shoot when a young female voice called out my name from behind and I turned to see a woman in her mid-twenties looking back at me. She had dark brown hair piled on top of her head in the fashionably untidy manner that seemed to be all the rage these days and was wearing a black jacket and skirt with a cream top and knee-high boots. Her eyes were a deep brown and there were a light scattering of freckles across the bridge of her nose. She looked oddly familiar but I just couldn't place her.

'You're . . . '

'Bella Rhodes,' she replied. 'We met last week. Dave Walsh on the arts desk introduced us.'

'Oh, that's right,' I replied. As a rule of thumb I tried my best to avoid interns on the grounds that if you paid them the slightest bit of attention they'd rope you into critiquing articles they'd written for their student paper and this one was no different.

'I remember now. How are you getting on? Settling in well?'

'Really well. I'm loving it.'

'So what can I do for you?'

She smiled, seemingly embarrassed by whatever it was she was about to say. 'I'm so sorry to bother you like this, Mr Clarke, and you're going to think I'm a complete stalker, but there's

29

something I've been wanting to ask since we were introduced.' She reached into her bag and took out a well-thumbed paperback. I recognised the book's cover immediately. It was *Hand in Glove*, the novel I'd written two years out of university which was based, give or take a few embellishments and a stock 'the bleaker the ending the more serious the writing' conclusion, almost entirely on the early days of my relationship with Penny. While not exactly a huge seller it had been a minor critical success, garnering praise from the literary pages of a few broadsheets, and at one point (long before I'd secured my staff job) I was even included on *The Weekend*'s Hot Young Things page along with a theatre director who's now an Emmy-award-winning screenwriter and a male model who presents Saturday night entertainment shows on ITV. Having long since boxed up in the loft the two dozen copies I'd been given by my publishers along with my rowing machine, video recorder and all the other things I own, don't use but haven't yet got round to selling on eBay, I hadn't seen a copy of *Hand in Glove* outside the shelves of a charity shop for at least a decade, let alone met someone who had actually read it.

She handed the book to me. 'I can't tell you how much I love this. It would absolutely make my day if you'd sign it for me.'

'Very funny,' I replied curtly. 'Who put you up to this?'

Bella looked stunned. 'I don't know what you're on about. No one's put me up to — '

'Don't insult my intelligence,' I snapped.

'You're telling me that you just *happen* to be a fan of a huge pile of overwritten angsty old tosh that's not even been in print in over a decade? I don't think so.'

Without another word, I abandoned the intern in the middle of the hallway and marched over in the direction of the desk of the *Correspondent*'s books editor, Dave Walsh. This prank had his fingerprints all over it for sure. He'd always been a bit sniffy about me having written a novel when from what I'd gathered over the years he'd written several without managing to secure a publisher. Did he really believe that I was gullible enough to believe that the young, pretty intern he'd sent over to wind me up was a fan of the one and only book I'd ever written? Not even I was that deluded.

'Nice try, Walshy,' I said, slapping the book down hard next to his overpriced coffee. 'But you'll definitely need to work harder than that to catch me out!'

Walsh's deep baritone laugh filled the air as he picked up the book between his thumb and forefinger like he was afraid of catching something from it. 'You're not trying to blame this old potboiler on me are you? It's your name on the cover!'

So, he was going to play dumb. Weak ploy. I'd make him admit it, if it took all day. 'Come on, admit it, you put her up to it.'

'Put *who* up to *what?* You'll have to be more specific.'

'That intern,' I replied. 'Pretty. Dark-haired. Started on the arts desk last week. You know the

31

one I mean. Come on Walshy, just admit it: you talked her into asking me to sign a copy of my book.'

Walsh roared so loudly with laughter that everyone within twenty feet of him turned around to get a better look at what was going on.

'You mean Bella? She's a fan of your distinctly limited oeuvre, is she? If I'd known that she certainly wouldn't be working for me!'

If he was lying his face wasn't letting on. I had a moment of doubt. Could I have got it wrong after all?

'Are you saying it wasn't you?'

'Hand on heart.'

'So the intern is . . . '

'A genuine fan of yours? It would certainly look that way.'

With the sound of Walshy's laughter echoing in my ears I returned shamefaced to the spot where I'd so rudely abandoned the intern and apologised.

'You must think I'm insane,' I began.

'I'm just confused, that's all,' she replied. 'Did I do something wrong?'

'It's just that, well, I thought that . . . actually, you know what, it doesn't matter what I thought. I was an arsehole to you and I shouldn't have been. Look, I feel terrible about this. Why don't you let me take you out for coffee this afternoon? I'll sign your book and we can talk about working on the paper and I can give you the benefit of the obviously minuscule amount of wisdom that I have.'

'I'd love to.' She smiled as though this was the

most exciting prospect that she'd ever heard and then opened her mouth as if she had something else to add but before she could say a word my boss Camilla appeared in my eye line.

'Joe,' she asked. 'Have you got a minute?'

I made my excuses to Bella and followed Camilla into her office. She told me to take a seat and handed me an espresso from the little machine in the corner. It had all the makings of someone about to deliver bad news.

'It's about the editorship of *Sunday*,' she said as if reading my thoughts. 'You didn't get it.'

So that was that. After three rounds of interviews, two presentations to upper management and numerous sleepless nights I hadn't got the job.

'Who have they given it to?' I asked.

'Hannah Bainbridge from the *Sunday Reporter*. She really dazzled them from day one.'

I'd met Hannah a few times over the years. She was just one of those people who were naturally adept at promoting themselves and everyone seemed to buy into it without question. It didn't help that she was pretty damn good at her job too. Even I would've struggled not to appoint her over me.

Camilla offered me a commiserative smile. 'For what it's worth you were my first choice but I just couldn't get anyone else to see you as anything other than a safe pair of hands.'

'That's me in a nutshell, isn't it?' I replied. 'That's everything I amount to: a pair of hands, not even a whole body.'

3

In the course of the past year alone I'd applied for at least a dozen senior positions on various newspapers and magazines and while I'd come close to getting them a few times luck never seemed to be on my side. Getting rejected by my own paper in favour of Hannah Bainbridge of all people, however, felt like a real slap in the face. Where could I go from here? Without me bringing in more money Penny couldn't give up work and we'd be forced to carry on at this manic pace that rendered us virtual strangers to each other. And while I knew it wouldn't always be so tough it was hard to imagine that day. Penny and I were stuck in the middle years in more ways than one. We were halfway through our lives, halfway through bringing up the kids and as far away from the beginning as we were from the end. It was like hitting the wall in the middle of a marathon and knowing that the only way out was to give up on everything or somehow find the strength to carry on.

That afternoon, still feeling beaten down by the disappointment of not getting the promotion, I reluctantly took Bella the intern to Allegro's, a cheap and cheerful Italian café favoured by journalists from my own paper and others round about. On our way to the only free table in the place I took care to acknowledge Faye Bonner from the *Correspondent*'s crime

34

desk, waved hello to Simone Patterson, senior features writer at the *Post*, and nodded a greeting to David Owen, arts editor of the *Sunday Reporter*.

'I'm feeling a bit star-struck,' said Bella as we took our seats. 'I can't believe I'm sitting in a café with the great and good of the media world.'

'I wouldn't go that far,' I replied. 'They're just people and anyway I'm sure one day, in the not-too-distant future, some new intern will be looking at you eating lunch in here and won't be able to believe they're in the same room.'

We ordered two cappuccinos and I tried to make up for that morning's mistake by showing an interest in her life. She was born in Kent but raised in Hereford by an army officer father, who she didn't really get on with, and a homemaker mother who divorced her father and remarried when Bella was nine. She did her first degree in modern languages at Durham then went travelling around Australia for six months, which had turned into eighteen before she realised that she needed to turn her attention to her career. On her return to England she decided that she wanted to practise law but by the time she'd trained up and got a job at one the big law firms in the City she realised that it wasn't for her and gave it all up at the age of twenty-five to get into journalism.

'Anyway,' she said in conclusion, 'that's enough about me. How about you? I can't believe you never wrote another novel.'

'It wasn't for me,' I replied. 'I think I only ever had the one story in me.'

'I don't think that's true for a minute,' dismissed Bella. 'And even if it is, I can't imagine a better book to have written: 'The image of her moved like liquid honey in my mind tracing all the words she never said to me and I knew from that moment on that neither life, nor love, would ever taste the same again.''

She was quoting a passage from *Hand in Glove* when the protagonist realises that the girl he's waiting for is never going to arrive. The idea had come from a row Penny and I had at Florence's Santa Maria Novella train station. It was during the summer break and I'd told her that I was thinking about dropping out of university and moving to London. She'd asked me what I thought the move would mean for us and I'd told her that I didn't know and that was when she'd run out of the station. I spent two hours alone with the luggage, wondering what to do, by which time I had made up my mind that if Penny ever did return then that would be the last row we would ever have.

I didn't know what to say. I was simultaneously flattered, self-conscious and not a little confused.

'I don't understand. You've committed lines from my novel to memory?'

'That's the sort of thing seventeen-year-old girls do when they read a book that changes their lives.' She laughed and briefly touched my hand. It was like a bolt of lightning ran straight through me. In an instant I felt alive, energised and strangely invincible.

And then it was gone.

'I've been carrying this book around with me hoping to see you since I started last week, just for a moment,' she said as I drew my hand away from the centre of the table. 'When I spotted you in the office today I thought I'd scream. I hope I didn't embarrass you, it's just that it was too good an opportunity to miss.'

'I'm not embarrassed,' I replied, 'I'm just . . . I don't know, but whatever it is, it's not embarrassment.'

* * *

We talked for just over an hour, mostly about the paper, but also the future of the industry, the difference between working on newspapers and magazines and even about our favourite books. I'm sure we could have gone on much longer but then I looked at my watch and remembered that Carl had booked a car to take us over to the shoot at two and so I paid the bill and we headed back to the office.

'I can't thank you enough for taking me for coffee, Joe,' said Bella as we stood outside the revolving doors to the building. 'It was really kind of you to take time out to talk to me.'

'It was nothing,' I replied casually. 'I'm just sorry that we got off on the wrong foot. Anyway, I really do hope your time on the paper goes well.'

She laughed, and tucked a stray strand of hair that had been caught by the wind back behind her ear. 'How could it not after a start like this?' she replied. A nearby car sounded its horn before

I could reply. I turned to see Carl and his assistant waving at me to hurry up from the back of a black Addison Lee minivan.

'I'd better go,' I said. She nodded and gave me a smile that if I hadn't known better I might have described as flirtatious, then headed back into work leaving me alone with my thoughts for the walk to the car.

'Who was that then?' asked Carl, leaning out of the window to get a better look at Bella. 'The next Mrs Clarke?'

'It was no one,' I replied, climbing in. 'Look, let's get a move on if we're not going to be late for this stupid shoot.'

★ ★ ★

The studio we'd booked was in one of the few parts of East London yet to be gentrified but was as overpriced and over-styled as any I'd been in. Hair and make-up had arrived, the stylist was at the ready and now all we needed were the stars of our show who were nowhere to be seen. I couldn't get a signal to call them from where we were set up and so cursing my brand-new state-of-the-art phone with its mega memory and superior processing power I headed out into the corridor to get a better signal when I saw a tubby guy in a stained sky-blue puffa jacket and grey supermarket tracksuit bottoms staring at me. He held an open bag of chips in his hands.

'Can't get a signal?'

'Not for love nor money,' I replied, assuming he was some kind of caretaker. 'I don't know what the point of these things is if you can't actually make calls with them.'

'I can't seem to go a month without killing a phone,' replied Tubby Guy. 'I'm like a phone serial killer.' He laughed, clearly amused by his own joke, and as I turned away to resume my signal search he coughed and said, 'I don't know if you can help me, mate. I'm looking for Joe Clarke, a journalist. I don't suppose you could point him out could you?'

'That's me,' I replied. I looked at him again. Maybe he wasn't the caretaker. Maybe he was some kind of delivery guy. 'Do you need me to sign for something?'

Tubby Guy looked puzzled. 'I'm not sure I . . .'

'You're here to deliver something aren't you?' I wondered if I'd missed an accent that might explain why he didn't understand English.

Tubby Guy laughed. 'No, I'm not delivering anything — I'm the star of the show!' He wiped one of his greasy hands on his tracksuit bottoms and held it out for me to shake. 'I'm Stew, I'm a neighbour of Gary Crossly from your IT department. I'm here for the shoot.'

I immediately thought back to Camilla's words on the day she'd commissioned the feature: *Readers never getting tired of good-looking guys who have made a mess of their lives.* When Tubby Guy's friend, Gary from IT, had responded to my appeal for divorced dads he'd assured me that not only was his mate Stewart a recently separated father of two but also good-looking in a 'poor man's Hugh Grant' kind of way. Even though my usual protocol was to demand a jpg upfront in order to verify the photogenic status of respondents, the studio, photographer, make-up artist and stylist had been booked and as I still had another two slots to fill I just said yes and decided to hope for the best. I looked at the lumpy, red-faced man smelling of vinegar standing in front of me. The only way he resembled Hugh Grant was that both he and Hugh had two eyes and a nose. I made a mental note to kill Gary from IT with my bare hands first thing in the morning.

At this point there was literally nothing I could do other than usher Stewart through to hair and make-up and hope for the best. But as I was about to do that I noticed something else about him — other than the ketchup stains on his sweatshirt — that wasn't quite right.

'Where are your kids? You do know we need them to be here for the photos?'

Stewart shook his head. 'Gaz never said anything about that. He just said that I needed to be a recently separated dad, which I am.'

This was great. Not only had I booked the world's least photogenic man for the shoot but his kids weren't even here. Camilla would burst a blood vessel the moment she saw the pictures. Wherever these kids were, whatever they were doing, I was going to have to get them to the studio in the next hour. 'Where do they go to school? I'll send a car round to pick them up.'

Stewart blinked and stared down at his chips and for an awful moment I thought he might cry. 'My kids, Thomas and Victoria, they're actually in Thailand. That's where their mum's from and where she's taken them. I'm trying to get them back but my solicitor says it could take months if not years.'

I couldn't have felt any worse than I did at that moment. This poor guy was stuck in the middle of an international custody battle, and here was me giving him a hard time. 'I'm sorry to hear that, Stewart, I really am. Listen, why don't you take a seat over by the coffee and pastries and I'll send someone to look after you.'

* * *

Five minutes later I looked up from my phone (still only one bar) to see a tall, stocky man accompanied by two sullen-looking kids, a boy and a girl, neither of whom was more than ten or eleven years old. They had to be my next interviewees. On the downside: in his long grey overcoat, rolled-up black jeans and Doc Marten boots, Tall Stocky Man looked like an overgrown student. On the upside: if I squinted it turned out that he was actually not bad-looking — not exactly Camilla's type, but the sort of squishy, slightly overweight amenable beta male that most men wouldn't mind their sister dating.

'You must be Paul Baker.' I recognised him from the picture he had emailed to me earlier in the week. 'Nice to meet you and these must be your kids . . . '

'Zach and Melody.'

'That's the one!' I replied, hoping he hadn't noticed that I'd completely forgotten their

41

names. 'Pleased to meet you Zach and Melody, just take a seat over there next to the — '

I was stopped in my tracks by the sound of bellowing. A huge hulk of a guy in his late forties with peroxide blond shoulder-length hair and the walk and demeanour of a retired WWE wrestler was yelling questions at the studio's pretty receptionist even though she was sitting less than two feet away from him.

'I'm here for a magazine shoot!' he boomed in a heavy New Zealand accent that was straight out of *Flight of the Conchords*. 'Bloke who's organising it is called Joe Cook . . . or Cart or something like that.'

The receptionist — presumably terrified that he was about to lift her up and throw her across the room — pointed in my direction.

'All right mate?' he yelled down the corridor as though he was attempting to be heard over a crowd. 'Don't mind telling you this place has been a right bugger to find!'

This couldn't be right. I had a photo on my phone of my last interviewee. He was a guy called Rajesh, in his mid-twenties, who looked a lot like an Indian Brad Pitt. This guy with his denim shirt open to the waist, leather trousers and cowboy boots looked like a stand-in for *Dog the Bounty Hunter*.

'I think there might have been some sort of mistake,' I said quickly as I noticed the two small sandy-haired denim-dressed boys trailing after him. I made a big show of checking my list in the hope that this might rein him in a little. 'What's your name?'

42

'Van Halen.'

Surely I couldn't have heard that properly. 'Sorry?'

'Van *Halen*,' said the man. 'Like the band.' He sang a couple of the opening bars to 'Jump' surprisingly well. 'I changed it by deed poll. You can call me Van though, everyone does.'

This was all too much. I needed it to stop this very second. 'The thing is . . . Van, I'm actually waiting for a Rajesh Bhatnagar.'

'Yeah I know, dude's my drummer and a bloody good one too. You should hear him do the solo from Iron Butterfly's 'In-A-Gadda-Da-Vida'. He kills it! Anyway, funny story: he was telling his ex-missus about the shoot last night and about how he'd need to take the kids out of school and long story short they've decided to give their thing another go. Knowing my circumstances he called me this morning and asked if I'd step in. I split up with my old girl a few months back, damn nearly killed me.'

I should've known better than to ask the next question but I couldn't help myself.

'Why did you split up, if you don't mind me asking?'

'She caught me with a groupie.'

I had to stop myself from laughing. Of course he was in some awful band. Either that or he was a roadie. Again, I couldn't help myself.

'What kind of music do you play?'

'We're called Man Halen. We're a Van Halen tribute band, formerly of Wellington, New Zealand, currently of Willesden Green.' He looked down at the children. 'And these are the

43

twins: Harley and Suzuki.'

If this had been happening to anyone other than me it would have made for the funniest story I'd heard in years. After all, what wasn't amusing about hearing how some journalist had laid out thousands of pounds hiring a studio, a top-notch photographer, stylist and make-up artist on behalf of his newspaper for a cover shoot and feature only to have the whole exercise undermined by the ropiest bunch of interviewees ever? But what could I do? I was under no illusions: Camilla would hate the results. Equally, if I cancelled everything and returned to the office empty-handed I'd be in even bigger trouble. For a moment I seriously considered begging some of the better-looking fathers I knew to come down to the studio with their kids and then making up their interviews afterwards but that was precisely the kind of escapade that would guarantee the sack.

I shuddered as I cast a final look over at my interviewees who were chatting and laughing together like old friends. How did people get themselves into messes like theirs? Pitiful examples though they truly were, these men were what I was stuck with, my Divorced Dads' Club. As I ushered them and the children towards the dressing rooms I took solace in the fact that as awful as the feature would undoubtedly be the one saving grace of the whole debacle was that this was one club of which I'd never have to become a member.

4

Despite Carl's comment at the beginning of the shoot that he had the retouching house on speed dial the shoot actually went a lot better than I'd expected and the results, while not brilliant, were far from poor. Relieved at this news I'd agreed to join Carl and his assistant for a drink and so once we'd waved off the Divorced Dads and their kids, we'd helped pack up the studio before heading to the Hop and Grape, a down-at-heel pub around the corner from the studio.

The guys, both single, clearly wanted to make a night of it but somewhere around my fourth pint I realised that if I didn't leave now there was every danger that I wouldn't make it home at all and so I said my goodbyes.

Drunk, tired and feeling oddly emotional I left the pub and started following directions on my phone to the nearest overground train station. As I headed up the road my phone pinged. It was a text message from a number I didn't recognise:

Sorry to text you out of the blue like this (I asked Dave Walsh for number, hope is OK?). Wanted to thank you again for being so nice today. Would love to take you out for a drink sometime to carry on the conversation. Hope to see you soon, Bella xxx.

Bella.

I'd been thinking about her — or more accurately, trying my best not to think about her and failing miserably — all afternoon. I wasn't mad was I? She had been flirting with me at the café. The coy smiles across the table, the way she'd hung on my every word like I was the smartest guy on earth and that touch, that touch had been electric and had left me feeling on top of the world. On the very day that my bosses had let me know just how little they thought of me I'd received validation from this smart, sexy, confident young woman. Where in every other sphere of my existence I felt like I was old news Bella had made me feel like I was worldly and interesting. To her I wasn't just an anonymous old hack with the best of my career behind me, I was a successful journalist at the top of my game, and a published author who happened to have written her all-time favourite book.

It was flattering. How could it not have been? She was gorgeous. But the truth is I wasn't at all in the market for an affair. Don't get me wrong: as a husband I was by no means perfect. And if I'm being totally honest I'll admit from time to time to having had minor crushes on women other than Penny. But these were crushes, nothing more, and while Penny might not exactly have been over the moon had she been aware of their existence to me at least they weren't signs of a desire to betray my wife; rather proof that I was still alive and kicking. I no more wanted these women in any real sense than I wanted to walk on the moon or score a winning goal for England in a World Cup final. It was the stuff of fantasy, pure and simple, but this thing with Bella felt different, it felt dangerous, and I

46

wanted no part of it.

I quickly tapped out a reply to her message: *Was good to meet you too. Not sure how I'm fixed for next week. Quite busy. Maybe another time* ☺

I pressed Send and breathed a huge sigh of relief as I thought about my afternoon with the Divorced Dads' Club. If flirting with a woman nearly thirteen years your junior wasn't a guaranteed way of joining the club then I didn't know what was. Turning her down was absolutely the right thing to do.

An electronic ping. A reply from Bella: *That's a shame* ☹. *How did shoot go?*

Nervously I tapped out a quick reply: *OK. Interviewees=ropey. Have been to pub to de-stress! On way home now.*

An electronic ping. Another message: *So you're still out? I'm out too! Have been for drinks for friend's birthday so am v. tipsy. Everyone's heading home now but I want to carry on. Why don't you join me and I'll buy you that drink we talked about!*

She wasn't making this easy was she? I tapped out another message: *I'd love to but I can't*, and in an instant I received her reply: *How about if I promise not to keep you out too late?*

It was time for a different line of defence. *Really I can't*, I wrote. *Have loads on at work tomorrow.* In a matter of seconds I received her reply: *You work too hard! Everybody needs to let their hair down a little! I'm only in the Sun and Thirteen Cantons. You could be here in no time.*

This was all too much for me. In spite of the

47

boost it was giving my ego I knew it couldn't go any further. I returned my phone to my jacket pocket. I had to get out of here, to somewhere safe where I wouldn't be tempted to make any stupid decisions. I scanned the street for a taxi to take me home but the only cabs I could see were already occupied. I resolved to just keep walking and continued on up the road but then there was that all-too-familiar electronic ping from inside my jacket. I made up my mind to ignore it. No good could come from becoming embroiled in a game of text tennis. If I didn't take part I couldn't get in any trouble.

I managed to get a good thirty feet up the road before the insistent ping of the phone got the better of me. I took out the phone and checked her message: *Pretty please?* This was getting ridiculous. She was practically begging me to meet her. Was she really as drunk as she was making out? She had to be surely. I never had that much confidence when I was twenty-five.

I stared at my phone wondering how best to reply and then finally it hit me. I could just switch off my phone and have done with the whole thing until morning, by which time she'd be sober and so would I meaning that we could just get on with the business of avoiding each other forever. As I pressed down on the button that would cut off our communication for good I received another text that proved impossible to ignore: *I promise you won't regret it!*

I promise you won't regret it.

Was she saying what I think she was saying?

I promise you won't regret it.

This wasn't just my imagination, was it?

I promise you won't regret it.

I was a thirty-eight-year-old failed novelist and hack and she was a young, attractive woman with her whole life ahead of her and if I wasn't mistaken she had just sent me a text outlining the fact that *she* wanted to sleep with *me*. Out of all the men alive in the world at this moment in time this beautiful woman wanted me and all I needed to do to make it happen between us was to jump in a cab and meet her.

But I couldn't, could I?

It would be wrong in every way.

I'd always sworn I'd never cheat on Penny.

I just wasn't that kind of guy.

I breathed a sigh of relief. I couldn't believe how close I'd come to crossing the line. Once again I determined to turn off my phone but then in came another message: *YOLO x.*

Her message brought me to a standstill. It was the phrase that had been rolling around in my head ever since the day of Fiona's funeral: You only live once. And it was true wasn't it? This was the only life I was going to get and here I was wasting it. Did I really want to die speculating about all the things I never did or the paths I'd never taken? Did I really want to look back on this moment in my old age and wonder: What if?

Racked with indecision I looked up from my phone to see a heavy-set young man of seventeen, maybe eighteen, dressed top to toe in sportswear approaching me. In his hand was an unlit cigarette.

'Got a light mate?'

I was momentarily confused. Around his neck on a silver chain I could quite clearly see a silver Zippo lighter. Maybe he'd run out of lighter fuel. Either way as a non-smoker I couldn't help him. 'No, sorry,' I replied. 'I don't — ' I stopped suddenly as I became aware of a heavy, sweet-smelling perfume and sensed someone lurking behind me. I tried to turn around but before I could I felt a short, sharp shock of pain across the back of my skull and everything went black and then the next thing I knew I was waking up naked in Bella's bed.

5

It was a little after six thirty by the time I reached the office having picked up a coffee on the way in a bid to sharpen my wits. Even though I was convinced that George, the security guard who often worked the reception desk in the early mornings, wouldn't remember which clothes I'd been wearing the day before let alone care that I was in them now I still felt it necessary to speed past him as quickly as possible, explaining that I was rushing because I was expecting an important call from Japan. George barely glanced up from his copy of the *Mirror*, making it clear to me that as long as I had my security pass my business held precisely no interest for him whatsoever.

The office was empty save for the guys in the post room doing their early rounds and so I made my way to the shower in the gents' toilets and was about to start getting undressed when my phone rang. I checked the screen. It was Penny. It would have been the easiest thing in the world to let the call go to voicemail but the guilt I felt was so intense that 'easy' made me feel like I was adding insult to injury.

'Hey you,' I said brightly. 'What's up?'

'Hey, Dad, it's me.' It was Jack. Hearing his voice threw me completely.

'What's wrong, son? Is everything OK? Where's Mum?'

51

'She's just here,' said Jack. 'She's getting the bowls out for breakfast. I'm having Frosties and Rosie's having Rice Krispies.'

'That's good,' I replied, still wondering why Penny had let him call. 'You like Frosties don't you?'

'I love them, they're my favourite.' There was a long pause and I could hear Penny whispering, 'Don't forget to tell Daddy why you're calling.'

'Oh yeah,' said Jack, who had clearly become distracted. 'Dad?'

'Yeah?'

'*Scooby Doo*'s not for babies is it?'

'No, son. Why?'

'Because Lucas at school said that it is, and it's not, is it?'

'Of course not,' I reassured him. 'They solve mysteries and they're always getting chased by ghosts and zombies. There's nothing babyish about zombies, is there?'

'I knew it,' said Jack victoriously. 'Lucas doesn't know everything, does he Daddy?'

'Absolutely not,' I replied. 'So is that it?'

'Yeah,' said Jack. 'Hang on because Mum wants to speak to you.'

I waited as Jack — who was clearly having problems concentrating on anything this morning — finally handed the phone to Penny.

'Hey you,' she said. 'Sorry about calling so early, it's just that he woke up at five and started on about this whole Lucas Taylor/*Scooby Doo* thing and was completely inconsolable until I said that he could call you. How's your head this morning? Heavy night was it?'

52

'You could say that. Rosie's OK?'

'She's fine, she's still up in her room. I take it you're heading straight to work?'

'That's the plan.'

'Well in that case, I'll see you tonight. Love you.'

I felt like a monster saying it back given what I'd just done. How could I say I loved her and mean it if I'd just slept with someone else? Regardless, I knew I had to force the words out.

'Love you too. See you tonight.'

Ending the call I had a quick shower and went back to my desk and turned on my computer. I needed to know why I couldn't remember anything at all about my night with Bella. A quick Google suggested a number of possibilities from mild stroke through to dementia, but the explanation that seemed most likely was something called dissociative amnesia: a temporary or permanent memory loss brought about by stressful or traumatic situations. This seemed to fit as I couldn't think of anything more stressful than having cheated on the woman I loved. Maybe my subconscious had reached the same assessment while I'd been asleep and had blocked out all memory of the previous evening in order to save me from having a complete and utter meltdown. Oddly enough, even having Google-diagnosed myself with a pretty major psychological disorder, I considered this the least of my problems and filed it away at the back of my mind to be worked on another day. As far as I was concerned, right now, my biggest problems were trying not to drown in the tsunami of guilt

I was feeling about cheating on Penny and worrying about how exactly I was going to deal with seeing Bella face to face for the first time since the night before.

Like the coward I was, I did everything humanly possible to avoid Bella that day. I avoided the arts desk like the plague, leaped at every opportunity to take a meeting out of the office and any time she so much as looked like she might be about to approach my desk I'd buttonhole the person nearest me and attempt to launch into a deep and meaningful conversation about life, the universe and everything. It was childish stuff, I'll admit, and not at all becoming to a man of my age and station but if I knew anything at all, it was this: I didn't want to talk to Bella again. Not now, not ever.

★   ★   ★

Leaving work just after seven, having waited a good three-quarters of an hour after I'd seen Bella packing up for the day, I felt sure I was safe but as I emerged from the office building through the revolving doors I spotted her leaning against the barriers near the main road. Though she didn't move I knew she had seen me and in saying nothing she was giving me one final opportunity not to disappoint her more than I already had.

'You must be shattered,' I said, forcing a smile. 'What are you still doing here?'

'Waiting for you,' she replied. 'Were you hoping I'd be gone by now?'

54

'No . . . of course not. Is that what you think? That I've been avoiding you? Of course I haven't, it's just that — '

'There's no need,' she said firmly. She reached into her bag and took out my watch. 'I only waited because I wanted to give you this.'

I took the watch from her, put it on and shoved my hands deep into my pockets. This was it. My moment of truth. There was nowhere left to hide.

'Listen . . . ' I had to raise my voice so as not to be drowned out by the sound of a passing articulated lorry. 'Do you want to go somewhere and talk?'

Bella shook her head. 'I've done all I wanted to do.'

'Are you sure?' I asked. 'Don't you think it would be better if we cleared the air?'

'And how would we do that exactly? Would you sit me down and tell me I'm a really sweet girl but that last night was a mistake and I deserve someone better in my life?'

I felt myself shrinking. I was the worst kind of walking cliché, the kind that was absolutely convinced they were anything but.

'I'm married,' I said redundantly.

Bella's eyes filled with tears and fury. 'This was a bad idea,' she said more to herself than me. 'I never should have waited for you.'

'Then why did you?' I hadn't meant the question to sound quite so abrupt. I genuinely wanted to know. Had I made her promises I couldn't keep? Had I said I'd find a way for us to be together? It was torture not knowing what I'd said or how I'd said it and frustrating that the only person who could help me piece together the events of the night before was the only person who would be outraged and humiliated by my inability to remember it.

'I waited for you because I wanted you to know there were no hard feelings,' said Bella, no longer able to hide the hurt in her voice. 'I waited because I wanted you to know that I understood.'

★ ★ ★

Playing with the kids at home that night was like waking up from a dream. This was who I really was, not the guy I'd been last night. I was going to put this whole episode behind me, which was easy enough given that I couldn't remember half of it. If no one ever found out about it how difficult would it be to convince myself that it had never happened? A life lesson would have been learned, no one would get hurt and there would be no chance of it ever happening again so, really, no one needed to know, did they? From then on I avoided Bella, kept my mouth shut and swallowed down every bad feeling that haunted me and everything might have been OK had it not been for the dreams.

★ ★ ★

They started not long after Bella's last day. I dreamed that Bella and I were in a park and she wanted to swim but I didn't because in my dream I was convinced that I couldn't. Somehow — I forget precisely how — I fell into the water and felt sure that I was about to drown when I woke up in the darkness, struggling to breathe. I'd tried to get back to sleep but it wouldn't come and so finally after an hour and a half of staring at the ceiling I got out of bed and went downstairs to watch TV. The following night it was a different dream. This time I was with a bunch of old school friends who I hadn't seen in years. They all started climbing a tree in the local park around the corner from my parents' house and even though I wasn't sure about it I followed after them. Halfway up however I lost my footing and started falling. I woke up before I hit the ground but after that sleep once again eluded me.

It had been the same pattern every night for the past fortnight: I'd go to sleep and some ridiculous dream would wake me. Recently however the dreams had become more intense and more frequent. My disturbed sleep was affecting my whole life. I was finding it difficult to concentrate in meetings and I'd been driving the kids to the local ice rink when I nearly drove through a red light as a gang of kids was crossing the road. They were fine; I put the brakes on in time for them to scatter out of the way but it really shook me and in the end Penny and I swapped seats at the edge of the road and she drove the rest of the way.

As a rule I wasn't superstitious at all. I didn't do horoscopes, believe in fate or karma and as much as I'd enjoyed studying the works of

Shakespeare at university I certainly wasn't a believer in any knee-jerk pop psychological beliefs that might see me cast as a tortured Macbeth plagued by a troubled conscience. Real people's minds didn't work like that. In the past I'd known friends who'd been having affairs, some for months on end, and until the point at which I'd learned of their transgressions I hadn't been the slightest bit aware of what they were up to. And so when the dreams started I simply wrote them off as the net effect of having been working too hard. The *Correspondent* had been trying out a bi-monthly supplement to the magazine which I'd been editing in addition to my regular job. So it made perfect sense that I should be having these dreams. I was knackered, hadn't been eating properly and the poor excuse I had for an exercise regime had all but gone out of the window. The rational evidence was overwhelming and yet even I didn't buy it. Knee-jerk or not, this was guilt talking, pure and simple.

★   ★   ★

Things came to a head after about a month. I'd woken from a deep sleep with a jolt and opened my eyes not knowing where I was. I'd been running. Someone was after me. They'd wanted something from me but I didn't know what.

'Are you OK?'

Penny's face was partially illuminated by the light of her bedside lamp. She was sitting up in bed next to me, a pile of folders on her lap.

She'd obviously been working for some time while I'd been lying next to her tossing and turning like some kind of chained lunatic.

'I'm fine, babe. You carry on with your work.'

Penny wasn't going to let it go that easily. It wasn't her style. As self-appointed chief medical officer for the family Clarke, the physical and mental health of both the kids and me fell under her remit. You couldn't get away with any of that, 'It's just a flesh wound,' crap with Penny. You either took your Calpol or you talked the problem out until a solution presented itself.

'You were having another one of those dreams again, weren't you?' she diagnosed with her usual clinical accuracy.

'No, it wasn't that. I just woke up funny, that's all. I must have heard a noise in my sleep. Didn't you hear it? Probably that new couple next door going to work. It's fair enough that they have to leave early but I just don't understand why they have to be so noisy about it.'

Penny was completely unconvinced. 'I didn't hear anything. Are you sure it was them that woke you? I think you were dreaming.'

'Says the expert.'

'Says your wife who shares a bed with you every night. You haven't been sleeping right for weeks now. In fact I think the last time you had a decent night's sleep was the night before that big shoot when you went out with Carl from work and didn't make it home.'

'I'm pretty sure it wasn't then,' I said quickly. 'What is it with women and their ability to always know what happened when?'

'It's probably the same thing that causes you to remember whole scenes from *Star Wars* but not a single one of your friends' birthdays. Do you want to know what I think the problem is?'

My breath momentarily caught in my throat. I'd never been a big believer in women's intuition but when it came to Penny and her curious ability to discern the indiscernible nothing would surprise me.

'Go on then, tell me.'

'I think you're working too hard and you need to get some rest. You're not looking after yourself properly. Starting from today things are going to change. You're going to start eating more healthily, going to bed at a decent time and you're going to book a couple of days off work and stay home and do nothing. That's an order.'

In that instant I was overwhelmed by the love I felt for Penny. She was so amazing, generous and resolutely on my side that she put me to shame without even trying. How could I ever have betrayed her? How could I have treated someone so badly who only ever wanted the best for me? I closed my eyes and turned over on my side; I just couldn't look at her any more. 'I'll be fine. I'm going to try and get back to sleep.'

6

Regardless of Penny's kindness or perhaps because of it, the dreams continued to the extent that there were some nights when I hardly slept at all. In the end however the answer to my problem came from a completely unexpected source: a conversation with one of the kids. It was a weeknight and I'd just arrived home from work to hear chaos reigning in the kitchen. Rosie was in floods of tears, Penny was nowhere to be seen and Jack was sitting alone on the stairs in his pyjamas.

'What's going on?'

Jack ran to me and jumped into my arms. 'Mum's just really told Rosie off and now Rosie's crying and Mum's got her angry face on and is sitting in the living room.'

'Why? What's Rosie done?'

Jack shrugged. 'I don't know,' he said plaintively. 'Mum sent me upstairs before the good stuff started.'

To be honest getting flung into the middle of a family row was the last thing I needed given how exhausted I was, but for Rosie to be so upset and Penny to have walked out of the room it had to be really bad and so I sent Jack back upstairs and opened the door to the living room to find Penny standing staring out of the window.

'What's up?'

Penny turned around. She'd been crying. She

walked over to me and hugged me tightly. 'I'm such a terrible mother.'

'No you're not. You're the best mum there is. Tell me what's going on.'

'It's Rosie. You know that vase your Auntie Pat gave us as a wedding present? Well Rosie broke it jumping off the sofa after I'd told her a million times not to. I was loading the dishwasher when I heard this almighty crash and I came in here to find it smashed into a thousand pieces. I asked her what had happened and she looked me in the eye and told me that she'd been walking past it and accidentally knocked it over. I told her to tell me the truth, and she insisted that she had and that's when I completely lost it. You know how much I hate lying, Joe, I can't abide it and to see her doing it so easily really hurts.'

'Well maybe she didn't do it?'

We both turned to look at the pieces of the vase; however we'd seen enough episodes of *CSI* to know that a vase knocked over by someone brushing past it doesn't shatter into anywhere near as many pieces as a vase that's been bounded into by a high-velocity child leaping from a sofa.

'Right,' I said to Penny firmly. 'Let's go and talk to her.'

I called Rosie down from her bedroom and sat her at the kitchen table. Aware that she was about to get what was coming to her she began sobbing even harder.

'I'm going to ask you once and once only. What happened to the vase?'

'I told Mum already, I walked past it and it

must have caught on my clothes.'

'So you weren't jumping off the sofa?'

She shook her head.

'Is that the truth?'

She nodded.

Penny drew a deep breath; she was moving in for the kill. 'You know this isn't going to be over until we get the truth, don't you? You know families work on trust and if I find out in the future that you're lying to me I won't ever be able to trust you again?'

She nodded once more.

'So I'm going to ask you one last time and then we'll say no more about it: did you knock over the vase jumping off the sofa?'

Silence. Then a barely perceptible nod of the head. And then it all came out. She was sorry. She never meant to lie. She was just scared of getting in trouble and she promised never to do it again. And as I watched her sobbing in her mother's arms I understood that when push had come to shove being in a state of truth with her mum had been more precious to Rosie than escaping punishment. Right there and then I knew what I too had to do if I was ever going to have any peace of mind even though the very idea made me feel physically sick: I was going to have to tell Penny the truth about Bella. It was the only way to make things right.

★   ★   ★

That night as we lay in bed, Penny deeply engrossed in some book club tome that her

63

friends were forcing her to read and me watching her surreptitiously while pretending to doze, I tried to imagine myself asking her to put the book down for a moment because I had something important to tell her. I imagined the look of concern that would flash across her features and the way she would turn to me without a moment's hesitation and say softly, 'What is it? What's wrong?' and how I'd try several times to find the courage to say what needed to be said before finally managing to get the words out. But although I could imagine her immediate reaction — hurt, shock, and humiliation — I couldn't begin to picture how things would ever get back to normal. Trying to see beyond that moment of revelation into our future together was like staring into a black hole. It just didn't bear thinking about. The truth was while confession might have brought me some relief it would be the beginning of a nightmare for Penny and I couldn't bring myself to do that to her. There was only one option for me: I'd have to keep it to myself. I'd have to live with the guilt. This would be my burden to shoulder, not Penny's.

That night, having made up my mind to be the best husband I could be, I slept a peaceful, dreamless sleep, my first in a very long time. Things would be different from now on. What was done was done; I couldn't undo it, but what I could do was change the man I'd be in the future. I made a vow to myself: I'd never betray Penny again and instead I'd dedicate the rest of my life to trying to become the kind of man of whom she could be proud.

★ ★ ★

My plan such as it was worked well over the course of the next few weeks, and those weeks turned into months until six months on I found myself at a Covent Garden hotel concluding a highly enjoyable interview with Johnny 'Wolfman' Morrison, the once-forgotten Delta bluesman whose career had been resurrected by the release of a new documentary. I thanked Niamh O'Connell, the PR who'd arranged the interview, like a professional and left the hotel room where it had taken place mentally conjuring up ways to structure the article.

It felt good to be back to my old self again. It felt good to spend a morning chatting with an attractive woman like Niamh and be completely indifferent to the experience. It felt good to have had an even prettier intern in the office than Bella for over a month now and to not know her name or anything about her; but more than that it felt good to be back firmly at Penny's side, to feel that surge of love for her whenever I looked at her, to know in my heart, without a shadow of a doubt, that she was all I wanted.

So many things had happened since I'd made my decision not to tell Penny about Bella: Penny's mum had had to have an operation on her knee; Rosie had been off school with a raging temperature for two days; the central heating had stopped working and we'd been quoted eight hundred pounds to fix it; Jack had sprained his wrist falling down some stairs at school; the car had failed its MOT and I'd been on a two-day trip to Stockholm to interview the creator and lead actress of a new Swedish crime series. It was the hectic nature of family life that made even the most recent of events feel like the dim and distant past to the extent that a day felt like a week and every week like a month. It was no wonder that time seemed as though it was on fast-forward. And while this may have given me the perfect excuse to forget the promise I'd made to myself to do right by Penny, I had steadfastly refused to let anything divert me from my mission. Nothing meant more to me than making her happy and the result of this was a renewed energy between us. Almost as if we were falling in love again — if such a thing was possible for two people who had never actually fallen out of love in the first place. For me at least, it was as though I was seeing her with fresh eyes: noticing all the things about her — her beauty, quick wit and kindness — which I had somehow become indifferent to over time. She was all I wanted, now and forever more.

★   ★   ★

I'd been back in my office for nearly an hour working on potential features ideas for the next issue of *The Weekend* when Penny rang.

'Hey, you. What's up? Everything OK?'

'Everything's fine. Are you busy?'

'Just the usual, why?'

'Because I want to take you for lunch,' said Penny. 'These past few weeks you've been so amazing — getting up early with the kids, buying

66

me presents, volunteering to take Jack and his friends to the never-ending stream of Tumble Jungle/Wacky Warehouse/Bumper Barn parties that they seem to be invited to every week — and I just wanted you to know how much I appreciate you and everything you do for us.'

'There's no need,' I replied. I meant it too. I didn't want credit for these things, I didn't want anything for them, I just wanted to get on and do what was right, but Penny wasn't having any of it.

'Of course there's a need! Whenever I tell my friends what you're like they think I'm making it up! Please let me do this one thing for you. It's only lunch, nothing special. I just want to spend some time spoiling you for a change. Where would you like to go?'

I had no choice but to relent. 'How about I see you in Allegro's at one?' I suggested.

'That,' replied Penny, 'sounds ideal.'

★ ★ ★

Allegro's was packed with regulars and I had to nod several 'hellos' to colleagues from other papers as Penny and I pushed our way past chairs and tables crammed far too close together to reach a free table in the middle of the café which had the benefit of the best view of the dessert cabinet in the house.

'I really don't understand why you all like this place so much,' said Penny as she glanced over the laminated menu. 'It's just like a million other cafés in central London.'

'I'll have you know that Allegro's is an institution in British print journalism,' I declared. 'The deals that have been made here over toasted sausage sandwiches and coffee are the stuff of legend. Without this place there would be no news, just page after page of white space interspersed with the occasional line about Jordan and the royal family.'

I called over a waitress and ordered the sausage sandwich and promised myself I'd go for a run that evening by way of compensation, while Penny opted for a grilled vegetable and hummus pitta.

Beaming like she was on a first date, she reached across the table and held my hand. 'I can't remember the last time we had lunch together on a weekday.'

Neither could I. 'That'll be never.'

Penny reacted with a good-natured tut and roll of the eyes. 'You have a memory like a sieve! We used to have lunch together all the time when I worked at ICM. Remember, you used to beg me to meet you for lunch at that little sandwich place around the corner from Victoria station because you missed me so much?'

It rang a bell, but only faintly. It was a story from a different era, pre-kids, pre-mortgage and pre-marriage. It sounded about right though: I never had liked being away from Penny for too long.

I squeezed her hand and grinned. 'What can I say? I was in love.'

★   ★   ★

Over lunch the main topics of conversation were entirely domestic — the kids, the house, the car. Penny was worried that Rosie hadn't got enough clothes to last her for an upcoming week-long field trip to an activity centre in Sussex; I was concerned about the fact that Jack had wet the bed the night before last and hoped that it wasn't going to become a regular thing again like it had the previous summer; and we were both worried about money, or rather the lack of it, and in particular how we were going to afford to have the boiler fixed once the novelty of boiling kettles to fill the bath every day wore off.

To an outside observer I was sure it must have seemed like the dullest conversation, the sort of practical exchange that as a young boy I had watched my own parents have a thousand times wondering how it was possible for two people to care so much about things that had nothing to do with *Star Wars* figures or Manchester United. I now knew that the things my parents talked about, the things Penny and I talked about, weren't simply a list of moans and gripes but an opportunity to bond, because dull as they might seem to the outside world, they were important to us. These weren't just my problems or Penny's either, they were *ours*, problems that *we* solved together in our roles as joint chief executives of this particular branch of the Clarke family tree. And in a world where so many people had no choice but to solve the problems life threw at them on their own it was a comfort to know that whatever came our way, we would deal with them together, as a family.

* ★ *

Lunch over, I asked for the bill. Penny had an afternoon of meetings ahead of her as did I; still, it was good to have had the opportunity to have a conversation with her that wasn't constantly interrupted by our kids and their seemingly never-ending stream of questions.

Penny put on her jacket wearing a look that bordered on shy as though she was embarrassed by the depth of her feelings for me. I felt it too. The giddiness of feelings of first love tempered by the realisation that we'd been together for over twenty years.

'This has been so good, don't you think?' said Penny. 'We should definitely do this more often.'

'Absolutely, I was thinking — ' Out of the corner of my eye I spotted Angela Towney, a former staffer at the *Correspondent*, now arts editor of the *Review*, heading towards our table. But that wasn't what had shut me up so abruptly. What had silenced me was that Angela wasn't alone. Trailing behind her, looking as horrified by the events that were unfolding as me, was Bella.

7

Bella.

I hadn't spoken to her since that day outside the office when she'd returned my watch. And just as I had made it my aim to have nothing whatsoever to do with her, each time our paths crossed at work she looked right through me as though I didn't exist. With every other person she was her usual charming, funny, self, but with me there was nothing. Not hatred, not bitterness, or discomfort. Nothing. It was as though she had permanently erased all memory of our time together.

After a few weeks of this I simply stopped seeing her around the office at all. At first I thought perhaps she was ill because her internship wasn't due to end for another two months but then curiosity finally got the better of me and I inquired about her at the arts desk to be told that she'd quit the internship for personal reasons. For a while I'd thought about calling her and finding out if she was OK but knew I couldn't afford to do even that without risking everything I'd achieved in the past few months with my relationship with Penny.

★ ★ ★

Angela greeted me with an enthusiastic kiss on the cheek. 'Joe! Long time no see! How are you?'

'I'm good thanks. You look great.'

Angela laughed. 'I do, don't I?' She turned to Bella. 'Let me introduce you to Bella, our new junior at the *Review*. She started last week and is a real star. She actually did part of an internship at your place though I don't suppose you remember her. You never could stand mixing with the interns.'

Were we friends or complete strangers? I looked at Bella, wondering how best to play it. She beat me to it though.

'Pleased to meet you, Joe,' she said, shaking my hand. 'Angela's told me a lot about you.'

I needed to take control of the conversation. I couldn't afford to let it roam wild and free given its potential to ruin my life. 'It's nice to meet you too. Let me introduce you to my wife, Penny.'

There, I'd said it. It was done. Now Bella would know that the woman with me wasn't a colleague, an interviewee or a PR who I was trying to sweet-talk into doing me a favour.

Penny shook Angela's hand and then Bella's. As their skin touched my stomach knotted so tightly I had to brace myself against the table to stop from doubling over. This was my worst nightmare playing out before my eyes. This was everything I never wanted to see happening right in front of me in 3-D complete with Dolby 7.1 Stereo.

'I can't believe I've never met you before now,' said Angela gleefully. 'I sat at the desk opposite Joe's for three years, taught him everything he knows!'

I laughed, determined to maintain the illusion

of normality. 'You wish! She basically forced me to make her coffee every day.'

'And he couldn't even do that very well!'

Penny laughed and addressed Bella. 'You must be thrilled to be at the *Review* after all that interning. It's a great first job.'

Angela, who was never short of a surplus of words, answered for her. 'She's over the moon, aren't you?'

'I couldn't be happier,' said Bella. She coughed nervously. 'Really I couldn't.'

My blood was pounding in my ears and I felt like I was going to throw up. Desperate though I was for this to be over I knew that it required a little more small talk to sound anywhere near convincing. 'So how are you, Angela? Keeping well?'

'As well as can be expected these days. We've been understaffed for months now and the only reason they let me hire a junior was because I told them I was going to leave if they didn't.'

Bella cleared her throat politely. 'I'm so sorry about this but I've just remembered I need to return quite an important call.' She shook Penny's hand again. 'So lovely to meet you, Mrs Clarke.' Then she turned to me and shook mine without meeting my gaze, 'And lovely to meet you too, Joe. Take care.'

With Bella gone there was an instant drop in pressure inside my skull. I no longer felt like I was going to burst a blood vessel. Although Angela chatted on in a bid to update me on all the industry gossip, I soon stopped listening to a word she was saying. All I could think was how horrific it was that Penny had just met Bella. I stole a look at Penny. Surely she hadn't guessed anything? I was pretty sure I'd kept my cool and Bella had barely said a word. Penny was listening to Angela, nodding and smiling in all the right places. Everything was fine. The danger had passed.

Angela concluded the conversation by coaxing me into promising to meet up with her at some unspecified point in the future for lunch. It would never happen, of course. As much as Angela and I had got on well together, I was pretty sure we didn't have much to say to each other now that we were at different papers. Still it was nice to pretend if only to distract myself from the enormity of Penny meeting Bella.

As Angela took her leave and made her way over to her table the waitress arrived with our bill. Once we had paid I watched as Penny casually glanced over at the table where Bella was sitting down opposite Angela.

'Well, they were nice, weren't they?'

I nodded. 'Yeah, they were.'

'What was the younger one's name again?'

'Bella.'

'And she was an intern at the *Correspondent?*'

'Apparently.'

'She's very pretty.'

'Is she? Can't say I've given it much thought.'

'Mind you, so is that other woman, Angela. How long did you work with her again?'

'Three years, give or take.'

'She's a bit of a force of nature isn't she?'

I shrugged. 'To me she was always just Angela.

But yeah, now you say it, 'a force of nature' is a good way to describe her.'

Penny picked up her bag from the back of the chair. 'I suppose we'd better be getting off.'

As we made our way across the café towards the exit, I attempted to engage Penny in conversation, refusing to look anywhere near Angela and Bella's table. On the way out Penny stopped at the door to wave in the women's direction, forcing me to join in too. My gaze met Bella's for a brief instant but there was no hint of recognition on her face. I was just another guy and this was just another day.

*   *   *

Outside I took Penny's hand in mine and told her I'd walk her to Liverpool Street. I tried making conversation on the way but she seemed lost in thought, only offering half-hearted responses to my questions. I asked her if she was OK and she offered me a half smile.

'I'm probably just tired, that's all,' she replied. 'Still, I finish early today so it's not too bad.' For a moment her face wore an expression that I couldn't quite discern. Was she upset? Was she mulling something over? I couldn't tell. Then all at once it disappeared. 'Don't forget the recital's at seven,' she continued. 'Jack's told all his friends that his journalist daddy's coming and will probably be writing a review.'

As her train arrived to take her back into central London we kissed goodbye but it felt cold and perfunctory, compared to the kiss with which she had greeted me outside Allegro's. Should I ask her one last time if everything was all right? It seemed like a good idea but before I'd even formed the question she had hopped on the train and taken her seat. As the train doors closed I stood waving goodbye but she didn't look up once. It was as though she was lost in another world.

★   ★   ★

Through no fault of my own I ended up being late for the recital. And by late I don't mean coming in halfway through the evening but rather having missed the entire thing — Jack's recorder solo, Rosie's group violin performance and everything in between.

Penny face was like thunder as she spotted me dodging through the hall full of proud parents gathering together their offspring. This wasn't going to be an easy sell at all.

'You wouldn't believe it, Pen; everything that could go wrong did go wrong. My meeting with Camilla took the whole afternoon and then she wanted me to prepare our efforts for a meeting first thing in the morning with the bigwigs upstairs, and once I'd finished that it was gone six and I still had a rewrite to do on some copy that was long past its deadline and then I was stuck on a tube for forty minutes because of an 'incident' on the line. Every time I tried to call I had no signal. It was a total nightmare. How did the kids get on?'

Penny didn't say a word. Instead she gestured

towards the front of the room where Jack and one of his friends were jumping on and off the stairs at the side of the stage. I scanned the room for Rosie and finally spotted her at the back of the hall talking with her friend Amelie.

I called over to Jack and he came running over dangling his recorder from his fingers. 'Why weren't you here, Daddy? Mum said you promised you'd come. Isn't it bad to break promises?'

I knelt down and gave Jack the biggest hug in my repertoire. 'It's the absolute worst thing you can do but sometimes these things are just out of your hands. I tried really hard to get here but I couldn't. You forgive me though, don't you?'

Jack's face lit up. Was there ever a better present for a child than the opportunity to tell off a parent? He adopted his sternest expression: it was adorable. 'Do you promise not to do it again?'

I held up my hand and crossed my heart. 'Never again.'

'Then I forgive you.'

Hand in hand we made our way over to Rosie who had just finished saying goodbye to her friend.

'I'm sorry I was late, Rosie. A whole bunch of stuff got in the way. Do you forgive me?'

Rosie shrugged. 'You didn't miss much anyway. Jack got nervous and kept playing the wrong notes. Everyone thought it was hilarious.'

I glared a first and final warning in Rosie's direction as Jack's face crumpled in sadness. 'Rosie, you know better than that. Apologise to your brother.'

She rolled her eyes for both Jack's benefit and mine. 'Fine! Jack, I'm sorry, OK?'

It sounded more like a threat than an apology and Rosie knew it. I glanced at Penny, who had come over to join us, hoping that she might jump in and say something, but she didn't. It was as though she'd decided to take the role of an impartial observer. Was she really so angry with me for being late? Or was this to do with something else?

Out of earshot the children gathered their instruments and so I took the opportunity to gauge her mood. 'Are we OK?'

A thin-lipped silence then she turned her back on me, picked up the kids' bags from the chair in front of her and left the room.

* * *

Any hope that Penny's mood might have lightened once we reached home evaporated the moment she got out of the car — having not said a word the entire journey home — and made her way inside the house without looking back. Even Jack, who had never been great at reading people's emotions, was prompted to ask if Mummy was all right. I told him she was just tired and he nodded solemnly as though he understood.

I took responsibility for the bedtime regime while Penny cleared the kitchen noisily. Left to his own devices Jack could easily take a good hour and a half to get ready for bed with a long shower, full-scale search of his room for missing pyjamas and several trips to the bathroom. I managed the lot, bedtime stories included, in forty-five minutes — which given that I was wild with tiredness myself was no mean feat.

On the way downstairs I passed Rosie's room; thankfully as a ten-year-old she pretty much put herself to bed these days. She was sitting on her bed in her pyjamas and dressing gown playing with her iPod.

'So what are you doing now? Are you staying up here or coming down for a bit?'

She momentarily lifted her eyes from the screen. 'Staying put. Are you in trouble with Mum because you were late?'

I couldn't help but smile; sometimes I loved how black and white my kids' worlds were. 'No one's in trouble with anyone. Mum's just tired and if you know what's good for you, you'll keep a low profile and get to bed tonight without any fuss.' I kissed the top of her head. 'Lights out by nine o'clock at the latest and I mean it.'

Downstairs I paused in front of the kitchen door, wondering what tack to take with Penny. Should I ask her outright what the problem was or wait patiently and hope she'd tell me in her own time? In the end I decided to play it by ear and entered the kitchen to find her sitting at the table. My eyes flicked from the half-empty bottle of Malbec in front of her to the full glass she held to her lips.

I sat down in the chair nearest to her. 'Rough day?'

'No more than usual.'

'It's just that you don't seem right. It's not just

because I was late is it?'

'It didn't help.'

'So what is it?'

'You tell me.' She looked away and took another long sip from her glass before setting it carefully down on the table. I tried to read her face. She was angry, possibly hurt too, and while I was the cause I couldn't work out why.

'You slept with her didn't you?' she said, her gaze fixed towards the view of the garden through the French windows.

For the second time that day, I felt my world imploding.

'What?'

'That woman today, the one we met at lunch, the tall willowy-looking one, Angela, that was her name wasn't it?'

'You think I'm having an affair with Angela?'

'Had, have, is that how you think you're going to get out of this — on a technicality? I was there, Joe. I saw the way she looked at you. There was something between you, I know it.'

Brimming over with righteous anger I bounded from the room only to return moments later clutching my phone, which I slapped down on the table so hard that it skidded across the surface and was only prevented from falling off by Penny's arm.

'If you really think that what you've just said is true then call her up, speak to her and make up your own mind,' I spat. 'Tell her what you've just told me. Her number's under Towney.'

I didn't dare to think, feel or move as we both stared at the phone. My entire life was held in the balance. One wrong move and it would all be over.

Penny pushed the phone away, stood up and buried herself in my arms. 'I'm so, so sorry, Joe. It's just that when we bumped into her today, I felt, I don't know, I just felt like something was ... off. I felt sure that there was something between you. I should never have said that. I should never have said something so horrible. You're not my dad. You'd never be like him.' Sobbing even harder she clung to me fiercely like a child apologising for her accusation over and over again. 'Please tell me you forgive me.'

'It's OK,' I reassured her, 'there's nothing to forgive. Everything's going to be fine.'

8

That night as Penny fell asleep in my arms I went over the all-too-surreal events of the day. The image of Penny meeting Bella was burned into my brain, as was Penny's accusation that I'd cheated on her with Angela. I'd escaped by the skin of my teeth but at what cost? Now Penny thought she was losing the plot. Seeing things that weren't there. But she hadn't been entirely wrong. I'd had an affair, just not with Angela. With all the time that had passed combined with my lack of memory of the night in question it was easy to kid myself that maybe it hadn't happened at all. That it was just a bad dream. But the evidence was overwhelming, not least the look on Bella's face when I asked her why she'd waited for me. It had been a look of hurt and betrayal of the kind that only former lovers use. It had happened. We'd slept together and nothing I said or did could change that.

*　　*　　*

The following morning over breakfast I announced to the kids that both Penny and I would be taking them to school. To Jack this was like hearing that Christmas and his birthday had arrived early.

'You're both taking us. How come?'

'Mum and I have both decided to take the day off work.' I looked over at Penny sitting next to

82

me and she squeezed my hand.

'It's one of the perks of being a grown-up,' said Penny. 'Every now and again you get to put your feet up.'

Never one to miss an opportunity when one presented itself Rosie's ears pricked up immediately. 'Can Jack and I take the day off school too?'

'Not a chance, Missy,' I replied. 'You've got a maths test today.'

Rosie's face became the very picture of despair. 'That's so unfair! How come you guys get the day off and we don't?'

'It's just the way it is,' I told her. 'Now go and brush your teeth and grab your bags because we're out of here in five minutes.'

Talking Penny into calling in sick had initially proved harder than I had hoped. Having had the idea during the night I had put it to her as we lay in bed that morning but she was still so racked with guilt about the accusation she'd made it was obvious that all she had wanted to do was escape to work. In the end she'd only relented because in the heat of the moment I said, 'If you don't take today off, sit down with me and talk through this mess you're going to end up wrecking this marriage for good.' As much as I regretted saying it, it did do the trick. 'You're right,' she said tearfully, 'I'll phone in,' and without another word she got ready for the day ahead, made the call and then joined the kids and me for breakfast.

★　★　★

The house was quiet and still as Penny and I removed our coats and shoes having dropped off the kids at school. It was so rare for the two of us to be home alone and even more rare for such a day to occur during the week. Even the light in the house seemed different, and for what felt like the first time I noticed the shadows the oak tree in front of our house threw against the off-white walls of the hallway.

We decamped to the kitchen. I made us coffee while Penny got out a plate on which she carefully presented the freshly baked pastries we'd purchased from the little bakery near the kids' school. These small routines were so commonplace and soothing, it was almost possible to believe that everything would be OK.

'Before we start,' said Penny, cradling her cup in both hands, 'I know you've probably got a lot you need to say about the horrible things I said last night but I want you to know here and now that I have never — and I do mean never — been as sorry as I am right now. What I said, what I accused you of was the worst thing I could ever do because the truth is in all the time we've been together you've never done anything other than give me cause to be grateful for having you in my life. I just want you to know that I love you and adore you and I will do everything in my power to make up for it.'

This was too much. Being told I was in the right when I was so clearly in the wrong was just too high a price to pay. I wasn't made of stone. I had a conscience and, when it came to Penny, I had a heart too. I couldn't bear to hear her say another word. It was as though something cracked within me and the guilt came flooding out.

'You were right,' I said, avoiding her gaze. 'You got the wrong person but I cheated on you all the same.' I dared a glance at her as she looked on in silent horror. 'It was a while ago — with Bella, the ex-intern you met the other day. It was a one-off, I swear. I was drunk, or not thinking properly. It'll never happen again. It's the worst thing I've ever done. I hate myself for it. That's why I'm telling you now. The guilt is eating me up.'

Penny didn't speak and somehow her silence and stillness were worse than any dramatic outburst could ever have been.

I took her hand in mine and although she didn't resist she didn't respond either. It was as though she wasn't there at all.

I started to panic. 'Pen? Please, please talk to me.' I squeezed her hand still tighter but she didn't move. 'I love you, Penny. I've never stopped. I just got confused, that's all. I made some really bad decisions but I swear on my life — on our kids' lives — that I'll never — '

'Don't you dare!' spat Penny as though a switch had just been flicked somewhere deep within her. 'Don't you dare bring our kids into this! You want to ruin your life, Joe, then be my guest, but don't try and manipulate me with the kids!' She stood up and ran from the room. Every fibre of my being wanted to go to her, to comfort her but I just couldn't move. It was like I was paralysed from the neck down and the only thing that worked was the one thing I wished would stop: my brain. I should never have told her. I should've kept my big mouth shut. The torture of keeping this from her was nothing compared to the memory of the look on her face when I'd told her. I'd see that look for the rest of my life; the look of pure shock that said, 'I never thought that you of all people would do this to me.'

It was impossible to know how long I sat there motionless in the chair but the sound of her returning down the stairs was enough to snap me out of it and bring me to my feet. I needed to see her, to talk to her, to explain that I still loved her and was prepared to do anything to make it right.

By the time I reached the hallway she was putting on her coat. At her feet was her overnight bag.

'Where are you going?'

'To my mum and Tony's.'

'But what about the kids?'

'Tell them I'll call later to kiss them goodnight.'

Outside, a minicab driver sounded his horn. She picked up her bag and reeled off a list of instructions about the kids. It would have been funny — a broken-hearted woman who even in the midst of her pain couldn't stop herself from entering the role that defined her — had this been a play, or a book, or a film. But it wasn't any of these. It was my life. Her life. Our life together. 'You need to write a cheque for Jack's dinner money,' she said, 'and make sure you read with him tonight as he's having problems with his 'th' sounds again. Oh, and check Rosie's homework diary. She's taken to declaring that she has none even when it's written down in black and white.'

She opened the front door. The territorial songs of blackbirds. A far-off siren of an ambulance. The low rumble of a waiting diesel engine. I grabbed her arm but she snatched it away almost immediately. 'Please, Pen, please don't go. Look, let's talk, let's talk and make this right.'

'I think you've said more than enough for now,' she replied, then picked up her case and slammed the door behind her.

For a moment I didn't do anything but stare at the back of the door. She couldn't have left. Surely any moment now she'd be back. But a moment passed and so did many others until the collective weight of all those missed opportunities came crashing down on me, forcing me to the floor where I sat sobbing uncontrollably. And there I remained, bereft of all hope until I smelled that same sweet heavy scent I'd smelled before I was mugged and turned my head to see the unmistakable form of Fiona Briggs sitting on the stairs.

'Well,' she said, 'you made a right cock-up of that, didn't you?'

9

Fiona Briggs.

The very same Fiona Briggs I'd dated all those years ago. More to the point, the very dead Fiona Briggs whose funeral I'd attended not so long ago. But she looked so real. So alive, so . . . Fiona. I had to be seeing things. I blinked. I looked away from her. I looked back again. She was still there. Perhaps there'd been some mistake. Perhaps they'd buried someone else that day and Fiona was still alive. But this didn't explain why she was currently sitting on my stairs examining her painted fingernails nor how she'd managed to turn the clock all the way back to the early nineties. The Fiona in front of me didn't look a day over eighteen, complete with too much eyeliner and the brown monkey boots she'd loved so much. I put my head in my hands: I was having a hallucination. It was the only thing that made sense. Penny's leaving me had pushed me to the very edge of sanity. I was in real danger of losing the plot altogether; perhaps I already had.

'Have you finished with all the soul-searching internal soliloquies or do you need another five minutes? It's not like I've got anything better to be getting on with.'

I raised my head, fixed my eyes on Fiona and rose to my feet determined to take control.

'You're not real,' I said firmly. 'I know you're

not real, so just go away, OK? You're a figment of my imagination. I'm freaked out because Penny's left, that's all. All I need to do is go upstairs and lie down and you'll be gone.'

Fiona laughed. 'That's brilliant! Your wife's just left you because you're a cheating low-life toerag and your response is to take to your bed! Now that *really* is insane! I always knew you were an idiot, Joe Clarke, but I'd hoped you'd have become wiser over the years, not more stupid.'

This was worse than I thought. The Fiona I'd hallucinated didn't just look like Fiona but spoke like her too. There was no point in trying to argue with this imaginary Fiona — I never could win against the real one so I had no chance now — but perhaps if I indulged this illusion a little I could find why I'd manifested it here and then make it disappear.

'Yolo,' said Fiona. She crossed her legs and pointed the toe of her right boot in my direction. '*That* is why I'm here.'

I was completely baffled. 'I have no idea what you're on about. What do you mean, Yolo?'

'You. Only. Live. Once. My dad said it at my funeral and you used it to justify your little dalliance with that girl — who incidentally isn't all that and a bag of chips. Her arse is HUGE and she's not half as posh as she makes out — anyway, where was I? Yes, Yolo. Ironic isn't it? There I was spouting platitudes like 'You only live once', and one altercation with the sharp edge of a tiled bench and I'm dead as a doornail and plaguing you from beyond the grave.'

'So you're saying you're a ghost?'

'We prefer the word apparition but yes, I suppose at a push ghost will do.'

I had to laugh. This was all just too ridiculous. 'Right, so you're an *apparition* and of all the places in the world that you could appear right now — like, I don't know, a spooky Scottish castle or a graveyard at midnight, you've chosen my hallway in South London in the middle of the day?'

Fiona smiled enigmatically. 'Let's just say for now that I have my reasons.'

'And am I meant to believe that one of them is that you're precious about people hijacking your catchphrases?'

Fiona's face changed in an instant. Her eyes narrowed, her lips thinned. She looked like evil incarnate. She uncrossed her legs, stood up and walked down to the bottom of the stairs. 'So you think this is funny, do you? You think this is all one big joke? Let's see if you're still laughing when I've finished teaching you a lesson.'

'What lesson?'

'The only kind that counts, Joe: a life lesson. You see, the thing about people like you is that you always have to learn the hard way. Wouldn't you agree?'

'No,' I replied. 'Not at all.'

'Really?'

'Yes, really.'

Fiona sighed and sat down on the bottom step. 'So, Mr I-Like-The-Easy-Way, what do you think would've happened if you hadn't got mugged that night?'

'What night when?'

'Don't play the innocent with me. I'm talking about the night before the morning after when you woke up in bed with that little trollop who isn't your wife.'

I closed my eyes again. This was getting weirder by the second. Why was this hallucination I'd conjured up talking about that night? My memory of it was patchy at best. This vision of a teenage Fiona Briggs was nothing more than my subconscious trying to work things out. It was trying to tell me that I had been mugged that night but I knew for a fact that this wasn't true. I hadn't been mugged. At least —

'At least what?' quizzed Fiona, arching a carefully plucked eyebrow. 'Is it all coming back to you now?'

'Look, I'm not having this conversation. I didn't say any of that out loud and the fact that you seemingly heard my thoughts just goes to prove I've made you up. I'm having some sort of breakdown and right now I'm alone in my hallway talking to myself.'

'Nice theory dimwit, but let's just park it to one side for a minute and concentrate on the matter in hand: were you mugged that night or not?'

I hesitated, unsure of whether or not to indulge this illusion any further. I sighed. I was this far in, I decided, so I might as well see it through.

'Well, the truth is when I woke up that morning I was convinced that I had been mugged. My memory of it was so clear. It seemed so real. But then when there were no cuts, no bruises, no

91

marks at all and I still had my phone and wallet, I realised it couldn't have happened. It had to have been some sort of vivid dream. That's all it was, wasn't it?'

Fiona held out her hand to silence me. 'Do I look like sodding Google to you?'

'No,' I replied.

'Then stop with the questions, OK? From now on you only speak when you're spoken to.' Fiona took a deep breath and tossed her hair back as if to compose herself. 'Right, where were we? Yes, that's it, I asked you a question: what do you think would've happened if you hadn't been mugged that night? And your answer is . . . ?'

'I don't know,' I replied, fighting back the urge to question her again, 'because as I've just explained I wasn't mugged that night.'

Fiona pulled a face. 'Shows how much you know then, doesn't it? Because, Idiot Boy, in fact you were. By me.'

'You?'

'Well me, and my friend Chaz — you know the one, walks with a swagger, likes sportswear?'

'The guy with the lighter?'

'Bingo. It was one of Chaz's favourite tricks when he was alive, a pincer movement with his mate Traps, he was good at it apparently but then Traps went and stabbed him in a row over a girl and it all got a bit messy.' Fiona grinned. 'I'm digressing aren't I? You probably want me to stick to the point, which is this: I was the one who hit you over the head with this.' She reached behind her and produced a cricket bat that I'd never seen before.

'You hit me with that?'

Fiona nodded. 'You should have heard the noise. Nothing quite like the sound of willow against numbskull.'

'I don't understand. Why would you hit me with a cricket bat?'

'Because a tennis racket wouldn't quite have done the trick.'

'So you're saying you wanted to hurt me? Why would you want to do that?'

Fiona laughed. 'Think about it.'

I thought hard. 'Because you're a mean and spiteful bitch who despite going out with me for eighteen months couldn't stand the sight of me?'

Fiona wagged a finger at me nonchalantly. 'Sticks and stones, Joe, sticks and stones.'

This had to be what a nervous breakdown felt like. Talking hallucinations. General madness. Things sounding like they made sense when really they made none at all. I took a deep breath and made a superhuman effort to remain calm.

'I apologise,' I replied. 'But try and see this from my point of view. My wife's just left me and for some unknown reason I'm having visions of a dead ex-girlfriend. I'm just trying to figure out what's going on.'

'Aren't we all?' said Fiona. 'The thing is, Joe, I actually saved you from yourself that night.'

'Saved me, how?'

'By stopping you from meeting Slag Face.'

'You mean Bella?'

'No, I mean Slag Face. I must say I thought you had better taste in women but obviously I was wrong. Anyway, I saved you. You should be thanking me, not casting aspersions on my character by trying to pass me off as a hallucination. Have you any idea how offensive that is?'

'But none of this makes any sense. I know I wasn't mugged that night. I almost wish that I had been because then I wouldn't have met up with Bella, or slept with her and made the biggest mistake of my life.'

Fiona clapped slowly. 'Finally, he gets it. Were you always this dense or is it a recent development?'

My head felt like it was going to explode. 'So are you saying that I didn't actually cheat on Penny?'

'Well not unless you've mastered the art of being in two places at once. You haven't, have you? I've got a new friend who can do that but she's been practising for years.'

'This is ridiculous. It makes no sense at all. How could I not have cheated on Penny when I know for a fact that I woke up in Bella's bed?'

'It's a real conundrum isn't it?' said Fiona sarcastically. 'Any ideas? No? Well, let me spell it out for you in a manner that even you will understand: you were mugged that night by me like I said. You never were in bed with Slag Face. And right now you're lying unconscious face down on a pavement in a dodgy part of East London, oozing blood from a cracking head wound. It's genius really.'

I stared hard at Fiona as she stretched out her arms triumphantly. It was incredible how intricate this hallucination was. The heavy-handed eyeliner, the detailing of her clothing, even the sweet heavy scent of her perfume was accurate for the Fiona I remembered. I tried to recall its name.

'Poison by Dior,' clarified Fiona. 'Best. Perfume. Ever.'

It triggered the sudden release of a fragment of memory from the depths of my mind. The morning I'd woken up at Bella's I'd smelled that same fragrance. But that didn't mean anything, did it? There could have been a million and one explanations for it, all of them more plausible than this. I laughed out loud. My imagination really was quite spectacular.

'So you're trying to say that none of this is real? That everything that has happened since that night has all been, what . . . some kind of dream?'

'If that's what your tiny brain can cope with at the moment then go with that.'

'That's ridiculous. This isn't Narnia, it's Lewisham! It's been months since then. So much has happened in that time, how can you possibly expect me to believe that it's still that same night?'

'I don't *need* you to believe anything. I've got a job to do and this is me doing it.'

'What job? What are you talking about?'

'The details aren't important right now. Just the facts. That night you stood at a crossroads: one path leading home to your wife and kids and the other leading to Slag Face. The thing about crossroads, Joe, is that no matter which path you take there's always part of you wondering about the road not taken. Thanks to me you're going to find out exactly what lies at the end of that road and the journey has already begun. You think you only get to live one life? Well, from now on this is yours. Enjoy.'

This was all too much. I shut my eyes, willing this whole thing to be over, and when I opened them again Fiona was gone.

10

I didn't move for an hour after the hallucination ended. I couldn't. It was like I was rooted to the spot. I'd obviously suffered some kind of post-traumatic stress episode brought on by Penny's leaving. What other explanation could there possibly be for my dead ex-girlfriend popping back for a visit? It had seemed so real and the idea that my brain was capable of doing something like this while I was fully conscious terrified me because while it wasn't exactly great that I'd blocked out the night that I'd slept with Bella, it was altogether a different kind of 'not great' to be conjuring up Fiona. And though my every instinct was to put the hallucination and everything that came with it into a file at the back of my mind to be worked on another day (along with my missing night with Bella), each time I tried to do so the same question would present itself: was that really a ghost or have I officially lost my mind?

Like any decent twenty-first-century man my first step once I'd gathered my wits about me was to sit down at the kitchen table with my laptop and Google 'Suffering from hallucinations why?' Within 0.2 seconds I was faced with 3.3 million potential diagnoses. I took a look at the first five to get a brief overview of my condition. According to everything that I read hallucinations took several different forms but usually

97

only ever affected one of the senses. For example someone might hallucinate a smell, or a sensation, even a sound, but rarely, if ever, all three. Yet my hallucination had been so real, so complete. I'd heard Fiona talking, I'd smelled her perfume and I'd seen her sitting on my own stairs looking as real as anyone I'd ever seen. Potential causes of hallucinations ranged from schizophrenia through to substance abuse but given that until this morning I'd never seen anything that wasn't actually there combined with the fact that I hadn't so much as touched a glass of wine since the weekend I doubted either of these could be the cause. One thing that did strike a chord with me was the mention of anxiety being a key factor. This made absolute and total sense. After all, what could be more anxiety-inducing than watching my wife leaving me? No, there wasn't anything seriously wrong with my mental health. I just needed to calm down and relax a little then talk to Penny and try to sort things out.

I reasoned that the best way to re-establish normality was to busy myself with mundane household chores. I stacked the breakfast things into the dishwasher, put a load of washing on, tidied the kids' bedrooms, cleaned the bathroom and then after lunch vacuumed the hallway and made a sizeable dent in the ironing pile. Although I was still unsettled, the performance of these tasks did soothe me somehow and had the bonus of showing Penny, when she did return, that I'd made an effort and kept the wheels turning. As feeble attempts to get on the right side of a woman wronged went it was pretty pathetic, but at that moment it was all I had.

★ ★ ★

I was already filled with dread as I stood in the school playground waiting for the kids to come out but when the bell went signalling their impending arrival I was nearly sick. They were going to want to know where Penny was and I didn't have the faintest clue what to say or how to say it.

Jack came through the doors first and on spotting me he bounded across the yard and into my arms. I scooped him, his parka, book bag, water bottle and sandwich box up into my arms and landed a big kiss on his cheek.

'Where's Mummy? Couldn't she come too?'

'She's had to go and visit Grandma and Grandpa because Grandpa's not very well,' I explained.

Jack looked up at me quizzically. 'What's wrong with him?'

'Nothing too bad but I think Mummy's a bit worried and wants to see for herself that he's OK.'

Jack thought about it for a moment. 'Mummy does worry a lot, doesn't she?'

'Yes, but only because she loves us all so much.'

I set Jack on the ground and we began walking over to the junior playground to pick up Rosie. 'Will we get to speak to her tonight?'

'Of course, and she'll want to know exactly how your day's been. So come on, how was it?'

99

Jack's face fell and he pushed out his bottom lip. 'Rubbish.'

'How come? That Lucas kid and his mates haven't been bothering you again, have they?'

Jack shook his head.

'I'm not scared of him anyway.'

'Never said you were. So what's happened to make your day rubbish? You were really looking forward to it this morning.'

'Mrs Millard told me off and sent me down the zone board because I told Kayleigh Sanderson that she was going to die.'

I stopped in my tracks.

'You said what?'

'I told her she was going to die and she started crying and told the teacher. But I was right, wasn't I? You said every living thing dies eventually.'

I cast my mind back to the previous weekend when the conversation in question had occurred. We had all just finished watching *The Lion King* and Jack — who for as long as I could remember had had a bit of a dark side — asked when he would die. Cursing Elton John and his 'Circle of Life' I'd reassured him that he wouldn't die for a long time. Then Jack asked when Rosie would die, to which I responded not for a very long time. Then Jack asked when Penny and I would die and so very much aware of my son's ability to continue this line of questioning long after bedtime I replied that while we wouldn't be going anywhere any time soon every living thing dies eventually.

To be fair to me it had seemed like the right

thing to say at the time, and appeared to satisfy Jack's morbid curiosity but it had obviously been percolating away in that brain of his ever since. I rubbed Jack's head affectionately, hoping that in the future he might focus his energies on Poké-mon cards rather than existential philosophy.

'The thing is, son, the important part of what I told you was the word: 'eventually'. Do you know what eventually means? It means one day way, way in the future but not right now. So while you were right in the sense that one day Kayleigh Sanderson will die, chances are it won't be for a very, very long time, so long in fact that it's probably not even worth mentioning it, all right?'

Nodding half-heartedly, Jack looked at me as if about to make a point of clarification but thankfully before he could the bell for the end of the junior school day rang releasing a deluge of rough and tumble pre-teens out of the main school entrance.

In contrast to Jack, Rosie's response to my presence at pickup time was typically muted: meandering through the playground chatting ani-matedly to her best friend Carly she had scanned the adult faces for her mum, spotted me and without a hint of surprise casually strolled over.

The first sentence out of her mouth was: 'Where's Mum?' And the second, 'I'm starving. Have you got any food?'

'Well hello to you too.'

Rosie sniffed haughtily and made a big show of waving goodbye to Carly. 'Dad's being a pain,' she called and then pulled a face — eyes crossed and tongue out — to illustrate exactly how much of a pain I was being. 'I'll text you later, OK?'

Carly giggled and waved goodbye. Given that from my experience there were very few moments in the day when they weren't communicating with each other in some fashion I wondered what they could possibly have left to say.

'So where is Mum then?'

'Granddad's not well,' interjected Jack, thoroughly pleased to know something that his sister didn't. 'Mum's gone to look after him.'

'How long will she be gone for?'

'I don't know. A day or two maybe.'

Rosie wrinkled her nose. 'I'll text her and find out.'

'No you won't. She's got a lot on her plate right now. She said she'll call this evening and you can ask her whatever you want then. But in the meantime no texts, understand?'

Rosie nodded reluctantly, signalling thankfully that she knew the difference between the kind of no that could be ignored and the one that would result in her phone being taken away if she even thought about disregarding it.

'Right.' I sighed — this day had gone on for far too long and I couldn't believe how much of it was left before it would officially be over. 'Let's go home.'

★   ★   ★

I made the kids a tea of pasta with a green salad, which Jack point blank refused to touch. I didn't have it in me to make him eat it but neither did

I have it in me to contravene Penny's wishes ('The kids eat what we put on their plates and that's that,') and so I compromised by allowing Jack to make such a mess of his plate that the majority of the salad ended up on the floor, thereby saving us both from doing the wrong thing where Penny was concerned.

Penny phoned after tea but didn't say more than a handful of words to me. All she wanted was to speak to the kids and so while she did that I busied myself in the kitchen. Afterwards as I took Jack upstairs for his usual bedtime routine I asked how he thought Mummy sounded but he just looked at me, puzzled. 'She sounded like Mummy. How else would she sound?'

Downstairs in the living room Rosie was doing her own thing, which seemed to consist of watching TV with the sound off, texting her friends and listening to music all at the same time, and once Jack was in bed I sat her down and attempted to help her with her homework. It was multiplying decimal fractions, something I hadn't encountered for the best part of twenty-two years. Between us both it took half an hour and a search on Google to answer the first question, and a further forty minutes for the next three by which time we both decided to call it a day.

After making the kids' sandwiches, and ironing their uniforms I settled down in front of the TV but couldn't concentrate on anything and so ended up going to bed. The next morning I called in sick again, partly because I needed to be around for the kids but mostly because I couldn't escape the fear that were Penny to arrive home unexpectedly she would interpret my absence as a sign that I didn't care. Anyway, I decided, if my hallucination had been a sign of anything it was that I needed to keep calm and I wasn't going to get much of that at work.

Three days into my sick leave and desperate to offer the kids something other than pasta for tea I'd ventured out to the supermarket to stock up with supplies and when I returned the first thing I saw in the hallway were Penny's silver glittery Converses at the bottom of the stairs. I called out to her but there was no response so I searched the house until I found her loading clothes straight from her suitcase into the washing machine.

'When did you get back?'

'About twenty minutes ago. Did you go shopping?'

'I thought it best to get a few things in. Is that OK?'

She said nothing.

'How are your folks?'

'Fine, though I really wish you hadn't told the kids Grandpa was ill. Poor Tony didn't know what they were on about.'

'I'm sorry,' I replied, 'I just thought — '

'I know,' said Penny. 'It's fine.'

I poured myself a glass of water from the bottle in the fridge door and stood closer to her. 'The kids have really missed you. This morning they could barely bring themselves to talk about anything other than when you'd be back. You are back, aren't you?'

Penny closed the door of the washing machine and turned the dial to start the programme. The kitchen filled with the sound of water flooding into the machine's stainless steel drum.

'I've been doing a lot of thinking,' she said, looking up at me.

I took her hand. 'Pen, I want you to know that I'll do whatever it takes to make this right. You name it and I'll do it, no questions asked. I love you. You and the kids are my world and I don't ever want to be without you.'

'Do you really mean what you've just said?'

'Of course I do,' I said quickly, fearing that the opportunity to make amends might pass before I'd had time to respond. 'I absolutely meant every word. Whatever it is you want, it's yours.'

Penny took her hand from mine. 'Then I want you to move out. You've screwed everything up, Joe, you really have, and right now what I need, what this family needs, is for you to go.'

This wasn't exactly what I'd been hoping for. My every instinct told me that if I left it might prove impossible to return. Perhaps I could talk her round and make her see the impracticality of her request. 'I get that you're upset, Pen, I really do, but you're not really thinking this through are you? I mean how long are we talking about here? What would we tell the kids?'

'I'll deal with them,' said Penny. 'They'll be fine.'

'But if I went that wouldn't be us saying it's over would it? Penny, I — '

The hardness of the look she cast in my direction cut me off completely. Wordless though it was, it spoke volumes about my inability to keep promises made even a few breaths ago.

'Tell the kids I love them,' I replied, 'and tell them that I'll speak to them soon.'

11

It was hard to describe with any degree of accuracy the multitude of feelings that manifested themselves as I stood looking up at the faded, peeling façade of the St Joseph's Guest House. Suffice it to say that none of them were good. From the outside alone it was clear that this was the kind of place where hope came to die and the interior with its sticky lino, yellowing paintwork, and strange aroma, only confirmed what I already suspected. I booked in for a night (my mind balked at the idea that I might be there any longer) and was shown to a dingy single room with access to a shared bathroom with the added benefit of breathtaking views of the Old Kent Road.

I packed with a surprising efficiency for someone who didn't know where he was going or how long he was going to be away. In fact I was almost proud of how well I'd done the job until, of course, I remembered that I wasn't going on a last-minute trip halfway around the world for a celebrity interview but rather was leaving the home I'd lived in with my wife for the past ten years all because I screwed up in the biggest way possible.

Hideous though the B&B was, the truth of the matter was that my sleeping options were limited. My parents divorced when I was nineteen and my dad died five years later. Mum was still in Swindon but I couldn't stay there for any significant period of time without driving us both up the wall, and although my brother Jim and I got on well, he was in Bristol which wasn't exactly within commuting distance. As for friends, most had long since moved out of London to the commuter belt with their families and even if any had been up for having a thirty-eight-year old man sleeping on their sofa for an indeterminate amount of time, I wasn't sure I could stand the pitying looks that would almost certainly follow. I would never have had this problem twenty years ago and even five years ago it might have been OK to knock on a mate's door and say that you'd been kicked out by your girlfriend. But now all the girlfriends were wives, and all the wives mothers, and no one really wants a reminder of how wrong life can get turning up in a sleeping bag on their living-room floor.

★ ★ ★

That evening as I heard the sound of the occupant of the room next to mine coughing loudly through the paper-thin walls I called Penny's phone, hoping to find out from her when I'd be able to speak to the kids. The only thing was, Penny didn't answer her phone, Rosie did. 'Dad! It's you! I can't believe you're in China! You sound like you're just down the road! Why have they sent you there?'

China? For a moment I thought it was just Rosie having a laugh but then I remembered the situation at hand. Penny had clearly had to do some quick thinking to explain my absence and in her anger she had sent me as far away as she could. Working quickly, I raked through the far reaches of my memory for an excuse that sounded sufficiently plausible. Film premieres sounded too exciting. A political investigation too dull. Finally I found it. A small article I'd done on the British Council a few years ago.

'I'm covering an arts festival. They've gathered together groups of British writers, actors and artists and they're working with their Chinese counterparts to make something new.'

'A bit like an exchange trip?'

'Pretty much.'

'Cool.'

'So when are you back?'

'I'm not sure. The festival goes on for a month but I'm hoping to be back before the week's out.'

We talked some more about my trip and Rosie asked a thousand and one questions about China, the answers to which I could only hope she didn't choose to verify via the internet. It was so good to hear her voice. I know it hadn't even been a day but I already missed her.

She asked if she should put Jack on the line but as much as I wanted to speak to him I needed to talk to Penny more.

'Can you put Mum on?'

'OK. Love you, Dad.'

'Love you too, sweetie.'

A short pause, then Penny's voice.

'Hi.'

'How are you?'

'OK. I'm sorry about before. Rosie must have heard my phone, saw who it was and was so eager to talk to you that she didn't bother telling me.'

'It did throw me a little . . . well, that and the fact that you've sent me to China.'

'Would you have preferred me to tell them the truth?'

'No, of course not, it's just . . . I don't know. I'm checking in, that's all. I need to know everyone's all right.'

'They're both fine.'

'And you?'

'I'm not doing this. If you want to speak to the kids speak to the kids but leave me out of it.'

She called for Jack and the next thing I knew he was on the line.

'Daddy!'

'Hey, son! You OK?'

'Yes, thank you. What time is it in China? Is it night-time?'

I had no idea. I took a guess. 'Yes it is.'

Jack let out a victorious roar. 'I told Rosie it would be night time and I was right! What are the people you're with like? Are they nice?'

Showing a knack for comic timing hitherto unknown, the man in the room next to mine produced one of his most bronchial coughs yet.

'They're lovely,' I replied. 'Couldn't be better.'

We talked about his day at school, his excitement about his friend Alex's upcoming birthday and why he didn't like girls. 'They don't like to play fighting games,' he explained, 'and they're always trying to kiss me.'

'Don't worry about it. Mummy's a girl and we both think she's brilliant, don't we?'

'Yes,' said Jack, yawning. 'Mummy is brilliant.'

'You sound shattered. You need to go to bed, sweetheart, so I'm going to say goodnight now. Love you very much.'

'Love you too. Do you want to say goodnight to Mummy?'

'Yes, please,' I replied and there was silence for a few moments before he came back on the line.

'Mummy says she's busy, Daddy, and she'll call you back in a bit.'

I said my goodbyes to Jack and then the line went dead. I tossed the phone on the bed next to me, painfully aware of the truth that Penny wasn't going to call back any time soon. The man next door had another violent coughing fit and was only drowned out by the siren of a passing police car. This was my life. And what a spectacular mess I'd made of it.

'And so say all of us!'

A sudden whiff of perfume filled my nostrils. I looked up to see Fiona leaning against the rickety wardrobe in the corner of the room. She smiled coquettishly at me as our eyes met, almost as if she were a bashful schoolgirl and not a figment of my imagination.

Having reasoned away my previous encounter with Fiona as a one-off brain malfunction brought about by extreme stress — and therefore nothing to worry a doctor about — it was disconcerting in the extreme that she was back. This couldn't just be written off as 'one of those things' like the time as a kid when I flipped a

111

coin ten times in a row and got heads, or the time Penny and I went on holiday to Marbella in our early twenties and ended up in an apartment next door to our actual downstairs neighbours back in London. No, if this was happening again then it was officially in the realms of the weird and therefore needed a strategy for dealing with it. I just couldn't afford to lose my mind on top of everything else. I had to stay sane. Whichever broken part of my consciousness had churned up Fiona it wanted me to engage with it, and so I reasoned that if I refused to do so there would be a pretty good chance it would get the message that I wasn't playing ball and would give up hassling me.

'Oh,' she said, 'so that's your game now is it? Ignoring me? Do you honestly think you can do that when I can quite clearly read your mind? You really are as stupid as you look, aren't you? You can't escape me, Joe, unless I want you to.'

I squeezed my eyes shut. She wasn't going to get to me that easily.

'Actually, that's where you're wrong,' she said in response to my unspoken thoughts. 'It is going to be easy. Have you any idea how many men tried to ignore me when I was alive? Quite a few, I can tell you. And have you any idea how many of those men succeeded in their endeavour? Absolutely none. So if you think ignoring me is going to make me disappear, you can think again. You may recall that I know all the words to every song from *Madonna: The Immaculate Collection*. Do you really want me to sing them in your ear every second of every hour that

112

you're awake — which believe me will be all of them — because I'm game if you are.' Just to underline her point Fiona started singing the opening lines to 'Crazy For You' in a voice that was eighty per cent honk, seventeen per cent screech and three per cent pure unadulterated caterwaul; exactly as I remembered it being. It was excruciating. I wouldn't be able to last sixty seconds, let alone a whole day.

'Fine! You win! What do you want?'

'What do we all want, Joe? Peace, happiness, goodwill to all men.' She strode purposefully across the room to the window and wiped her hand across the glass to clear the condensation so that she could look out, but then she glanced at her hand and pulling a face of disgust proceeded to dry it on my coat that was hanging off the back of the chair next to her.

'Where did you find this dump? Is this really all you can afford? I know you're broke and everything, but come on, have some respect why don't you? I wouldn't send my worst enemy to a place like this.' She turned and took a few steps forward until she was only a couple of feet away from me. I stared at her as hard as I could. She could not have looked any more real than she did.

'That's because I am real,' she replied clearly, doing that mind-reading thing again. 'Or at least as real as I need to be for what I have to do.' She paused. 'I guess you're missing Penny and the kids right now.'

'Of course I am,' I snapped. 'How could I not be?'

'Do you think you'll make up eventually?'

'Why wouldn't we?'

Fiona shrugged. 'Who can say? We women are funny creatures. We never know what we really think about anything until it happens.'

'But she loves me. We have a family. All she needs is a bit of time to understand that I'll never do this again.'

Fiona laughed. 'Says you.'

'But I wouldn't!'

'Says you.'

'You're saying you think I would? You're the one out of your mind, not me.'

Fiona shrugged. 'We'll see about that.'

'Are you suggesting that I am mad?'

'Those words never left my lips.'

'So what are you saying?'

'I've told you. I'm dead, you're alive, and I'm here to save your marriage.'

I looked around the room, pointedly making a special effort to linger over the threadbare carpet. 'Well, you seem to be doing a spectacular job so far.'

Fiona tutted loudly. 'Joe, Joey, Joe, is that any way to talk to someone who's trying to help you out?'

'But you're not helping me out, are you? As far as I can work out all you're doing is taking great pleasure in being a one hundred per cent grade A bitch to me.'

Fiona offered me a cheeky wink that was every bit as annoying as it was hateful. 'Why don't we put a pin in that for another day? For now what I really want to do is talk about that night.'

114

'What night?'

'*That* night, Dumbo!' Fiona rolled her eyes with exasperation. 'The night you cheated on your wife.'

'But last time we spoke you said that I didn't cheat on Penny and that seems to make a kind of sense because I don't remember doing anything wrong. I remember texting Bella — '

'And that isn't cheating?'

'What? Sending a text?'

'There are texts and then there are *texts*, aren't there? And those were definitely *texts*. Would you be happy if Mrs Clarke saw those? Because I can make it happen if you like.'

'No, no, don't do that!'

'So, you're not so blameless after all?'

'I never said I was blameless. I just don't understand why you're here if I never actually cheated on Penny.'

'Teaching you a lesson,' replied Fiona. 'Weren't you listening last time?'

'So you're telling me I'm being punished for something I didn't do?'

'No, I'm telling you you're being punished for something you would've done had I not stopped you.'

'That makes no sense! How could you possibly know what I would or wouldn't have done without it happening? I'll admit that yes, I let myself get carried away for a minute with the texts. And yes, I was flattered by Bella's interest in me but I would never have actually gone to meet Bella. I'm just not that type of guy.'

It felt like a huge relief to say these words

115

aloud. To admit — no matter how barking — that this could actually be a reality, that I didn't cheat on Penny, that I had been faithful after all.

'I didn't do anything wrong,' I said aloud. 'I always knew there was something off about that night. It just wasn't like me. *I* don't do things like that. *I* didn't cheat on Penny!'

Fiona snorted. 'Says you.'

'But it's true! You know it is!'

'Says you.'

'Look, just because I entertained the thought of meeting up with Bella that night doesn't mean that I did anything wrong. I was simply trying on the idea for size for a second . . . just, I don't know, trying to work out how I felt.'

'Says you.'

I felt my sense of exasperation increase sharply.

'Look, just because you keep adding 'Says you' to everything I say doesn't mean you're right. Just because I *thought* about sleeping with Bella doesn't mean that I *would* have slept with Bella. Penny and the kids are my world. I'd never do anything to hurt them.'

Fiona laughed. 'Says you.' She cleared her throat theatrically. ' 'Is whispering nothing? Is leaning cheek to cheek? Is meeting noses?' '

Now I really did know that this was a hallucination. At sixth form Fiona studied maths, physics and chemistry because she thought the arts were 'pointless', so the idea that she might actually be able to quote lines from *The Winter's Tale* was simply too much to believe.

'Says you,' said Fiona out loud as though she'd read my thoughts again. 'I'll have you

116

know that I got quite into the arts after I dumped you. In fact I played Dorcas in a university production of *The Winter's Tale* in my final year to rave reviews, thank you very much.'

It was impossible to keep her on track. 'But what's your point?' I asked. 'In the play Leontes falsely believes his wife, Hermione, has been unfaithful to him with his friend, Polixenes. The 'whispering' and 'leaning cheek to cheek' lines were him misinterpreting innocent actions. You haven't made your point, Fiona, you've proved mine because like Hermione *I* didn't do anything wrong.'

Fiona arched her left eyebrow disdainfully. 'Didn't you? Do you really think Penny would be happy with the way you've behaved? 'Let every eye negotiate for itself, And trust no agent; for beauty is a witch, Against whose charms faith melteth in blood.''

'That's Claudio from *Much Ado About Nothing*,' I said.

'No,' said Fiona. 'That was you after your coffee date with Slag Face. You wanted her. She wanted you. Even if by some miracle you'd managed to escape her clutches that night it still would've happened because your ego wouldn't have been able to resist the temptation. But we'll get there, Joe, you and I will definitely get there.'

From behind me I heard the door slam hard. I turned around to see what was going on but the door was locked and bolted as I'd left it and when I looked back Fiona was gone.

I made a decision on the spot that this would

be the last time I would ever see her. I picked up my phone and called Dr Frank Bennett.

'Hi, Frank,' I said when he picked up. 'It's Joe Clarke here from *The Weekend* magazine. I was wondering whether you might be free for lunch at the Grange tomorrow?'

12

Every journalist worth their salt has someone like Dr Frank Bennett in their phone book, a medical expert who can be relied upon to offer an authoritative opinion on any health-related matter you care to mention.

I'd first met Dr Frank about ten years before when he was promoting his book, *I'm Sane, You're Sane — A Light-hearted Look at the Mental Health Industry*, and we'd hit it off so well that he'd quickly become my go-to medical expert. The last time I'd used him was when I'd needed him to make a few informed suggestions about a politician's state of mind following a big scandal about eighteen months ago. He'd provided me with all the quotes I'd needed and the reason I hadn't called him for anything since was because Camilla had spotted his picture in a feature of mine and commented to the entire floor, 'He looks about ninety-three!' After that I'd used Dr Caroline Westbury for all my medical quotes, a funky-looking twenty-seven-year-old with a look of Angelina Jolie.

'How have you been keeping?' asked Dr Frank between wheezes as we sat down to lunch. 'I'd assumed you must have forgotten my number. It must be a couple of years since we last spoke.'

'That can't be right,' I bluffed breezily. 'And if it is then it's something we'll have to get around to correcting. But for now I have a few questions

I need to ask you in relation to a sort of hush-hush feature I'm working on at the moment: it's about a guy I've met who's been having hallucinations.'

This was my plan to get rid of Fiona once and for all. Rather than go to my GP and run the risk of having an official note made on my permanent record or being sectioned on the spot I'd reasoned that the next best thing would be to fake an interviewee for a feature, attribute my exact symptoms to them and see what a medical professional of Dr Frank's calibre might have to say about the situation.

'So,' mused Dr Frank, once I'd given him a rough outline of the facts, 'you say this young man is seeing things?'

'Yes,' I replied. 'His dead ex-girlfriend to be precise.'

'And is it significant that it's his ex?'

I shrugged. 'It's hard to be exact. It's been over twenty years since they were together but she did die not so long ago and he did attend the funeral.'

Dr Frank nodded sagely. 'Was it a long-drawn-out death? I mean was she ill?'

'No, it was very abrupt. An accident. But they weren't in touch at the time or anything.'

'And so this young man believes that he can see her?'

'Yes, he does, he's seen her twice now.'

'And does she talk to him?'

'Yes,' I replied, shifting in my chair. 'She talks a lot.'

'About what exactly?'

'Well, apparently, she's mainly very offensive towards him, calling him names and so on. Oh, and claims she's a ghost.'

At this Dr Frank's brow furrowed until it resembled a corrugated roof.

'Oh,' he said, 'I see.'

I looked at him warily. 'What does that mean?'

'What that means is that this young man is more likely than not having some sort of psychotic episode. Is he a substance abuser by any chance?'

'Not even the odd swig of Benylin,' I replied. 'He's just not the type.'

'How about a trauma? Has he been in any kind of accident?'

'There was a sort of accident,' I said, thinking back to the mugging, 'but he's not even certain it actually happened. His memory of that night is hazy to say the least.'

'But he hasn't seen his GP?'

'Well, no, because he couldn't find any actual evidence of having been in an accident. There wasn't a scratch on him so he assumed that he must have dreamed it.'

'Dreamed it?'

'Also, there's another odd thing about this case. Every time he sees his dead ex-girlfriend not only is she twenty years younger than she should have been but there's also a smell that follows her, a perfume — Poison by Dior, to be exact. Is that unusual?'

Dr Frank raised his eyebrows. 'Very.' He gently massaged his temples as if trying to alleviate an oncoming headache. 'This case really does sound quite peculiar. Are you sure I can't meet this person?'

'No chance,' I spluttered, 'absolutely not! He's . . . he's got a very important job. If it got out that he was seeing things it could ruin him for life.'

'Well,' said Dr Frank, 'this is all rather unusual and I'm not quite sure what it is you'd like me to say. Maybe you could point me in a particular direction?'

'It's not like that,' I replied. 'I genuinely want your actual opinion.'

'In that case I'd have to say that this person is not very well at all.'

I nodded. This wasn't helping me. 'Right. I get that. But what should he do about it? Take a couple of paracetamol, lie down in a darkened room, what?' Dr Frank's face fell and I immediately apologised. 'I'm so sorry Dr Frank, I don't know what came over me. I think I'm just worried about this chap, that's all.'

'The first thing he should do is see his GP because it's impossible to get any real sense of what's going on without an examination. Then hopefully once he's done that his GP will refer him to a psychiatrist who will possibly commence a short course of antipsychotic drugs to get the problem under control.'

'Antipsychotics,' I repeated. I was pretty sure I wasn't going to be able to get them over the counter at Boots. 'What if he's not psychotic but just really stressed?'

'Is he really stressed?'

'Very stressed indeed.'

122

'With work?'

'Relationship problems.'

'I see. And he won't see a GP?'

'I could ask him again but I'm pretty sure he won't go.'

'Do you feel that he's a danger to himself or to others?'

'I'd stake my life that he isn't.'

'And it's only happened twice so far?'

'Correct. And in between he's as right as rain. Not a problem.'

'Well if he categorically refuses to consult a medical professional the only thing I can really suggest is that you advise him to relax and de-stress as much as possible and hopefully the hallucinations will disappear as the stress subsides.'

'So in short you're saying he should just chill out a bit?'

'Absolutely,' smiled Dr Frank. 'What this young man needs to do is try his very best to — as they say — kick back and relax.'

★   ★   ★

As I left my meeting with Dr Frank assuring him that I'd contact him the next time I needed any advice, I wondered quite how I was going to properly 'kick back and relax', when all I had to look forward to was another night in Bed and Breakfast Hell. What I really needed was for Penny to forgive me and ask me to come home but given the fact that she hadn't replied to a single one of my texts or phone messages I couldn't see that happening any time soon. So it was that evening as I headed back to the St Joseph's Guest House that I found myself taking a detour ending up in front of a block of graffiti-scrawled local authority maisonettes next to a small shopping precinct with a row of grille-covered shops, one of which was a mini-market and off-licence. Not only was I hungry, lonely and in need of my own toilet paper, but it also occurred to me that I could do with a drink. A drink might relax me. A drink might stave off any more hallucinations. It was, I was fully aware, a twisted logic given what I'd read about hallucinations and alcohol abuse, but I wasn't planning on becoming an alcoholic, just having a drink or two to help me sleep and anyway, right now it was all I'd got. After waiting for a group of youths to pass by I wandered into the mini-market, picked up a basket and walked the aisles in search of anything that caught my fancy. A short while later, satisfied that all my basic needs were covered by the contents of my basket — a packet of bourbon biscuits, some cheese strings and a bottle of vodka, I joined the long queue at the till and it was here that something rather odd happened.

At first it was a feeling that I was being watched, closely followed by the certainty that this was indeed the case when I looked over my shoulder to see a tall, bald man wearing a denim jacket, leather trousers and cowboy boots staring at me from the booze aisle. My eyes met his and I immediately looked away. The last thing I needed right now was to be stabbed to death by some drug-addled lunatic spoiling for a fight and

I steadfastly refused to look in the man's direction again even though the feeling of being observed continued. I told myself that I'd just get my things, leave the shop and run back to the B&B at full tilt.

The shopkeeper rang my goods through with a dead-eyed efficiency that spoke volumes about the kind of area I was in. Not for him the smiles and small talk of the jovial local shopkeeper; he didn't care who I was or what story I had to tell, all he wanted was my money and as quiet a life as possible.

Still aware that I was being watched, I took my bags and made as if I had forgotten something in the canned food aisle before quickly doubling back so as to fool my shadow but then as I reached out to grab the door I felt a hand on my shoulder. I turned to see the tall bald man grinning widely in my direction. 'You're Joe Clarke, from the *Correspondent*, aren't you?'

The man's Antipodean accent sounded oddly familiar.

'You're . . . '

'Van Halen,' he replied. 'You interviewed me a while back for your magazine. The Divorced Dads' Club article.' He beamed at me with a slightly manic glint in his eye and gave me an over-enthusiastic man-hug. 'It's so good to see you, dude, it really is.'

'For a minute there I thought you were some sort of nutter the way you were staring at me.'

'I get that a lot,' said Van, 'especially since I started chemo.' He pointed to his bald head and the alarming lack of eyebrows that made him

125

look completely otherworldly.

'You've got cancer?'

'Of the balls. Only finished the treatment a month ago. Would've been lost if it hadn't been for, you know . . . *the guys*.'

'Which guys?'

'You know, Stew and Paul, the guys from the article.'

'You mean you still see each other?'

'Every week. I know it sounds weird. On paper it doesn't work at all. I mean Stew's a bit of a slob, Paul's a real brain box, and well, I'm me, but we all get on really well together. I guess that's the thing about being a single parent, it's the great leveller, isn't it? Doesn't matter who you are, when you haven't seen your kids for a while and your ex hates you, you need mates around you who know what you're going through.'

'Listen, I'm really pleased that you all get on so well,' I replied. 'It's nice when that sort of thing happens but anyway, I've really got to — '

'I've got an idea! Mate, you've got to come out with us sometime! The guys would be absolutely mad for it. Paul even has your article framed on the wall in his bog, mind you I think he only does it to wind his ex up — he's not been too good since she announced her engagement. Still, at least his kids live with him full time.'

My life was crazy enough as it was. There was no way I was ever going for a drink with him and his mad loser friends. 'I'm sorry to hear about Paul, and obviously about you being ill and everything — '

126

'What am I doing? I haven't given you my number yet. Where's your phone?' He pulled out his and handed it to me saying, 'And don't bother making one up because I know where you work!'

He chuckled so hard at his own joke that he failed to notice me deleting the fake number I'd started to type in. Even after chemo this guy was still big enough to snap me in two without breaking into a sweat.

Van stared at his phone seeming genuinely chuffed.

'That's brilliant, mate, expect a call from me and the boys real soon.'

He shook my hand and I left the shop and immediately I was swallowed up by an overwhelming feeling of loneliness. For a moment I almost headed back into the shop to take Van up on his offer because what I really needed right now was a friend, a comrade, a drinking buddy. Someone with whom I could offload all my problems, who'd put everything into perspective, who'd show me that the light at the end of the tunnel wasn't necessarily a train coming the other way.

The problem was however that I hadn't heard a single word from any one of my so-called friends for a long time, and while I appreciated the fact that they had busy lives to lead involving work and partners and the raising of children I was surprised not to have heard from my closest friend Mitchell, especially as his partner, Katie, was close enough to Penny for me to be in no doubt at all that news of the split would have reached his ears by now. Why hadn't he called? I'd been there for him when he and Katie went through a rough patch over his reluctance to start a family a few years back. I'd taken Mitchell out to the pub, acted as a sounding board for him as he worked out how he wanted his life to be, and when they finally did start a family and found themselves in need of godparents it had been me and Penny they'd turned to. We were friends for life. I was sure of it, and as a sign of just how much confidence I had in this fact I made the decision to turn up at his house and invite my old friend Mitchell out for a beer.

13

It was after eight o'clock as I reached Mitchell and Katie's Victorian two-bed terrace in Finchley. The last time I visited their house had been back in the summer with Penny and the kids for their daughter Molly's third birthday party. We'd all stayed over because both Penny and I had drunk too much to be totally sure that we weren't over the limit. The following morning we'd all had a lazy breakfast together before taking the kids to the local park for an hour on what turned out to be one of the sunniest days of the year. The thought struck me as I rang the doorbell that I might never enjoy a weekend like that again.

* * *

Mitchell was barely able to hide his surprise when he saw me standing on his doorstep.

'Joe, what are you doing here, mate?'

This was the point at which I was going to have to lie if I was to keep even a shred of dignity. 'I was in the area interviewing someone for the paper. Thought I'd drop in on the off chance you'd be free for a quick beer.'

'No can do, mate. Katie's out at her Zumba class. You could come in for a drink though. We can have a proper catch-up.'

I followed Mitchell into the kitchen and took a

seat at the large wooden table that reminded me of my own at home — right down to the magazines, children's drawings and unopened bills piled up at the opposite end.

'How are the kids?' I asked as Mitchell rooted around in the fridge in search of beer.

'Couldn't be better,' said Mitchell, pulling out two cans of Stella. 'Molly's just started at pre-school and after a bit of a bumpy start — she hated being away from Katie — she's finally started to settle in. As for Cameron, he's great. He's really getting into his reading. It's like a lightbulb has suddenly gone off in his head and he gets it. He's reading everything. Signs on bus stops, advertising hoardings, in fact only last week I caught him reading the back of a pack of tampons that had fallen out of the bathroom cupboard. Had a few awkward questions to dodge after that, I can tell you!' Mitchell took two glasses from a cupboard and brought them along with the beer to the table, pausing to clear a box of crayons and an abandoned Furby from his chair before he sat down. Reverentially, he poured out the beers into the glasses, making sure that each had the perfect amount of head, and then we clinked glasses and both took a sip.

Mitchell wiped his mouth and set his glass down. 'Listen mate, I'm sorry I haven't been in touch. Obviously I've heard about . . . well, you know, and I know I should've at least called or sent a text and it's bang out of order that I haven't.'

'It's fine,' I replied, somewhat relieved to know that I wouldn't have to go through the whole process of telling Mitchell what had happened. 'I know how it is, life's busy.'

'Yeah, it is actually. Katie's eight weeks' pregnant.'

'Congratulations, mate, I didn't even know a third baby was on the list.'

Mitchell laughed and took another swig of beer. 'Technically it wasn't but now the little blighter's on its way I couldn't be happier. Anyway, enough about me, how are you faring?'

'As good as can be expected. When did you hear?'

'A couple of days ago. Penny turned up here with the kids and I was put on babysitting duty while she and Katie disappeared to the kitchen for about three hours. I knew something was up but I never imagined this. I'd always thought you and Penny were solid.'

'We were. It was me who messed everything up.'

Mitchell raised a knowing eyebrow. 'So I hear. A twenty-two-year-old blond intern wasn't it?'

'Twenty-five,' I corrected. 'And she was a brunette but before you ask, no, it wasn't worth it. Hand on heart, mate, I've never regretted anything more in my life. I've ruined everything, Mitch, absolutely everything.'

Mitchell nodded sagely. 'It's a killer, mate, no two ways about it. And apparently you've moved out? Where are you living?'

I laughed. 'You don't want to know. Grim doesn't even begin to cover it.'

Mitchell played with his glass, gently pushing it around the smooth surface of the table with his forefinger. 'I don't know what I'd do if it happened to me. For what it's worth Katie's told me in no uncertain terms that if I ever get caught doing anything like that she'll gut me like a fish, pack her bags, and take the kids with her. I believe her too, she can be ruthless when her back's up. Do you remember that time — '

The sound of keys in the front door. Mitchell checked his watch. 'Katie's back early. You need to go, mate.'

'What do you mean, go? I haven't even finished my — '

Katie — who had always done angry pretty impressively — came into the room. She looked first at me, then at Mitchell and then she let rip, talking about me as though I wasn't in the room.

'What's he doing here?'

'He just dropped by.'

'I told you I didn't want you seeing him and I meant it!'

Mitchell held up his hands in defence. 'Babe, there's no need to be like that! Joe's just here to say hello.'

Katie threw a look of real disgust in my direction. Finally an acknowledgement. 'Well I hope he's said it because either he goes or I do.'

Mitchell tried to stick up for me. 'Joe's a mate, he's godfather to our kids, you can't just kick him out of our lives like that.'

'I'm going for a shower. If he's not out of here by the time I come back down you'll find out exactly what I can do.'

Katie exited the room, almost sucking all the air out of it as she did so. I finished off my beer

132

and turned to Mitchell.

'I ought to be getting off.'

'No, stay,' said Mitchell with equal parts fear and conviction. 'I shouldn't be spoken to like that in my own home.'

I wanted to say that at least he was in his own home but I thought better of it. 'No, mate. You don't need the hassle and to be honest I don't either. I'll see you around sometime.'

He walked me to the door.

'I'm sorry about this, mate, I really am. You know how these things are: people take sides even though it isn't anyone else's business. She's decided that we're on Penny's side and she won't listen to anyone who says otherwise.'

I nodded. I'd suspected that this would happen and now it had I felt more than a little sorry for myself. 'It's fine, it's good to know that Penny's being looked after.'

★ ★ ★

Just to prove a point, once I was back at the B&B I texted every last one of my and Penny's mutual friends asking if they were free for a drink. I didn't get any replies that night but the next day I received one from my friend Simon (of Simon and Laura) who pretty much summed up the situation at hand with a pithy: *Mate, right now you're so toxic the missus would sooner see me hanging out with Satan at a strip bar than you in a pub. Keep your head down and I'm sure it'll all blow over soon. Take it easy, S.* That was the truth. I was toxic. Potentially hazardous waste material that would contaminate the blissfully happy lives of any couple with whom I came into contact. It was official. I had reached rock bottom. I pulled out my phone and scrolled through my missed messages until I found Van Halen's number. It was positively ridiculous how much he and his friends wanted to spend time with me; what did they hope to gain from a night out with a boring hack they met once over six months ago? Hadn't they got lives to lead? Things to do and achieve? I stared at Van's number, hoping it might somehow magically disappear thereby saving me from what I was about to do; but it stubbornly refused to do anything even remotely supernatural. I was tired and lonely and I wanted to be back in the world, fully functioning like a real person, but to do that I needed friends, and right now it didn't look like I had any — or at least any that wanted to be around me.

That night I tapped out the following text: *Hi Van, Joe Clarke here from the Correspondent. Turns out I'm free for a drink tomorrow night, if you're up for it. Let me know, JC*. Rock bottom? It looked like I had a little further left to go.

14

It was a little after eight as I arrived at the Red Lion, a scruffy, down-at-heel drinking establishment just around the corner from the studio where the Divorced Dads' Club shoot had happened all that time ago, and having scanned the room for anyone I recognised I ordered a pint and got comfortable at the bar.

I felt ill at ease for a myriad of reasons, not least because I hadn't the faintest idea what these guys actually expected of me. I hadn't done anything special by introducing them to each other. It wasn't as though it was part of some plan of mine to create a miniature support group for divorced dads. All I'd been trying to do was make the best of a very bad job, and yet here I was waiting for a bunch of guys who wanted to personally thank me for bringing them together. It occurred to me as I took the first sip of my pint that there was probably a feature idea in here somewhere — the accidental friendships formed out of media encounters — but I was pretty sure I wasn't the man to write it. This felt weird. And desperate. The fewer people who knew about my little night out the better.

My relatively optimistic mood had collapsed to such an extent that I'd been in the process of finishing up my pint ready to go home when out of the corner of my eye I saw a tubby guy in a beige mac and jeans heading towards me with a sense of purpose. Reaching me, he grinned and held out his hand: 'Joe, really good to see you, mate!'

As much as I recognised the man's face from the day of the shoot I couldn't for the life of me remember his name.

'It's good to see you again,' I replied. 'You'll have to forgive me though. It's been such a long time since I saw you last. You're?'

'Stewart.'

'And you're the stay-at-home dad?'

Stewart laughed. 'I wish. I'm the painter and decorator whose kids live in Thailand.'

'So no news at all there?'

He shook his head. 'None.'

Of all of the interviews from that day Stewart's should have been the one I remembered given how moving it had been. Stewart was a hard-working devoted father of two little girls who just happened to be married to a nightmare of a woman. Having left him three times in a row for men she'd met on the internet, one day she finally left for good to travel around her native country of Thailand and after twelve months and thousands spent on legal fees he had yet to see even a photograph of his kids.

I had to buy the man a drink, it was the only decent thing to do, but he seemed horrified at the thought of me dipping into my own pocket when the whole idea of the evening was to thank me for bringing them together. 'Van would never forgive me if I let you get a drink in,' said Stewart. 'He sent me a text earlier saying that you're not even allowed to pay for your own crisps.'

Reluctantly I agreed to allow him to get me a pint but just as he had ordered our drinks another man arrived. It was the tall studenty-looking guy. He was wearing a green parka and jeans and looked like he had just stepped out of the union bar — albeit one from 1994.

'Joe,' he said, shaking my hand, 'I couldn't believe it when Van said you actually wanted to come out with us. He didn't browbeat you into it, did he? He means well but he can be a bit overbearing when he's — let's say — over-focused.'

I laughed. Overfocused was exactly what Van was. 'He was fine actually, er . . . what was your name again?'

'Paul, I'm the bloke who was full-time carer for my kids.'

That was it. Paul had been a history teacher. His ex-wife ran a big marketing firm in the city earning far more money than he could ever hope to make. They started a family, a boy and a girl a couple of years older than my own, and he stayed home to look after them but after six years of drifting further and further apart they finally split up. For the sake of continuity they decided that he would stay in the family home and be primary carer just as he always had been.

I asked after his kids and he laughed. 'Hateful, the older they get the less they seem to like anything that hasn't got a screen. Sometimes I think I drew the short straw having them live with me.'

Stewart laughed nervously as though he thought I might be secretly recording the conversation and corrected his friend. 'He's only joking. Truth is he wouldn't have it any other way. Isn't that right, Paul mate?'

'Yeah, I suppose,' replied Paul. 'They can be all right when the mood takes them. I just wish they'd stayed small though. They were really lovely kids when they were small.'

Stewart asked Paul what he was drinking and he pointed out one of the guest ales and was about to start telling some kind of story attached to it — which he prefaced with a grin and the comment, 'As a man of words you'll like this' — when a voice bellowed across the room: 'Joey, mate! You're here!' All of us at the bar (and for that matter the entire pub) turned to see Van, resplendent in a denim shirt, leather trousers and cowboy boots, striding across the floor towards us. He threw his arms around me and kissed me on both cheeks.

'Sorry I'm late, Joey mate,' he said with his arm around my shoulder. 'Bit of a domestic issue: my ex's washing machine gave up the ghost this morning so I ended up spending all day fixing it.'

I was confused. 'You fix washing machines? I thought you were in a tribute band?'

Van laughed. 'You know how it is mate, even a guy like me has to eat!'

★   ★   ★

'So how did it happen?' I asked once we were all assembled around a table. 'How did you guys move from being a bunch of strangers to the mates you are now?'

'It's hard to say,' said Van Halen. 'We just clicked at the shoot, and our kids seemed to get on OK, and at the end of the day I think it was Paulie who said we should meet up again, and basically we never looked back. Honestly, Joey, these guys right here . . . they've been my rock.'

Paul shrugged. 'He's exaggerating. We just helped out where we could.'

Van laughed. 'Helping out would be picking up some shopping for me. You drove me to chemo twice a week for three months!'

'Only because you didn't mind me banging on about Lisa when she announced her engagement,' replied Paul. 'I must have bored you senseless with all that whining!'

'Well if we really are going to have a love-in, how about the way you guys helped me out with everything that's been happening with my kids? I had debts up to my eyeballs because of all my legal fees and Paul here stumped up a grand to help me pay my rent, just like that, no questions asked, and when I thought I was going to lose my business because I couldn't afford to fix my van who spent three and a half days sorting it for me at zero cost? Only Van-the-bloody-man, right here! I'd sooner lose a limb than be without these guys!'

It was impossible not to be impressed at the strength of the bond that had formed between these men, especially given that I was the one who had inadvertently brought them together.

'I'm impressed. You're practically a support group for single fathers.'

Van raised his pint in the air. 'Yeah, but one that likes a drink.'

'And doesn't mind the odd curry either,' added Stewart.

'Oh, and we have been known to visit a racetrack from time to time,' said Paul finally. 'But apart from all that, we're *exactly* like a support group for single dads.'

★   ★   ★

We stayed at the Red Lion for another pint and then moved on to a nearby curry house that they frequented so often that on entering the proprietor greeted them all by name before showing them to their 'usual' table. They ordered without even glancing at the menu and not wanting to feel left out I did too: a lamb pasanda, lime rice and a naan, which much to my relief was met with nods of approval by my dining companions, clearly all experts in North Indian cuisine.

'So come on Joe,' said Van, dipping a huge chunk of naan into his rogan josh, 'what changed your mind? You're a pretty hard guy to read and correct me if I'm wrong but even I could tell you were a bit reluctant to come out with us. What did we finally do right?'

I looked at Van Halen and grinned. I should have expected this kind of frank questioning four rounds and a curry into the evening. Nice as the guys were — I don't know what it was exactly but there was *something* about them — I was nowhere near ready to start opening up to them

140

about my troubles. Or at least that's what I thought as I started conjuring up a story about how I was supposed to be meeting some mates who had cancelled on me at the last minute. Suddenly I found myself putting down my fork and saying: 'I've just split up with my wife.'

No one spoke. Not even Van. Instead they all sat staring at their food as if waiting for me to continue, which I did.

'I miss my kids like . . . like an amputee misses their limb. Nothing feels right without them. I don't feel whole.'

Van leaned in next to me. 'Mate,' he said in a voice barely registering above a whisper, 'whether you're a man or a woman, whether you were the cause of the problem or just an innocent bystander, splitting up when you've got kids is always going to be a massive ball-ache.' He put his arm around my shoulder. 'You did the right thing meeting up with us. If anyone's going to get you through this, we will.'

Up until this point in the evening I hadn't quite been sure of what I'd hoped to gain from this encounter with the Divorced Dads' Club. Van, when he settled down, was actually quite a funny guy who was forever coming up with ideas for things that might be a bit of a laugh and Stewart, if you gave him long enough and didn't interrupt, had a good line in amusing painting and decorating anecdotes; and Paul — who could chat about the latest foreign language film releases and argue about which of the *Die Hard* films was his favourite with equal vigour — was the most normal of the bunch, and the one guy,

141

if I was in the market for such, I could actually imagine becoming friends with outside of these current circumstances. But the thing that made me believe that I'd done the right thing in coming out with them was the way they talked about their kids like they were actually important parts of their lives. Stewart mentioned his kids continually, almost as if to keep the memory of them vivid in his head, and while Paul preferred to grumble about his two there was no mistaking how much he loved them. As for Van, he was the biggest surprise of all. He adored his little boys and never said a word about them that didn't make it clear to the listener that they were his proudest achievements. And in a world where most of the guys I encountered barely even acknowledged their kids' existence, let alone talked about how they were developing and changing, what they were into and what made them laugh, this was a rare thing indeed. Even though to the outside world these guys might have looked — Van notwithstanding — like the biggest bunch of beta males this side of a comic book store, to me at least it was clear they were the bravest bunch of guys I'd met in a long time. Most of all, however, they gave me hope for a life beyond the towering mess I'd made of it so far. Maybe I could do this after all.

My phone rang. It was Penny's number. It was all I could do not to scream like a teenage girl. Making my excuses to the guys I left the table and took the call outside.

'Joe, it's me,' said Penny. 'Are you free to talk?'
'Of course I am,' I replied, willing it to be

good news while almost certain that it would be bad.

'I've told the kids you'll be flying home tomorrow,' she said, her carefully measured voice seemingly loaded with so many different levels of meaning that I couldn't begin to decode any of them.

'That's brilliant news. What time do you want me home?'

'Will eight o'clock do?'

'That's quite late. Can't I come earlier?'

'No,' she replied. 'No, you can't.'

'Actually you're right,' I said. 'I'll see you at eight.'

I was going home.

After one of the weirdest episodes of my life and nearly a week out in the wilderness, I wouldn't ever have to join the Divorced Dads' Club because I was finally going home.

15

In all my life I'd never felt quite as nervous as I did as I walked up the front path to my own house the following evening. Although it had been less than a week since I'd left it had felt much longer and the fact that I had my suitcase with me and a carrier bag full of souvenirs I'd picked up in Chinatown all added to the impression that I was returning from an epic tour of Asia rather than a five-day sleepover at a B&B in South-East London.

'Daddy, I've missed you millions!' screamed Jack, running to me in his pyjamas. 'Last night I thought I was going to faint if I didn't see you soon.'

'Dad, you have to promise not to go away for this long ever again, OK?' said Rosie, who was also dressed for bed. 'The house feels weird without you.'

It was good to be back, and even better knowing I'd been missed, but then Penny appeared from the kitchen still wearing her work clothes and the ground shifted beneath my feet. In an instant I went from knowing exactly where I was to being lost at sea. She briefly joined the kids in their embrace and said: 'I'm glad you're home.'

Her words were for the kids' benefit, even I could see that, and yet they gave me hope. Yes, I'd done wrong, and yes, we were still a long way

144

from being right with each other, but with me home now we were on the road to recovery. At least we could come up with a plan to work things out.

Rosie spied the carrier bag, and smiled mischievously as she whispered in Jack's ear what she thought it might be. The excitement was too much for him and he practically exploded. 'You've got us presents, Dad, thank you!'

I doled out the kids' gifts first. Jack tore into the wrapping surrounding his in a matter of milliseconds. He stared in awe at the pointy-headed futuristic-looking superhero in the brightly coloured box in his hands. I'd come across it while peering through the window of a shop that specialised in Chinese toys on Shaftesbury Avenue.

'Who's this?'

'He's called Ultraman, and he's the coolest superhero in China. His eyes glow and I'm pretty sure he can talk too.'

Jack ripped open the box and with my help managed to free Ultraman from his cardboard prison. Victorious, Jack held him aloft. 'Dad, he's awesome! Taking her turn, Rosie, squeezed the package in her hands. 'What is it? It's some kind of clothes isn't it?' She tore open the paper to reveal a shiny black and gold dress. She held it up against herself and stroked the material. 'It's gorgeous, Dad. It feels really smooth. Is it made of silk?'

'It's called a *qipao*. Traditionally Chinese women used to wear them when . . . ' I stopped myself. Maybe every moment in life didn't need

145

to be turned into a learning opportunity after all, especially when her special Chinese dress was from the owner of a Chinatown market stall. 'All you need to know is you'll look great in it.'

Rosie grinned. 'Carly is going to be seriously jealous when she sees this, especially when she finds out that it's all the way from China. I can't wait to see what you've got for Mum.'

I reached into the bag and took out the final package, a long, velvet jewellery box, and handed it to Penny. 'It's not much but I hope you like it.'

Penny smiled and kissed my cheek, and while I knew it was yet another show for the kids I couldn't help but think that at least some small part of her meant it. 'That's really sweet of you, you shouldn't have.' She opened the box and showed the jade butterfly pendant to the kids. 'It's lovely, Joe, thank you.'

At Rosie's insistence Penny put on the necklace and admired it in the hallway mirror. It was identical to the one I'd bought for her twentieth birthday back when we were students. She'd worn it all the time until it got lost somehow in the move from Sheffield to London. If she recognised it, she didn't say, but it was good to see that the gifts from my fake work trip seemed to have hit the spot for everybody else. Grateful to have done something right for a change I began collecting up the wrapping paper and boxes and as I did so a tiny slip of paper fell from inside the jewellery box the necklace had come in and fluttered to the floor. Rosie picked it up, read it and her expression changed so much that for a moment I was convinced she'd found a receipt and that I was about to get caught out. But it was worse. Much worse.

She read aloud from the paper in her hands. 'It's like an information thing to tell you what the necklace means. 'The butterfly represents fidelity between lovers, an undying bond of true love.''

Rosie laughed and Jack — who hated anything remotely to do with boys loving girls — pulled a face but it was the look of desolation in Penny's eyes that really did me in. Was there nothing I could do that didn't seem like yet another twist of the knife?

★ ★ ★

I helped put the kids to bed and kissed them both goodnight before going downstairs to talk to Penny. I didn't have to wait long. As I was making a coffee she came into the kitchen carrying a duvet, pillow and a set of covers, which she placed on the counter.

'The weather reports are saying it's going to be cold tonight,' she said. 'Just make sure you're up before the kids and that this is all packed away out of sight by the time they come downstairs.'

'You want me to sleep on the sofa?'

'Would you rather it was the other way around?'

'No of course not, it's just that — '

'What? You thought that after a week away I'd calm down? I'm not anywhere near calm, Joe. No, you're back for the kids' sake, not mine. You'll sleep here, I'll cook your meals and wash your clothes as usual but that's it. And come the

147

weekend we'll alternate. I've booked this weekend away to be with some old uni friends so you need to make sure you're away next weekend, OK?'

'You've thought all this through haven't you?'

'I'm just doing what I think is best.'

'How can this be for the best? Don't you even want to try and work this out? Look, I'll do whatever it takes — therapists, counselling, the whole thing.' I took her hand. 'Come on Pen, I know you're angry, and you have every right to be but please, let's at least try and talk this out.'

'I can't,' said Penny. 'I just can't.' Then she left the room, leaving me staring at the duvet and bedclothes absorbing everything they represented: the beginning of the great deception. From this moment onwards the only thing keeping our marriage alive would be the lengths we would be prepared to go in order to keep up appearances for the sake of the two people who mattered to us most.

★   ★   ★

For the next month the sofa was my home. I'd get up early and pack away the duvet and pillows and then join the family for breakfast before heading to work and then in the evening once the kids were in bed Penny would go upstairs to our room to read while I'd stay in the living room watching TV and arranging my bed for the night. At the weekends, just as she requested, we alternated looking after the kids using a whole variety of excuses to justify the need to go away. One week Penny was visiting her friend Annabel in Ipswich whose cat had died; the following week I was in Bristol helping my brother board out his loft; the week after Penny was helping her cousin buy a new car; then finally I went to Swindon — allegedly to help my mum clear out her garage. As plans went, it obviously wasn't the greatest, and even Jack was asking almost daily if we were ever going to have a weekend under the same roof again; but I couldn't see any other way around it, at least not while Penny refused to talk.

★ ★ ★

On the final night of my stay at my mum's she went to bed early with a headache leaving me in the armchair dressed only in a T-shirt and pyjama bottoms working through some of the programmes she'd recorded on her satellite box. So far I'd watched ten minutes of an episode of *Murder, She Wrote*, the first half-hour of *Cat Ballou* and was about to see how much of an episode of *Escape to the Country* I could stomach before giving up and going to bed myself when suddenly I smelled the now-familiar waft of Dior's Poison and I turned to see Fiona sprawled along the full length of the sofa.

My hallucination was back.

Given that I hadn't seen anything of Fiona since my temporary residence at the B&B I'd hoped that I'd somehow cured myself. After my conversation with Dr Frank, I'd concluded that my hallucination of Fiona was down to the extreme stress I'd been under with everything falling apart at home. I'd thought that if I tried to relax and calm down then that would be an end to it. But now here she was again. However this time, although things with Penny were still awful, I'd been doing nothing more stressful than watching retired couples mooching around their dream houses. Why then was I seeing visions of Fiona again?

'You should have stuck with *Murder, She Wrote*,' she said with a nod towards the TV.

I stared hard at her. She seemed so real that I was sure I could have reached out and touched her. What was happening to me? How was it possible to be so ill that I was experiencing talking hallucinations and yet be completely normal in every other way? Was my mind really this broken? I had to stay calm if I had any hope of stopping this from happening again. I closed my eyes and thought back to my conversation with Dr Frank about how stress played a key role in these episodes. If Fiona was here again then perhaps I wasn't quite as relaxed as I thought I was. Without opening my eyes I crossed my legs and tried my best to recall the breathing exercises Penny had taught me during her brief flirtation with yoga about five years ago.

Keeping my eyes firmly shut I inhaled deeply through my nostrils and exhaled through my mouth, repeating the exercise over and over again until I heard Fiona's unmistakable cackle right in my ear.

'Are you seriously trying to yoga me out of your life?'

I carried on breathing. In. Out. In. Out. In. Out.

'Have you any idea how ridiculous a notion this is? I'm a ghost, Joe, a ghost whose job it is to save your marriage; a bit of deep breathing's not going to get rid of me, you daft git.'

I sighed heavily and opened my eyes to see Fiona staring right back at me, her nose less than an inch from my own.

'What do you want?' I asked.

She smiled, knowing full well that she had won, and then returned to the sofa opposite.

'I want to know how you're doing,' she replied.

'I'm great. Wonderful. Couldn't be better. Isn't it obvious?' I threw my arms open wide, encouraging Fiona to fully appreciate the glory of my mum's interior decorating skills. Floral wallpaper, matched with floral carpet and curtains with a floral three-piece suite just to ram the I-like-flowers message home.

'So what are you doing about it?'

'About what?'

'Getting home.'

'You're not going to start with that nonsense again are you? This is home . . . well not this exactly, but this is my life and I don't care what you say, I know for a fact that I'm not lying bleeding on a pavement in East London, OK? I'm sat on a sofa in Swindon watching crap TV.'

'So you don't want to go home then?'

'Look, Fiona, you know as well as I do that you're not real. You're a figment of my stressed-out mind and first thing in the morning I'm going to see a doctor and get myself sorted out. I don't care what they do. They can fill me up on Diazepam, send me to the funny farm or electro-shock me until the cows come home as long as I don't have to see you any more.'

Fiona laughed. 'Aww, Joe, you're so sweet when you're angry. I think that's why I used to like having you around. You really feel things, don't you?' She swung her feet to the floor in one fluid movement, walked over to my chair and sat on the arm. 'What if I could prove to you that this really is all a dream and that you are still lying crumpled on the pavement where I whacked you?'

'And how would you do that?'

Fiona gave me a wink. 'Come on Joe, you know me. How did I used to get things done when we were together?'

'Sheer force of will?'

She smiled, oblivious to my tone. 'Exactly.'

She stood up and took me by the hand. 'Let's go into the kitchen, there's something there I need to show you.'

I couldn't possibly imagine what she might want to show me in my mum's kitchen but I was too tired to resist. I stood up and followed her but as we walked through the door to the hallway I suddenly felt cold and it was only when I looked back that I noticed the door we'd come through wasn't there any more. In fact nothing was there any more. We were no longer in my mum's house. We were in the street. The street where I'd been mugged, and I knew this because lying next to my feet was my own body, unconscious, blood pouring from a gash in my head.

'That's me.'

Fiona nodded. 'It sure is.'

'But how do I really know that's me?'

Fiona shrugged. 'How do any of us know anything, Joe? We touch, we feel, we experience.'

I knelt down and felt the body. It was still warm.

Across the road a young couple walked by. This was my opportunity to test this reality. 'Over here!' I yelled. 'This man needs help!'

The couple carried on walking. It was as if they hadn't even heard me. This was a dodgy part of the city though and it was how most sane people would react to a prone figure and his shouty doppelganger.

'They didn't hear you,' said Fiona.

'But I shouted.'

Fiona tutted. 'Silly boy. How can you shout when you're lying on the floor unconscious?'

I began to panic. What if this wasn't a hallucination? What if this was real? What if everything I'd experienced since the mugging was some kind of dream after all? A dream I was having while lying right here on this pavement. What if no one found me? What if I never woke up? Would I stay trapped in this world?

A ringing phone.

I opened my eyes, which was odd because I'd been absolutely sure that I hadn't closed them. I'd been dreaming. I must have nodded off in front of the TV. The phone continued to ring. I looked down to see that it was my own. I answered the call. It was Penny.

'I've booked us in to see a counsellor,' she

said. 'It's at six thirty on Monday evening in Clapham. Is that OK?'

I thought about the dream. It had all seemed so real. And for a brief moment I wondered if it might actually be true. After all my life as it stood right now seemed pretty surreal. This time last year I couldn't have imagined any of this happening and yet here I was, estranged from my wife, away from my kids, watching OAP TV in my pyjamas at my mum's.

'Joe, can you hear me?' Penny's voice was more insistent now. I'd been so lost in thought I'd forgotten I was talking to her. 'I was asking you if six thirty on Monday is OK for the appointment with the counsellor?'

'Yes,' I replied, coming to my senses. 'Six thirty sounds fine.'

16

Countdown2Counselling was based in a grandly named double-fronted retail unit called the Majestic Centre just around the corner from a Sri Lankan takeaway. Despite its name the outside of the premises brought to mind a down-at-heel suburban dental practice whose owner had been locked in a decade-long battle with his professional body not to be struck off. It didn't look like any work had been done to maintain the place in the last twenty years. The paint around the windows had long since flaked away, the presumably once-cream Venetian blinds had faded to a sickly yellow as had the leaflets advertising the centre's various businesses (Reiki healing, one-to-one yoga sessions, lunchtime meditation classes and an osteopathy clinic). It seemed like every man and his dog could hire rooms here at £28.00 per hour (plus VAT) and set themselves up as whatever they wanted and no one would bat an eye.

I reached out and touched one of the windows. The glass felt cool and smooth just like glass was supposed to. I knelt down and thumped the pavement with my fist, not so hard that I would break my hand but hard enough to scrape my knuckles. Odd as it might sound, with the memory of the dream I'd had at my mum's still very fresh in my mind and unable to shake the shocking image of my own body lying unconscious on the pavement, I'd tentatively felt the need to test reality somehow. Had I been dreaming then or could it be that I really was dreaming now? The thing I couldn't get over was the question of the mugging. I remembered it all too clearly. The feel of my phone in my hand, my surprise at the youth's request for a light and then finally the blow across the head. It was so vivid it couldn't have been a dream, could it? In contrast to this was my night with Bella. I couldn't remember any of it. Not the journey to Soho, anything we'd talked about that night or even the details of how we'd ended up in bed. It was as though none of it had happened. It just didn't make any sense.

I opened the door to the premises and stepped inside. Penny was sitting on one of the plastic chairs in the tiny waiting room. She'd been in bed when I got back from Swindon the night before and that morning with Rosie needing to go into school early to rehearse a play and Jack unable to decide if he felt sick or not we hadn't had the chance to talk at all.

'Hey you,' I said, sitting down next to her.

'So you found it OK?'

'Yeah, your directions were great. You?'

She nodded. 'No problems.'

Penny picked up her phone and started checking her messages as though to signal that this was the end of the conversation. Was this something the real Penny would've done or was it what I imagined she'd do in this situation? It was impossible to tell. I hadn't the faintest idea how she would react in a situation like this. Perhaps she wanted to save her energy for the counselling and didn't want the cosiness of a domestic conversation to dissipate the resentment she was preparing to release. Maybe she just couldn't stand the sight of me.

I attempted to distract myself by reading the community noticeboard on the wall opposite. Maybe I could find a flaw in the items pinned there, a clue or some detail that would prove that this was just a long and unusually involved nightmare. But if these posters advertising mother and toddler groups, drop-in cafés for the over fifty-fives and art therapy classes were made up by my subconscious then I couldn't tell. They seemed completely authentic to me right down to the occasional spelling mistake and over-enthusiastic use of commas.

'Mr Hanley is ready to see you now.'

Penny and I both looked up at the receptionist and followed her along a dimly lit corridor through to a tiny consultation room. In the far corner against the wall was a desk. The majority of the floor space however was taken up by two blue upholstered chairs positioned side by side and a brown armchair facing them. Standing in front of the brown armchair and smiling beatifically was a tall, bespectacled bearded man who looked to be in his mid-sixties. My stomach flipped over. This man looked a lot like my dad. Not an exact carbon copy but more like a relative of some kind. He had similar-shaped eyes and exactly the same prominent nose although this guy's face was longer and thinner.

'Joe, Penny, I'm so glad to meet you. Please, take a seat.'

Now that really was weird. He didn't just look like my dad. He sounded like him too. Or at least the way I remembered him sounding — he'd been dead for years. Was it possible? Could this really all be an elaborate dream? I was already seeing visions of my dead ex-girlfriend, wasn't it a bit much to be seeing my dead father too?

While Mr Hanley checked our details I gave him the once-over. He was sporting a cream linen jacket and button-down white shirt, dark brown linen trousers and sandals. He wasn't wearing socks and his toes were so long and hairy that I really wished he had been. I looked over at Penny to see if she saw the resemblance because she'd passed by the framed photo of my old man in the hallway at home enough times to know what he looked like but she was too busy staring straight ahead as if this was the first day of school and she was keen to impress the teacher.

The man who looked like my dad started off the session by telling us to call him Rob and that he liked to keep things as positive and informal as possible. To this end he laid out some ground rules for this and any future sessions. 'Firstly,' he began, 'I think it's really important you understand that I'm not here as a referee or to take sides. I think the best way for you to think of me is as a facilitator. I'm here to help you guys get the results you're looking for. Secondly, it's important that we don't play the blame game because believe you me there can never be any winners in that scenario. What we do here is communicate with each other about how we feel and our understanding of certain situations.

There is no right and no wrong here. And finally, and I think most importantly, we listen, to each other, to ourselves, with the aim of trying to understand what the core of the issue really is.' Rob/Dad stopped and looked at us both. 'How does that sound?'

Penny and I nodded in silent agreement.

'Good,' he said, rubbing his hands together as though he was looking forward to getting stuck into our session. It was a gesture I remembered my dad using countless times. 'Now, which one of you would like to tell me why you felt the need to come here today?'

I stared at Rob/Dad. Surely this was too much of a coincidence. The resemblance was uncanny and Penny didn't seem to see it at all. Was I having another episode? Was this yet another hallucination and if so why did it have the face of my father? To the best of my knowledge my parents' marriage broke up because they didn't like each other very much, not because he'd played the field. Of course there was an alternative explanation: I was dreaming after all.

A polite cough. I looked up to see Rob/Dad and Penny looking at me expectantly. They were waiting for a response from me to the big question.

'I had an affair,' I replied. 'I was unfaithful.'

Rob/Dad nodded sagely. 'I see. And how did you find out about this, Penny?'

'Joe told me,' replied Penny. 'But only because I'd incorrectly accused him of sleeping with someone else.' She looked at me with real hurt in her eyes and then back at Rob/Dad. 'That's not me playing the blame game. That's exactly how it happened.' She turned back to me. 'You must have thought me such an idiot, tossing your phone to me like that, hoping I'd call that woman just so you could hide what you'd done.'

'It wasn't like that,' I replied, feeling sick at the thought of having to return to that moment. 'It wasn't like that at all.'

Penny shrugged. 'So what was it like? You had me doubting myself, Joe. I knew there was something wrong with you at that lunch. Your whole demeanour changed the moment those two women came over to our table. But you had me thinking I was mad, you had me thinking I'd got it all wrong. And after everything that Mum went through with Dad too.'

Rob/Dad raised an eyebrow. 'With your father?'

'He was a serial cheater. Nearly broke Mum's heart with his behaviour. The day he left was the best day of our lives.'

'I see,' said Rob/Dad. 'And you feel this informs your relationship with Joe?'

'Fidelity is everything to me,' she said.

'I know it is,' I replied. 'And I've never regretted anything more than what I did. It was terrible of me. There's no defence at all.'

Rob/Dad jotted something down on a pad by his side and turned to Penny. 'Perhaps you should continue from where you were before we spoke about your father. You were talking about how you felt when you found out.'

'I felt stupid. And belittled. Especially as I'd actually met the woman.' Penny looked at me.

160

'Was your little girlfriend in on the big joke? Was she laughing at me behind my back as I tried to be nice to her?'

'Of course not! That day was the first time I'd seen her in months. It happened just the once and then I cut off all contact with her. I wanted her out of my life.'

Penny shook her head with disgust. 'Ever the gentleman.'

'It wasn't like that,' I said again, even though it was exactly like that. 'I just let myself get carried away, that's all. I didn't love her. I didn't care for her. I didn't even really know her. I just let myself get carried away.'

Penny laughed. 'And that's supposed to make me feel better, is it? Am I meant to take solace from the fact that the kids and I weren't even a consideration? You've ruined absolutely everything, Joe. We had the best thing ever and you ruined it with one selfish act. Don't you think I've had offers? I've had plenty if you want to know. Only last week an old boyfriend of mine messaged me to see if I'd like to meet up when he's in London for business.'

I bristled. 'Which old boyfriend?'

'You're missing the point! He's not important. That I didn't even reply to his message is. That's what you do when you're married. You don't dip your toe in to test the water. You don't put yourself in harm's way. You don't do anything at all that could hurt the thing you love the most. But you did, Joe. You just jumped in there with both feet and you didn't give a damn about the consequences.'

Rob/Dad, sensing that our discussion was in danger of getting out of control, took the opportunity to intervene. 'Right, there's certainly a lot of food for thought in what's been said. But I think going forward we probably need to unpack some of it and see what we can tease out.' He looked over at me. 'Joe, why don't you go first? What I'm hearing from Penny is that the affair has caused her a great deal of heartache and — correct me if I'm wrong — that she feels let down by the explanation you've offered for your actions. As Penny was speaking I found myself jotting down the following question: 'Why does Joe think he chose to have an affair?''

It was a good question. One that got to the very heart of the matter. And if it hadn't been asked by a man who bore such an uncanny resemblance to my deceased father maybe I would've bought it, but this along with everything that had been going on of late was just one step too far. This really was a dream. I wasn't losing my mind after all. I was coming to my senses. I'd been mugged and was unconscious and had created a whole nightmare landscape populated by people from my past. There was nothing real about this world. Not a single thing. So it stood to reason that if I challenged it directly it would disappear and I'd wake up where I'd fallen after the mugging.

I took a deep breath. I had to do something drastic if this was going to work. I looked at Rob/Dad.

'Do you really want to know why I did what I did?'

Rob/Dad smiled. 'That's why I asked the question.'

'And you want me to tell the truth? I mean, there's no point in any of this if I just make it up is there?'

'No,' said Rob/Dad. 'There would be no point at all.'

'OK,' I replied. 'Well here it is.' I turned to Penny and took a deep breath. 'I know that what I told you the other day must have really hurt and I'm more sorry about that than you'll ever know but when I said I'd had an affair I wasn't telling you the truth, I was telling you what I thought was the truth. I know it's going to sound weird but hear me out. That night — the night that y'know — well, I was attacked by — and I know *this* is going to sound *really* mad — Fiona Briggs, my dead ex-girlfriend. She knocked me out with a cricket bat but she did it to save me . . . to save us, and right now I'm lying unconscious on a pavement in a dodgy part of town and I'm hoping that telling you all this will help me to wake up.'

There was a long silence. Penny and Rob/Dad exchanged awkward glances. Clearly neither of them knew what to make of this. Was I joking or was I insane? Even I had to weigh the question up in the light of their reaction and the more horrified they became the more my confidence faltered. Did Rob/Dad really look like my own father? They had slightly similar features, but so had a million other old men. And yes, his voice had sounded familiar at first but now I thought about it I wasn't so sure.

163

I'd been so convinced of my own argument but now my words were out there all they served to do was make it clear just how bonkers an idea this was.

The longer the silence went on, the more I doubted what I'd said. This was horrible. Truly horrible. If I continued to insist that the world wasn't real, when it clearly was, Penny would have no choice but to get me hospitalised, maybe even sectioned, and who knew where that would end? Like Bruce Willis in *12 Monkeys*, babbling on about being from the future and locked up in a mental institution? Did Rob/Dad have a panic button hidden somewhere behind a box of tissues which he'd reach for at the next opportunity? I needed to think fast.

They always say that the most straightforward answers are most likely to be true. How likely was it that my dead ex-girlfriend had attacked me to save me from cheating on my wife? Wasn't it infinitely more plausible that I'd actually done it and was so overwhelmed with guilt that I'd blocked it out and the episodes with Fiona were my way of dealing with it? Surely this was a case of extreme stress and nothing more: the mind doing odd things to keep itself from short-circuiting. It didn't mean that I was mad or in danger of losing my mind. It simply meant that I had to get out of here, grab a good night's sleep and get back to being my old self. I needed to rest.

I sat forward in my chair, the tension palpable, then I laughed and held my hands up in surrender. 'Anyone would think you'd never

164

heard a joke before.'

Rob shifted uncomfortably in his chair. 'I think the most politic thing to say here, Joe, is that when it comes to humour context is everything.'

Penny stood up, her face livid. 'I can't believe you, Joe! You begged me to work on our marriage, made me feel guilty for giving up on us and now this? Is this all just one big joke to you?' She shook her head. 'I wasn't going to say this until the end of the session but seeing the way things are going I don't see the point in keeping it to myself any longer: I want you to move out. I'm tired of lying to the kids every day, I'm tired of all the subterfuge. I've had enough.'

Rob held up his hand. 'Maybe we should take a break? In my experience decisions made in the heat of the moment aren't always the most helpful.'

'No,' said Penny. 'I want you out, Joe. I want you gone.'

17

Saturday. Mid-afternoon. The seventeenth floor of a high-rise block of flats not far from Lewisham station. A two-bed ex-council flat that had three things going for it: a bedroom each for Rosie and Jack (so long as I slept on the sofa), a living room large enough for me to imagine the kids and me spending a rainy afternoon playing games in without tripping over ourselves and most importantly the fact that I could just about afford it. On the other hand, of the several things it had going against it — being a high-rise, the lifts not working, and the smell of urine in the stairwell — the thing that was really putting me off right now was the sound of the couple in the flat next door hurling expletive-riddled abuse at each other.

'How much for this place again?'

The estate agent grimaced. 'Let's just say,' he replied pointedly, 'that the rent is definitely up for negotiation.'

★   ★   ★

Despite days of me apologising Penny had absolutely refused to budge on her request that I moved out of the family home. I had explained away my attempt to tell her what I saw as the truth saying it was a stress response to the situation, a bit like laughing when someone dies.

166

Following, I suspect, a phone call to the counsellor she had come to accept this, albeit begrudgingly, and even agreed to return to counselling. Not however with me still at home. From her point of view my moving out was the only way forward. How could we ever hope to return to normal when my being around the house did nothing but make the situation worse? Every morning we ate breakfast together like a normal family was just another reminder that we were pretending to be something now that Penny didn't feel we were and she hated it. I couldn't stand to see her so unhappy and so I agreed to start looking for somewhere to live.

Desperate to stay close to my family but acutely aware of my meagre budget, my choices were seriously limited. Like most London couples Penny and I had mortgaged ourselves to the hilt in order to get the most for our money and with Penny working part-time there wasn't a lot of spare cash floating around. That said, as relatively cheap as the B&B had been in the short term returning there in the long term wasn't an option and so while Penny took the kids to her Mum and Tony's for the weekend, I started my house search in earnest.

The second place I saw that day was another ex-local authority flat, five minutes away from the first property. It was in the middle of a large council estate and the area reminded me of the kinds of places Penny and I had first looked at when we'd decided to move on from house shares to getting a place of our own. The overwhelming impression I had of the flat was that it stank, of cigarettes, grease and desperation. It seemed to be ingrained in the walls and the carpets, and sewn into the very fabric of the back street charity shop-style furniture. Seeing the disappointment on my face the estate agent had offered me a deal where the rent would be discounted significantly if I was prepared to spruce the place up a bit at my own expense but I think we both knew that little short of knocking the whole building down and starting again would make it habitable.

I spent what remained of my weekend and the week following looking at flat after flat and being so disappointed that I began to wonder if there was any decent rentable accommodation left in London. I saw flats that had chronic problems with damp, ones that overlooked railway lines and others with a full generational set of antisocial neighbours. It started to look like I was never going to find a home. Then at my boss's suggestion I posted a request on the *Correspondent's* online internal bulletin board, and as luck would have it by the end of that afternoon I received an offer from an ad sales executive from the fifth floor.

'My fiancée and I have just bought the place,' he explained over coffee at the local Starbucks — ever since my run-in with Bella I'd avoided Allegro's like the plague. 'It's structurally sound but in need of updating and we can't do the work until my flat in Enfield is sold which could take at least six months because we're having problems with the lease extension. In the interim I'd be happy to let it to a fellow *Correspondent*

168

employee for a reasonable rate just to keep it occupied. You're more than welcome to come and take a look tonight if it sounds up your street though I must stress it isn't in a great state.'

He wasn't joking. The house was a wreck. A deceased estate, previously owned by an elderly man who though obviously a keen gardener hadn't exactly been an interior decorating wizard. The orange and green carpets, sludge-coloured anaglypta walls and brick-built fireplace complete with fully functioning fake-log-effect gas fire made me feel as though I'd travelled back in time to the late seventies — and not in a good way — but the house's one saving grace was that it was only ten minutes from Penny and the kids. It was a winner.

The ad sales guy and I shook hands on the deal. A guaranteed six-month lease at minimal rent and given his plans to totally renovate the place I could decorate it any way I wanted in the meantime. As deals went it was the best I could hope for.

'I feel bad charging you anything for this place,' he said as we left the house. 'It's a total tip. You must really be up against it to want to live here.'

'You don't know the half of it,' I replied.

* * *

At the end of our counselling session the following week I asked Penny if she had time for a coffee as I had some news I wanted to share. She agreed and we went to a little place just around the corner. We ordered our drinks at the counter and then took up seats near the window. Penny must have sensed how difficult this conversation was going to be because for the first time in what felt like forever she made small talk.

'How's work?' she asked.

'OK,' I replied. 'Nothing much to report really; I interviewed quite an interesting guy at the start of the week. He's a director who for the last year or so has been making a series of films about his family and posting them online. Fascinating stuff. How about you?'

'Same as ever: too much to do, too little time to do it.' She smiled awkwardly. 'That was a good session wasn't it?'

'It was,' I replied, even though for me it had been anything but. In the middle of the session Rob had asked us if, prior to the affair, we'd thought we were happy. I'd said yes straight away because I'd assumed that he meant happy as a couple which I had been because as far as I was concerned my problems had been with myself, not with my marriage. When Penny took her turn however she revealed that there had been times when she'd wondered if she hadn't made a mistake getting married, which had completely been news to me.

I looked at Penny. 'Did you mean what you said?'

'About what?'

'About sometimes wishing you hadn't married me?'

'That's not what I said. What I said was that sometimes I wished I'd never got married — not

170

just to you — to anyone.'

'Because . . . what? Marriage is a terrible institution?'

'No, of course not,' she replied. 'I loved being married, I loved our life together it's just that . . . I don't know, when you're that close with another person it's easy to lose sight of who you are . . . what you want . . . what you need.'

'Like how?'

'Like work for instance, it was never my great ambition to be a social work team leader bogged down in paperwork. I wanted to have a career that meant something. We both did. You wanted to be a writer. I wanted . . . well I know at one point I talked about working for Greenpeace but the truth was I didn't care all that much; I just wanted my career to be special. But then you compromise, don't you? The book you write doesn't sell well, or the dream job you wanted doesn't materialise — and before you know it the job you took to pay your half of the rent has become your career. I think part of me always felt that if I'd been single I wouldn't have compromised on my career just as you wouldn't have either. We would have just ploughed on trying to make it work because we'd only have had ourselves to worry about. I don't think I'm saying anything controversial. I'm just saying that meeting the love of your life when you're young changes things, doesn't it? After graduating from university at twenty-one we made decisions that most people wouldn't have to make until much later in life because we wanted to be together and it felt like the right thing to

171

do.' The waitress arrived with our coffees, interrupting the flow of conversation. By the time she'd put down the drinks and asked if we wanted anything else I could see from Penny's face that the moment had passed and that I needed to get to the point of why I'd asked her here.

I picked up a packet of sugar and poured the contents into my cup. I hated sugar in coffee but right now I needed the taste of something sweet in my mouth.

I stirred in the sugar and looked at Penny. 'I've found a place.'

'Where is it?'

'Crofton Road.'

'Near the park?'

'Just around the corner.'

We sipped our coffees silently. I could tell Penny was thinking the same as me: how would we tell the kids? It was an impossible situation.

'I was thinking we'd tell them it was just a temporary thing,' said Penny as though reading my mind. 'That yes, we are having some problems but that we are trying our best to sort them out. Then we can ask if they have any questions.'

I felt sick. This was really happening. Despite Fiona's assertions to the contrary this wasn't a dream, this was my life, and it was disintegrating for real. 'I can't imagine telling them, can you? Penny, please, I'm begging you, let's sort this out between us.'

'That's what we're trying to do isn't it?'

'But do we have to tell the kids?'

'What should we do instead? Carry on deceiving them? Rosie's not stupid Joe, she knows you've been sleeping downstairs.'

'How do you know?'

'She asked me why we weren't putting the burglar alarm on at night any more but she did it in that way where I knew she was asking something more. She's a bright kid, Joe. Treating her like she's not does us all a disservice.'

I could barely get the words out. 'When would we do it?'

'The sooner the better,' said Penny. 'The longer we leave it the worse it'll be.'

18

As much as I needed to say goodbye to my family, I think Penny did too, and the idea of a reprieve seemed too good to turn down. So for the week that followed both of us put aside our differences and played happy families for all we were worth: the kind that went to Nando's on a weekday, let their kids stay up late when they had school next day and spent a small fortune on a last-minute two-night break to Center Parcs. Rosie and Jack loved every minute of it and Penny and I would have too if we hadn't known the truth. But as it was even as we laughed and joked with the kids all I could think was that I was witnessing nothing less than the end of their innocence.

On the following Thursday night, just as Penny and I had arranged, I left work early, picked the kids up from school and brought them home to a feast of takeaway pizzas ordered by Penny that we ate huddled together on the sofa in front of the TV. Towards the end of the evening as Jack was requesting just one more episode of *Scooby Doo* I switched off the TV and announced that I had something important to tell them.

'What is it?' asked Jack. 'Are we getting a PlayStation?'

'No, son,' I replied. 'It's about Mum and me.'

'What about you?' asked Rosie.

'Well, the thing is we've been having some problems.'

Rosie's brow furrowed. 'What kind of problems?'

'Grown-up problems,' I replied.

'Daddy and I still love each other very much,' added Penny. 'And we love you guys more than the world and we're doing everything we can to make things right. But while we do that Daddy's going to be living somewhere else.'

Jack looked stricken. 'But Daddy can't live on his own. It's not right.'

Rosie looked me straight in the eye. 'Are you and Mum getting divorced?'

'Of course not,' I said quickly and to my relief Penny backed me up.

'We just need some time apart, that's all,' said Penny. 'You'll see Dad all the time. He'll pick you up some days and cook you tea, it'll be like he's still here.'

'I don't like it,' said Jack.

'I don't like it either,' said Rosie.

'I know my lovelies,' said Penny, her eyes brimming with tears, 'but right now it's just the way it's got to be.'

★ ★ ★

I moved out the following afternoon while the kids were still at school. Penny had said that I should feel free to take whatever I wanted but when it came to it I didn't want very much of anything at all. I took my clothes of course; two silver-framed pictures of the kids, some bedding and a couple of box files filled with bank and credit card statements but that was it. Partly I

175

didn't take any more because I couldn't fit it into the car but mostly I left stuff behind because I wanted to send a clear message to the kids that this was temporary; one day sooner or later I was coming back.

At Penny's request I stayed away from the house for a while to give the kids a chance to settle into the new routine; wanting to keep the peace I agreed to make do with daily chats on the phone. Rosie barely said a word during these calls. I'd ask her question after question about her day and got nothing in return other than one-word answers punctuated with long sullen silences but as awful as they were they paled in comparison to the conversations with Jack. Every call was pretty much the same: he'd demand through angry, snotty tears that I should return home immediately and when I told him I couldn't he'd just sob his heart out. I normally had my first drink of the day after I had spoken to the kids in the evening in the vain hope that the alcohol would make life bearable.

★   ★   ★

Finally however Penny called to suggest that I should spend some time with the kids so the following evening I left work as early as I could and headed over to the house of the childminder who picked up the kids after school whenever Penny was working.

★   ★   ★

Jane Cairns was a hippyish but harmless woman who had been childminding on and off for Penny and me ever since Rosie was born. Jane loved the kids like they were her own and even Rosie, who frankly found most interactions with adults something of a chore, would happily chat to her for hours without ever resorting to sarcasm.

'I can't begin to tell you how devastated I am for you both,' said Jane, smothering me in a tight hug. 'It's such a terrible thing, the end of a marriage. Penny didn't go into details, and I don't really want to know them either, I just wanted to say that if you need a shoulder to cry on, I'm here for you.'

'Thanks, that's really kind of you,' I replied as Jane finally released me from her grip, 'but would you mind if I went and saw the kids now?'

Rosie and Jack were watching TV in the living room along with two of Jane's other charges. Like that day in the playground, the moment Jack realised that it was me in the room and not the parent of one of the other kids he leaped to his feet squealing with delight and showering me with kisses.

'Daddy, Daddy! I've missed you so much!'

'And I've missed you too, little man,' I said, blinking away tears.

I called over to Rosie, who was sitting watching me as if waiting for her turn. Without speaking she came over and hugged me but it wasn't until she stopped that I realised she was crying.

'She misses you like I do, Daddy,' explained

Jack. 'Sometimes she cries in her bedroom when she thinks no one can hear but I do.'

Rosie glared at Jack, and he took a step backwards as though wanting to be sure that he was out of range of her fists. 'No I don't!' she snapped. 'I don't cry, you take it back!'

The last thing I needed when I had such little time with them was to have to get tough with them both. 'He's not teasing you darling, he's worried about you. You need to look after each other, OK? These are tough times and we need to stick together.'

★ ★ ★

At home the children took up residence with me in the kitchen while I prepared tea the ingredients for which Penny had labelled in the fridge. Rosie told me about an argument that she had had with Petra Goodman, a girl in her class who had accused her of saying things about her behind her back; while Jack's lowlight of the day was having to hold Lettie Harrison's hand in country dancing. As I tossed chicken and vegetables in the hot spitting oil of the wok I did my best to offer fatherly insight into both predicaments. To Rosie I advised ignoring the girl making the accusations, reasoning that she was probably only making them to get Rosie in trouble; and to Jack I suggested that the best way to deal with his situation was to imagine that he had a robotic hand, because everyone knows that there's nothing romantic at all about a girl holding a robotic hand. Rosie thought that my advice wouldn't work because the girl was too annoying; Jack however thought my robot hand idea was the best he'd ever heard.

★ ★ ★

I turned off the flame under the wok and distributed the steaming hot food between three plates. It was hard not to be thoroughly pleased with myself to be doing something so obviously constructive for my children.

'Grub's up!'

Jack ran to the kitchen sink and began washing his hands without being asked.

'What are we having?'

'Your favourite.'

Jack's eye's widened in delight. 'Chicken stir-fry? I love chicken stir-fry! You're the best dad in the world!'

I knew I wasn't. I was far from it. But even so it was nice to think that Jack, however misguided, actually believed it was true.

★ ★ ★

The kids had long since gone up to their rooms when I heard Penny come home. Guiltily I switched off the TV and snatched up a magazine from the coffee table as though reading as an activity might make me appear less like I was making myself at home than watching the BBC news channel.

I called out to her and she came into the room. She was wearing her gym kit, and had her

179

hair tied away from her face in a ponytail.

'How did it go?'

'Fine. Rosie's up in her room tackling her homework and Jack's asleep — that said, he's been downstairs to see me about half a dozen times in the last half-hour.'

Penny sat down in the chair opposite, her keys still in her hands. 'Aches, pains, and strange noises in his room?'

'You've guessed it.'

'He's been at this for weeks now. He's going to be so shattered in the morning and on top of that he's still having trouble settling at school.'

This was news to me. 'Still?'

'It's just the usual,' replied Penny. 'Tears in the morning, not wanting to go in . . . according to Miss Brown he seems to be calming down more quickly than last week but it's still not great.'

Not great. That was the understatement of the century. It killed me to know the separation was hurting Jack so much. I looked over at Penny. 'Are you sure this is what you want?'

'What I want?'

I apologised immediately.

'Look, I didn't mean it like that . . . obviously I'm the one to blame here but — '

'You're absolutely right about that! Do you seriously think any of this is what I wanted? This is all you, Joe, and don't you ever forget that. It wasn't me who broke my vows. It wasn't me who tossed away twenty years without a second thought. It was you, and only you, and don't you dare forget that.' Penny stood up. 'I think you should go.'

'But I need to talk to you about when I'll next see the kids.'

'Then we'll have to talk tomorrow because do you know what? Now is not a good time.'

I'd lived with Penny long enough to know when she could be talked round and when she couldn't and this was definitely one of those situations when she wasn't going to budge an inch. I left the room and grabbed my coat only to look up and see Jack in his Spiderman pyjamas sitting on the stairs.

'What are you doing, Dad?'

'It's time for me to go.'

'Can I come too? I won't be any trouble.'

'I know you won't son, but you live here with Mum.'

He stuck out his bottom lip, pouting. 'I don't want to live here any more. I want to live with you.'

It took all the strength I had not to snatch Jack up in my arms and smuggle him out of the house. Thankfully Penny appeared in the doorway, and Jack and I both looked at her, and then back at each other. It was time to say our goodbyes. I kissed his head.

'I promise I'll see you soon.'

Jack began sobbing, clutching on to my legs. 'But I want to see you always, Daddy!'

I picked him up and hugged him one last time but he was inconsolable. Finally I handed him over to Penny and without saying anything to me she whisked him upstairs leaving me alone in the hallway. I didn't move. I just wanted his tears to stop. Grabbing my coat I headed out to my car, but as I opened the driver's door I was hit by a waft of Poison.

'Guess who's back?' said a voice from behind me.

I turned around to see Fiona sitting cross-legged on the next-door neighbour's wall. She was holding a packet of prawn cocktail crisps and every now and again she'd take out a handful and crunch down on them loudly.

'You're actually quite sweet when you're upset, aren't you?' said Fiona between crisps. 'Why did I never notice that before? You're like a little boy . . . I almost want to hug you.'

'Go away!' I yelled, and then immediately regretted having done so. Nothing was going to drive Penny even further from me than she already was than reports that her husband was yelling to himself in the street.

I got into the car and started up the engine but then Fiona opened the rear passenger door and climbed inside.

'Nice motor.'

I ignored her.

'Could do with valeting though, eh?'

I continued to ignore her.

'That said, I'm guessing money is a bit tight at the moment.'

I couldn't ignore her any more. I turned off the engine.

'You don't exist.'

Fiona laughed. 'Says the man who's just stopped to talk to me.'

I wanted to scream but in the end I settled for scraping my fingernails over my scalp out of pure frustration. If this was what it felt like to lose your mind I didn't like it at all.

'Why won't you just leave me alone?'

'Because I'm not done with you.'

'You've broken up my family — what more can you do to me?'

Fiona smiled wryly. 'Believe me, you'd be surprised.'

'So that's it?' I replied. 'You're just going to carry on like this?'

'I told you it's for your own good,' she replied.

'How could this be for my own good? Have you seen how upset my kids are?'

'I know,' said Fiona. 'It's tragic and they're dead cute too. But business is business and like I'm always telling you I've got a job to do.'

'Which is what exactly? You've never once given me a proper explanation for why you're doing any of this. What's your motivation?'

'I've got plenty of motivation thank you very much. But since we're on the subject how about yours on the night you were texting Slag Face? Was it plain and simple lust or was your fragile ego in need of a bit of a boost?'

Seemingly out of nowhere raw emotion worked its way into my voice. 'I don't know why you keep going on about that night. I've learned my lesson a million times over! If I could go back and have my time again I'd never even talk to Bella let alone think about sleeping with her!'

Fiona rolled her eyes and yawned. 'Are you quite finished with the histrionics? Because I'll tell you what: your mawkishness is really making me gag.' Fiona emptied the last of her crisps directly into her mouth and then discarded the packet on Jack's car seat. 'The thing is, Joe, as much as I'm sure that we'd all like to throw our hands up in the air when things get tough and say, 'Please let me erase my own stupidity and get back to normal,' life doesn't work like that. Do you want to know how life really works? It works like this: you do something stupid and that stupid thing comes back to bite you on the arse not just once or twice but again and again and again until you've got no arse left. And while you might be feeling a little tender at the moment you, Joe Clarke, have got a little way further to go until you're arseless but I'll make you a promise here and now — we'll definitely get there.' Fiona opened the car door and then stopped and looked at me. 'Thirty seconds after I get out of the car you're going to think to yourself that the only thing you can do is turn up at the local Accident and Emergency and tell them that you're having hallucinations. So, word to the wise, here's what will happen to you if you do that: they'll do loads of tests but they'll find nothing wrong with you but they'll section you anyway because, well, you can't be right in the head if you say you're seeing dead people can you? And after that, well, maybe you'll get released, maybe you won't. Maybe the HR department at work will get involved and you'll get pushed out of your job, or maybe it won't. Maybe social services will get involved and you'll have a plump middle-aged woman called Joanne supervising all your visits with your kids, or maybe you won't. But what you've got to ask yourself is this: is it really worth the risk?'

She was right. There was no way that telling anyone in authority about Fiona wouldn't somehow impact upon me for the worst.

'Fine,' I replied. 'You win.'

Fiona grinned. 'I always do in the end.'

19

This latest encounter with Fiona had really shaken me. For the few days until my next visit with the kids, I resolved to make more of an effort to take better care of myself. Fiona would only make another reappearance if I allowed my stress levels to get the better of me and so I tried to eat more healthily, get out of the office at lunchtimes for a bit of fresh air and even started drinking Holland & Barrett branded chamomile tea in a bid to calm my obviously frazzled nerves.

By the time my next midweek visit to the kids came around, I was feeling a lot better. I picked them up from the childminder's, took them home and spent a good few hours of real quality time with them. We played half an hour of Hungry Hippos followed by a couple of rounds of snap — at which Jack consistently cheated — then I prepared a tea of fish fingers, peas and potato waffles after which we watched TV for a while before bedtime. It was good having this time with them but I wanted more: each visit I noticed something about one of them had changed and I hated it. If I could see the changes then it meant I wasn't close enough to them. I wanted their growing up to be as imperceptible to my naked eye as a field of daisies opening in the warmth of a summer's day. And with the house ready I now had somewhere to take them that wasn't our old family home or a fast food restaurant; so when Penny returned home that night I decided to broach the subject as she made the kids' packed lunches.

'I just thought I'd let you know that I'm off now,' I said, popping my head around the kitchen door, 'and Rosie has a maths test next week that she needs to revise for.'

'I'll make a note of it,' she said chopping carrot sticks and dropping them into the lunch boxes. 'Are you still available to do something with them on Saturday afternoon?'

'Actually,' I replied, 'I was wondering how you'd feel about me having them overnight — you know, picking them up on Saturday morning and bringing them back on Sunday afternoon.'

Penny stopped chopping. 'Oh,' she said as though it hadn't occurred to her that this moment might ever happen. 'So the house is ready then?'

'As it'll ever be.'

'It's not cold there though is it? Rosie's been a bit snuffly all week and I don't want it to develop into anything. Maybe we could do it when it gets a bit warmer?'

'The house does have central heating. Admittedly it's not the most efficient, but it's there, plus I'll make sure she's wrapped up warm at all times.'

'But Jack's not been sleeping very well and he'll miss his room too much. You know how he is, he likes to have his things around him.'

'Then I'll make sure he brings everything with him that will make him happy.'

'But what if — '

'They'll be fine, Penny, I promise. I'll have my phone on me all the time, I'll make sure they call you to say goodnight and — I know you know this already — I won't let anything bad happen to them.'

'I know that, you're their dad, it's just that . . .'

'You'll miss them?'

Penny nodded and started to cry. I went to put my arm around her but thought better of it.

'I know you will,' I replied. 'Believe me, I know.'

★ ★ ★

It was Rosie who answered the door when I went to collect the kids that weekend for their first sleepover at my new place. She kissed my cheek and told me how Jack had been packed and ready to go since five thirty that morning. I picked him up and gave him a kiss as he ran to greet me and as I set him down I noticed he was holding a medium-sized teddy bear under his arm that I'd never seen before.

'Who's this?' I asked.

'Oscar,' he replied. 'He's my friend.'

Jack had so many soft toys that fell in and out of favour at whim it was impossible to keep up with them.

'Nice to meet you, Oscar,' I replied and solemnly shook the bear's paw. Keen to get the weekend off on the right note I was about to ask a few more bear-related questions when Penny appeared at the kitchen door.

'They're all packed,' she said.

I told Jack and Rosie to give their mum a big hug and say goodbye. Jack told Penny that he had packed a picture of her in his bag so he could look at it at night and Rosie told her that she would text her. I handed Rosie the car keys and told her and Jack to wait in the car while I loaded up their bags.

'I was thinking about bringing them back after lunch tomorrow if that's OK?' I said once the kids were out of earshot.

'Of course,' said Penny, 'that's fine.'

'And, like I said before, you can call them any time you like.'

'I know, thanks.'

'So you'll be all right then?'

Penny shook her head. She had tears in her eyes.

'No,' she said, ushering me out of the door, 'I don't think I will be but the kids need this so I'll work on that.'

★   ★   ★

The kids' reaction to the outside of my new home was typically unrestrained in its honesty.

'It looks like the kind of place a witch would live,' said Rosie.

'I think that too,' said Jack, tucking his bear under his arm. 'Did an actual witch used to live here, Dad?'

'No,' I replied, even though I could see exactly what they meant. Their home — by which I mean the home I used to live in — was the complete opposite of this house in every way and despite my efforts at modernisation and refurbishment it still looked like the dated, rundown home of a housebound octogenarian with an interest in spell casting.

The kids demanded a tour of the house and so once we'd unloaded the car we started upstairs in Rosie's bedroom. As she was older I'd given her the big bedroom that overlooked the garden so that she could spread out and make it her own.

'What do you reckon? I've just given it a couple of coats of white for now but I was thinking you could decorate it any way you like. I don't know, maybe put up some posters and make it feel homely?'

Rosie looked around the room as it was. It had a single bed and not much else — the very definition of prison cell chic — and somehow the pastel-coloured duvet set which I had bought seemed to make matters worse.

'It's great,' she said, but in the same voice that she uses to thank my mum whenever she knits her a jumper out of leftover wool. It was a voice that said, 'I appreciate this, and I love you because we're related, but this simply isn't going to work.'

I tried my best to salvage the situation.

'Maybe you could bring round a few of your things next time. You could leave them here so that you don't have to keep dragging stuff back and forth.'

'Yeah, cool,' said Rosie but it didn't take a

190

genius to see that her heart wasn't in it.

As spartan as Rosie's room had seemed it was practically a palace compare to the only other bedroom in the house, which was technically mine. I still had the old carpets down and the original owner's faded orange curtains at the window. In the middle of the room was the double bed I'd ordered from Argos which had taken me a whole evening to put up and at the far end was a half-built flat-pack wardrobe surrounded by black bin liners filled with my clothes. It looked like a squat.

Jack shot me a worried glance.

'Dad, where am I sleeping?'

'Here,' I replied. 'I know it's not perfect but Rosie's room took longer than I thought to sort out. But this one's definitely next on the list.'

Jack shook his head fearfully.

'Daddy, Oscar doesn't like it.'

I was completely thrown.

'Oscar? Who's Oscar?' Then I remembered the bear. 'Oh, you mean your teddy?'

Jack nodded and clutched Oscar just that little bit tighter.

'How come I've never seen Oscar before, son? Did Nanny get him for you?'

Jack shook his head.

'He's the school bear, Daddy, and it's my turn to have him for the weekend.'

My heart sank. I remembered the school teddy bear from when Rosie was in infants. He came with his own suitcase and clothes which was fine, but the real killer was his diary. Every day you had him had to be recorded in the diary with pictures and writing describing his weekend, which wouldn't have been so bad had parents not tried to constantly outdo each other. By the time it came to Rosie's turn to have the bear he'd already been skiing in Switzerland, boating on Lake Garda and met the cast of *Les Misérables* backstage at a theatre in Covent Garden. I flicked through Oscar's diary to see if anything had changed in the world of weekend bears since our last trial. The previous one he'd been to London Zoo, the weekend before that Kenwood House, and, unbelievably, the weekend before that a garden party at Buckingham Palace, but this was the least of my problems. I'd got the bear on my very first weekend with my kids as a single dad and so it wouldn't matter if I booked him on a return trip to the Bahamas because all the other parents in Jack's class would be too busy reading between the lines of a small boy spending his first weekend away from his mum after the end of his parents' marriage. Infidelity, it appeared, really was the gift that kept on giving.

★   ★   ★

Determined to give Weekend Bear Oscar the best twenty-four hours of his life, I ditched my plans to spend the day at home in the hope of encouraging the kids to treat it as their own and instead took them into the centre of London without much of a plan at all. We started off at the National Portrait Gallery because at the very least I reasoned it would be educational but after ten minutes of staring at paintings of — according to Rosie — 'fat men with beards' it became clear that I'd made the wrong choice when Jack started crying saying that the museum lights were hurting his eyes. In the end I took a quick snap of Jack and the Weekend Bear standing in front of a portrait of King Charles II, making a hasty retreat before we could be apprehended by the tiny but irate security guard heading our way.

Teatime was ruined when the cooker broke down in the middle of baking a pizza; bathtime by virtue of the fact that neither of them would get into the tub because they said it was too dirty — it *was* a bit grimy-looking although I'd scrubbed it half a dozen times to no avail — but bedtime was the biggest disaster of all. Having taken an hour to coax them into bed they were both up and out again within a few minutes because independently they both claimed to have heard strange noises in their rooms. This went on — me checking their rooms for ghosts and them refusing to be comforted — for a good two hours after which I sat down on Rosie's bed and admitted defeat.

'You want to go back to Mum's, don't you?'

They both nodded and without another word on the matter, we started packing.

* * *

To her credit, Penny couldn't have been more gracious. Refusing to gloat as I stood on her doorstep in my pyjama bottoms, she reminded me of how it had taken three attempts before the kids would even countenance staying over at her mum and Tony's without us, but as much as I tried to take solace in this fact I just couldn't find any. As far as I was concerned it was fine for them to find Penny's mum's place weird because it was never meant to be their home, but I'd tried my best to make a home from home for them and it just hadn't been enough. If my attempt at throwing a sleepover for my kids had proved anything, it was that I'd failed at the first hurdle of the newly single parent: make a home for your kids that they actually want to be in.

The real killer however came a few days later while I was babysitting the kids at the house because Penny had a conference to attend. With the kids in bed and nothing on telly I'd idly flicked through a pile of the kids' school work on the table and come across Jack's entry in Oscar the Weekend Bear's diary. Under the picture I'd taken of Jack and Oscar in the National Portrait Gallery Jack had written: 'Oscar enjoyed his weekend with me and we did lots of fun things. He did find my dad's house a little bit scary but he loved being with my daddy very, very much.'

20

Van Halen put a reassuring hand on my shoulder. 'It's a novice mistake, buddy, and an easy one to make at that. Things don't go right the first time you have your kids over and you convince yourself that you've messed up for good. First time I had my Harley and Suzuki overnight they bawled their eyes out for three solid hours because they missed their mum and then when I took them home they bawled for another three hours because they missed me.'

Stewart nodded. 'At least yours came though, Van. When Chris who used to work with me had his kids over for the first time they took one look at the outside of his crappy little flat in Croydon and said, 'Cheers Dad, but maybe we should just stick to Saturdays at Nando's.''

'The thing you've got to remember,' said Paul, fingering the open packet of crisps in front of him and shoving a couple in his mouth mid-sentence, 'is that it's always going to be weird for the parent who moves out. Whoever stays in the family home gets to define normal because normal is what the kids know. If you're the one who leaves then not only have the kids got to handle the separation but now they've got to cope with a new normal which inevitably means them getting used to being somewhere with you that's nowhere near as nice as the place you left.'

I looked around the table at my drinking companions, still barely able to believe that we had anything in common. On my left was chubby Stewart, now for some reason sporting a faint blond moustache; across the table was Paul, who for reasons known only to himself had turned up at the pub wearing a fisherman's cap; and on my right, larger than life and bald with it, was Van, wearing a leather biker jacket and a vest top emblazoned with the legend: Coke is the real thing. Sitting in the midst of this motley crew in a designer suit, fresh from covering a charity book launch at 10 Downing Street, was me. From an onlooker's point of view we couldn't have been more mismatched and yet from the moment I'd finished telling the guys the story of my weekend I knew that I had done the right thing in accepting an invitation to join them for one of their regular nights out. It felt good being with a bunch of guys who understood my situation. It made me feel that perhaps I wasn't quite so alone in the world after all.

'The thing is,' continued Van, warming to the topic, 'in the early days you feel like you have to try really hard with your kids to keep things the same — I know I did with my boys — but the truth is you just can't because you're in a completely different situation. Before you and your wife split up, how many times were you in sole charge of the kids for more than a day? I bet it wasn't many.'

He was wrong. I was sure of it. Just to be on the safe side however I counted them up. There was the time when Rosie was still a baby and

Penny went on her friend Nikki's hen weekend up in Edinburgh; then there was the time when Rosie was a toddler and Penny had a conference to attend for work; then there was the time just after Jack was born when Penny had had to have her appendix out; then there was the time a few weeks after Jack's first birthday when Penny went to Brighton for the weekend for a reunion with her old university friends and ended up coming home early because she missed the kids too much; and then finally there was the time after that when Penny's cousin split up with her boyfriend and invited Penny to join her for a weekend in Paris that she had already booked and paid for. Hard as it was to believe, Van was right: the number of occasions I'd had my kids for over twenty-four hours in the course of their lives before the split was five.

'I don't get it. How could I have been a father for a decade and only ever had my kids overnight on my own five times?'

Paul shrugged. 'It's just the way it is. Once you have kids neither of you goes away all that much if you can really help it and when you do it's usually work making the demands meaning you have no choice in the matter so one of you gets left holding the baby, which in my case was me.'

'So what do I do? I want my kids to want to stay with me but I can't afford to move anywhere else.'

'You need to sort your place out,' said Van. 'I'm free Friday night if you want some help getting it straight.'

'And I've got a tonne of paint that might be a

better choice for kids' rooms than brilliant white,' offered Stewart.

'This is beginning to sound like a party,' said Paul, grinning. 'You can definitely count me in.'

★   ★   ★

True to their word the guys turned up at mine on Friday night armed with paintbrushes, toolboxes and all manner of DIY equipment to help sort out the house. They divided up tasks between themselves with some on painting and others building flat-pack furniture while I seemed to do very little other than get in the way to the extent that an hour in they sent me out with a list of errands — at the top of which was beer and a rogan josh (×4) — just to get rid of me. The whole evening was like a scene from a barn-raising only instead of being in Amish country we were in my two-bed terrace in Lewisham and by the time we called it a night in the early hours of Saturday morning my former hovel resembled the sort of place that an actual real live woman might have approved of, and if she didn't I was almost definitely sure that her children would. The once barely furnished living room now looked like somewhere the kids would want to hang out in: it had a TV (on loan from Paul), a PlayStation (an old version, on loan from Stewart) and even a couple of framed arty-looking black and white pictures on the wall (thanks to Paul again). And the rest of the house couldn't have looked better either. Rosie's room now had lilac walls — her favourite colour — a wardrobe and a desk; my room (which would double up as Jack's bedroom when he stayed over) also had a fully assembled wardrobe, a chest of drawers and was painted a cheery shade of sky blue. While there wasn't a great deal I could do about the bathroom ('the whole thing needs gutting,' was Stewart's opinion) I did have a fully functioning cooker thanks to Van's efforts.

What the guys had done for me was amazing and I was in their debt. I felt quite moved and wanted to explain just how grateful I was for this true act of friendship but my overly effusive thanks were dismissed by Van with typical aplomb: 'Mate, if I hadn't been here helping you I'd have been out on the lash celebrating my bassist's forty-third birthday. The way I see it you've saved me about fifty quid and stopped me waking up tomorrow with the mother of all hangovers, so let's just say we're even.'

* * *

I waited until my midweek visit with the kids to pop the question about staying over at mine again. We had the radio on for a bit of background noise and they were tucking into the jacket potatoes and beans I'd rustled up and Rosie had just finished telling me a long and involved story about why it was annoying that Rebecca Crossly had made it into the netball team when she hadn't when I finally came out with what was on my mind.

'What do you think of giving it another go at mine this weekend? I've had a real tidy up and me and some . . . well, friends have done a brilliant job on the place. You'll love it.'

Jack chewed thoughtfully on the mouthful of potato he was working on. 'Would we get to sleep here in our own beds at night-time?'

'Well, not really, son. I was thinking that it would be like before. Rosie would sleep in her room and you'd sleep in my room, and I'd sleep downstairs on the sofa.'

Jack speared a solitary bean on his fork and contemplated it like he was studying a diamond through a magnifying glass. 'Well in that case I think I'd rather stay at home if that's OK with you, Daddy. I still really want to see you on Saturday but I don't think I'd like to stay over.'

I looked at Rosie, who was helping herself to seconds of coleslaw. If I could talk her round to wanting to go then Jack would easily fall into line for fear of missing out on a good time.

'And what about you, sweetie? You'd like to sleep over at mine wouldn't you? I tell you what, we could stay up a bit later than normal and I'll order in pizza.'

She wrinkled her nose like my offer was about as appealing as a week-old fish that had been left lying out in the sun. 'It sounds really great what you've done to your place, Dad — and I like the idea of the pizza — but do we have to stay over? Couldn't we just come for the day, eat pizza and then come back here?'

'Of course you can. You guys can do whatever you like. The important thing is that we get to spend proper time together.'

Rosie gave me a kiss on the cheek as a

thank-you and Jack chomped down on his bean with gusto and let out a victorious, 'Yes! Pizza at Dad's house on Saturday!' like he'd just scored in a cup final while I tried my best to look pleased with the result. There really was no point in forcing them to do anything they didn't want to do. After all, being with me wasn't meant to be a punishment but although I tried to put a brave face on it, the fact they didn't want to stay over hurt like a punch in the face. My kids loved me, but not enough to want to rough it at mine for one night every two weeks.

At the house that evening as I tucked away the brand-new bedding I'd bought for the kids back in the wardrobe Penny phoned to talk to me.

'Rosie and Jack said you've invited them to stay over again.'

My heart sank. It wasn't enough that my kids had rejected me for a second time, now she was about to have a go at me for inviting them without clearing it with her first.

'Listen, before you say anything . . . they don't want to come, OK? They're not interested in staying over.'

'And you're just going to leave it at that?'

'Well I thought — '

'You thought what, Joe? That it's OK for our kids to dictate to us because you think they've had it a bit hard of late? They never told us what to do when we were together and I'm not about to let them start just because we're apart. It's the thin edge of the wedge, Joe. We feel guilty about what's happened and so we let them walk all over us because we want them to like us. Well

201

it's tough luck for them because we're their parents. They don't have to like us but they do have to do what they're told. Pick them up first thing Saturday morning and I'll have them and their bags ready for you.'

★ ★ ★

Whether it was something Penny had said or the makeover the Divorced Dads' Club had given the place, the kids seemed to really enjoy their second visit to my house. Rosie loved her room so much that she spent the weekend texting pictures of it to Carly, and Jack thought that Stewart's old PlayStation was better than anything he'd ever seen. But the best thing about our weekend together, the thing that made me think that perhaps there was hope for us all, was seeing how quickly they felt at ease in the house, padding around in their socks, flopping on sofas, and generally treating the place like it was their own private hotel.

Over the next few weeks I began to feel like life had turned a corner. I stopped drinking to excess, started going to the gym and, bizarre though it sounded, in the Divorced Dads' Club I now had some real friends. To my very great relief there had been no new encounters with Fiona and even work was going well. The week after the kids came round I managed to bag a world-wide exclusive interview with British actor and Hollywood star Jonah Lloyd-Hughes who was hot property since being arrested in LA on assault and battery charges against his fellow

Hollywood actor Ray La Havas whom he'd allegedly attacked after witnessing La Havas striking his model girlfriend Casey Fields. Now that Lloyd-Hughes was back in London every publication in the world had wanted an interview and I'd landed it for the sole reason that back when he was a struggling actor I'd been the only journalist to review his one-man play at the Edinburgh Festival and praise the actor as a 'star in the making', a favour which, according his PR, he had never forgotten. In fact the only thing left on my to-do list was to work out exactly where Penny and I were heading — something that was a lot harder than bagging an interview with one of the biggest stars on the planet.

One of the most remarkable things about the separation was how quickly I'd gone from feeling like I knew her inside out to not being sure whether in fact I knew her at all. Outside our weekly counselling, whenever we spoke — normally while dropping off or picking up the kids — it seemed as though we were both so desperate to keep the fragile peace between us that in the process we failed to be ourselves. I was over-formal, Penny was needlessly polite, and the result was that even the kids noticed we were treating each other like relative strangers. At the time I had politely laughed along with Penny about this but afterwards when I went to say goodbye to her I could see that she understood what was happening just as well as I did. Without the day-to-day intimacy there was no familiarity and without familiarity it felt like we were on the fast track to becoming total strangers. Still, before I could even begin to think about dealing with that I had to face down the biggest challenge so far: Jack's seventh birthday, the first big family occasion to have taken place since I'd moved out.

21

It wasn't just that I didn't want to feel like an outsider at my own son's birthday party, or even that I knew all of the family and friends gathered at the house would be gossiping about me behind my back; it was more that I hadn't been sure whether I was going to be invited at all. I'd seen it happen before. One of the sub-editors at *The Weekend* had split up from the mother of his kids six weeks before his son's ninth birthday and because he'd managed to fall out with her family in the process he didn't get an invite. He'd had to make do with seeing his son for an hour and a half two days earlier in the week and ended up spending the actual anniversary of his son's birth staring at the walls of his poky flat in Putney. It had been, he assured me, the single worst day of his life.

Thankfully, Penny wasn't like that. Three weeks before the big day, without prompting she brought up the subject of Jack's birthday herself. 'He wouldn't be happy if you weren't there,' she'd said, handing me Jack's invite handwritten in purple felt tip. 'No matter what's happened we're still a family and we need to remember that.'

★   ★   ★

It was Penny who answered the door. She was wearing jeans and the grey mohair Whistles

205

jumper I'd bought her for Christmas. She'd had her hair done, a short choppy style that made her look even younger than she already did. If she was trying to make me feel bad by looking like she could pull any man she pleased then she had accomplished her mission. However much as I appreciated that I wasn't her desired audience I found it almost impossible to stop looking at her.

'You look great. New hair?'

'Just fancied a change.'

'Well it looks amazing.'

'Thanks.' She smiled. 'Come in.'

I stepped past her, tapping the present under my arm with my index finger. 'Where's the birthday boy?'

Penny closed the door and gestured up the stairs. 'On the loo. He's been so excited that he hasn't been for a poo since the day before yesterday. He'll be there forever.'

'And Rosie?'

'On her way back from a sleepover at Carly's.' The doorbell rang and she turned to answer it. 'I'd better get this. Why don't you go and say hello to everyone in the kitchen and I'll send Jack in when he's done?'

The kitchen.

The one full of Penny's family. The family who'd heard me make my vows in front of a packed room to 'forsake all others.' Family who were doubtless aware that I was no longer living at home and why. I didn't want to face them, I couldn't. I hadn't seen Fiona since that day in the car when I'd moved out of this very house. What if the pressure of being back here surrounded by people who hated me made me see Fiona again? I was supposed to be staying calm, avoiding stress, and this situation was anything but. As potentially hostile environments went this was right up there with an afternoon stroll through an Afghan minefield.

I looked at Penny. 'Maybe it's best if I just wait here.'

Penny shook her head. 'No Joe, you're going to have to face them all sometime and it might as well be now.'

It was like one of those moments in a Western when the bad guy walks into the saloon and everything pauses. The showgirls stop dancing. The fat guy on the piano stops playing and the drinkers cease their chatter waiting to see what will happen next. Penny's mum glared at me, her stepdad stood, arms folded, wearing a look of disgust and her brother Simon refused to look at me at all. However Simon's girlfriend, Ruth — much to the mortification of everyone in the room — marched over and gave me a huge hug. I'd always enjoyed Ruth's company and the fact that she wasn't allowing family politics to stop her doing what she'd always done made me like her even more.

However my conversation with Ruth was brought abruptly to a close by the arrival of Rosie, who launched herself into my arms. It was a Clarke family tradition that on a sibling's birthday the other child got a present too and this year was no different. I gave Rosie a twenty-pound voucher to spend on her phone on games or downloads or whatever it was she was into at that moment. She was so happy that she screamed to the entire room that I was the best dad in the world. The look on Penny's mum's face was enough to let me know that it wasn't an opinion shared by anyone else. Thankfully before anything could be said the doorbell rang again and a harassed-sounding Penny yelled down the stairs, 'Can you deal with that, Joe? Jack's had a bit of an . . . accident.'

It was the kind of message I didn't need to hear twice and so I answered the door to half a dozen parents and their overexcited children. It was party time and it would be all hands on deck until the issuing of party bags in some three hours' time. Grateful to finally be of some use I pointed the children towards the crisps and drinks, the adults towards the beer and wine and announced to anyone who cared to listen that the first game of pin the tail on the donkey would be starting in five minutes' time.

The afternoon went well, helped in no small part by the free flowing of alcohol from the kitchen that helped all the kids' parents to get along and the fact that I was an excellent master of ceremonies, making sure that the kids were constantly entertained. Having said that, even I was relieved when, at just after six, Penny called an end to the gathering with the classic: 'Right everyone, come and get your party bags!'

* * *

'I know sometimes I'm guilty of being too subtle,' said Penny later, returning to the kitchen as I finished loading the dishwasher once everyone else had gone, 'but honestly little Zachary's dad just wouldn't take the hint. Half a bloody hour I've been trying to turf him and his son out. It was like he didn't want to go home!'

Penny laughed but I didn't join in. Was this her subtle way of saying it was time for me to go? I'd had such a good time being back at home. I just didn't want the day to be over.

'I suppose I'd better be heading off too . . . It's been really great. Thanks for inviting me.'

Penny looked at me, puzzled. 'What?'

'You were saying about Zachary's dad overstaying his welcome and well . . . '

Penny sighed. 'And when did you get so sensitive? I wanted Zachary's dad to go because all he ever talks about is how much money he makes. Do you talk about how much money you make?' I shook my head and smiled. Chance would be a fine thing. 'Good,' said Penny. 'Now go and watch some TV with Jack. He's been so distracted having his friends around he's barely seen you all day.'

'Are you sure?' I asked. 'Jack and I can catch up some other time.'

'Of course I'm sure,' she replied, 'and if you've got any other plans think again because he already asked at breakfast if you could be in charge of bath- and bedtime.'

* * *

It was after nine as I came downstairs having kissed both Jack and Rosie goodnight. Penny was standing in the kitchen scrubbing at a particularly stubborn greasy handprint on the glass door.

'Can you tell me why the kids feel the need to touch the glass when there's a handle they can reach right there in front of them?'

'I'm still trying to work out why we bother giving them shoes with laces,' I replied. 'The last time they were at mine I watched Rosie spend a good five minutes trying to shove her feet into her sparkly trainers without undoing them. Halfway through I said to her, 'Wouldn't it just be easier to undo the laces?' and she just rolled her eyes as if I was deliberately being dense and carried on about her business.'

Penny nodded. 'She's so lazy sometimes I wonder how she's ever going to get on in the real world, but then I'll find her in her bedroom happily beavering away on some project she's invented for herself just because she's a bit bored and she convinces me that there is hope after all.' Penny stopped rubbing at the glass and inspected it with a satisfied look on her face. She gave it one final wipe before placing the sponge and spray back under the kitchen sink. 'How did you get on upstairs with his Highness?'

'He fell asleep in the middle of telling me all about the plans he has for his next birthday — apparently it's going to be in a tree house and all his guests will have to swing to it from his bedroom.'

Penny rubbed her eyes and yawned. 'Do you think he had a good day? It was hard to tell with everything else that was going on.'

210

'Are you joking? He was still singing the praises of your football cake even as he drifted off to sleep. You did an amazing job today, you really did, even Rosie said so and you know how hard it is to get a compliment out of her these days.'

Penny smiled, headed over to the fridge and opened the door. 'I've got this that needs finishing if you're up for it,' she said, holding up a half-empty bottle of Chardonnay. 'Or there's some beer lying about somewhere if the dads didn't polish it all off.'

'A beer would be good if you've got one,' I replied.

'A beer it is. You flick on the TV and I'll bring it through.'

★ ★ ★

It was dark in the living room and so I shut the curtains and turned on the lights, but the room seemed too bright so I turned them off and switched on the table lamp instead; but the light from that seemed too intimate somehow. I needed the kind of light that didn't say or mean anything. I needed light without subtext and so I switched the main light back on, and sat on the sofa flicking through the channels.

I switched the TV off again just as Penny entered the room shielding her eyes as she came in.

'It's like Wembley stadium under floodlights in here! What's wrong with you?'

'I thought . . . never mind.' She handed me my

211

beer and switched on the table lamp, turned off the main lights and sat down on the sofa next to me. She was right. This was much better.

'Nothing on then?'

'Not that I could see.'

Penny put her feet up on the coffee table and took a sip from her glass. 'I'm so shattered. I was up 'til midnight last night Googling designs for children's cakes and baking half a dozen cake alternatives for his friends who are either gluten intolerant or allergic to something or other. Remind me again why it is we bother with children's birthdays?'

'Because we're too scared not to,' I replied. 'We'd never hear the end of it if we didn't throw them a party.'

Penny smiled. 'There have been some good ones though, haven't there? Do you remember Rosie's third?'

'How could I forget? Sixteen three-year-old girls in their best party dresses sobbing hysterically at the sight of the Fun Barn's Birthday Bear.'

'That poor teenager in that horrible flea-ridden suit was more terrified than they were. And he must have wet himself when Rosie's friend Ella started screaming at him and kicked him in the shins.'

'Another first for the Clarkes. How many families can say they've been banned for life from their local Fun Barn for GBH?'

Penny laughed so much that she spat a mouthful of wine down her top. 'And how about Jack's Spiderman party last year? Was there ever a funnier sight than them all sat around the table with their masks halfway up their faces shovelling away jelly and ice cream?'

'How about the vision of two of them peeing in the garden because they wanted to water the plants?'

'That was that evil child Oliver Holland and his oddball sidekick, Reece Owen. That rose bush never did recover from their interference. I'm so glad Jack's not friends with them any more.'

'But you're right, there have been some good birthdays.'

Penny didn't respond and so I just sipped on my beer wondering if she was thinking about how best to ask me to leave but then as if from nowhere she asked me a question I hadn't been expecting at all.

'Do you think we're good parents?'

'Of course, I think we're great parents. Why?'

She didn't say anything. She didn't need to. I felt myself slump into the sofa. We'd had a great day. The first in what felt like forever but now she wanted to ruin it by talking about everything that had gone wrong. Unlike most separated couples I was pretty sure we were making a good fist of a bad job. We were civil to each other; always put the needs of the kids first; and refused to make each other out to be the enemy. Surely these were the things to focus on along with the fact that we were working on getting our marriage back together, not all the bad stuff.

'I think we're doing the best we can with a bad situation,' I said.

'But what about what we're doing to the kids though?' said Penny. 'Jack and Rosie miss you so much it's hard to bear. I didn't tell you this because I couldn't see the point but I was half an hour late picking them up from the childminder a few weeks back and Jack was in absolute hysterics. When I got to the bottom of it he said it was because he thought that I'd left him like you'd left us. I tried to correct him, Joe, I really did, but he was inconsolable. The whole thing made me feel like the worst parent in the world.'

I took Penny's glass from her hand as she started to cry, set my beer down on the table next to it and took her in my arms. This was the first time since I'd moved out that she had allowed me to show her any kind of affection and it made me miss her and want her with an intensity I hadn't felt for a long time. Penny must have felt it too because while I was weighing up the pros and cons of going with the moment she leaned in and kissed me and then a small voice called out from upstairs: 'I feel sick!'

And that was it. It was all over before it began. Penny unwrapped herself from my arms and began straightening her clothing. The moment and everything that was riding on it had gone.

'I'd better go and check on him,' said Penny, refusing to meet my eye as she stood up.

'Of course,' I replied. 'I think there's some of that kids' antacid stuff in the bathroom cabinet. I'll go and get it.'

Penny held up her hand. 'Don't worry, I'm sure it's nothing a kiss and a little tummy rub won't solve but if it doesn't I'll find it. I'll

214

probably be a while though so if you wouldn't mind letting yourself out that would be great.'

'Of course,' I replied, rising to my feet. 'Give him a kiss from me and tell him I'll speak to him in the morning.'

22

'It's because you haven't been getting any,' said Van.

'Plus, it was your kid's birthday,' said Paul, shaking his head sadly.

'Plus you haven't been getting any,' said Van.

'Plus you said you'd both been drinking,' said Stewart.

'Plus you haven't been getting any,' repeated Van. 'It was like a perfect storm. Acute emotions, plus booze, plus neither of you getting any: if that kid of yours hadn't interrupted proceedings there's a good chance that the two of you would have exploded before you'd even reached the sack.'

'That's all fine,' I replied, 'but it's not exactly the issue is it? The issue is what do I do about it now it's happened? Do I bring it up? Do I ignore it? What would she want me to do?'

'If you want my advice,' said Paul, 'I'd say don't go there. It's not worth it.'

'Dude's right,' said Van. 'All you're doing is stringing out the inevitable.'

'But we kissed!' I protested. 'We actually kissed. That's got to mean something, surely? She's not come anywhere near me since this whole thing started.'

Stewart nodded. 'It's a tough one, mate — and I speak as someone who took his ex back at least half a dozen times. On the one hand the boys are right: all it does in the end is string out the pain but on the other hand it doesn't matter what they say because if you love her, you're going to do it anyway. At the end of the day there are some things in life that you can only find out the hard way.'

When I first thought about calling together an emergency meeting of the Divorced Dads' Club in the pub on Sunday afternoon to discuss what had happened with Penny it hadn't once occurred to me that any one of them let alone *all* of them would be so convinced that getting back together with Penny would be such a bad idea. It didn't make sense and yet so far they'd been right about every piece of advice they'd given me.

'It's a newbie mistake,' explained Van. 'And believe me I made it a few times with my girl. I think over the course of the last year we ended up falling into bed half a dozen times and on each and every one of them I was fully convinced that we were getting back together and each and every time we split up again. And they take their toll you know, the break-ups — each one shatters your heart just that little bit more. In the end for the sake of the kids we both made the decision not to let it happen again. Some things are just too dangerous to mess with.'

Paul nodded. 'It took me and Lisa three attempts to separate properly. It was terrible for the kids because they never really knew where they stood.'

'It's true,' said Stewart. 'The kids come off worst of all. Every time my ex came back I could see in their eyes that even they didn't believe they'd be home for long and sure enough they never were. Kids need stability. They need to know where they stand. They need to know that if you say you're going to stay together you mean it.'

'Of course I mean it,' I replied. 'Do you really think that I ever want to go through this again? I can hear what you're all saying and I understand completely, but this is different. I want Penny back so much it hurts and if I don't take this chance just because things might not go my way then I might as well give up now.' I drained my pint glass. 'Thanks for coming out, guys, you've been a real help, but my mind's made up: I'm getting my family back.'

★   ★   ★

It was just after three as I arrived at the house. I didn't know what I was going to say but I knew exactly how I was going to say it: with power and conviction so that there couldn't be any other response from Penny except, 'Let's work this out.'

I reached up to ring the doorbell but before I could the front door opened revealing Penny, Rosie and Jack dressed as though they were about to go out.

'Joe,' said Penny. 'What are you doing here?'

'He's here to come to the park with us,' said Jack excitedly.

'Don't be a lame brain, Jack,' said Rosie. 'How would Dad know we were going to the park unless Mum invited him?'

Simultaneously Penny and I both reprimanded Rosie for her 'lame brain' comment. It was nice being in sync about this even if we were out of sync with everything else.

'I'm here to speak to your mum,' I said, looking at Penny.

'Actually, now's not a good time,' she said quietly, bending down to adjust Jack's hood.

'But we need to talk,' I replied. 'You know . . . about that thing that happened last night.'

The kids looked at me and said in unison: 'What happened last night?'

'Dad's talking about some trifle that got spilled on the sofa,' said Penny quickly.

'I didn't see anything,' said Rosie. 'Where was it?'

'It doesn't matter,' said Penny. She looked at me. 'I've sorted the problem so there's no need for you to worry.'

'Oh,' I said, finally getting the message. So that was it, was it? Last night was an aberration. A mistake. A moment of weakness. 'Well, if you've got it sorted then I won't bother you.'

'But you can still come to the park though,' said Jack brightly.

'No, I can't, son,' I replied. 'Not today.'

'But you have to,' he insisted. 'I want to show you how good I am with my new scooter.' Jack turned to Penny. 'Mum, tell Dad he has to come to the park with us.'

Penny and I exchanged embarrassed glances. She'd obviously been hoping for a quick and easy half-hour of fresh air with the kids without the unnecessary complication of her estranged

219

husband with whom she'd shared a kiss the night before. As much as I wanted to go with them I had to give her a way out of this if she wasn't to use it as another one in a long list of reasons why she was never going to take me back. I knelt down next to Jack. 'I'd love to come with you guys but I don't think today is the best day. I've got lots of stuff to do . . . but listen, we'll do it soon, OK? You have my word.'

Jack pouted indignantly. 'You always say that now and it's not fair!' He turned to Penny with determination etched across his little face. 'I know it's not my birthday any more but please Mum, please, please, please can Dad come with us? I promise I won't ask for anything for next year's birthday if you say yes.'

'It's up to Daddy,' said Penny, her voice neutral. Whatever happened next was all on me. 'He's said he's busy and so we should respect that.'

'Please Daddy?' said Jack.

Rosie looked at Penny. 'He won't come unless you ask him to. That's how it works when you don't live together.'

'It's true,' said Jack, even though it was obvious from the vacant expression on his face that he had no idea what she was talking about. 'That's how it works.'

More embarrassed glances. The kids had run absolute rings around us with their subtle but exacting use of emotional blackmail and detective work. Penny sighed, clearly wishing that she hadn't left this trip until so late in the day. 'Joe, will you come to the park with us?'

Even without looking at them I could feel the kids' eyes boring into me.

'Doesn't look like I've got much choice really, does it?' I replied.

*　★　★*

The park was crawling with kids. There were kids kicking footballs, kids pulling wheelies on their BMXs, kids swinging dangerously off vertiginous climbing frames and kids screaming at the top of their voices for no other reason than it seemed like a cool thing to do. Then of course there were Penny and I sitting on a bench, barely saying a word to each other as we watched our two — Jack zipping up and down the smooth tarmac of the main path on his new scooter and Rosie zigzagging on her bike near the cool kids doing tricks on their skateboards. I turned to look at Penny and even though she was staring straight ahead I knew that she knew exactly what I was doing.

'Listen, about last night . . . ' My voice trailed off as I knew it would; after all there wasn't any need to spell it out. It was obvious that it was the only thing either of us was thinking about.

'It was a mistake,' said Penny. Her eyes remained fixed ahead; her voice was small and low. Anyone observing us would have us down as two spies making a drop. 'I let myself get carried away,' she continued. 'I'm sorry if you feel it was anything more.'

I shook my head. 'It wasn't a mistake and you know it. Last night was the first bit of real hope

221

we've had — a small chink of light after months of gloom — we can't just ignore it. It meant something.'

Penny turned to me for the first time. 'No, it didn't. It was just two stressed-out parents who had probably drunk more than they should coming over a bit sentimental because their youngest wasn't a baby any more.'

'I don't believe you.'

Penny shook her head. 'We don't need to get into all this, Joe. All we need to do is concentrate on being the best parents we can be for our children and what happened last night . . . and what would've happened, well . . . it, like this conversation, would've been just another stumbling block to get in our way.'

'You're wrong,' I replied. 'You've never been more wrong. This could be our chance to — ' I stopped at the unmistakable sound of Jack crying. I looked over. His face was crumpled, tears were streaming down his cheeks and he was running over to us clutching his elbow. I loved Jack dearly but what was it about him that meant he knew exactly the worst time to interrupt a conversation?

Penny ran over to Jack and swept him up into her arms as he sobbed: 'I was trying to do a stunt like the big boys and I fell off my scooter.'

Penny sat him on a bench and rolled his sleeve up to check the damage.

'I don't think I want to play on my scooter any more today,' said Jack once he'd calmed down. 'Can we go home now?'

'Yes,' said Penny, relieved. 'Of course we can.'

★ ★ ★

My usually gloomy hallway glowed with the golden light of the setting sun as I kicked off my shoes. Hungry and fed up I dropped a couple of slices of bread in the toaster before emptying a can of beans into bowl and shoving them into the microwave. As the beans heated up I tried to distract myself from the maudlin thoughts waiting in the wings with plans for what the kids and I might do next weekend. I was determined to make it a good one. Instead of just sitting around the house getting bored we would all go out to do something cultural. There was a new exhibition about theatrical costumes at the V&A, which I was pretty sure Rosie would get a real kick out of and which I could get Jack to tolerate as long as it was done in under an hour and ended with a visit to Pizza Hut. And then maybe on Sunday I'd cook a proper Sunday lunch, just like the ones my mum used to make: roast chicken, roast potatoes, carrots and broccoli, maybe even Yorkshire puddings too. And then when I took them back to Penny's they'd be so full of excitement about the amazing weekend they'd enjoyed that she'd feel, if only for a moment, that she had missed out on something special. I couldn't help but laugh. It was pathetic really. Trying to get back at Penny by making her jealous about an imaginary weekend that I hadn't a hope of pulling off. I'd have enough trouble selling the idea of museums as entertainment to Rosie let alone cooking a chicken in an oven which last time I used it had filled the kitchen with so much smoke that it set off my neighbour's smoke alarm as well as my own.

My toast popped. I walked to the fridge, took out the margarine and then my phone rang. I checked the screen hoping it would be one of the Divorced Dads' Club at a loose end as I could have done with the company, but it wasn't, it was Penny, no doubt calling to read me the riot act for hijacking her afternoon with the kids. I was tempted to let it go to voicemail but the age-old fear that something bad had happened to the kids stopped me.

'Joe, it's me,' she said. 'I want to talk about earlier.'

'Don't worry,' I replied. 'I got the message. You're probably right: the last thing we need to do is screw things up while we're sorting things out in counselling.'

'Well actually,' said Penny, 'I've been thinking that . . . well maybe we could do with spending some time together outside of counselling without the kids doing something, I don't know . . . fun.' She laughed self-consciously. 'I don't know, like a date.'

'A date?' I rolled the idea around for a moment. I used to be good at dates. Not that I'd been on one in about twenty years but the idea of spending time with Penny outside of Rob's office and away from the kids really appealed. 'Do you know what? That's a brilliant idea and I know exactly what we should do.'

23

As the house lights dimmed and a shirtless Van resplendent in tight bright red PVC trousers, furry white boots and the worst blond rock mullet wig I'd ever seen strode across the stage to join the rest of his band, Penny — who was laughing so hard that the contents of her pint glass were spilling over her hands — leaned into me. 'This guy is actually a friend of yours?' she yelled into my ear over the opening bars of 'Hot For Teacher'. 'Where did you find him?'

'Long story,' I yelled back, 'and yeah, he's a little wacky on the outside but on the inside he is a true diamond in the rough.'

It had been years since Penny and I had been out together to see a band play live at a small, amateur pub gig like we used to back when we were students and so the idea of taking her to see Man Halen supporting the Gary Numan tribute band, Numan's Humanoids, in a down-at-heel King's Cross boozer had been something of a gamble but thankfully Penny had warmed to the idea straight away. 'It'll be like the old days,' she'd joked. 'I might even dig out my black woollen tights and eyeliner just for the occasion.' She had however turned up at the pub looking incredibly cool in a baggy grey jumper, skinny jeans and calf-length boots. With her hair swept up under a hat, she looked ten years younger and as she strode across the room searching for me it was impossible not to clock the half-dozen guys in my periphery straining their necks to get a better look. I was so nervous I felt sick and as I waved her over I mused how surreal this experience was and wondered whether there was any date in the world more difficult than a first date with your own wife. But this was exactly what we needed: an opportunity to remember that we weren't just parents, or estranged husband and wife, but rather two people who a very long time ago met and made the decision that they wanted to be together forever.

'So, I'm intrigued,' said Penny as the song ended and Van — without the merest hint of irony — asked the twenty-plus-strong crowd who weren't queuing at the bar for a drink if they were ready to rock. 'What's his story?'

'New Zealand guy likes Van Halen so much that he moves to the UK, gets married, changes his name by deed poll to that of his favourite guitarist and starts South London's premier Van Halen tribute band.'

Penny laughed. 'Where's his wife? I have to see her. Is she all Spandex and big eighties hair?'

'She's not here,' I yelled as the next song started. I grabbed Penny's hand and we moved towards the back of the room so that we could talk. 'They're divorced,' I explained. 'That's sort of how I know him,' and then I reluctantly proceeded to tell Penny a truncated version of the story of the Divorced Dads' Club. 'It's weird how it's all worked out,' I said in conclusion, 'me getting friendly with a bunch of guys I interviewed for an article but somehow it just works.'

I wondered what was going through Penny's mind. Would she think worse of me knowing that I was hanging out with a bunch of divorced guys? That I was somehow picking up their bad habits by social osmosis?

'These past few months have been tough for all of us,' said Penny thoughtfully, 'and if the guys you've told me about have helped you to cope then I'm pleased for you.'

We turned back to the stage and watched the rest of the gig in awe as much to the — mostly Numanoid — crowd's delight, Van, channelling the spirit of David Lee Roth, sprinted through hit after hit, the set culminating with a blistering version of Van Halen's biggest hit, 'Jump', that Penny enjoyed so much she even dragged me to the front so that we could dance. We jumped up and down like idiots and it was the best feeling ever as it reminded me that youth wasn't like the skin of a snake that you sloughed off and never saw again but rather a feeling that you tuck away because you think you don't need it any more and it's only when you come across it by accident that you realise just how much fun it really is.

When the band finally left the stage with a 'Thanks, King's Cross, you've been a great crowd!' Penny and I whooped and cheered so loudly that you'd have been forgiven for thinking we'd just seen the Rolling Stones play at Hyde Park in 1969 rather than witnessed a bunch of middle-aged rockers living out their fantasies. But that was how we felt. Triumphant. Victorious. Like we were back at the beginning of our lives together when everything was fresh and new.

'That was the best fun I've had in years,' said Penny, wiping the sweat from her brow with the back of her hand. 'Can you imagine what the kids would say if they could see us now?'

'Easily,' I replied. 'Rosie hates it when I sing along to the radio let alone add in a dance routine, so the sight of both her parents displaying exhibitionist tendencies in public would be enough to put her off interacting with either of us for life.'

Penny laughed. She had such a gorgeous smile. 'But Jack would like it, wouldn't he?'

'He'd love it,' I replied, wondering if they were asleep yet. They were staying over at Penny's mum's house for the night and they tended to go to bed later there as a treat. 'But then again he's not exactly what you'd call discerning.'

In need of a drink we made our way to the bar and were soon joined by Van, still shirtless, bewigged and dripping with sweat.

'Dude, you came!' he bellowed and enveloped me in a sweaty overenthusiastic man-hug.

'Of course I did. Wouldn't have missed it for the world. You were amazing.'

'We were weren't we?' said Van. 'Must have been something in the air.' He looked over at Penny. 'Is this the missus? You never told me she was so bloody gorgeous!' He gave a dramatic flourish with his hands and kissed her on both cheeks. 'Great to meet you! I'm Van and Joey here is one righteous dude.'

Penny — clearly amused at the incongruity of

a mild-mannered mother of two chatting to a shirtless six-foot-tall New Zealander wearing a blond mullet wig — succumbed to a fit of the giggles. 'I need to buy you a drink,' she said to Van once she'd composed herself. 'You've cheered me up more in the last forty-five minutes than any pair of shoes, box of chocolates or bottle of wine has ever done.' She kissed Van's cheek. 'Thank you!'

★   ★   ★

It was late as Penny and I stood outside the house watching the minicab that had brought us from King's Cross to Lewisham pull away.

'I can't remember the last time I was out in town this late,' said Penny, the flickering streetlight casting strange shadows on her face. 'It's almost like being a student again.'

'I wish we were students,' I replied. 'Compared to now we were practically millionaires. Do you remember the pound-a-pint nights down at the union?'

Penny laughed. 'I'm surprised you can the way you and your mates used to knock them back. Didn't I wake up one morning to find you asleep in the bath?'

'I was on the loo and I wasn't asleep. I was just dozing.'

'Dozing? You were practically unconscious!'

We both laughed and she put her arms around me, resting her head against my chest. I closed my eyes taking in the moment: the smell of her hair, the sensation of her body against mine, the warmth between us. This was the place I wanted to be forever. Hers were the only arms I wanted to hold me from now until the end of time. How had I ever taken anything about this woman for granted? She was unique. A one-off. And though I didn't deserve her I knew that from this moment onwards I would do everything I could to treasure her. Things would be different this time round. I would be a better husband, a better father, and I'd never hurt her again for as long as I lived.

Penny looked up. 'Listen, I really want to thank you for a great night. I know that we said we'd talk about . . . you know, everything . . . but it's been so good to — '

'Just be normal for a while?'

Penny smiled. 'That's it exactly. So thank you, Joe, thank you for that.' She kissed my cheek lightly. 'I suppose I'd better go in. Will you be all right getting home?'

'I'll be fine, but I think that if I am going to be the perfect gentleman the very least I should do is walk you to your door.'

'I'd be delighted,' smiled Penny. She took my arm and together we walked up the path. She opened the front door.

'I suppose this is goodbye,' I said hopefully.

Penny looked down. 'I think it's for the best. But we'll talk soon, OK?'

'Of course,' I said breezily, hoping the disappointment didn't show. 'We'll definitely talk soon.'

For a moment neither of us moved and then Penny said something like, 'It's getting a bit chilly,' and leaned in to kiss my cheek and as she did I pulled her into me and before either of us knew exactly what we were doing we were inside the house pressed up against the hallway wall removing each other's clothing. Gradually we manoeuvred our way into the living room, flopping onto the sofa as overwhelmed with desire we began making the kind of love that we hadn't made in years. This was young love, urgent love and new love all rolled into one. It was all-consuming passion, at least I thought so until sensing that something was wrong I opened my eyes to see tears streaming down Penny's face.

I wiped away her tears with my hand. 'What's wrong? I didn't hurt you did I?'

Penny shook her head as though unable to speak.

'Penny, please, tell me what's wrong. Whatever you say, it'll be OK.'

'I still don't trust you,' she said in a voice barely above a whisper. 'I thought I could but I can't. I don't think I ever will.' She stood up and began to put on her clothes.

'Penny, wait, let's talk about this.'

'I'm tired of talking, Joe,' she said through tears. 'The counselling isn't working is it? You must see that too? Every time I think I've moved on I find myself getting pulled back to the moment you told me what you'd done. I can't keep going around in circles. I can't keep thinking that this is just Mum and Dad all over again. I think we should draw a line under this and both try to move on.'

'What do you mean? Move on? Move on how?'

'I want a divorce.'

'You don't mean that. You can't.'

'That's just the thing,' she said. 'I do, Joe, I really do.'

★ ★ ★

I'm not at all sure how I got home that night; I felt like I was in a daze the whole way there so when I opened my front door to see Fiona waiting for me in the hallway I wasn't in the least surprised.

'Where have you been?' she asked, letting the magazine she'd been reading fall from her hands. 'I was worried about you.'

I stared at her wordlessly.

'Had a bad night?'

Without speaking, I walked past her into the kitchen and took out a bottle of vodka from the freezer and grabbed a glass from the cupboard next to it.

'Come on Joe, it can't be that bad, surely? What answers do you hope to find at the bottom of a booze bottle?' She delivered the line with the deliberate addition of a northern accent as though she were reading it straight from a vintage *Coronation Street* script.

I poured myself a large shot of vodka, knocked it back in one go, poured another and headed into the living room.

'Penny wants a divorce,' I announced as Fiona followed me into the room.

'I know,' she replied, sitting down on the sofa

next to me. 'I honestly didn't see that coming . . . ' She stopped and laughed. 'Who am I kidding? It couldn't have been any clearer. To be honest, I'm actually surprised she's not said it long before now.'

'It was just one night and it never meant a thing. I don't understand. Why can't she just forgive me?'

'Was that what you were banking on then? Penny being so forgiving that she wouldn't hold it against you?'

'I wasn't banking on anything.'

'Not even a little bit?'

'Of course not.'

'Didn't a tiny bit of you think that even if you did get found out Penny would have to forgive you because she had too much to lose?'

I found myself getting angry. 'No, of course not, I didn't think like that. I . . . '

Fiona smiled wryly. 'Wasn't thinking?'

She'd taken the words right out of my mouth.

24

To say that relations between Penny and me broke down after our date and the events which followed would have been an extreme understatement. It was almost as though we became two completely different people. In an instant all the warmth and affection we'd managed to build up over the past few days evaporated and now every exchange between us was either perfunctory to the point of rudeness or suffused with unconcealed bitterness. And while there was no immediate action on the divorce front I didn't take that as a sign that things were going to get better any time soon because true to her word she unilaterally cancelled all of our future appointments with Rob the counsellor. It was like being thrown back to the beginning in those nightmarish days after she first found out about Bella. We hadn't moved on an inch and for days on end I felt so low that I wouldn't have been surprised to find that Fiona had taken up permanent residence in my living room but, it seemed, even she'd abandoned me.

As for the kids I didn't like to think too much about what they were making of the frosty silences and obvious resentment. Mostly I hoped they were still so young that it was all going over their heads but I'm not sure I ever believed that even at my most optimistic.

The only bright light on the horizon was work.

With the rumours of job cuts at the *Correspondent* meaning that everyone from upper management right through to the post room was fearing for their livelihoods, I reasoned the best thing I could do was concentrate on making myself invaluable and so I started getting in early and leaving late and for the first time in years felt as though I was actually on top of things. Moreover, unlike every other part of my life, here at least I knew how to deal with the problems that came my way. A month into this new regime I began to feel as though I was getting my confidence back but then I came home one evening to find a thick, crisp white envelope waiting on my doormat amongst an avalanche of pizza takeaway menus. I tore it open and read the contents and on white, heavyweight paper Penny's solicitor, a Ms T.L. McNally, informed me in perfect legalese that Penny was suing me for divorce.

★   ★   ★

The letter hit me like a wrecking ball. Divorce. I couldn't believe she'd gone through with it after all. I'd known she was hurt, I'd known she was angry, but the idea that she would be willing to give up on the life we'd built together so easily hurt like nothing else on earth. Couldn't she see I was a changed man? Couldn't she see I'd never do it again? Wasn't she factoring the kids into any of her decision-making? After all the time that had elapsed I'd assumed it had just been an idle threat issued in the heat of the moment but now I knew better.

I called Penny's mobile half a dozen times but each time it went straight through to voicemail. I toyed with the idea of going round to the house but knew I couldn't trust myself to keep calm. I called her number again but again it went straight through to voicemail. She was ignoring me, she had to be. I poured the first of many glasses of Jack Daniel's and wondered if her solicitor had told her to avoid making contact with me. I looked at the letter again and drew a mental picture of the hard-faced, bitter woman being paid by the hour to pull my life apart. I imagined her making notes as Penny revealed the story of what had happened, handing her a box of tissues at appropriate points. The final paragraph of the letter advised me to 'appoint my own legal representative' — as if this would make any difference at all to the outcome. I'd get screwed if I found a solicitor and I'd get screwed if I didn't and given that I was happy for Penny to have everything as long as I could carry on seeing the kids all I really stood to lose was a couple of grand in legal fees that I couldn't afford to pay anyway.

I had to talk to Penny. I had to stop Ms T.L. McNally from ruining both our lives. Setting down the drink in my hand I picked up my phone and tried Penny's number once more but when I got her voicemail yet again I was so angry I nearly threw the phone against the wall. I stopped at the last moment and tapped out the following text:

Just got solicitor's letter. Well done! Obviously you enjoy playing the victim so much that you'd rather screw over this family than move on from the past. Hope you're happy now, Joe x.

I thought I might feel better once I'd sent it but like so many things done in haste I actually felt a lot worse. In retrospect I could see it was a stupid, selfish, and spiteful thing to do and perfectly illustrated why Jack Daniel's and despondency should never mix but it was how I felt. Penny and I had come so close to getting back together, so close to making a new start, and I hated the fact that she was prepared to turn her back on that. Yes, I understood she was hurt but surely she believed our family was more important than her hurt or my own. I wanted things back to how they used to be and I thought that my short, sharp, shock-style text might bring her to her senses. I couldn't have been more wrong however, a fact to which her reply by text perfectly attested:

If that's what you really think then there never was any hope for us. It was you who caused this, Joe, nobody else. So let me be clear: I'm done with blaming myself about this. You were right about one thing. I do need to move on from the past. And your text has helped infinitely with that. Penny x.

I reread the text over and over again, and each time my eyes lingered over the last part of the sentence, 'I do need to move on from the past and your text has helped infinitely with that.'

What did she mean? Would she ever speak to me again? Would she let me see the kids? All I knew for sure was that in one fell swoop I'd managed to eradicate any hope there was of us ever getting back together.

★ ★ ★

When I eventually met up with the Divorced Dads' Club early the following week and told them what I'd done they all had their own horror stories to share. Paul recalled how at one point his ex-wife was talked into labelling him as unfit to look after the kids by her solicitor so that she could get full custody. Paul got so angry that he went as far as purchasing two bagfuls of manure to dump in the reception area of the solicitor's office but chickened out at the last moment. Stewart told us how after receiving a bill from his first solicitor even though he hadn't had so much as a postcard from his kids he'd torn it up and posted it back to them. And Van revealed that when his ex told him she was divorcing him he set fire to his entire record collection because it was the only thing he thought was worth any money. 'The worst of it was,' he added sadly, 'when we started getting into who got what she didn't mention my vinyl once.' The message was clear: of the top ten things that will make a normally sane person crazy divorce was there right at the head of the list.

'So what are you going to do now?' asked Van. 'Hire yourself a solicitor? Those buggers can be mega expensive.'

'And it's almost impossible to find a good one,' said Stewart. 'I'd give you my bloke's number but I reckon he's only got a couple of weeks left before I sack him and find someone new.'

'My guy was the business,' said Paul, 'but he cost a fortune. Ironically the only reason I could afford him was because my ex was absolutely loaded.'

I told them my plan to do the whole thing on my own and not fight Penny on anything other than access to the kids.

'That's probably the dumbest thing I've ever heard,' said Van, 'but I get where you're coming from. I get it completely. Sometimes when you've made such a colossal mess of things it's better to own up to everything just so you can get it all over and done with.'

★   ★   ★

In spite of my initial fears, Penny let me have the kids to stay that weekend and in a bid to blot out everything that was going on I went all out to make sure we had a good time. I pulled a couple of strings through work and on the Saturday managed to get us tickets to Harry Potter World in Watford which the kids had been begging me to take them to for months, then on the Sunday we went into central London and mooched around Hyde Park for the afternoon followed by tea at the Rainforest Café. Those two days cost me a fortune but it was worth it to see them happy for a change.

* * *

'Sounds like you had a lovely time,' said Penny politely when the kids told her what we'd been up to. 'Don't forget to give Daddy a big hug and kiss for making it happen.'

The kids piled on top of me covering me in kisses before Penny finally called time and instructed them to get ready for bed. They reluctantly headed upstairs and as they did so I recalled the fact that my and Penny's cordiality was merely an act for their sakes and currently we were still very much at war.

'I suppose I'd better get off then,' I said, unable to prevent the usual frostiness entering my tone. 'Can you tell them I'll call them tomorrow at the usual time?'

'Of course,' replied Penny, 'but before you go could I have a quick chat with you about something?'

My gut instinct was to say no because the last thing I needed was for the whole weekend to be ruined by a row but then it occurred to me that perhaps I'd got it wrong, maybe Penny wanted to call a truce. Perhaps she was as tired of the arguing and acrimony as I was and wanted to make amends. I followed her into the kitchen with my fingers crossed. One quick conversation about how sorry each of us was for our behaviour these past few weeks, and maybe peace would reign once more.

'Listen,' I began, keen to make this as easy for Penny as possible, 'I'm pretty sure I know what this is about and I just want to say that I'm sorry.

240

I should never have reacted the way I did and that text I sent was awful. Being at each other's throats like this is getting us nowhere. You were right, I — '

'That's not it,' interrupted Penny. 'That's not what I want to talk to you about.'

'So what then?'

She sighed heavily. 'This isn't an easy thing to say, but I think you're best hearing it from me rather than anyone else: I've met someone new, Joe. I've started a new relationship.'

I didn't speak. I couldn't. This wasn't what I'd been expecting at all. All I'd wanted to do was drop off the kids, apologise to Penny for being such an idiot and go home. I certainly hadn't wanted to be taken unawares like this by the news that the woman I loved, the mother of my children, the woman I was still legally married to, had taken a lover. This was not the kind of news I would ever be ready to hear, not in this world or any other.

I was determined not to let the emotions bubbling up inside me burst through the lid that I was tightly screwing down. After all, if losing my temper with Penny in a text was enough to make her start seeing someone new who knew what losing it in person might result in? Running away to join the circus? Getting a Mike Tyson-style tattoo across her face? The list of possibilities was endless but there was no way she could drop a bombshell like that and not have me say a word about it. And of the many words I wanted to say, there were three that were top of the list by some considerable distance.

241

25

'Who is it?' I asked once my wits had returned.

'It doesn't matter.'

It was as if I couldn't hear her. 'Someone from work?'

'I've told you, it doesn't matter.'

So it wasn't someone from work. Where would Penny have met someone outside of work? At a bar? Through friends? At the school gates? That was it. The school gates. Jack's friend Riley's dad was a single parent and pretty good-looking too if you liked the whole stubble and olive skin look. When the kids were younger he was forever encouraging Penny to bring Jack round to his for a playdate even though Jack thought his son was a bit weird. Was that it? Had she hooked up with weird Riley's dad?

'You have to tell me, Penny. Who is it?'

'Look Joe, can't we just leave it for another time? The kids are upstairs and this is obviously something of a shock to you. Maybe it would be best for both of us if we slept on this and talked about it later.'

'I don't want to talk about it later. I want to talk about it now. I need a name.'

'Fine,' she said, 'it's Scott.'

She said the name like I was supposed to know who it was but I hadn't got a clue. I personally didn't know any Scotts, and I was pretty sure Penny didn't either apart from her old boyfriend, the guy she had been dating before she met me at university . . .

'You're back with your ex?'

The embarrassment on Penny's face said it all. I was right. The Scott she was dating was her ex-boyfriend from over twenty years ago.

'I don't understand. You haven't seen him in at least two decades.'

Her gaze moved to the floor like she couldn't bear to look at me. 'He got in touch.'

Got in touch? Of course, it was the curse of Zuckerberg striking all over again. I had to laugh. A few years ago it felt like a week didn't pass without some story appearing in the papers about couples splitting up because one of them had hooked up with an old partner after accepting their friend request on Facebook. In the end it was happening so often that Camilla actually commissioned me to write a piece for *The Weekend* about it which I did with the help of a dozen couples who had been reunited thanks to the irrepressible rise of social networking.

I tried to recall everything I knew about Scott. He was two years older than Penny. His parents were quite well off. Penny had been fifteen when they met. He'd studied modern languages at Bristol. Five years into our relationship he'd sent a Valentine's Day card to Penny's mum's house. Penny being the kind of person she is had shown it to me. He'd put his telephone number inside the card along with a message telling her he still thought about her. I asked her if she felt the same and she joked that if I thought I was going

243

to get rid of her that easily I was mistaken. The last thing I heard about him was when Nicky, an old school friend of Penny's, came to stay with us not long after Rosie was born. I overheard Nicky telling Penny she'd bumped into Scott and that he was teaching at a private school somewhere up north.

'Are you really telling me that you're sleeping with some guy you used to know a lifetime ago who contacted you via Facebook?'

Penny went to the fridge and poured herself a glass of wine. 'I've said all I want to say, Joe. You're obviously upset so let's leave it.'

She was completely out of luck on that one. 'Is that how things are now? Are we just jumping into bed with the first guy who asks and calling it a relationship to cushion our egos? He's using you, Penny. He's using you and you're going to get hurt if you're not careful.'

It was a mean and bitter thing to say which given that I was brimming over with both emotions was exactly why I'd said it. And as much as I meant every word, I regretted them too. Penny was a beautiful, wonderful woman and any guy would be lucky to have her and while there was a case to be made that she should be careful — I know, ironic, me warning her about what men are really like — this wasn't the time or the place. And as far as egos went, hers didn't need cushioning, it was fine as it was. It was mine that had been crushed and was in need of some padding. This right here was the beginning of the end, I could feel it in my very core, and I just wasn't ready for it. Still, an apology was in order.

'I'm sorry, Penny, that was completely — '

'Get out.' Her voice was sharp and yet controlled like she was a headmistress and I her pupil. 'Get out of this house before I say something we'll both regret. Stay out of my life, Joe, stay away from me!'

★ ★ ★

Back at home all I could do was torture myself thinking about how Penny and her ex got back together and the role I had played in helping it happen. Sitting on my sofa staring at the hideous brick fire surround I imagined the initial tentative exchanges on the internet, followed by long late-night outpourings of emotion where she'd fill in the gory details of her failed marriage only to have Scott do the same in return. Gradually they'd open up to each other further, overwhelming each other with honesty, and then of course there would be the suggestion that they meet up for the day, no pressure, maybe a trip into the centre of London on a Sunday afternoon. Perhaps they would take in an exhibition or two and then naturally lunch somewhere nice, after which he'd walk her to the tube where there would be an extended goodbye and then that first kiss, which would lead to a second and third after which it would be all about the planning of weekends away and . . . thankfully a buzz from my phone derailed that particularly devastating train of thought. It was a text from Paul asking if I fancied a drink.

I checked my internal diary. Between half-eight and midnight I'd planned to torment myself by imagining Penny and her new lover in bed together but with a bit of juggling I was sure I could shift it to later in the evening given the fact that I couldn't imagine ever sleeping again.

★　★　★

'What's up?' I asked as we sat staring at our pints.

'I could ask you the same question,' replied Paul. 'You've barely said a word. Everything OK?'

'It's Penny,' I explained. 'Apparently she's started seeing someone. And you know what the real killer is? The thing that's so galling that even thinking about it gets my blood boiling? It's the fact that my whole world is coming down around my ears because of some stupid social networking site!'

'It's the way things go these days,' said Paul. 'It's just easier isn't it? Have a few beers one night, jab the name of some girl you used to know into the internet and wait to see what it spits out. It's not a nice way to lose someone but then again what is?'

I nodded. Paul was right, what did it matter that Penny had reconnected with her ex this way? It wasn't as if I would have been any happier if she'd got together with someone from work.

'You're right, the how is the least interesting part,' I replied. 'I suppose the point I was

246

focusing on was how easy it's been for this guy to come back into her life. Even after a twenty-year break it's a whole different thing dating someone you used to go out with compared to a total stranger. At least with a stranger if things started going too fast you'd put the brakes on . . . '

'Whereas with someone from the past if things speed up they're just making up for lost time.'

'Exactly. So what do I do?'

Paul shrugged.

'There's nothing you can do. I learned that the hard way with Lisa. She's going to do what she's going to do whether I like it or not.'

'Is that why you texted? I know from what the other guys have said you're pretty cut up about her engagement.'

'I wish it was just that,' replied Paul. 'As of yesterday she's talking about wanting custody of the kids again.'

'But I thought she worked full time?'

'She told me that her career has put paid to one relationship and she's not about to let it happen a second time so she's selling the business and wants the kids to go and live with her. I told her I needed time to think about it but I know she's not going to let it go. I don't know what to say.'

'But the kids don't have to go?'

Paul shrugged. 'But what if they want to?'

'They won't. They love living with you, don't they?'

'They're so moody it's impossible to tell.'

'But yours is the only home they've ever really known. Surely that will go in your favour if it goes to court?'

247

'She's their mum, she's giving up a successful career to be with them and when she wants to she can be very persuasive indeed. What family court judge wouldn't find that appealing?'

Paul and I talked through the problem for over an hour without coming to any conclusions. I was of the opinion that he should get a solicitor involved straight away but Paul was afraid that any talk of legal experts would result in an escalation of hostilities from which neither of them would walk away unscathed. 'It's hard,' said Paul, as we parted company, 'it really is because she keeps saying to me: you've had your turn why can't I have mine? And when she puts it like that I can't help thinking that maybe she's got a point.'

★　★　★

It was late when I reached home with a head full of thoughts about Paul's situation illustrating as it did that there was no such thing as a civil divorce. Divorce by its very nature was a bloody, uncivil process that brought out the worst in people and now that hostilities had escalated between Penny and me it would only be a matter of time before we would start tearing into each other too, unless I could find some way to temper the hurt that I felt knowing that she had started afresh with someone from her past. I needed to move on quickly if I was ever going to be in with a hope of breaking out of the cycle in which I found myself.

In an effort to get outside my head for a while

I poured a drink and collected together the weekend papers I'd bought that morning but had yet to open. Picking up the first from the top of the pile I began flicking through one of the sections and stopped suddenly when an article caught my eye. It was a feature about a new movement in low-budget films by up-and-coming young US directors unwilling to wait for Hollywood to come knocking on their door before committing their art to celluloid. As well as containing interviews with all of the main players there were quotes from a number of well-known industry names. It was an interesting, well-rounded piece but the most interesting thing about it was its author: Bella. I could barely tear my eyes away from her byline photo. She was even more beautiful than I remembered and seeing her face again after all this time made me wonder if perhaps everything wasn't falling into place. OK, so I couldn't actually remember our night together but there had been a connection between us, hadn't there? And even though I couldn't remember that night no one could doubt that I'd paid a high price for it — too high a price by far — but if we got together, if we managed to forge something good out of something so bad then maybe everything I'd endured would not have been in vain.

She was the answer, she had to be, and so the following evening I did the only thing I could do under the circumstances: I left work early, made my way to the offices of the *Review* and after an hour waiting in the rain wondering if she was even still at work I engineered what was perhaps the least convincing 'accidental' meeting in the long and illustrious history of 'accidental' meetings.

'Joe,' she said, moving the yellow umbrella in her hands forward to protect me from the rain, 'what are you doing here?'

It was a good question given that I was soaking wet and hadn't so much bumped into her as called out her name. But the longer I looked at her the more I realised how wrong this was. Not just because we weren't suited — in the harsh light of day that seemed patently obvious — but rather because I knew in my heart I didn't want anyone but Penny.

Bella stood staring expectantly waiting for me to speak.

'I've come to see you,' I said, more than a little shocked by the words coming out of my mouth. This wasn't quite the slick performance I'd rehearsed in my head. 'I've come to apologise.'

'You don't have to do this. It's water under the bridge. I've moved on.'

There was no inflection in her voice but I couldn't help imagine the only thing meant by this was that she had long since found herself another lover.

'That makes perfect sense,' I replied, reasoning that it had been wildly optimistic to have even thought otherwise. Bella was quite stunning and so the idea of her being single seemed like an affront to nature. 'Still, if you're not in a rush I'd really like the opportunity to explain my behaviour if I can. I'm not saying that it'll undo what I put you through or anything but if it could make you hate me just a few degrees less I'd consider it an hour of my life in the rain well spent.'

Bella smiled in spite of herself. 'You can have half an hour but that's all. I'm meeting friends soon and I don't want to be late.'

26

'How's work?' asked Bella as we sat down at a table in a busy pub that was so generic it could have been anywhere in the world. 'I saw your Jonah Lloyd-Hughes piece a while back. You must have been over the moon to have landed that.'

'It was definitely what you'd call one of my better days,' I replied, glad she'd at least had some awareness of me since we'd parted. 'Sadly it pretty much came down to luck rather than journalistic skill. And anyway if we're passing out the compliments, how about you? Every time I pick up the *Review* your face seems to pop out at me.'

'I've been more than a bit lucky too. They've been very supportive. I never imagined getting quite so far so quickly. Nearly everyone I know from my course is still looking for work.'

I looked at her across the table, barely able to believe that we'd once been together. She really did look incredible. She picked up her drink, a Coke, ordered I suspected to indicate the strictly functional nature of our meeting.

'So what's this all about, Joe?'

'It's exactly as I said. I want to apologise. The way I acted after we . . . well you know . . . was despicable. I was in a pretty weird place in my life at the time and while that doesn't excuse how I acted I hope it goes some way to explaining why I behaved the way I did.'

'You were a pig,' said Bella.

'I was,' I replied. 'And like I said there is no excuse.'

'Why the sudden need to apologise?'

'Because my wife is divorcing me.'

Bella looked horrified. 'Not because of what happened between us?'

'No,' I said quickly. She didn't deserve to shoulder any of the blame for how I'd screwed things up with Penny. 'She's divorcing me because at the end of the day I'm an idiot.'

'I don't know what to say,' said Bella.

'I doubt there is much to say really,' I agreed.

'And there's no chance you'll get back together?'

An image of Penny together with Scott flashed up in my head. 'It's looking increasingly like we're past that point. I've got a place ten minutes away from the house so I can be there for the kids. It's not ideal but it beats not seeing them at all.'

'You have kids?' She didn't know. I knew I hadn't mentioned them when we had coffee that day but it was news to me that I hadn't mentioned them at all on the night I'd met her in Soho. 'I have two, Rosie and Jack. Rosie's ten and Jack's seven.'

'And how have they reacted to the split?'

'Not well at all. Jack seems to have taken it the hardest, mainly because I don't think he fully understands what's going on. As far as he's concerned all that happened was one day I was living with them and the next I was gone and now he can't always see me when he wants to.'

'And your daughter?'

'She's growing up and has changed so much over the past few months it's hard to tell exactly what's going on with her.'

'I was the same at her age,' said Bella. 'I shared everything going on in my life with my friends because I felt like they really wanted to know me and it was almost as if the more I gave to them the less I had to give to anyone else.' She touched my arm, albeit briefly, and the lightning bolt that shot through me took me back immediately to that day in the café. 'I was nine when my parents spilt up. It's a tough time for everyone involved and obviously no matter what I say you'll be worried about them but they'll be OK.'

Her parents' divorce. She had told me all about it when I'd taken her for coffee. One day after school her mum had explained to Bella and her sister over steaming hot platefuls of spaghetti Bolognese that her dad was going to be living somewhere else. Neither of the girls would believe her until they went to his study and saw that all their father's books had gone along with the bookcases that had held them. 'He couldn't have made it any plainer just how little we meant to him,' concluded Bella. 'He took his books because he couldn't live without them but my sister and me — his own flesh and blood — he could take or leave. We didn't see or hear from him again for a year and a half.'

'And how are things these days?'

'Not great. Dad was briefly engaged to some

254

divorcee that he met online but now he's with the ex-wife of one of his old friends; I think they might actually even be engaged. It's hard to tell when all you get is text messages.'

He sounded like an idiot of the highest order. 'Do you think he's happy?'

'I'm not even sure if he knows what happiness is,' said Bella. 'That was always his trouble. He could never tell when he was on to a good thing.'

The words were out in the open before she'd realised their significance and never one to miss out on an opportunity to publicly flail myself I joked, 'Sounds like we have a lot in common.'

Bella shook her head. 'No,' she replied. 'You're nothing like him.' She finished her Coke and stood up. 'I'm going to get a proper drink. Do you want another?'

'So you're staying then?'

Bella smiled. 'For one more drink, at least.'

★ ★ ★

It was after ten by the time Bella and I thought about calling it a night. Having spent the evening discussing everything from politics to our least favourite Beatles album, talk had inevitability turned to the lateness of the hour.

'I can't believe the time,' said Bella. 'I'm reporting on a new exhibition at Tate Liverpool tomorrow and I'm booked on the six eighteen a.m. out of Euston.'

'Plus I don't think your friends will be too pleased you didn't meet up with them.'

She smiled. 'There were no friends. I just

didn't want to spend all night with you.'

'And now here you are,' I replied.

'Yes,' she said, 'here I am. And what's worse is I'm starving.'

'Why didn't you say? We could've gone for something to eat.'

Bella shrugged. 'We still could. A friend of mine has been raving about a new Mexican place that's opened up in Covent Garden. It's late enough to have missed the evening rush. We could try there if you like?'

'And what about the six eighteen to Liverpool?'

She grinned. 'Don't worry, I'll get on it. I'll be dead to the world for the whole day but I'll make it for sure.'

We grabbed our coats and bags and left the pub and as we stepped out into the street joining the late-night milieu on Tottenham Court Road I felt Bella's slender fingers intertwine with my own. As much as I tried not to read too much into this simple act it was hard not question her motivation. I'd treated her dreadfully, leaving her bed in the early hours and avoiding her the day after; why was she being so forgiving? It made no sense.

Still holding hands we headed in the direction of the restaurant pausing only to allow a trio of taxis to pass by before crossing the road. As we waited Bella briefly glanced up at me as though she had been about to say something and then changed her mind.

'What?'

'Nothing.'

'It didn't look like nothing. It looked like you had something on your mind.'

'It was nothing really, it's just I think you should know that you really hurt me.' Her eyes were now fixed straight ahead.

'I know I did. It was a mess and I should never have let it happen.'

'But it did.'

'And I handled it badly.' I squeezed her hand. 'Generally speaking how do you feel about second chances?'

'As a concept? I've never been a big fan. I'm a believer in getting things right first time.' Bella laughed and looked right into my eyes. 'There's something irresistible about you, Joe Clarke, I felt it the moment I met you. It's like you're lost and you're desperate to find someone to show you the way home.'

'And you think that person might be you?'

'I don't know,' said Bella and she smiled. 'But now that you're free I think I'd like another opportunity to find out.'

The kiss was long and slow and exactly the kind of kiss that could turn even the worst of days into the best. Still, it was Bella who broke away first, and as the traffic slowed we continued across the road towards our destination. It felt odd being with her like this. Out in the open where anyone could see. Everyone we passed would assume that we were together, a couple, and would treat us accordingly, wondering about our story and what had drawn us together. It felt as though all the dots of the evening — our initial meeting, the things we'd talked about, the kiss we'd shared — were joining up to form the anecdote we would tell friends and family in the future, the story of how we got together.

At the restaurant we peeked in through the windows at the dimly lit cavernous canteen that was quite clearly still operating at full capacity. There was no way we'd be getting a table any time soon.

'We could try back in Soho,' I suggested. 'There's a pretty good Turkish place that stays open until late.'

'Or we could just go back to mine?' countered Bella. 'My flatmates are out tonight. We could order in and have the whole place to ourselves.' She squeezed my hand as though she genuinely imagined I might need some encouragement.

'What do you say?'

'I say let's find ourselves a cab.'

★   ★   ★

On the way over to Bella's place I couldn't help but wonder if the journey would somehow jog my memory of the night we'd slept together. Maybe the taxi would take a similar route, or I'd see a building that looked familiar. Perhaps even Bella would say something that would make me think, 'Ah, yes, I remember that now,' but there was nothing. It was as though I'd never made this journey before and not for the first time I began to wonder how that might be.

As I paid the cab driver I looked up at the house, a three-storey Victorian conversion. I recognised it immediately: not from my previous journey to Bella's house but rather from my memory of leaving it. How could it be that I could perfectly recall one and not the other? Even if I factored in the amount I'd had to drink that night it still didn't add up. Maybe I was suffering from dissociative amnesia after all.

'You look worried,' said Bella, taking my hand, 'there's no need to be.'

'I know,' I replied, even though a sense of unease continued to linger over me like a black cloud.

★ ★ ★

Once inside the flat Bella told me to take a seat in the living room and disappeared into the kitchen. After a few moments she popped her head round the kitchen door. 'Beer or wine?'

'I'll stick to wine if that's OK.'

Bella reappeared a short while later carrying a plate laden with bread, olives and hummus. She handed me a bottle of Merlot that she had tucked under her arm and a corkscrew.

'What do your flatmates do?' I asked as I opened the bottle.

'Fran's in her final year of medical school,' said Bella, taking two wine glasses from a cabinet near the TV, 'and Kimberley's a trainee womens-wear buyer for Selfridges.'

They were all still on the thresholds of their respective careers. Everything was new and fresh for them just like this night was for me. I filled the glasses while Bella closed the blinds and switched on a lamp.

As we ate and drank we talked more about work but then Bella asked me about my early days as a novelist again and it reminded me of the present that I had brought for her. I pulled out an envelope from my jacket pocket.

'What's this?' she asked as I handed it to her.

'I don't know,' I replied. 'A present to go with the apology. I wouldn't get your hopes up though. I can't imagine anyone else in the world who would want it apart from you.'

Bella ripped open the envelope and her eyes widened in surprise. 'Is this what I think it is?'

'All eight hundred words of it,' I replied. 'I was never really sure where it was going. In the end I handed back the advance to my publisher just so that I didn't have to torture myself any more.'

'The first chapter of your second novel — I don't know what to say.'

I suddenly felt sheepish. 'Chuck it if you want.' What was I doing showing her my old work like that? She must have thought me an idiot. 'Like I said, I don't know where I thought it was going.'

'I love it,' said Bella, putting down the pages and leaning towards me. 'Sometimes it's good not to worry too much about what will happen next.'

We kissed, gently at first then with increasing intensity as each moment passed, our hands running across each other's body, but as Bella whispered something about moving to the bedroom I thought about my last time with Penny and how right it had felt being with her. Suddenly this felt different, alien, and I wasn't nearly so sure what I was doing here.

Bella stood up, tugging on my hand.

'Joe, come on. What are you waiting for?'

I thought about telling her the truth. That I was waiting for myself to wake up. That incredible as she was I wanted to open my eyes and find that this was all a dream and that I was safe and happy with the only woman I'd ever love. But I didn't of course because that would have made even less sense than a guy like me turning down a girl like Bella when there was effectively no reason to do so. So instead I spun her a yarn about how I was confused and didn't feel ready for a big commitment and was wary of doing the wrong thing. She said that she understood, she even said that I could stay and sleep on the sofa, but in the end I kissed her on the cheek and said a final goodbye.

★ ★ ★

As I closed the front door to the house determined to head to the high street so I could get a cab I looked down at the front gate and spotted Fiona waiting.

'Come on then,' I said, refusing to stop, 'I'm ready to take whatever insults you're waiting to throw at me.'

Fiona laughed and followed me. 'Who said I'm here to insult you?'

'Isn't that what you do?'

'Yes, when it's needed. But it's not needed right now is it? I'm impressed, Joey Boy. For a minute back there when you were rifling through Slag Face's underwear I'll admit I was thinking,

'What an idiot! He hasn't learned a thing!' but you proved me wrong didn't you? Which — I'll have you know — is something that doesn't happen very often. I'm almost proud of you, Joe, you're growing.' She pretended to dab her eyes with a handkerchief that she produced out of nowhere. 'I think I'm actually coming over a bit emotional.' She laughed and tucked the handkerchief up her sleeve. 'It feels good though doesn't it?'

I stopped and looked at her. 'What?'

'Knowing for a fact that out of all the women in the world you only want Penny.'

'And a fat lot of good that's going to do me. She's with Scott, she's not going to come back to me.'

'I wouldn't be so sure about that.'

'And what's that supposed to mean?'

Fiona shook a finger in my face. 'I've already said too much. But you're nearly there, Joe, you're so very nearly there.'

27

'Right then you two, kiss Mum goodbye and we'll get off.'

A month had passed since the night I'd tried to rekindle things with Bella. Thankfully I hadn't seen any more of Fiona but other than that, very little had changed. Things between Penny and me were frosty but civil and she was still very much with Scott. Thankfully however a distraction came my way in the form of an idea of Stewart's. On a low after having missed out on yet another one of his children's birthdays he'd needed a project to focus on and when he'd shared his idea — taking our kids camping in Suffolk over the summer bank holiday weekend — with the Divorced Dads' Club and me we'd agreed to it unanimously.

★   ★   ★

Rosie and Jack gave Penny their biggest kisses and squeezes before racing to the car. They were practically fizzing with excitement at the prospect of three nights under canvas and seeing them so happy made me happy, albeit briefly, given that Penny and I were still not really speaking.

I looked at her, wondering what she was thinking, something I never had to do when we were together. Penny had always been such an open book, so easy to read. Not any more.

'Right, if that's everything, I think we'll be off.'

She didn't speak and so I turned away, ready to head down the path, but then she called after me.

'I've given you Jack's hay fever medicine haven't I?'

'It's in the glove box.'

'And you'll remember to keep an eye on that patch of eczema on Rosie's shoulder? It's really been irritating her lately.'

'I've got it all under control. Her cream's with Jack's medicine and it goes on twice a day. I'm not stupid, Pen. Give me some credit will you?'

Instead of getting angry at my barbed comment her face softened. She seemed distracted. 'Of course, yes, I'm sorry. I'm just . . . it doesn't matter.'

I started down the path again.

'Joe?'

'Yes?'

'Is there any chance we could have a chat sometime? Maybe when you drop the kids back on Monday? There's some stuff I could do with talking to you about. Nothing major.'

I felt my heart sink. Was there really any such thing as a 'quick chat' when you were in the middle of a divorce? 'I don't know, Pen, after a weekend under canvas with the kids I'm guessing I'll be good for nothing. Can't it wait until next week sometime?'

'Not really, no.'

'Fine,' I sighed, and wondered if this was some tactic her solicitor had devised to mess with my head. 'I'll see what I can do but I'm making no promises.'

I carried on to the car and started up the engine while the kids frantically waved Penny goodbye through the window and then finally, after what had been three-quarters of an hour of 'Oh-I've-forgotten-this,' and 'Oh-I've-forgotten-that,' we were on our way to the Suffolk coast for our first break as a single-parent family.

★ ★ ★

It was a little after two as we pulled up in the car park at the Sunny Sands camp site, following a somewhat traumatic journey during which I'd been forced by Jack to stop at the side of the road twice for unscheduled wee breaks — to complement the four I'd already planned — dealt with a leaking Tesco bag of Jack's vomit while driving at sixty m.p.h. on the A12 outside Colchester and battled Rosie for control of the car stereo because apparently listening to my own music in my own car was 'unfair'.

Grumpy, hungry and considerably crumpled, the kids and I got out of the car and stretched and just like that our foul moods lifted. The keening of seagulls far above our heads, the salty sea breeze and the constant chatter of songbirds in the hedgerow made it clear that we weren't in Kansas any more.

As we began unloading our bags I saw Paul and his kids Zach and Melody walking up the hill towards us. Paul was dressed in shorts and an old Nirvana T-shirt while his two moody-looking children were wearing long-sleeved T-shirts and jeans.

'So you made it then?'

'Took a bit longer than I'd hoped getting out of London but after that it was plain sailing. Where are the others?'

'Van's taken his kids to the beach — we were actually just off there when you arrived — and Stewart's still sorting out the tents, or at least that's what he says he's doing. I tried to talk him into coming with us but he said he'd rather get himself organised.'

'I thought he was bringing his sister's kids with him this weekend? Wasn't that the plan?'

'They cancelled at the last minute — sickness bug. It's just one of those things I suppose.'

I looked down at my kids, suddenly overwhelmed by the urge to pick them both up and smother them with kisses. I just didn't know how Stewart coped not seeing his kids. If I'd been in his position I don't think I would have.

I introduced my kids to Paul's but the two sets of children barely raised an eyebrow and instead contented themselves with staring at each other like members of a rival gang.

'They'll warm up,' whispered Paul as he picked up a couple of our bags and headed towards the tents. 'My two pretty much hate everyone to begin with. It's just their way.'

* * *

At the tents I introduced Jack and Rosie to Stewart and he showed us where we'd be sleeping. He had organised everything from the borrowing of tents to the purchasing of food. I hadn't even managed to buy sleeping bags. The

266

kids had borrowed theirs from school friends while I'd been loaned one by Van.

'Honestly mate, the kids and I would be sleeping under the stars if it wasn't for you. You've done such a great job.'

Stewart smiled but there was a real sadness behind his eyes. 'I just want everyone to have a good time, that's all.'

'And we will,' I replied, 'but only if you relax too. Paul was saying you didn't fancy going to the beach.'

He shrugged. 'I like to keep busy. My ex used to say it kept me out of mischief.'

Paul and I exchanged knowing glances. If anyone had needed keeping out of mischief it was Stewart's ex-wife.

'Listen, we're on holiday, mate, you should be free to get into as much mischief as you like so why don't we sort out the tents together and once we're done all head down to the beach?'

Reluctantly, Stewart agreed and, once the tents were sorted, we all made our way along a short stretch of road to the steps that led down to the beach. At the top of the steps however was a hotdog stand and waving frantically at us from the queue was Van with his sons Harley and Suzuki.

'Are they your real names?' asked Jack as I greeted Van and we introduced our kids.

The two boys stared at Jack and shrugged.

'I think they're cute,' said Rosie, who like most girls her age liked young children because they made them feel grown-up.

'They're named after my two favourite

motorcycles,' explained Van, kneeling down next to Jack. 'If you were a grown-up and had two kids of your own what would you name them if they had to be called after your favourite things?'

Jack thought very hard. ''Scooter' and 'Dad',' he said without cracking a smile.

Van grinned. 'After an answer like that you should definitely get a raise in your pocket money.'

★　★　★

The kids, having bonded with Harley and Suzuki over a mutual love of ketchup, spent a good hour running in and out of the sea and building sandcastles after which Van started up a game of kids versus dads football which proved so entertaining that even Paul's moody pair deemed it worthy of their participation. It was heart-warming watching the kids laughing with their new friends with an expanse of empty beach to play on. This was the kind of outdoor freedom that Penny and I had always wanted for our children, the kind that we would talk about late at night in bed lying in each other's arms taking it in turns to paint pictures of what a perfect life might look like if money, jobs and all the other stuff that got in the way of dreams, were no longer an issue.

★　★　★

'Doesn't look like I'm going to get much of a look-in in this match,' said Stewart, wandering

268

back towards me in goal from his position as defender. One of the kids had kicked the ball into the sea and every time someone fished it out one of the other kids would kick it back in again.

'Doesn't look like it,' I replied. 'Can't say it matters much on a beautiful day like this.'

'It really is a cracker isn't it?' said Stewart, sitting down on the sand next to the goal post. 'My nephews would've loved to have been here playing football.'

'I'm sure they would. I'm sorry they couldn't come.'

'It's fine. It can't be helped. It's my kids I'm really missing.'

'How long has it been since you've seen them?'

'Just under eighteen months. If I saw them now I'd probably struggle to recognise them. Kids change so much when they're young, don't they?'

I nodded. 'I don't know how you handle it, Stew, I really don't. I'd be lost if Penny took the kids to a different county let alone a different country.'

Stewart picked up a handful of sand and let it spill out between his fingers. 'I used to think like that,' he replied, 'but you learn that you can't give up. I know that one day I'm going to get to see them and when I do I know I'll be able to look them in the eye and tell them that I never stopped fighting for them.'

We talked more, about kids, and life, and where we thought we'd gone wrong in life and how best to correct it. It was a real turning point in our friendship, and it made me feel like I wasn't quite so alone, so much so that later that night as I was sitting by the campfire listening to the guys swapping ghost stories for the benefit of the kids I found myself asking him a question that I never thought I'd hear myself ask.

'Do you believe in ghosts?'

Stewart laughed. 'I know Van's stories are good, Joe, but they're not that good! Are you a believer now?'

'No of course not,' I lied, even though prompted by the watching of box sets of *Britain's Most Haunted* I was slowly coming round to the idea that perhaps I wasn't mad after all. That perhaps Fiona was telling the truth about her being a ghost. It would certainly have gone a long way towards explaining the weird things that had been happening in my life, and would have brought me a great deal of relief in finally knowing what was going on, but the one thing that my over-rational brain couldn't get over was the fact that I didn't believe in ghosts.

'I was watching a TV programme a few nights ago,' I explained to Stewart, 'and they interviewed a guy who claimed that he'd seen one and he seemed absolutely straight up and trustworthy.'

He coughed and wrinkled his nose as a change in the breeze momentarily swamped us in bonfire smoke. 'My mum claimed to have seen the ghost of her great-granddad when she was a kid but then again she's always been a big believer in the spirit world and all that rubbish.'

'So are you saying you don't believe they exist?'

He shrugged. 'I don't know. I've never seen

one. But you only have to have a quick look on the internet to find plenty of folk who do. Truth is there's a lot of weird things that go on in the world so at a guess I'd say anything's possible.'

I was about to come out with a follow-up question that I'd planned to segue into a no-holds-barred confession about Fiona when Van announced that he was tired of ghost stories, pulled out his acoustic guitar and started up a rendition of 'Hot For Teacher'. Everyone, the kids included, was so entertained by the song and the completely inappropriate dance that went with it that, as far as ghost talk went, the moment was lost and never returned. Still, somehow it didn't seem to matter too much any more because the weekend as a whole was idyllic: the perfect mix of sunny days, barbecues and late-night singing sessions around a campfire. When it came to the last day none of us wanted it to be over and we all vowed to make it an annual get-together.

★   ★   ★

It had long since gone dark as I pulled up outside Penny's. Both the kids were curled up asleep beneath their borrowed sleeping bags and I was reminded of all the family trips in years gone by when they'd had to be carried into the house and put to bed. When she was younger Rosie especially had been such a deep sleeper that I'd once completely undressed her and put her into her pyjamas without her once stirring whereas Jack would always rouse long enough to have a long and involved conversation that rarely made any sense before falling back into deep slumber. These days however they were both too big to be carried any more. In the past year alone Jack seemed to have almost doubled in size and yet was as skinny as ever and Rosie's last growth spurt had left her only half a foot shorter than her mum.

I roused them gently.

Rosie rubbed her eyes. 'Are we home?'

'We are,' I replied even though my response wasn't strictly true. This wasn't my home now no matter how much I wanted it to be. 'Come on, let's go and see your mum.'

Penny could barely hold back her tears as she hugged the kids and wrapping them both in her arms refused to let go no matter how they struggled as she kissed and hugged them as if they had been away for weeks, not days.

Inside the house Jack reeled off his highlights of the trip: 'We stayed up after midnight, Mummy, and we caught some crabs and then let them go because they were too small and we met all of Daddy's new friends and one of them has a bald head and tattoos all over his arms and we made lots of friends too, like Suzuki and Harley and Zach and Melody and yesterday we ate beefburgers for breakfast and I was sick on the way home — but only a little bit.'

Rosie rolled her eyes and sighed. 'Jack's making it sound like it was a lame weekend but it was really cool. Zach and Melody are a bit older than me but they said when I'm seventeen they'll take me to a music festival.'

Penny smiled and the kids disappeared into the living room to watch TV leaving us alone together in the hallway.

'Sounds like they had a good time,' said Penny.

'They did,' I replied.

Penny sat down on the stairs. 'I need to ask you something.'

'Fire away.'

'It's about the kids.'

I felt my heart began to pick up pace. 'What about them?'

'I'd like your permission for Scott to meet them,' she said. 'I met his kids a few weekends ago and I feel like the time's right for him to meet Rosie and Jack. He's part of my life now and the kids need to know that the person I choose to spend my time with is a genuinely nice and caring man.'

My throat tightened. My mouth went dry. With Scott living and working in Harrogate I'd never believed they'd get so serious so quickly.

'How can you ask that? You've been with him for five minutes.'

'No, Joe, it's been three months.'

'So what happens if I say no? You'll set your lawyer on me?'

Penny shook her head even though I knew for a fact that her lawyer had been negotiating with my freshly appointed lawyer over points of the divorce for some time now. 'Look, all I'm asking is that you'll think about it, OK?'

'You can leave it with me for as long as you like,' I replied, 'but know this: I'm never going to change my mind.'

28

I put the whole question of Scott meeting my kids in the trash can of my mental desktop and pressed Delete, deciding instead to focus on being the best dad that I could be which meant of course having the kids to stay or — as was increasingly becoming the norm — having to fit in family time around their own busy social rounds of parties and sleepovers.

The following Saturday afternoon was no different and Jack had a playdate. It was with some kid I'd never met called Harry Reed whose parents were fairly new to the area and lived in a three-bed flat on Eliot Park just ten minutes away, and would be taking place between two and four p.m. I knew all of this because Penny had written it in a note which Rosie had thrust into my hands the moment she had opened the door the previous evening. 'Mum said I should give this to you,' she'd said before I even had the chance to say hello. There was other stuff in the note too: a mention of the fact that Rosie needed to be dropped off at Carly's before Jack's playdate because of a prearranged sleepover; another about how to apply the verruca cream to Jack's foot; and yet another about a maths test happening first thing on Monday morning that Rosie needed to practise for. The contents of the note didn't bother me because the kids always had stuff going on whether it was school work to be completed or ailments to keep an eye on. What did bother me was the note itself, or, more specifically, the fact that since I'd refused my permission for the kids to meet Scott it had become my and Penny's sole method of communication. We no longer spoke on the phone or in person or even texted because none of these conveyed the anger and animosity we felt towards each other quite like scribbling a note on a sheet of A4 and using our children to deliver them. Despite my feelings for her the Scott situation had enraged me so much that we were well on our way to becoming the kind of warring parents we had always despised — those who used their kids as a means of getting back at each other.

★   ★   ★

As I picked up Jack so he could press the Reeds' door buzzer it occurred to me that I wasn't as well versed in the etiquette of the modern playdate as perhaps I should have been. Although prior to the birth of Rosie both Penny and I had been adamant that we would both share in the rearing of our family, the truth was once we became parents that all pretty much went out of the window. Of course I did my fair share of nappy changes and middle-of-the-night bottle feeds but the social stuff, the birthday parties, baby groups and playdates, became solely Penny's domain. It made sense for many reasons, not least the fact that these gatherings were on the whole opportunities for female bonding and as such held no appeal to me whatsoever. 'You'd be bored senseless,' Penny would reassure me whenever I had a day off work and suggested taking Rosie to Rattle Time at the local community centre or offered to man a playdate. To add insult to injury she'd always add: 'Anyway there's plenty for you to be getting on with here,' and she'd hand me a long list of jobs that needed tackling around the house while she was sipping herbal tea and putting the world to rights with her new mum friends. I didn't resent this on the whole because it made sense — mums quite clearly needed the support of other mums — but it did feel odd that after so many years of mixing it up in terms of our gender roles (Penny knew her way around a toolkit far better than I ever did) the arrival of a baby should have led us to adopt such stereotypical roles. Now all that was in the past. Now we were both homemaker and breadwinner which wasn't half as liberating as it might sound.

★   ★   ★

I needn't have worried about my lack of playdate experience because Harry's mum welcomed Jack and me both in so warmly and talked so freely ('Hi, I'm Addy. You'll have to excuse the smell in the hallway, Harry's been farting for England all morning!') that all the anxiety I'd felt — just how exactly was I going to fill two hours of conversation with a couple I'd never met before? — faded away. She was incredibly easy to talk to and after a short period of acclimatisation on the

276

part of Jack, who always got a little bit shy in new places, the boys ran off to play in Harry's bedroom leaving his mum and me alone in the kitchen with our cups of tea and small talk about the perils of young boys' flatulence.

'So, is your husband . . . Chris isn't it? Is he out for the afternoon?' I asked after a while of us chatting about the children.

'Didn't Penny tell you? Chris and I have separated.'

I thought long and hard about how best to respond to this news. Most of me wanted to say something bland like, 'Oh, I see,' in the hope we could get back to a safer topic of conversation like the weather or how much we hate wheelie bins so it was as much of a surprise to me as anyone else when I found myself saying, 'Funny you should say that because Penny and I have separated too.'

Addy's eyes widened. 'Really? I had no idea. Penny didn't say a thing.'

'Well, she probably didn't want everyone in the world knowing.'

'No,' replied Addy, 'I can understand that. Mums at the school gates can be such busy-bodies sometimes. How have your kids taken it? You've got an older girl too haven't you?'

'Yes, Rosie, and well . . . neither of the kids took it well to begin with. Now I think they're just about getting used to it which somehow seems even more heart-breaking. How about you?'

'Harry took it really badly, he just wants everything to go back to normal. Chris and I are having counselling so who knows, maybe it will,

277

but right now the whole thing couldn't be more of a mess. And the worst of it is that this was supposed to be a new beginning for both of us. Chris had just got a new job, we'd made the move from Leeds, Harry was starting at a new school . . . ' Her voice started to falter. 'I don't know, I just feel like I've let Harry down really badly, like maybe all this is my fault somehow. That I didn't try hard enough.' She laughed self-consciously. 'I'm so sorry to unload on you like this, Joe. Here you were expecting some idle chitchat for a couple of hours on a Saturday afternoon and instead you're talking failed relationships with your kid's friend's batty mother! You're never going to want Jack to play with Harry ever again!'

'It's fine,' I replied. 'Truth is it's quite nice talking about all this with another parent. Makes me feel like I'm not in it on my own.' I stood up and smiled. 'Listen, why don't I make us another cup of tea and then you can tell me your life story.'

★   ★   ★

Aided by a mug of tea and the posh Marks & Spencer biscuit selection I'd brought with me on Penny's instruction, Addy told her story. Born in Leeds, she'd met her husband, Chris, a recruitment consultant, while out clubbing with friends when she was twenty-four and working as a nurse in the obstetrics department of Leeds General Infirmary. They'd moved in together two years later, married three years after that at a

278

country house hotel near Ullswater and a while later Harry was born and Addy believed that she had her fairy-tale ending.

Things were good between them for a few years but then Chris started to climb the career ladder which resulted in him getting moved all around the country for work meaning that he was never at home and soon the arguments began. The move to London was supposed to be the answer to all their problems. Chris would be away from home less, yet still able to advance his career, but he ended up being away more than ever and finally they had a huge row and Chris moved out. Addy was desolate, thinking he had gone for good, but a few days later he came round and they talked and for the first time in their relationship he acknowledged that they had a problem and needed outside help to solve it. That had been six weeks ago, and now once a week on a Monday evening in East Greenwich they were meeting with a grey-haired counsellor called Kate who listened as they carefully laid out the intimate details of their married life before her.

'I think that's why I started telling you my life story before you'd even asked,' Addy explained as she wound up her tale. 'The thing about counselling is once you start talking to complete strangers about your love life it's really hard to stop.'

Embarrassed to have, in her eyes, dominated the conversation, Addy tried to get me to talk about my own situation but I felt far too self-conscious to even consider it. So I did the only thing I thought I could do in the circumstances: summed the whole thing up in a single sentence ('Basically we were having problems and she asked me to move out,') and hoped she wouldn't push me further. Addy was a good sport and thankfully just laughed. 'You're exactly like Chris,' she commented, 'he used to think talking about your problems was pointless too.'

I should probably have left it at that but I didn't. Or rather I couldn't. Somehow it didn't seem right presenting myself as a potentially injured party when the truth was somewhat different.

'I had an affair,' I said quietly. 'It was just the once, with a colleague at work. Penny found out. Like you and your husband we tried counselling for a while but it didn't seem to take.'

Addy raised any eyebrow. 'How come?'

'She's met someone else.'

'You really have been in the wars haven't you?'

'Just a bit.'

She looked at me thoughtfully. 'How old was this . . . colleague of yours? Younger?'

'A bit.'

'And by that you mean what? Thirty? Thirty-five?'

'Twenty-five.'

Addy rolled her eyes in a what-is-wrong-with-men kind of way. 'Have you any idea how hot your wife is? I saw her in the playground the other day picking up Jack and while she might not be twenty-five any more she's absolutely gorgeous.'

'I know.'

'So why do it?'

I smiled. For some reason I couldn't quite pinpoint it felt good to be interrogated like this. Maybe it was because she was a woman and I missed talking to a woman in a frank and forthright fashion; then again maybe it was because I hadn't quite done with feeling bad about what had happened. 'I have no idea,' I replied. 'I really don't. Sometimes you just do things and you think no harm will come of them and it's only when you've done them that you realise the only person you've fooled is yourself.'

'You still love her don't you?'

'I never stopped.'

'Does she know?'

'I don't think it would make any difference.'

Addy put down her mug and looked at me thoughtfully. 'Do you want my advice?'

'Not really. I've got a feeling I won't like it.'

'Maybe you will, maybe you won't, but I'm going to tell you anyway. You need to go and make peace with her. Whatever it is that she wants, give it to her. You know better than anyone what you've put her through so the very least you can do is stop playing the victim and apologise. I'm not saying it will bring her back to you, I'm not even saying that it'll make her want to talk to you, but I guarantee you if you do this, the one thing you will gain is her respect.'

As hard as it was to admit it she was right. I rubbed my eyes and looked at her. Being honest was exhausting. 'Is that what you want from your husband? Respect?'

'It's what I've always wanted,' she replied.

'That, and for him to tell me that he loves me and look like he means it.'

*   *   *

It took me two days to pluck up the courage to call Penny, but I eventually did and we arranged to meet at the house once the kids had gone to bed.

'So what's this about?' asked Penny, putting two mugs of tea down on the kitchen table.

'I want to talk, which is something I know I haven't exactly been too good at of late . . . and well, I want to say that if you want the kids to meet Scott, it's fine by me.'

Shock flashed across Penny's face. This hadn't been what she was expecting at all. 'Are you sure?'

I felt myself wavering but I pushed on through with my decision. 'Yes.'

'Why the sudden change of heart?'

'It doesn't matter,' I replied. 'At least not now anyway.'

*   *   *

Although when I called to speak to the kids on the following Monday evening I wondered if the children would mention their meeting with Scott and how it had gone, both failed to do so. Jack, who at times had trouble recalling what had happened five minutes ago let alone several days before, only mentioned it in passing with reference to the dessert he had eaten at Pizza

Hut. Rosie didn't bring it up at all and although she went into great detail about the sleepover she'd had at Carly's on Friday night, and the Saturday afternoon she'd spent playing laser tag at a party and her Monday at school in its entirety, it was as though she had completely erased Sunday lunch and her meeting with Scott from her brain.

Keen not to push things I didn't mention the meeting again until the following weekend when the kids stayed over at mine. It was Saturday night and Jack and Rosie had long since gone to bed. I'd been watching a DVD that I'd picked up from work when I'd heard a knock on the living-room door and turned to see a pyjama-clad Rosie standing in the doorway.

'Can't sleep?'

She shook her head and joined me on the sofa, making sure she was cuddled up against me as close as she could be. She stared at the paused screen: a man running down an alleyway in New York, being chased by police.

'I met Mum's new friend last week.'

'Oh yeah.' I tried my best to sound casual but I wasn't at all sure that it worked. 'You mean Scott? What was he like?'

'He was really nice.'

It was just four words and she obviously meant nothing by them, but each and every one was like the stab of a knife through my heart.

29

Saturday morning in the tinned goods aisle of my local Tesco. Graham Leith, the boorish financial adviser father of Jack's friend Arthur, was in full-on whinge mode about his day.

'I've been on duty since six this morning,' he was saying. 'Suzy left at eight for a spa day with her mates, I've just dropped the eldest at swimming and then I've got to pick him up to take him to a party. The baby's got colic and is off her food and this one,' he looked down at the toddler by his side who was busy trying to liberate a can of beans from the shelf next to her head, 'has been in a foul mood all morning just because Daddy wouldn't let her watch twenty-five episodes of *Angelina Ballerina* back to back. Chances are I'll be dead by the time Suzy gets home.'

Listening to Graham left me conflicted. On the one hand, having been in his situation in the past I could sympathise with the strain that being alone on duty with the kids on a Saturday morning could cause. After a gruelling week at work there was no denying that a couple of bickering kids and a wonky shopping trolley was enough to bring the worst out in anyone. But today of all days I just couldn't muster a single iota of sympathy for Graham, at least not when I would gladly have swapped the next forty-eight hours of soul-crushing emptiness that I called a life for just five minutes of the stuff Graham was clearly so sick of.

Saturdays never used to be like this. Saturday used to be the day I would long for more than any other. The start of the weekend, a day of freedom, the first opportunity of the week to divest myself of any title that wasn't husband or father. While I was still half asleep the kids would pile into bed with Penny and me and after a long chat and snuggle we'd enjoy a leisurely breakfast secure in the knowledge that even if there were parties to attend or sleepovers to be dropped off at there would still be plenty of time for us all to be together curled up on the sofa in front of the TV at the end of the day. But not today. Today I was alone. It was Penny's weekend to have the kids and I could only imagine that they were out celebrating the one-month anniversary of Scott's introduction to the children's lives because so far the kids had yet to say a bad word about him. I would've been happy with an occasional 'He's a bit dull,' or even a 'He's fun but not as much fun as you, Dad,' but instead all I seemed to hear was what great adventures they had together and 'Scott says this,' and 'Scott says that,' to the point where had Scott said anything more I'd lose it altogether. The Divorced Dads had tried their best to reassure me that what I was experiencing was nothing unusual. 'Kids like new stuff because it's new,' Van had explained, 'but in the end they always go back to the stuff that's stood the test of time.' And yet as much sense as Van's comment had made it had provided me — their father who wanted his

285

family back *now*, not at some unspecified date in the future — with little in the way of the consolation I craved.

Conscious that my disheartened disposition was taking a distinct turn for the worse I made my excuses to Graham and escaped to the tills. On the way home I planned out the day ahead in a bid to distract myself. Step one would be making a show-stopping breakfast with the bacon, eggs and orange juice I'd just bought, step two would involve tackling some of the domestic tasks I'd been ignoring — there were rooms to tidy, clothes to be ironed and wardrobes in need of repair — and then, finally, after lunch, step three: head into town and catch up on any one of the half-dozen films I'd been meaning to see at some point but never found the time to get round to. As empty Saturdays without my kids went, it could have been a lot worse but then my phone rang. It was Rosie.

'Dad, you need to come quick,' she said. 'Mum and Scott have had a massive argument and he's gone and now she won't stop crying. I don't know what to do, Dad, I don't know what to do.'

The panic in her voice tore at my heartstrings. 'You don't need to do anything other than wait for me to arrive, OK?' I told her as I calculated the logistics of getting over to Penny's in the shortest time possible. 'I'll look after you, and I'll look after Mum too. Don't worry about a thing: Dad's coming and he'll sort everything out.'

★　★　★

286

When I arrived at the house the kids opened the door and raced at me with such force that they nearly knocked me off my feet. The relief they felt now I was there was as palpable as the guilt I felt that they'd had to deal with this problem without me for a single moment. I was their dad, I was supposed to stop bad things happening in their lives. If I couldn't do that then what use was I?

'Mum's upstairs,' said Rosie with tears in her eyes. 'She just won't stop crying and I didn't know what to do. Did I do the right thing calling you?'

She started to cry and I held her to me tightly. 'Of course you did,' I said, stroking her hair. 'Mum's going to be fine. Just tell me what happened.'

'Well, she was on the phone to Scott and they were talking for a while and I could hear her getting more and more upset and then the next thing I knew she'd gone upstairs and slammed the door. I knocked and she told me to go away but I could hear that she was crying and that's when I called you.'

I kissed Rosie's head. 'You did exactly the right thing. Now what I need you to do is take Jack and go and watch some TV while I talk to Mum. Help yourself to some biscuits and make yourself a nice drink. Just relax, everything's going to be fine.'

The kids did as I asked and once they were safely ensconced in front of the TV I went upstairs and knocked on the bedroom door. There was no reply but I could hear Penny crying and so I went in. She was curled on top of

287

the covers sobbing uncontrollably. It was heart-breaking. She was always so strong, so vital, so unwilling to let life get her down. Whatever the source of her argument with Scott, it was irrelevant. Penny would never have been in this state if it hadn't been for me. If I'd stayed away from Bella. If I'd never had an affair. If I'd just been satisfied with what I'd got instead of scrabbling around for something more. They say you get what you deserve but Penny didn't deserve any of this. I, on the other hand, deserved to be shot.

I asked her what was wrong, what had happened. She couldn't seem to or perhaps didn't want to tell me and I couldn't blame her. It was me who'd made her so vulnerable. My affair had made her feel like a failure, as a wife and subsequently as a parent, and this thing with Scott — whatever it was — had reopened wounds that I had inflicted.

Tucking her into bed I quietly closed the bedroom door and explained to the kids that Mummy was fine but was having a really bad day and that the best thing they could do would be to spend the night with Penny's mum and stepdad. Although Jack was excited at the prospect of seeing his grandparents Rosie was reluctant to leave her mother's side, almost seeing it as an act of betrayal. 'I don't want her to think we don't care,' she explained. 'I don't want her to wake up and wonder where we've gone.' I reassured Rosie all I could. 'She's your mum, sweetheart, she knows you love her. But right now, she needs a rest. Sometimes the best thing you can do for someone you love is give them the space they need to get well again.'

★   ★   ★

I helped the kids pack their overnight bags into which they piled all of life's essentials. For Jack it was his latest Lego set, a picture book about space travel and the Chinese superhero action figure I'd bought him from Chinatown; for Rosie it was a couple of books, her iPod and a small green furry frog that had been her bedtime companion from the day she was born. It was very worn and ragged now and though Penny washed it often it still smelled musty. Once a few years earlier having noticed the state of it I offered to buy her a new one. She didn't even reply, just looked at me askance as though she couldn't believe I would even entertain the question. I picked up the frog from the bed and stroked its fur and Rosie snatched it from my hand and put it back in her case. She might have had to call me to sort out the situation in which we found ourselves but that didn't mean she didn't blame me for it on some level.

★   ★   ★

The afternoon was all but over by the time I returned from dropping the kids with Penny's mum and stepdad. I let myself into the house with the spare keys I'd taken from the kitchen drawer near the back door where they'd always lived. I was about to head upstairs to check on

Penny when I heard a noise from the living room and as I poked my head around the door I saw that she was sitting, legs curled up, on the sofa underneath a throw.

She looked up. Her eyes were red and swollen but at least she'd stopped crying. 'I'm so sorry you had to see me like this . . . and the kids too. You must think I'm the worst mother in the world.'

'I'd never think that. You just had a bad day, that's all. We've all had those.'

'Are the kids all right? What did Mum and Tony say?'

'The kids are fine,' I replied. 'Jack was straight in the garden with Tony and when I left Rosie and your mum were playing backgammon.'

Penny looked puzzled. 'Backgammon? Since when has Rosie had any interest in playing that?'

'By my reckoning since about an hour ago. You know what your mum's like, she can't stand Rosie listening to her iPod or as she calls it the 'i-music-thingy'. She likes to get the kids doing old-timey stuff.'

Penny smiled. 'But they're OK?'

'They're fine. They told me to give you this.' I reached into my pocket and pulled out a sheet of A4 folded into the shape of a card. On the front Rosie had drawn a bunch of tulips and underneath in Jack's unmistakable scrawl were the words *Mummy's favourite flowers*. Inside it read: Sorry you're not feeling well, get better soon, love and squeezes, Rosie and Jack. Rosie had drawn three neat crosses after her name but Jack being Jack had covered the bottom of the card and the entire back of it with wonky kisses.

As a rule I wouldn't say I'm an overemotional man but even the most hastily thrown together of my kids' art projects brought a lump to my throat. All it took was some glued-on pasta, a scattering of glitter and some scribbled kisses and I was complete mush in their hands. It was something about the unfettered honesty of their intention that when combined with the rudimentary nature of the card's construction got me every time.

Penny took the card from me and sobbed as she read it.

'That's so beautiful. They're such good kids. They don't deserve any of this. I have to call and let them know how much I love them.'

'You can,' I replied. 'But not right now. I told them I'd call them tonight and you'd call them first thing in the morning and they were fine with that. And as for your folks, I think they knew something was going on but knew better than to ask.'

Penny wiped her eyes and moved to get up. 'I have to let them know I'm OK. They'll worry otherwise.'

'No, you don't,' I insisted. 'You've been through a lot. All you need to do right now is sit down and rest. I'll call in a minute if you want and tell them whatever you want me to.'

Penny nodded and sat back down. 'Maybe you're right. I don't think I could face their questions right now.'

I sat down on the armchair opposite. 'Is that your way of saying that I shouldn't ask what happened? Because I won't if you don't want me to.'

'There's not much to say really. Scott finished with me.'

'He did what? Why would he do that? I thought he was mad about you.'

Penny shrugged. 'The why doesn't matter. It's done and it can't be undone.'

The more selfish part of me wanted to agree and spend the rest of the evening conducting a thorough character assassination of Scott but I knew I couldn't destroy her hopes.

'It's only a stupid fight, just give him a night to come to his senses and he'll be back.'

Penny smiled sadly. 'Dating advice from my husband . . . I don't think this day could get any more weird. This time last year I could never have imagined we'd be here, could you?'

I couldn't look at her. The guilt was too much. 'I'm sorry, Penny. I'm so sorry.'

Penny reached out and took my hand.

'I know,' she said. 'I know.'

*   *   *

Dropping around at Penny's became a sort of habit after that. I'd come home from work, make a quick tea and then pop over for an hour or two on the pretext of checking in with the kids. And while it didn't take a genius to work out that I was unconsciously pinning all my hopes for a happy future on these occasions, at the same time I was just glad to be a comfort to her.

A few nights into this new pattern I turned up

at the house with a Chinese takeaway in response to a throwaway comment of Penny's about how desperate she was for a chicken chow mein. It seemed like a no-brainer: purchase takeaway, take said food to Penny, make her happy and while she was getting the plates out tell her that I still loved her and wanted a chance to make things right.

As steam rose up into the evening air from the takeaway carrier bag I rang the doorbell with my free hand and prepared to declare my love in the most convincing way I could to the only woman in the world who mattered to me. After a moment or two of tortured waiting I saw movement through the stained glass panel of the door followed by the fumbling of locks as the door opened to reveal Scott.

I have to admit I hadn't seen it coming at all.

'What are you doing here?' I spluttered.

'I think this is one that Penny needs to explain,' he replied.

Penny came to the door as Scott slipped back inside the house. She looked nervous and embarrassed. 'Joe, I'm sorry, I . . . well Scott dropped by, and . . . '

'You're back together aren't you?'

Penny nodded and I put the takeaway down on the doorstep. 'Here,' I said, 'dinner's on me.' I started down the path with Penny calling after me. Finally, she ran out of the house and up the street after me in her bare feet.

'I'm sorry you had to find out this way but it's literally only just happened,' she said, grabbing hold of my arm. 'I was putting the kids to bed and next thing I knew Scott was on the doorstep.'

'But you told me it was over.'

'I thought it was.'

'So what's changed?'

Her voice was barely above a whisper: 'He told me he loved me.'

'And do you love him?'

Penny didn't reply, but she didn't have to. The pity in her eyes directed towards me pretty much said it all.

★   ★   ★

As I walked home that night I fully expected to see Fiona. Surely if there was ever a moment for my mind to manifest her it was now. But there was nothing. Not on the way home, that sleepless night or at any point over the week that followed. Even the arrival of my decree nisi — which was in effect little more than an official-looking sheet of A4 paper with various sentences amended and dated for the specifics of my and Penny's circumstances — didn't cause a relapse. After I read it through there were no talking dead exes, no visions of me at death's door or anything even vaguely supernatural. Just the very real sense that my life was changing beyond all recognition:

The petitioner: Penny Elizabeth Clarke has sufficiently proved the contents of the petition herein and is entitled to a decree of divorce, the marriage having irretrievably broken down,

294

the facts found proved being the Respon-
dent's adultery.

I read that final word several times: adultery. It
didn't seem to matter any more that I couldn't
remember my night with Bella taking place, in
fact somehow it seemed more fitting given how
much I still loved Penny, as though it hadn't
happened at all. Maybe that was what my
unconscious mind had been trying to tell me
through 'Fiona' all along: to let go, to move on,
because that was exactly what Penny was doing.
It still hurt though, it hurt like nothing else on
earth. In fact I'm not sure that I would've got
through the weeks that followed its arrival had it
not been for the Divorced Dads' Club proving
the truth of the maxim that the best way to
forget your own problems is to help someone
else with theirs.

30

It started with Van.

It was the end of an unusually quiet night out in the Red Lion. With the kids still very much on my mind I'd barely said a word all evening which wouldn't have been so bad but Van had also been oddly quiet; seeing as he was usually the life and soul of our get-togethers, this succeeded in putting a real dampener on the proceedings.

I'd been too lost in my own thoughts to pay much attention to what was going on but then Paul returned from a trip to the loo, glanced around the table and said, 'Is this it? Is this the end of us? Is there no point in us hanging out together any more?' He looked from me to Van. 'You two have barely said a word all night. If you didn't want to come out why did you bother? I turned down tickets to see a mate in *Oklahoma!* for this. You're making me wish I'd gone and I cannot stand musicals. What's wrong with you both?'

Van replied to Paul's question before I'd even got my brain into gear: 'I'm sorry mate, I'm just feeling a bit off my game tonight.'

There was something in Van's voice that made us all sit up straight away. Even Paul stopped looking quite so annoyed. 'What's up, mate? Everything OK?'

'It's nothing,' he shrugged. 'I'm fine. It's just, well, I'm getting my test results back tomorrow.'

'I don't get it,' said Stewart. 'When you had them done you said it was just a formality. What makes you think you're not going to get the all clear?'

Van shrugged and drained the last of his beer. 'I think I've found another lump,' he said.

* * *

The following afternoon all three of us accompanied Van to his hospital appointment to get his results. This was yet another downside to being separated or divorced: having no one to hold your hand when you're preparing for bad news. I had to cancel a couple of meetings and put off an interview I'd been chasing with a well-known actor but despite the earful I got from the actor's PR it never once occurred to me not to go with them. To me Van was family now; in fact I felt the same about all the guys. They had proved themselves to be such good mates who always had my back that I was glad to have the opportunity to prove myself worthy of their friendship, no matter how small the gesture.

The nurses at the oncology department all appeared to know Van — or at the very least had failed to forget such a large personality — and laughed when he informed them that he'd brought his 'crew' along for emotional support before pointing us in the direction of the waiting room. His consultant was running late so his two o'clock appointment came and went without any relief from the tension of not knowing. While he didn't say a great deal it was easy if you knew him like we did to see how worried he was. His bravado put on for the nurses disappeared the moment they were out of earshot and suddenly the big man we knew him to be seemed almost small. He'd told me one night after a visit to the pub that one of the best things about having cancer had been that it had made him appreciate life, the bad bits as well as the good, because that was what living was all about. He'd also told me that the worst thing about having cancer had been the thought that he might not see his kids grow up. As we all sat in silence in the waiting room I knew exactly what he was thinking.

Finally a nurse appeared and called Van's name and as one we all rose to our feet.

'You guys do know that you can't actually come in the room with me, don't you?' chuckled Van. 'I don't think we'd all fit.'

Stewart spoke first. 'We just . . . ' His voice trailed off but it didn't matter. We all knew what it was he wanted to say.

Van nodded, acknowledging Stewart's valiant effort at saying something meaningful in this most desperate of times, and then looked over at the nurse holding the door open for him.

'I'll see you guys on the other side,' he said, and we watched as he crossed the floor and disappeared inside the room leaving us alone to silently contemplate the magnitude of what he must have been going through.

For thirty-five minutes none of us spoke. Instead we played about with our phones, flicked through long out-of-date magazines or simply stared into space but the longer we waited the more the guys and I began exchanging coded looks which at first simply asked: How long does it take for a doctor to say 'Everything's fine?' but as the time went by became increasingly concerned. Surely he had been in there far too long for this to be anything other than the worst kind of bad news.

I'd just decided to go and ask the nurses what was going on when the consultant's door opened and out came Van grinning like the Cheshire Cat.

'All clear,' said Van, wrapping his arms around Stewart and picking him up as though he weighed nothing. 'Turns out the lump was just a blocked skin pore.'

'So you're fine?' I asked. 'Completely fine?'

'Not a trace of anything dodgy in any of my tests. The consultant was so chuffed that he called in about half a dozen students to come and take a look at my results! That's why it took so long.'

Paul patted Van on the back. 'We should go and celebrate. News like this always tastes better with a pint.'

'Mate, I'd love to,' said Van. 'But I can't right now.'

Paul looked confused. It wasn't like Van to turn down a pint when one was offered. 'How come? Where are you going?'

'Where do you think? I'm off to see my kids. Just me, them and all the chocolate chip ice cream they can eat.'

★   ★   ★

Once we'd had our celebration with Van a couple of days later, Paul revealed a problem he'd been wrestling with alone, not wanting to take the attention away from Van and all he had been going through. Paul's ex was getting married. His kids wanted to go and he didn't but no matter how many different alternatives his ex came up with the kids had made it clear that they were only going if Paul went too and so this was the compromise: Paul would go but only if he could bring three complete strangers with him. Paul's ex told him that he could bring along a troupe of performing seals if he liked as long as the kids came and he warned her that although he probably wouldn't be doing that one of the guys was a tall, bald New Zealander called Van Halen and there was a very good chance that if he got drunk he could cause some real fireworks. Later that day Paul pitched the idea to us over a series of group texts:

Paul: *Who wants to come to my ex's wedding?*
Me, Van and Stewart: *Not me.*
Paul: *There'll be free beer.*
Van: *OK.*
Me and Stewart: *Still no.*
Paul: *I wouldn't ask but I've got a feeling it's going to be a tough day.*
Me: *In that case count me in.*
Stewart: *I'll be there.*
Van: *Dude, I don't know what's wrong with these guys, you had me at free beer!*

It was just after midday as Stewart and Van and I arrived at the Royal Metropolitan in Knightsbridge. All three of us looked up at the plush, marble-clad building in front of us.

'Paul's ex-missus and her fiancé aren't short of a few bob are they?' commented Stewart, straightening his tie self-consciously.

'You're not wrong there, mate,' replied Van, who although he was wearing a second-hand dinner jacket matched with a white vest top, jeans and cowboy boots couldn't have been any more blissfully unaware of the looks he was attracting. 'She must have really wound up Paulie for him to want to give up this kind of lifestyle. She's obviously loaded.'

I shrugged, and thought back to my Father's Day interview with Paul all that time ago. 'Somewhere along the way,' he'd said, 'we just stopped loving each other and by the time we realised there just wasn't anything anyone could do about it.'

We arrived late but the ushers were still busy getting everyone to sit down in time for the bride's arrival. We tried to find somewhere to sit at the back of the room but then one of the ushers asked me who I was, checked my name against the list in his hands and then — with the whole room looking on — promptly marched us to a row of chairs at the front of the room where Paul was sitting with his kids.

'Glad you could make it,' said Paul in a stage whisper.

Once we'd all settled down I nudged Paul and gestured to the tall, fair-haired guy chatting at the front of the room. He looked nervous and excited.

'Is that the groom?'

Paul nodded.

'What's he like?'

'That's the most galling thing about him: he's actually OK.'

I stared hard at the groom and in spite of myself an image of Scott popped into my head. Would that be him one day in a room packed with friends and family waiting for Penny to walk up the aisle and promise to love and adore him for the rest of their lives? I couldn't imagine any situation that would make me sit through that no matter what.

I leaned into Paul. 'You know, if you want to slip out before she gets here no one will think any the worse of you. I'm happy to look after the kids until it's all over.'

Paul shook his head. 'It's fine, really. This is something I need to do, not just for the kids but for me too.'

★ ★ ★

Later that night, after the food and the speeches had finished, Paul and I stood at the bar watching the bride and groom take to the floor for the first dance of the evening, Paul turned away and took a sip of his beer.

'Are you all right mate?'

'I'm fine, or I will be. It's just been a weird day and I don't quite know what I feel. They say that divorce is toughest on the kids, and it's true, it's really hard for them, but I'll tell you what, it's not easy on the parents either, not easy at all.'

★ ★ ★

A few weeks later, I was finishing off some work at home when I got a call from Stewart. 'It's the kids,' said Stewart, barely able to get his words out. 'I've just heard from my solicitor: my kids are coming home!'

For as long as I'd known Stewart he'd been trying to get his kids back from his ex-wife in Thailand without success. The battle to bring them home had taken its toll, financially and emotionally. I couldn't even begin to imagine how he was feeling.

According to Stewart the news had come completely out of the blue. He'd got in from work to find an email from his ex saying she wanted to talk. Stewart had called the number she had given him straight away and she told him that the kids were homesick for the UK and she would send them back to him if he'd pay for the flights. We all told him to be careful in case she was just after his money but he wouldn't listen. For him this was too good an opportunity for him not to hope to with all his strength that it was true. He'd told her he'd find the money and had so far managed to scrape together all but five hundred quid of it from family and friends.

I didn't wait for him to ask. Broke as I was, this was a cause I could really get behind.

'Give me your bank details and I'll transfer it now.'

303

The following evening Stewart called to say he'd bought the tickets but added that there was one last favour he needed from me.

'Name it.'

'I could do with a bit of company while I wait to pick them up,' he said. 'I've asked Van and Paul already but they're both working. I don't suppose you could come with me could you?'

'I'd be honoured,' I replied. 'Leave it with me and I'll sort it out.'

Three days later I found myself in my car with Stewart in the passenger seat on our way to Heathrow's Terminal Four. I still wasn't quite sure how I'd been invited to witness the single most important day of his life but I was glad he wasn't doing this alone.

Stewart was a bag of nerves as we waited in the arrivals lounge. He'd bought a coffee and let it go cold and then another and then let that go cold too. He'd pace the floor underneath the screen showing flight arrivals only stopping to check that he'd got the correct flight number even though I guessed he knew it off by heart. Finally however the news came through that he had been waiting for: his kids' plane had landed.

'What do you think I should say to them first?'

asked Stewart as we waited at the gate. 'I haven't seen them for so long, I want it to be right.'

'It will be,' I replied. 'You're their dad and throughout all this time you've never given up trying to see them. Your actions have said more than any words ever could. You just enjoy this moment and know that they're going to be absolutely mad about you no matter what.'

★　★　★

As the first flurry of passengers from Bangkok began to filter through the sliding doors even I felt my heart beat that little bit faster but not even this could prepare me for the lurch I felt in my chest the moment Stewart locked eyes on his kids. The kids and their chaperone didn't really know what had hit them when this chubby, dishevelled-looking bloke dressed in baggy jeans and a coat that was several sizes too big for him suddenly appeared in their line of vision with his arms outstretched ready to scoop them up and for a moment I feared that they might run away or, worse still, cry. But then the tallest of the two, a little girl no more than eight or nine at best, opened up her arms and hugged him and then her brother, who must have been around Jack's age, ran forwards and hugged Stewart too. As life-affirming moments went I doubted that they got any better than this: hope fulfilled, a fractured family reunited, a hole in the heart sewn up for good.

★　★　★

Wiping away tears with the back of his hand while dozens of passengers looked on wondering at the story behind this emotional reunion, Stewart called me over.

'Joe, I want you to meet Thomas and Vicky: my kids. Kids, this is Joe, one of my best mates.'

As I said hello I couldn't help but think back to the day at the studio when I'd first met Stewart. Who would've believed that all this time later Stewart and I would be not just acquaintances, but good friends? The older I got the more unpredictable life seemed to become. There was never any telling what might happen from day to day let alone from minute to minute. There was always something unexpected lurking around the corner.

★   ★   ★

That night I reached home long after it had gone dark. I opened the mail as I kicked off my shoes. A gas bill, a dentist's appointment card, two bank statements, the new issue of *Men's Health* and then, finally, my decree absolute. I sat down heavily on the bottom of the stairs. It was official: I was no longer married to Penny and in that instant I missed her more than ever.

31

It was early evening and the last embers of April sun were shining through the kitchen window casting shadows across the cupboards. I was in the middle of making a bowl of pasta when the phone rang. I'd been waiting for a call from Penny all day. Today was the single most important day of our daughter's life so far: today was the day she would find out which secondary school she would go to in September.

Since the previous September this had practically been the sole topic of conversation amongst parents at the school gates. Some had already made up their minds to move into the right catchment areas or out of London altogether, others were cashing in nest eggs and sending their kids to private schools and still others — like Penny and me — had chosen to simply cross our fingers and hope for the best.

Much like every other parent in the borough of Lewisham we wanted Rosie to go to Watermill Lane Comprehensive, a school that was so oversubscribed it had a waiting list to get on to its waiting list. Watermill Lane's Ofsted report was outstanding, its pupils regularly attained the kind of exam results any elite private school would be proud of and it had an incredible reputation not only for sport but also the arts. Parents had been known to rent houses in the catchment area months in advance for exorbitant fees and move their whole families there just to secure a place and others who had lied or cheated their way to the front of the queue were regularly caught out and splashed across the front of the local free paper. Back in October when Penny and I had filled in the online application form we'd convinced ourselves that even though we lived three miles away from the school, just outside last year's catchment, it was madness to up sticks and sell just to get a much more expensive house a mere 0.6 miles closer to the school and so we reasoned — or rather, hoped — that somehow we'd be OK. And with everything that had happened over the past few months, it was fair to say that we had taken our eye off that particular ball. But now that the day was here when we'd finally find out Rosie's fate it was a lot harder to be quite so easy-going, especially since West Gate Community College, the undersubscribed, fresh-out-of-special-measures secondary school was just minutes down the road.

Unfortunately however the call wasn't from Penny but Van trying to sell me on the virtues of going out with his sister Makayla, who had just arrived in London fresh from Auckland.

'She's amazing, mate! Gorgeous face, great personality and legs to die for!'

'Let me stop you right there, Van,' I protested before the conversation could get any more uncomfortable. 'You do realise this is your sister you're talking about?'

'Of course I do, but that doesn't stop her from being hot does it? Obviously she's not hot to me. To me she's still the little squirt who used to sneak into my room and nick my AC/DC tapes but take it from me, to regular guys who aren't related to her she is definitely one hot chick! I'll send you a photo if you don't believe me.'

The line went silent and I winced with embarrassment as I pictured Van talking his sister into the indignity of posing for a photograph: 'Don't worry, it's for a mate so he can see if you're all right-looking,' I could imagine him saying. 'I won't use a flash and I'll make sure to get your best side!'

My phone pinged just at the moment the boiling pot of pasta spat scorching water in the direction of my shirt. I lowered the heat under the pan then returned my attention to the phone as, with eyes half closed, I opened the picture attachment. The pretty brunette in the picture looked nothing at all like the blond-wigged Van in drag I'd imagined. She had a kind face, deep green eyes and looked exactly like the sort of woman I could fall for given the right circumstances. It was hard to believe that Van had been in the same room as this woman, let alone the same womb. There had to be something more to it. I called him back.

'And this is actually your sister?'

'Ha! Same mother, same father. I'm guessing she got a better pick from the gene pool though! Anyway, I told you she was hot and it looks like you think so too so let's do this. She's single, she's here for a month and I've talked you up a storm. All you need to do is say the word, and — prebooked sightseeing trips notwithstanding — I'll sort out a date.'

'Honestly, I'm really touched,' I said, and I meant it. I couldn't imagine any of my friends outside the Divorced Dads' Club taking this much of an interest in my life. 'But I'm just not in the right place at the moment.'

'And you never will be if you don't get out of the rut you're stuck in,' said Van. 'I know it's hard to hear but it's time to move on, mate. If me and the guys can do it then so can you.'

It had been over a month since I'd received my decree absolute and while all I wanted to do was curl into a ball and die Van had been determined to keep me in the land of the living to the extent that in this past week alone I had been to one of his gigs, out bowling with him and even to the cinema. 'You've got to keep putting yourself out there,' he'd told me as we'd left the cinema having sat though ninety minutes of a by-numbers action movie, 'otherwise you'll shrivel up and die.'

★ ★ ★

Telling Van I'd get back to him I returned to my meal preparations. I stuck a fork in the pasta and took a bite of a twirl. It was overcooked and waterlogged but nevertheless I drained the pan, tipped on the half-bottle of pasta sauce I'd found in the fridge and grated most of a block of cheese over it. I dumped the whole lot unceremoniously on to a plate and then my phone rang again. This time it was Penny. There was only one question on my mind.

'Did she get in? Did she get Watermill Lane?'

'No,' said Penny. 'They want to send her to West Gate.'

'I'll be with you in ten minutes,' I said and then I scraped the contents of my plate into a bin bag on the floor and grabbed my coat.

West Gate Community College. Even hearing the name was enough to send a shiver down my spine. Sometimes if I was off work I'd see kids in what passed for West Gate's school uniform hanging out by the station. More often than not however it was the smell of weed I noticed before I saw them. At first I thought I was imagining it but then one day when they were obviously feeling extra confident I spotted one of them lighting up a joint as openly as if it were a cigarette. Then of course there was the local newspaper, the *Lewisham Gazette*, which seemed to alternate articles about muggings with stories about school pupils raising money for local charities. Without fail the muggings involved kids from West Gate and the stories about philanthropy featured kids from Watermill Lane. As liberal as my politics were and as disadvantaged as I knew some of the kids at West Gate to be, I knew that there was no way any child of mine was ever going to go to West Gate Community College. This wasn't just a middle-class parents' nightmare. It was every parent's nightmare.

* ★ ★ ★

'We have to appeal,' I told Penny as we sat in the kitchen while the kids watched TV.

'On what grounds?' she asked. 'Rosie doesn't have any special needs, we're well outside the catchment area and as much as I'd love for things not being fair to be considered a legitimate argument I don't think that will cut it.'

'So you're just going to give up?'

'I don't know what else there is we can do, Joe. We haven't got the money to go private so other than moving out of the area altogether — and who knows how long that will take let alone whether we'll even get into a school that we like somewhere else — I don't see a way out of this.' A tear slid down her cheek. Instinctively I leaned across the table and put my hands on hers. 'Whatever it takes to make this right we'll do it, OK?'

Penny nodded and withdrew her hands guiltily. 'I know,' she said. 'I just wish it wasn't like this. I wish something would go right for a change. I mean how could they even think it was acceptable to send our little baby to that horrible place?'

Penny left the room in search of a tissue leaving me to think not just about the problem at hand but also my relationship with Penny. Even for the sake of our daughter it was hard being around her knowing that she was with someone else. Every time she got upset I wanted to take her in my arms and comfort her and yet I knew I couldn't trust myself to be so close to her and not do or say something that would drive an even bigger wedge between us than the one that already existed. This was one of the key things that films, books and TV fail to tell you about life after the end of a marriage: that the job of being a parent is no respecter of personal circumstances. It doesn't give a toss if as an ex-couple you're in one of those phases when you're not speaking to each other; it is frankly indifferent to how uncomfortable you might find the process of having to sit down across from each other while your kid's teacher informs you of how well your child is doing at finger-painting and it certainly doesn't give a crap if your ego's still bruised following the news that your other half has found someone new. Being a parent wants what it wants, it needs what it needs and right now, in the middle of the chaos of our fractured family life, it needed us to be the best parents we could be.

Penny returned to the kitchen. Her eyes were still red and puffy. I stood up and without a word put my arms around her and held her close. I could feel her heart beating against my chest. I was never going to recover from being in love with Penny, I could see that now, but as odd as it sounded, the truth was that I wouldn't have had it any other way. Penny would haunt me forever, but, unlike Fiona, I would be glad of the ghost of her in my life if that was all I could have.

'Everything's going to be fine,' I said, as we finally let go of each other. 'I know it all looks dark right now but hand on heart I promise you we'll get through this. We just need to stay strong. And rather than listening to all the rumours about West Gate I think our next move should be to take a look at the school for ourselves.'

313

It was raining as I arrived at the main entrance of West Gate Community College a few days later to meet Penny for our tour of the school. As we walked up the path towards reception it occurred to me that from the outside at least it looked no more threatening than the average British comprehensive and certainly less run-down than the school I had attended in my youth. Yes, there was the odd bit of graffiti scrawled across the school sign and certainly there was more than the average amount of discarded cigarette butts and chip wrappers on the floor than one might have hoped but on the whole it seemed not bad. And then we went inside.

It wasn't so much the exhausted and demoralised teaching staff we encountered or the cramped classrooms containing far too many kids or even the fact that an entire wing of the school was labelled 'The Detention Unit'. The real problem with the school was its atmosphere: housing fifteen hundred pupils at a time it was far too big to offer even the slightest impression of being a community. As Penny and I wandered the empty corridors taking in the pupils' dirty, damaged and in many cases long out-of-date work displayed on the walls I could easily imagine the kids who came here getting lost not only in the building itself but in the system too. The general air of despair that hung about the place, along with the aroma of cannabis in the toilets, made this a school I wouldn't be happy to send any child to, let alone my beautiful baby girl.

At the end of the tour we thanked Mrs Nardini, the school's harried-looking head teacher, for her time and shook hands. 'As a parent myself I completely understand the need to come and find out more about the school your child will be attending, especially one that's previously had — how shall we put it? — such a colourful reputation,' she said, smiling. 'But as I said earlier I can assure you as one parent to another that the West Gate Community College of the present is a completely different creature to the West Gate of the past. Thanks to new management structures, the hard work of its many dedicated members of staff and hopefully the presence of children like your daughter Rosie, we here at West Gate are all looking forward to a bright new future.'

Mrs Nardini pressed the green exit button on the wall and the huge glass entrance doors slid open. Penny and I thanked her once again for her time and started walking down the drive towards the main school gates in silence. It was only when the doors had fully closed behind us and we had put sufficient distance between ourselves and anyone who might be able to overhear our conversation that I finally spoke.

'Rosie goes there over my dead body. I mean it Penny, someone will literally have to kill me stone dead before I will let her set foot in this school.'

'I'm with you all the way,' said Penny. 'All the time she was talking about the changes they've

315

made and how they're hoping to attract kids like Rosie to 'inspire' the less able pupils I kept thinking: You are not going to use my kid like that! That was awful, I don't want anyone's kid to go there let alone mine. I'm scared Joe, I really don't know what we're going to do.'

'We're going to come up with a plan,' I replied.

32

I spent the next few days either on the phone to the local education authority or in front of the computer collecting information about how to make an appeal to the school board. It quickly became clear that we were far from being the only parents in Lewisham whose kids hadn't gotten into Watermill Lane. There were at least fifty or so irate mums and dads voicing their opinions about the education authority across half a dozen message boards and most seemed to know exactly what to do next: put in an objection, make your case in due course but don't hold your breath that you'll get the result you're looking for. Determined not to give up I made up my mind to try every route possible no matter how off the wall and so when Van called and asked if I was free to join the Divorced Dads' Club for a curry on the following Thursday night I saw it as an opportunity not just to meet up with my friends but also to discover whether any of them — ex-teacher Paul especially — might have any kind of information that could help our situation.

'It sounds to me like you're doing everything possible,' said Paul. 'You've lodged an appeal with the local authority and you're cold-calling schools in the area for places and keeping your eyes and ears open. Other than moving and taking your chances with what you get I don't think there's much more you can do.'

'I was worried you'd say that,' I said. 'I know I shouldn't have got my hopes up, it's just that I thought you might know someone.'

'I wish I did. The only reason my kids got into the school they're at was because we put down my ex's address on the forms as she was in the catchment area. All the schools round by me are terrible so I don't know what we would have done had we not split up — ironic really isn't it?'

'Truth be told we should have thought about this much earlier,' I said. 'I can't believe we didn't. I think with everything that was going on with the separation, and not knowing what the future would look like, we just took our eye off the ball a moment too long.'

'I wouldn't worry about it mate,' said Van. 'I'm planning to home school my two when the time comes.'

For the first time in what felt like forever I laughed. 'You're going to home school them?'

'Absolutely. I'm going to teach them all the stuff I think is important instead of the stuff the government's always trying to ram down their throats.'

'Mate,' said Stewart, 'you can't just teach them what you want. They set you guidelines to follow. Isn't that right, Paul?'

Paul could barely keep a straight face. 'I think they'd probably make an exception for a man of Van's standing. What would be on your curriculum? Soft metal stagecraft for beginners? How to give yourself tinnitus before the age of thirty? The art of wearing cowboy boots and cut-off T-shirts in the twenty-first century?'

My phone rang as everyone around the table including Van burst out laughing. I checked the screen. It was Penny.

'I'm sorry to call you so late.'

'It's fine. I'm not doing anything special.'

'You sound like you're out.'

'I'm just with the guys. In fact, hold on a minute . . . ' I gestured to my friends that I was going to take the call outside. 'Right,' I continued, shivering slightly; it was much colder outdoors than I had expected it to be. 'That's better, I can hear you now. What's up? Is it news about Rosie's school?'

'Sort of . . . '

I felt a tingle in the pit of my stomach as though I was about to get bad news.

'What is it?'

'Listen,' said Penny, 'before I tell you, I need to talk to you about Scott and me.'

I closed my eyes, waiting for the blow to fall. 'What exactly about you and Scott?'

'I wanted to tell you that as serious as Scott and I are we have no plans to live together. As far as I'm concerned the kids never asked for you and me to split up, this was something that was our fault, not theirs, and I don't see why they should have to put up with someone outside of their family coming in and sharing their home. This is their home, and it always will be, and I want for them to be sure of that.'

'That's good to hear,' I said warily. 'But why does all this sound like a precursor to you doing something I'm not going to like?'

'I'm not doing anything,' said Penny, 'at least not without your permission. It's just that Scott and I were talking tonight and he made a suggestion that I wouldn't feel right turning down without at least presenting it to you. You remember he's the headmaster of a boarding school up in Harrogate? Well, he's very kindly offered Rosie a place there.'

'I don't get it. You want to send Rosie away without us?'

'No,' clarified Penny, 'of course not, I wouldn't dream of it. Scott's school is a prep and senior school which takes day pupils and well the idea is that — '

'You're not just talking about Rosie are you?' I said as it dawned on me what she was getting at. 'You're talking about you and the kids moving up to Harrogate to live with Scott.'

Penny was quick with a rebuttal. 'No. I've told you that's not going to happen and I meant it. He's got a house on the outskirts of Harrogate that he rents out sitting empty which he's offered to us for free and in the meantime he'll stay at the headmaster's house that he's living in anyway, and I've checked with agencies and they're practically crying out for experienced social workers so I could easily find work. And before you say anything Joe, I just want to remind you that I'm not trying to pressure you into this at all. The kids need to see you as much as they need to see me and I wouldn't have it any other way but I can't see what other option we have. There's no way we can let Rosie go to West Gate and the last thing I want is to put all our hopes into an appeal that we both know is going to fail. We need to think practically about this. I understand that this is going to cost you more than it will me but please, Joe, please don't dismiss it out of hand. We always said the kids have to come first. Well this time we really have to mean it.'

It was a well-thought-out argument constructed by someone who knew exactly which buttons to press and which to steer clear of. It was an appeal to both the head and the heart presented in such a restrained yet forceful manner that a positive response wasn't just called for, it was demanded.

'You're right,' I replied, 'everything you've said is right but I just can't do it, Penny, I can't say yes. Call it selfish, call it short-sighted, call it what you like, but I love them too much to let them go that far away from me.'

* * *

'It's not fair,' said Jack in case I hadn't already got the message from his crossed arms, jutting bottom lip and sulky demeanour. 'Why are you taking Rosie to school but not me?'

How many times had I told him what was happening today? I sighed and picked him up. 'I've told you, Rosie's not going to normal school today, she's trying out the big school she's going to in September.'

'But it's just for a day isn't it?' asked Jack. 'And then she'll be back at normal school?'

I kissed his forehead and wondered if part of

the reason Jack got so sulky was because there weren't enough moments when we could just hang out with each other. I whispered in his ear so that Rosie couldn't hear: 'Do you think you'll miss her today?' and Jack whispered back gravely, 'Yes, I don't like it when she's not there.'

Rosie wasn't going to junior school as normal because she had been invited to a taster day at West Gate, a one-off event the school was holding for all the junior aged children who would be starting at the school in the coming September. Rosie had been distraught when we had broken the news that there was no choice for her but to go to West Gate but as distressing as it was for her, I felt her pain all the more keenly knowing that it wasn't strictly true. There was a school that she could go to, a school set in the greenest of fields with more facilities than even the most overeducated, overachieving kid could ever wish for, and the only thing standing between her and this fabulous opportunity was me, her own father.

★   ★   ★

I was still holding Jack in my arms when Penny came downstairs. She was wearing a smart suit and heels and her hair was up.

'You look nice. Big meeting?'

'First thing.'

Was there a note of frostiness in her voice? She turned to Rosie and hugged her tightly before I could decide one way or the other. 'Is my big girl all ready?' she asked.

Rosie scowled. 'I'll be fine, Mum.'

'And you'll call me if you need anything?'

'I've already said I will.'

'And you'll text me when you're leaving this afternoon?'

Rosie nodded, seemingly resigned to the fact that resistance was futile. Penny kissed her again and told her to have a good day.

'I'm making no promises,' said Rosie, and then she picked up her bag and made her way out to my car.

I gave Jack one final kiss and told him that I would see him later then looked over at Penny who was still standing in the doorway staring at Rosie in the car.

'She'll be all right,' I reassured. 'She will, just wait and see.'

'She'll have to be,' sighed Penny. 'She doesn't have any other choice.'

★　★　★

Rosie didn't say much on the way over to West Gate despite my best efforts to make conversation. So many of my opening gambits were met with grunts, shrugs, or silence that in the end I simply gave up talking altogether and turned on the radio.

I thought back to my own youth. Family trips to the coast in our Austin Allegro with my dad refusing to switch on Radio One, instead torturing the whole family with his cassette tape of Buddy Holly's greatest hits. I glanced over at Rosie, close enough to touch yet miles away, and once again realised how much I missed my own father. It was hard being a parent, not just because of the time kids demanded or the resources they used up. For me, the real stress came from the hundreds of decisions that needed to be made every day, each one seemingly innocuous until life stepped in and made it the origin of some future calamity which could never have been foreseen. Few things were more wearing on the soul than making decisions for which any negative consequences would be borne by someone else. If only I'd had the opportunity to share this insight with my dad while he was alive. I would have thanked him for every decision made, good or bad, in a bid to give me and my brother a better life.

★ ★ ★

We pulled up in front of the school gates and neither of us spoke. Instead we watched as streams of kids headed up the path to the school. They all seemed much bigger than Rosie and radiated an air of worldly wisdom which Rosie, even at her most streetwise, displayed very little of at all.

'I'll see you later then,' she said, reaching for her bag.

'No,' I replied and I pulled her to me and kissed the top of her head.

'What are you doing?' she asked.

'I'm not sure,' I replied, starting up the car. There was no way I was going to let her spend even five minutes in this place. No way at all. If it was Scott's way or this one I'd take Scott's every time. 'But I think it's called making stuff up as you go along.'

* * *

It was just after one on the following Sunday afternoon and Penny, the kids and I were finishing up a surprise lunch in Pizza Hut.

'I couldn't eat another thing!' said Jack, pushing away his dessert bowl which, fifteen minutes earlier, had been filled with ice cream, whipped cream and several handfuls of Smarties.

'Me either,' added Rosie, who had opted for a Mississippi Mud pie slathered in cream. 'I don't think I'll need to eat again until at least teatime tomorrow.' She licked the back of her spoon, dropped it into the bowl and then flopped back in her seat. 'This was the best surprise ever.'

'The absolute best,' added Jack. 'And the bestest bit is having Mum *and* Dad here. We used to do things together all the time but now it never happens.'

'I know,' I replied, exchanging guilty glances with Penny. Why couldn't we have made more of an effort to have some regular fun times with the kids instead of only when, as now, we had bad news to deliver? 'I'll have a word with Mum and we'll make sure we do things like this much more often. How does that sound?'

'Ace!' said Jack. 'And next time I'm not going to eat for a whole week before we go so that I can fit more pizza in my tummy!'

Everyone laughed and for a brief moment I

was free of the anxiety that had dogged me all week. The moment was here though and there was no going back.

I sat up straight in my chair and cleared my throat. 'Kids, your mum and I have got some news we need to share with you. Partly it's about school but mostly it's about the future and how things are going to be from now on.'

'What do you mean?' asked Rosie, sitting up straight in her chair. 'Have you got me into Watermill Lane?'

There was real hope in her voice and it killed me to have to disappoint her. 'Not exactly, but I think we've managed to sort out something even better. You know that Mum's friend Scott is the headmaster of a school? Well the plan is in a few weeks both you and Jack will be going there.'

'But that's in Harrogate!'

'You, Jack and Mum will be moving up there.'

Panic filled Rosie's eyes and she looked to Penny for confirmation. 'Mum, what's Dad on about? We're not really moving away are we?'

Penny nodded and put her arm around Rosie. 'I know it's a shock, sweetie, but your dad and I have done a lot of talking and we both agree it's for the best.'

Rosie's eyes filled with tears. 'How can moving away from all my friends be for the best? I don't want to go. I want to stay here. I don't understand why everything has to change just because you and Dad don't love each other any more. It's not fair you're making us move. It's not fair and I'm not going!'

While Rosie sobbed in her mother's arms Jack

questioned me. 'Am I going to a new school too?'

'It's a really lovely place. Mum will show you lots of pictures of it when you get home.'

'And will we get a new house?'

'It won't be ours, it actually belongs to Scott, but you will be living in it and Scott will be living somewhere else.'

Jack thought for a moment. 'And will you still take us to school sometimes?'

I shook my head in despair. Jack wasn't getting any of this at all. 'Sweetheart, I'm going to be staying in London so it's too far for me to be able to take you to school and I'm afraid you won't be able to stay over with me during the week any more. But you'll still see me some weekends and on holidays like Easter or half term. I'll come up to Harrogate and bring you back down to London with me and we'll get to spend the whole holiday together doing fun stuff.'

Jack shook his head making it clear that he thought this was officially a bad idea. 'If I can't see you when I want then I don't want to move away, Daddy, and that's my final word on the matter.'

Under any other circumstances I would've found great amusement in Jack repeating such an adult phrase with the gravest of intonations but today it simply served to grieve me in the most painful way possible. Yet again my kids' lives were being turned upside down against their will and all I could do was wonder if they wouldn't be better off without me after all.

33

As much as we hoped that the kids might warm to the idea of moving they completely failed to do so but resistance was futile. With so many preparations to make and so little time to get them done it was impossible not to get swept along by the momentum. The children's school was given notice of the move, a removal lorry booked, appointments made with letting agents and a farewell party for Rosie and Jack's friends planned. Penny took the kids up to Harrogate to look at their new home and let them spend a day with their new classmates, new uniforms were purchased and old ones given away to friends. At the time I wondered how we would ever get everything done by the moving date but as the days passed by the list of things that needed doing got considerably shorter until the Friday of the actual move I found myself standing in my former home — now devoid of all its furnishings — with one last job to do: take my family on a two-hundred-mile trip to their new home in Harrogate.

★   ★   ★

It was a little after six o'clock in the evening as the removal men who had spent all afternoon unloading furniture and boxes into Scott's Edwardian terrace waved goodbye to the kids, climbed into their lorry and pulled away leaving us alone for the first time that day.

As Penny closed the door behind her, Rosie and Jack asked if they could make a start on sorting out their rooms and without waiting for an answer they raced upstairs.

'You want to be careful,' I warned Penny. 'If you leave it up to them you'll be lucky to end up with the boxroom.'

'Thankfully the bedroom issue has long been settled,' said Penny. 'After some tortured debate they've both agreed that I might be allowed the largest one on the grounds that one of them will inevitably want to share it with me at some point.' Penny surveyed the boxes lying in the hallway which the removal men hadn't known where to put. 'I never want to do this again. I never knew we had this much stuff.'

I chose not to read anything into her use of the word 'we' as she'd likely said it more out of habit than anything more significant. 'It looks worse than it is, but knowing you, you'll have everything in its place by morning.'

Penny cast a glance in my direction, that if I hadn't been so unsure of myself I would have interpreted as tenderness. 'It's been so good of you to help like this. I don't know what we would have done without you. Will you stay and eat with us before you head back to London? I'm thinking some kind of takeaway — fish and chips maybe? — that is unless you want to spend the next couple of hours searching for saucepans?'

I laughed. It was good that we could still joke with each other even though we both knew what today represented. 'Fish and chips will do me fine. You start unpacking and I'll see if I can't sniff some out.'

Penny headed to the kitchen to search for plates while I took fish and chip orders from the kids. Heading out of the house I closed the door behind me just as a silver Audi pulled up in front.

'Joe, good to see you,' said Scott, getting out of the car. He stretched out his hand and I had no choice but to shake it when all I really wanted to do was slap it away. I'd hoped that he might have had the good grace to stay out of sight at least until I had gone. After all, he had won, hadn't he? He'd not only got the girl, but the family that came with her. All I'd wanted was to see my family safely into their new home and allow myself to indulge in the fantasy that Penny's life with Scott was little more than a bad dream.

'How was the journey up?'

'Fine, nothing to report.'

'And everyone's settled in?'

'You can go and have a look if you like.'

'Actually, I'm sort of glad I've managed to catch you without Penny being around. I just wanted to say that while obviously I'm overjoyed at having Penny and the children here I appreciate how hard it must be for you and . . . well, I want you to know that you won't have to worry. I'll look out for them.'

I wasn't sure if Scott was being sincere or whether he was trying to get a rise out of me. Regardless, it felt as though he had just spat in my face and called me a loser.

I drew a deep breath. I needed this day to go well not just for my family but for myself too, and if that meant being nice to Penny's boyfriend rather than swinging a punch in his direction then nice was exactly what I would be.

'Thanks,' I replied. 'That's good to hear.'

★ ★ ★

Scott was long gone by the time I returned with the food, and so we ate and drank in peace until I looked around at the kids — who were clearly shattered — and announced that it was time for me to go.

'Can't you at least stay until the morning?' asked Jack.

'I'd love to but I can't. I'll be up to see you soon though and when I do you'll have to remember every last thing you've been up to because I'll want to hear all about it.'

Jack flung his arms around me and hugged me tightly and even Rosie joined in, aware of the fact that this would be the last time for some weeks that we would be able to say goodnight in person.

Rosie stood on tiptoe and whispered, 'I love you, Dad,' into my ear. I couldn't remember the last time she had said this to me without being prompted. I closed my eyes and held them both tight and told them that I loved them more than the world.

★ ★ ★

Penny walked me to the car. 'Thanks for today, Joe, really. I don't know what we would have done without you. Today could've been horrible but your being here and the way you've reassured the kids . . . well, it's made all the difference and I know it hasn't been easy for you, so thanks.'

I held her close and as I let go I saw that she had tears in her eyes. 'In case you're having any last-minute doubts,' I said, wiping away a stray tear with my thumb, 'this is the right thing to do. It'll take a while but the kids are going to be happy here, I know it, and maybe one day we'll look back and wonder why we ever thought otherwise.'

★　　★　　★

It was late by the time I arrived home to an empty house that seemed all the more empty for the knowledge that the two little sparks of life that I'd so often shared it with wouldn't be in it for a long time to come. I poured a Scotch, and then another, and then another and then reaching across to the coffee table I flicked open the lid of my laptop to reveal the video file open on the frozen image of a four-year-old Rosie, the chubby features of her toddler years not yet fully formed into the face that I knew so well. She was holding her newborn brother, a lurching, gurgling, bundle of life in her arms, for the very first time. 'This is your baby brother, Jack,' I had told Rosie, handing him to her as she positioned herself on the bed ready to receive him, 'and he's already told me that he loves you more than you will ever know.' I pressed the play button and the image sprang to life with the added dimensions of movement and sound. The lightness of my daughter's laughter and the sheer look of bliss on her face as Jack gurgled were a wonder to behold. What I wouldn't have given to be able to step inside that frame and hold them right now. What I wouldn't have given to be able to tell them to their faces how much they were loved and adored.

* * *

In retrospect it was a wonder how we ever thought this arrangement would work in practice. My nightly calls to the kids, which were supposed to be the highlight of my day, turned out to be the complete opposite. My calls would leave Jack so distraught that after a week Penny asked me to stop calling to allow both him and Rosie to settle in.

As much as I had found these conversations with the kids emotionally draining and as much as I could see exactly what Penny was getting at, I still found it impossible not to be angered by her suggestion. Was she trying to push me out of their lives altogether? Wasn't it enough that I was hundreds of miles away from them?

'You want me not to talk to the kids because I remind them of home? If the tables were turned what would you say to that?'

'I'd tell you that they were my kids,' said Penny, emotion working its way into her voice,

'I'd tell you that the only thing keeping me going was the thought of speaking to them at night and catching up with their lives. I'd tell you that I'd already made enough sacrifices to last a lifetime and that this was one sacrifice too far. But then again if the tables really were turned and it was you who had to console the kids every time they spoke to me on the phone then I'm pretty sure you'd be asking me to do the same. This is a horrible situation for all of us, Joe. There aren't any winners here, not a single one.'

And that was how we left it. But then a week into the new regime while I was in Hamleys on Regent Street with Stewart looking for presents for the kids to celebrate my first visit to them at the weekend Penny called me and the moment I heard her voice I knew that something was wrong.

'It's the kids,' she said. 'They've gone.'

'What do you mean gone? Gone where?'

Penny was choking back her tears so hard she could barely breathe. 'I think they've run away.'

My stomach turned over in panic. This was my worst nightmare.

'Just tell me what happened,' I said, trying to remain calm.

'I went to pick them up as usual from school,' began Penny, 'and they weren't there so I went to the school office and they said that they hadn't been expecting them as they had a note from me on file saying they would be absent. They even showed it to me. Rosie must have typed it on the computer and signed it herself. I've tried calling Rosie's mobile but it just goes straight to voicemail. I rushed home to see if they were there and that's when I found the note. It was on her bed, waiting for me. She says that she and Jack have gone home — that has to mean they're on their way to London doesn't it? She's taken her birthday money from the jar above her bed and Jack's money's gone too. I'm out of my mind with worry. Please, please, tell me that they've at least tried to contact you.'

'I haven't spoken to them since you asked me not to last week,' I replied, raking over the last conversation I'd had with them, searching for clues. 'What have the police said?'

'I haven't rung them yet. I just wanted to check that they weren't with you first.' She started to cry. 'This is all my fault,' she sobbed. 'If anything happens to them I'll never forgive myself.'

'Listen, this is no time for blame. We're going to find them and they're going to be all right, but what you need to do right now is end this call and speak to the police. Don't let them fob you off, Penny. Tell them they need to find our kids and when you've done that call me back and let me know what they've said.'

I shoved my phone in my pocket and started dodging through the crowds in an effort to get back to Stewart. I felt sick. My kids were either in or on their way to London without anyone to look after them. I couldn't bear to think what might happen to them if they got lost or took a wrong turning let alone if they met the wrong people on their way. Why had I ever agreed to let them go so far away? Why had I ever thought it might be a good idea? If this was anyone's fault it was mine. None of this would have happened if it hadn't been for me. None of this would have happened if I hadn't been so self-centred. I had to find them, I had to know that they were all right, and when I got them back I'd never let them go again.

The speed of my approach made Stewart look up.

'Everything OK, mate?'

'It's my kids,' I said quickly. 'Penny went to collect them from school and they weren't there. She thinks they've run away to London. She's talking to the police about them right now.'

'And you think they're heading to your place?'

'Either there or the family house, I can't think of anywhere else they'd go.'

'Do you know when they went? Morning? Afternoon?'

'We've got no idea. Could've been first thing this morning or it could've been later. We just don't know.' I felt myself beginning to shake. This was too terrible for words. 'I just want them to be safe.'

Stewart rested a hand on my shoulder. 'I'll call Van and Paul and get them out looking straight away,' he said. 'We'll start with train and coach stations with links to Harrogate. As soon as you can, text me a picture of the kids and I'll forward it to the guys so they can get it up on all the social networks while you're heading over to your place. Wherever they are we're going to find them, mate, I promise you.'

34

It was after five as I reached the house having spoken to the police several times on the phone. There was no news of the children yet. The police were checking CCTV footage at Harrogate station and also King's Cross. I wondered how two children could travel to London alone without anyone noticing them. Just thinking about all the people who must have seen them and not thought to question where their parents were made me angry beyond words. What hope could there be for the world when people stopped caring about children?

The house was shrouded in darkness. The Canadian couple and their two kids who were renting the house were due to move in at the weekend. They were both teachers who had moved to the capital for work. The husband had told me that he was a particularly keen gardener and it had been our outdoor space which had attracted them to the house. I'd told him that the garden had been the reason we'd bought the house but that we had lacked the green fingers necessary to make plants grow. 'Our only success story was the rhubarb,' I'd joked as I'd shown him around. 'It comes up year after year without fail, which would be great apart from the fact that we all hate the stuff.'

As I searched for my keys I tried Rosie's phone again. Straight to voicemail. Her giggling

337

message in a faux American accent: 'Can't talk right now. Leave a message after the beep!' In her absence the lightness of her voice stung me every time and yet I couldn't not listen to it all the way through. This was how my baby was meant to sound — joyful and carefree — and I wanted her to always be like this.

I unlocked the front door. The house was silent. I checked all the rooms from top to bottom, my heavy footsteps echoing against the floorboards in the empty rooms. There was no sign of the children; there was no sign of anything at all. This used to be the house where my family lived but now it was an empty shell waiting for another set of people to bring it back to life.

★ ★ ★

I called Penny as I returned to the car. She'd be on the motorway now. At least that was the plan. She was going to come down to London while Scott remained at the house in Harrogate in case the kids went back. As angry as I was at myself, it was hard for me not to be angry with Penny — after all she was supposed to be in charge of them — but it was an impotent anger that had no bite or edge to it, born purely out of frustration. If anyone loved the kids more than me it was Penny and I'd get no pleasure at all from making the one person who understood what I was going through feel bad about something they were powerless to correct.

'It's me. I'm at the house. No news.'

'Well then they must be at your place,' snapped Penny. 'Why didn't you go there first? They've got to have gone to see you. They must have.'

'It's next on my list. I'll be there in a matter of minutes. I just . . . don't know . . . I had a feeling, that's all. In the note they said they were going home, and my place is a lot of things but I don't think they'd ever think of it as home.'

'I'm sorry. I shouldn't have jumped down your throat like that. You're only doing your best. Please hurry and call me when you hear anything.'

★ ★ ★

I checked every room at my place twice, but nothing. The only change to have occurred during the twelve hours I'd been out was the arrival of half a dozen takeaway leaflets and a bill from Thames Water. I called Penny to let her know but I almost wished I hadn't. She'd pinned all her hopes on them being safe at mine. Now the only image in her head was of them lost and alone in the big city.

'What about Carly's?' I suggested, thinking about Rosie's best friend. 'Maybe there's a chance that Rosie told her what she was doing?'

'I tried her after I spoke to the police,' said Penny, 'but she wasn't answering her phone. I've left messages but I haven't heard anything since.'

'Well, I'll go round to her house. Maybe Rosie told her what her plan was. You never know. It's got to be worth a shot.'

'And what if the kids have only just got to London and are on their way to yours now?'

'I guarantee you, Penny, if the kids are only just reaching London the police will pick them up straight away. They've been on the news here. And if they're on their way to mine I'll make sure the neighbours keep a lookout for them. But I have to try Carly.'

★   ★   ★

Carly looked like she was about to burst into tears at any moment as she stood next to her mum in the hallway of their house. 'I don't know where she is, Mr Clarke, honestly. You've got to believe me. I wouldn't lie to you about something like this.'

'I know you wouldn't,' I said. 'We just need to find her and Jack as soon as possible and anything you can tell me that might help would be really useful.'

'But I've told the police everything I know.'

'Well they haven't told me, so it would be great if you could tell me what you told them. Maybe it'll trigger something. When was the last time you spoke to Rosie? What did you talk about?'

'The usual. School. Homework. What people had been saying. Things that had been on telly. Oh . . . and we talked about you.'

'Me?'

'She was saying that she wouldn't have had to move away if it hadn't been for you and Mrs Clarke splitting up. She said that she didn't know what it was that you did but she was sure that it was your fault. I told her that parents get divorced all the time without it being anyone's fault but she wouldn't listen.'

Rosie knew. She knew that I was to blame for everything. Was that why she had wanted to come to London? To confront me about breaking up our family?

'And that's all she said?'

'About you?'

'About anything.'

'The last thing I heard from her was a text that I got on the way to school. All it said was that she missed me loads and she'd see me soon. I thought she was talking about coming to see me during half term. I never thought that she was going to come down to London on her own.'

'I know you didn't,' I replied. 'But will you promise me something? Will you promise to call me — whether it's day or night — if you even so much as get a missed call from her?'

'I will, Mr Clarke. I'll call you right away.'

★   ★   ★

My phone rang as I reached my house. It was Penny. I hoped she had good news.

'The police have just called,' she said. 'They have CCTV images of Rosie and Jack taken at nine twenty a.m. at Harrogate station and getting off at King's Cross just after twelve thirty.' It was a small relief, but a relief none the less. They were definitely in London. How many times had I taken Rosie on the tube over the years? Was it too much to hope that she'd know how to get

341

from King's Cross to Lewisham on the underground and by the DLR?

'How did you get on with Carly?' asked Penny. 'Did you manage to get hold of her?'

'The police had already interviewed her. Apparently the last thing she heard from Rosie was a text saying that she'd see her soon. Carly thought she was talking about the holidays.' I thought about telling Penny what Rosie had said about me but decided against it. This was neither the time nor the place.

'Where are you now?'

'Back at my place trying to work out where to try next.' My phone buzzed. I had another call coming through. It was Van. 'I'd better go, another call. Call me when you reach London.' I switched calls. 'Any news?'

'None yet,' said Van. 'Paul's made up some flyers and brought them over to me here at King's Cross and is on his way to Victoria coach station now.'

'Tell him not to bother,' I replied. 'I've just had word that they definitely came in at King's Cross so concentrate your efforts there if you can.'

'Will do,' said Van. There was a pause and then he added, 'Listen mate, I don't care how long it takes, I'm not going home till we find them. How you holding up?'

'I'm fine, honest. I just — ' I swallowed hard. 'I don't know where to look next. Part of me thinks I should wait here in case they turn up and then another part thinks I should carry on looking.'

'You should trust your gut,' said Van. 'No one knows your kids better than you do. Whatever you do will be the right thing.'

I ended the call and stared at my phone. Van was right. No one did know our kids better than Penny and I so where could they be? I'd already tried all the obvious places and yet they weren't at my house, their grandparents', Carly's or the family home. How could it be that they'd just disappeared? I had to have missed something. Rosie would know that Penny would be worried sick about her, that's why she'd left the note on her bed, so why would she have written that she was going home and then not gone there? There had to be an explanation. She'd run away because she wanted to be home and with Jack with her it would have to be somewhere she'd think was safe, somewhere she'd be sure they'd both feel secure. I felt a tiny click in my head as thoughts slotted together. There could only be one place that she could be. I was sure of it. I couldn't waste another second. I ran into the hallway, flung open the front door and without bothering to close it behind me started running like my very life depended on it.

* * *

How old had Rosie been when Penny and I had first discovered her favourite hiding place? Four? Five at the most, I was sure. Jack was just a baby then, and had been down for his afternoon nap when Rosie had requested that we play hide-and-seek with her. She would take the first

343

turn to hide — she had been insistent about that — and then after the count of ten Penny and I would try to find her. I'd been so certain that we would find her instantly I'd insisted that Penny give her an extra ten seconds before we yelled at the top of our voices, 'Coming! Ready or not!' I had gone straight to the living room, checking behind the sofa and chairs, underneath the coffee table and behind boxes of toys before yelling up to Penny, 'She's not downstairs!' and joining her in a search of the bedrooms. After ten minutes of looking absolutely everywhere — underneath beds, inside wardrobes, and behind every piece of furniture we owned — it was as though she had vanished. That was when the panic set in. She did understand the rules of hide-and-seek didn't she? She did know it was an indoor game not an outdoor one? In a panic I'd ran to the back door but it was locked as were the French doors in the living room. Penny called from the front of the house. The latch was still on the front door and she would have had to climb on something to reach it anyway. We began calling out to her. Rosie, where are you? Rosie, we give up. You've won, the game's over. But there was nothing. Penny began to panic, what if something had happened to her? What if she was lying unconscious somewhere? It was a mother's duty to always fear the worst and Penny was no different. I reassured her that Rosie was fine, and I was sure that she was, I could feel it in my gut. 'She's just found the best hiding place there is and she doesn't want to give it up without giving us a run for our money.'

We continued calling out her name, Penny's cries becoming increasingly frantic. We returned to each of the rooms we'd already checked. Sofas and bookcases were pulled away from walls, tables were upturned, and the clothes basket emptied on to the floor. No idea of where she might be was deemed too ridiculous to rule out and we searched everywhere so long as it ticked another potential hiding place off the list.

'We need to think like a five-year-old,' I'd said as we stood in the hallway, Penny close to tears. 'Where would a five-year-old think is the best hiding place?'

'Somewhere dark maybe, where they couldn't be seen or heard.'

'Like a wardrobe,' I mused. 'As a kid my brother and I used to hide in ours all the time.'

'But we've checked — ' Penny suddenly rushed up the stairs with me chasing after her. We came to a halt outside our bedroom and without any hesitation Penny went to the airing cupboard and flung open the door. Rosie was inside the cupboard, sitting on top of a pile of blankets, surrounded by cushions from her room reading one of her comics by the light of her pink princess torch.

'This is my favourite hiding place,' she'd said proudly. 'I knew you'd never find me here.'

Penny had swept her up into her arms while I inspected the cupboard, which had clearly been commandeered for her own personal use some time ago. There were books, spare batteries for her torch, a tub of raisins, her pencil case and a colouring book too. It was like a home from home.

'This is the best place in the whole house,' Rosie had explained, completely oblivious to the terror she had caused. 'I like it because it's dark and cosy like a mole's house.'

★ ★ ★

Entering the family home once more I called up the stairs but there was no reply. Had I got it wrong? Surely they would have said something by now if they had been here? I didn't dare breathe as I took the stairs two at a time. I didn't know what I was going to do if I was wrong about this. Every last shred of hope I had was pinned on them being behind the door to the airing cupboard. I turned on the light. The house was as silent and still as it had been on my last visit but as I opened the airing cupboard door and peered inside there they were, huddled together underneath their outdoor coats. In front of them was a half-eaten loaf of bread, two packets of custard creams and a two-litre bottle of lemonade. They both looked petrified as if they were about to be on the receiving end of the mother of all admonishments but telling them off was the furthest thing from my mind. All I wanted to do right now was hold them both in my arms and never let them go.

I lifted them out of the cupboard and set them down on the bare floorboards. They looked exhausted but it was nothing a decent meal and good night's sleep wouldn't sort out. I hugged them tightly and Rosie, who already looked tearful, started to sob, which set Jack off too.

'Everything's fine, now, you're both safe,' I whispered. 'There's nothing to worry about now that Dad's here.'

There was so much to do now that I had found them, so many people to call. I thought about the police scouring the area around King's Cross, my mum and Penny's mum and stepdad waiting anxiously by the phone, and the Divorced Dads' Club handing out homemade leaflets in the dark to passing Londoners. They all needed to be contacted, but as deserving as they all were, none was more so than Penny. I had to call her, and put her out of her misery.

She answered after the first ring.

'It's me,' I said. 'I've found them. They're with me and they're safe.'

35

It was late and the kids were safely tucked up in bed and the Divorced Dads' Club and I were all sitting in the living room enjoying a celebratory beer — the least I could offer them given how much they'd done for me. Van took a sip from his bottle and looked at me. 'So have you found out why they ran away?'

'They haven't been explicit but it's easy enough to read between the lines. I think they missed their home and friends and life here and thought sneaking away would be the easiest way to get it back.'

Stewart laughed. 'I bet now they wish they'd just called you on the phone instead of deciding to pay you a visit!'

'I think we all wish that,' said Paul. 'I've never seen so many dodgy things in my life as I did handing out flyers around King's Cross after dark. It's a different world out there.'

'Talking of which,' I replied, setting down my bottle on the coffee table. 'I know you're going to say it's nothing but, genuinely, hand on heart I can't begin to tell you guys what it's meant to have you help me out like this. It's been — ' I stopped, unable to continue as I found myself getting choked up.

'You don't need to say a word, mate,' said Van. 'You would have done the same for any of us. That's what we're about. That's what we've always been about.'

Overwhelmed with gratitude I was about to thank them all once more when the doorbell rang. Closing the door on the chatter in the living room I made my way along the hallway and opened the front door to find Penny standing on the doorstep. She looked small, fragile and completely exhausted and the sight of her stirred a deep desire within me to protect her for all time. From this day forward I'd never let anything bad happen to her. From this moment on my only wish would be to make her happy. Without saying a word she dropped the bag in her hands and threw her arms around me.

'They're OK, they're OK,' I said, stroking her hair as she sobbed with relief. 'Everything's fine now. We're all home.'

★　★　★

Penny stayed upstairs with the kids for so long that the mug of tea and plate of toast I'd made for her had gone cold. I began to wonder whether she had fallen asleep on the bed next to the kids but just as the guys were beginning to talk about heading back to their own homes and relieving the friends, neighbours and family that were looking after their kids, Penny came into the room.

'They're both fast asleep. Sorry I've been so long. I'm not disturbing anything am I?'

From the look on her face it was easy to tell that she didn't quite know what to make of the motley collection of men standing in her ex-husband's living room. Obviously she knew Van already but the badly dressed tubby chap and the guy who looked like an off-duty geography teacher were clearly new to her. I made the introductions. 'You've met Van before and well, this is Stewart and this is Paul and they've been amazing, Pen. They printed up flyers and spent the whole evening handing them out to people around King's Cross. They're an incredible bunch of guys. That's the only way to describe them.'

Penny opened her mouth to speak but, overwhelmed with emotion, tears started rolling down her cheeks. I went over and put my arms around her. Drying her eyes with the back of her hands she said, 'I can't begin to thank you all for everything you've done. Joe's so lucky to have friends like you.'

Van laughed and the moment I looked over at him I knew exactly what he was going to say. 'Truth is,' he said with a grin, 'I don't think Joey was all that keen on us to begin with but we kind of grew on him, you know, like athlete's foot or a verruca. I doubt that he could have gotten rid of us even if he'd wanted to.'

★ ★ ★

After one final toast to happy endings, the guys gathered their things together and said their goodbyes to Penny.

'It was great to meet you again,' said Van. 'And remember any time you and your friends fancy a night of top-flight entertainment courtesy of London's premier Van Halen tribute act, just say the word and I'll pop you on the list.'

'Thanks,' she said, and kissed him on the cheek. 'And that goes for all of you.' Penny planted a kiss on Paul and Stewart in turn. 'You really have been amazing today. You'll have to let me cook a meal for you all sometime soon so I can say a proper thank-you.'

★   ★   ★

As the guys put on their coats out in the hallway I took my turn to say a final thank-you. 'Listen,' I began, 'I don't know what I did to deserve a bunch of mates like you but whatever it is I'm glad that I did it. Once we're all settled we should have a proper blow-out, pub, curry, and then maybe back to the pub again, my treat.'

Van laughed. 'You do know that I can drink quite a lot in a single sitting, don't you?' He patted my back and everyone laughed. 'Joey, we'll be happy just to get our regular night at the Red Lion back up and running. Don't worry about anything else mate, we're as low-maintenance as they come. Just concentrate on looking after that family of yours. Right now they're all that matters.'

Van's words were still ringing in my ears as I returned to the living room in search of Penny. The room was empty and as I walked into the hallway wondering if she had gone upstairs I spotted her in the kitchen just coming in through the back door.

She looked up as I came in. 'Just emptying your bin.'

351

'You needn't have done that. I was going to tackle it in the morning.'

Penny smiled. 'I wanted to do something.'

'You must be starving. What do you fancy to eat? I did a quick shop earlier. I could do you beans on toast if you like or rustle you up some pasta.'

'Toast will be fine.'

I dropped a couple of slices of bread into the toaster and filled the kettle. 'Coffee or tea?'

'Tea, thanks.'

I got out a mug from the cupboard and deposited a tea bag into it. In the background the kettle roared as it boiled. The silence between us was awkward; I could practically feel the nervous energy crackling in the air.

Was this it? I wondered. Was this how we were going to get back together? Our kids run away and travel over two hundred miles to reach their former home and we as parents realise the error of our ways and kiss and make up, right here in the kitchen?

I was hoping that there would be a look on her face, a glint in her eye, a slight smile, even a raise of the eyebrow that would somehow signal I wasn't alone in seeing hope in our current situation, but Penny's face was neutral, her eyes tired, there was nothing at all about her that even hinted we were thinking along the same lines.

Seeing me staring she suddenly became self-conscious. 'What's wrong?'

'Nothing.'

'Are you sure?'

I nodded. 'I was a million miles away, that's all.'

'You must be shattered. You should get to bed.'

'I'm fine.'

The toast popped and the kettle boiled. I buttered her toast, made her tea, and followed her into the living room.

* * *

'It's the first time I've actually been in this room,' said Penny, clutching her mug to her chest as she looked around. 'It reminds me a lot of that place we lived in during our final year at uni, do you remember? Sixty-five Blakeland?'

'The party house! I knew there was a reason I liked this place. We had some good times there. Remember that summer party we threw where the police turned up because of the noise and your friend Harriet got all shirty with them and ended up getting nicked?'

'How could I forget? She missed a really important exam because of it and was inconsolable for days.' Penny laughed. 'Still, they were good times, weren't they?'

I nodded, wishing, not for the first time, that it was in my power to transport us back to the past before life became so messy. 'The best, the absolute best.'

Penny finished off her tea and toast and then took her empty plate and our empty mugs to the kitchen, washing up everything in spite of my protests. Once she was done she dried her hands on her jeans and made her way to the hallway.

'I should probably be getting off,' she said,

putting on her coat. She kissed me on the cheek. 'Thanks for everything today. You've been . . . well, you know how you've been. Tell the kids I'll be over first thing in the morning.'

'I don't understand. Where are you going? To your Mum and Tony's? That makes no sense at all. You should stay here. You can sleep in Jack's room. I'll be fine on the sofa. Given everything that's happened I know they'll be a lot happier if you're here in the morning. Anyway, you must be exhausted. The last thing you need to do is make another journey.'

I could see that she was wavering. 'Are you sure? I'd hate to be kicking you out of your own bed after a day like today.'

'You'd be doing me a favour,' I replied. 'If you're in with Jack that means he'll wake you up rather than me.'

Penny smiled, went out to her car and returned with a small overnight bag. She took the bag upstairs and I heard her on the phone to her mum. She then disappeared into the bathroom and I could hear her brushing her teeth. While she was in there I imagined her texting Scott, telling him the kids were safe and that she would talk to him in the morning. I wondered too if she'd tell him where she would be sleeping tonight.

As she emerged from the bathroom I handed her fresh towels. 'For the morning,' I explained, 'in case you, you know . . . want a shower.'

Penny smiled, amused by my attempt at being a good host. 'It's almost like staying at a posh B&B,' she said, taking them from my hands.

'Well then, goodnight, sleep tight and let's hope that tomorrow is a much less eventful day.'

I wanted to say more. To ask her what all of this meant. To ask her what tomorrow would bring but instead I just wished her sweet dreams and started to go back downstairs. I was halfway down however when I heard her call my name.

'Joe? I know you must have questions about us, about the future, and I want to say thank you for not bringing them up right now. I just don't know where my head is at the minute. Nothing makes sense any more and I don't feel like I know what to do for the best about anything. But I promise you, we will talk, just not tonight.'

She walked down a few steps until we were almost level and then, closing her eyes, she kissed me once, tenderly, on the lips. The moment felt like it was over before it had even begun but, regardless, the hope that I now felt was as real and tangible as the floor beneath my feet. Overwhelmed with emotion, I whispered a barely audible, 'I love you,' and then watched as she went back upstairs without responding.

Returning to the living room I made up a bed on the sofa and as I lay there listening to the far-off siren of a passing emergency vehicle I thought about Penny upstairs and wished I was lying next to her. But it didn't matter; I had something I hadn't had in a long time: hope.

36

I was making scrambled eggs.

'Just pass me that wooden spoon will you, Jack?'

Jack handed me the spoon and continued helping Rosie with the buttering of four slices of bread on four separate plates.

'All done,' said Jack, brandishing a butter-laden knife in the air. 'I'm hungry. Can we eat now?'

The kids had been up for several hours watching TV with me in the living room and while I'd let them have a bowl of cereal each it had been my hope that we would all sit down to eat breakfast together. I looked up towards the kitchen doorway hoping that a sleepy-eyed Penny might appear but she didn't; and having checked on her just five minutes earlier and found her sleeping so soundly I hadn't the heart to rouse her.

I checked the pan. My scrambled eggs looked perfect.

'OK, we can eat,' I told them. 'I'll make sure that Mum gets a fresh batch the moment she wakes up.'

★　★　★

The kids and I ate breakfast on our laps in front of the TV. It was some new-fangled version of

Scooby Doo Jack found so captivating that several times I had to threaten to turn it off so that he would finish the breakfast he'd been begging for since seven o'clock that morning. But it was so good to have them with me, to be able to do something as simple as make them breakfast, and it was only now as they chatted next to me that I realised just how much I'd had to harden my heart in order to survive being away from them for so long. Now there was no hardness left in me and there never would be again. I was vulnerable, without protection, but, terrifying though this was, I actually preferred it. At least I was no longer numb to my emotions.

Once breakfast was over the kids and I cuddled up underneath my duvet and continued watching TV but after half an hour or so they began to get restless.

Rosie turned to me. 'Dad, what are we doing today?'

It was a good question but sadly one to which I didn't have an answer. All I wanted was for Penny and the kids to stay and never leave; surely that wasn't too much to ask for after all we'd been through? Yes, there was the Scott problem, and the school problem, and more likely than not a million different other dilemmas that would demand our attention, but at least the main issue of whether or not we should be together had been decided. What was it that Penny had said? 'We will talk, just not now, not yet.' That had to mean her plans had changed. Surely that had to mean she wanted us all to be together.

Both the kids were staring at me waiting for an answer to Rosie's question.

'I don't know.'

Rosie pulled a face. 'How can you not know what we're doing? That makes no sense.'

Jack stretched his hand up in the air, desperate to join the conversation. 'I'd like to go to the park. There are parks in Harrogate but I don't like them as much as our one here. Dad, can we go to our park?'

Rosie chimed in, warming to the theme. 'And after we've been to the park can we have lunch at Pizza Hut? We haven't been there for ages.'

Jack nodded enthusiastically. 'Yes, I'd like to go to Pizza Hut too. I'd also like to see my old school friends because I lent Jake Flanagan two of my best pencils in class and he never gave them back to me and I'd really like them back because the red one was my favourite one and — '

I felt momentarily overwhelmed. If it were up to me I'd give them all these things and more. 'Guys, guys, you need to calm down. We can't make any plans yet, not until Mum's up.'

Rosie wasn't at all satisfied with this answer. 'But don't you want us to stay?'

'Of course I do but it's not that simple.'

'Well it should be,' said Rosie.

I switched TV channels as a means of distraction and as the kids settled down to a new programme Penny came into the room. She'd had a shower but with the absence of a hairdryer had tied her wet hair up in a ponytail. Her face looked somehow different from the night before

358

in a way I couldn't quite put my finger on.

'Mummy, you missed breakfast,' said Jack without lifting his eyes from the TV. 'Dad made his special scrambled eggs. He said he'd make you some too.'

Penny shook her head. 'As appetising as that sounds I think I'll stick to coffee if there's any around?'

'It's pretty much the only thing I am guaranteed to have in,' I replied. 'Why don't you sit down with the kids and I'll sort you out a cup?'

'Actually,' said Penny, 'I'd better not get too comfortable. We've got a long journey ahead of us and the kids really need to get ready if we're not going to spend all day in traffic.'

Rosie stood up, hands on hips, eyes defiant. 'Are you saying we're going back to Harrogate right now?'

Penny took no notice of the outrage in her voice.

Rosie began to get upset. 'But Jack and I don't want to live there. That's why we ran away — we want to be here where we belong with Dad and our friends.'

Penny was unmoved. 'That's just not possible right now. But don't forget, sweetheart, you'll be back for the holidays and you can catch up with all of your friends then.'

Wide-eyed, Rosie turned to me as the voice of reason. 'Dad? Aren't you going to say anything? Tell Mum we need to be here.'

I looked over at Penny, silently begging her to change her mind, but there was no response to my plea. Penny's decision was made. Whatever the change of direction that had been incubating in her heart it had died overnight. I wanted to challenge her, to make the case to stay, but to have done so in front of the kids would have made Penny the enemy here, and while she was undoubtedly many things this was one role she most definitely wasn't carved out for. I on the other hand had proved it was a part that suited me just fine.

'Mum's right, the sooner you get back into the swing of things in Harrogate, the better. You need to get settled there, sweetheart. It's your home now.'

Rosie sobbed. 'You don't want us here! That's why we have to go. I wish we'd never run away. I wish we'd just stayed where we were.'

She ran from the room and headed upstairs. I went to go after her but Penny stopped me. 'Just give her a bit of time. She'll be fine. I promise.'

'Will she?' I said sharply. I glanced over at Jack. 'Son, as your sister's packing it's probably a good idea if you start too. Just gather your stuff together and wait upstairs while I chat to Mum.'

Jack nodded solemnly and left the room head down, shoulders slumped. This was the most mournful of his repertoire of sad walks, reserved solely for the worst of times.

I waited until Jack had closed the door behind him before I spoke. 'I don't understand. Why are you being like this?'

'Like what?'

'Do you really want me to spell it out for you? Last night you were on the verge of staying here for good. I know you didn't say that exactly but I could feel it and I know you felt it too. This is it Penny, we're supposed to get back together and I know it's complicated, and I know that there are still problems to overcome, but there are two things I have no doubt about: the kids don't want to live in Harrogate and neither do you. You might not think you do, but you still love me, Penny, and your running back to Scott isn't about you loving him, it's about the guilt you feel because he's done so much for you. It's about feeling like you ought to do the right thing instead of the thing you really want.' I reached out and held her hand. 'I'm begging you, don't go, stay here with me and let's work this whole thing out.'

Penny snatched her hand away. 'I can't. I just can't.'

A knock at the door prevented the conversation from going any further.

'Jack's crying because he can't find one of his action figures,' said Rosie.

Penny moved towards the door. 'Are you packed?'

Rosie nodded. 'Do we really have to go, Mum?'

Penny picked up her bag. 'Yes we do. Say goodbye to Dad and I'll meet you in the car.'

It was impossible for me to say any more to Penny with the kids around and between Jack sobbing over his missing action figure and Rosie's tears over not wanting to return to Harrogate I wasn't sure that I'd be heard anyway. As it was, Penny had clearly made her decision. She had committed to Scott and a life away from me, away from London, and there was nothing I could say or do to change her mind.

Penny sat in the car with the engine running while I said my goodbyes to the kids. I promised them that I would be up to see them the weekend after next and I asked them to call me the moment they reached Harrogate. Clutching on to the Ultraman action figure I'd bought him all that time ago for comfort, Jack assured me that he wouldn't smile again until the next time he saw me. This hit me so hard that I had to look away before I could hug him and tell him that I needed him to smile every day otherwise I'd be sad too. Rosie meanwhile was sobbing too much to say anything at all. Even when she hugged me and I whispered in her ear that I loved her, she looked up at me with red and swollen eyes to reply but the only sound to come out of her was the anguished sob of a broken heart.

At the door Jack turned and ran back to me. 'Daddy, I want you to keep this,' he said, thrusting Ultraman into my hands. 'I want you to keep him so that you'll never forget me.'

He was gone before I could even form a reply and so at the front door I stood rooted to the spot watching Penny's car pull away, all the while clutching his favourite toy to my heart. I was still there long after they had gone and it was only when I heard my neighbours coming out of their house that I finally went back inside, closing the door behind me. For a moment I stood in the hall-way, not quite knowing what to do next, the house that had been so noisy and alive just

362

moments before now reverberating with silence. It was empty and so was I and in that same instant I dropped Jack's action figure and I fell to my knees as wave after wave of searing pain crashed over me. This was it. I was at the end of the road. I just couldn't take any more.

A sudden gust of wind blew across my face followed by the noise of distant traffic in my ears. I opened my eyes fully expecting to see the front door that I thought I'd closed now open but there was no door and even more oddly there was no house: I was somewhere else entirely.

37

I recognised my new location immediately: the top level of Lewisham Shopping Centre's multi-storey car park. The view across Hilly Fields Park and beyond was one I knew well from the times I'd reluctantly parked here when the shopping centre was reaching maximum capacity. This level was the last resort of the casual Saturday shopper, the place you only came to when there was nowhere else to go and here I was without a clue about how I'd got there.

'So they're gone, are they?'

A strong waft of Poison filled the air. Fiona was behind me, sitting on the bonnet of a silver VW Golf less than six feet away. This time, unlike every other, she was dressed — from her cardigan and blouse down to her jeans and shoes — entirely in black, and at her feet was a black cabin-sized pull-along suitcase. Everything about her changed appearance unnerved me greatly. Something was going on and I had a strong feeling that I wasn't going to like it.

'What am I doing here?'

'You didn't answer my question,' she said firmly. 'I asked about your family. Are they gone?'

Straight away I was close to tears as I pictured Jack and Rosie in the back of Penny's car driving away from me. They were my world. I was never going to get used to being away from them.

I looked at Fiona, who was casually brushing lint from her jeans. 'Yes, yes, they're gone.'

'And there was me thinking that this was going to be your happy ending. You must be heart-broken.'

Fiona's manner was different from how it had been the last time I'd seen her on the night of my date with Bella. Then she'd seemed almost maternal towards me, but everything about her now seemed harder, meaner, more spiteful, as though she had made up her mind that she'd got a mission to complete and was going to take a great deal of pleasure in seeing it finished. This new incarnation unsettled me deeply, and the last thing I wanted to do was antagonise her, but I needed some answers.

'Fiona, please, tell me what I'm doing here.'

'Penny doesn't love you, Joe.'

I wasn't going to let myself get sidetracked.

'Come on, Fiona, just tell me what I'm doing here!'

'To be honest, Joe, I'm not sure that she ever did.'

I still wasn't going to take the bait.

'Look, I get that you're in control but please tell me why I'm here.'

'And now another man's going to be raising your kids. How long before they start calling him Dad?'

I couldn't help myself. 'That's never going to happen!'

Fiona grinned, thoroughly pleased to have provoked me into a reaction. 'Says the man who claimed he'd never let his kids move away.'

'I didn't have a choice!'

'Joey, Joe, Joe, there's always a choice. I thought you would have learned that by now. Makes no odds though, sending the kids away was the first smart thing I've seen you do. You know as well as I do that they'll be better off without you.'

'That's not true.' Even I was surprised by the lack of conviction in my voice. 'It isn't.'

'Oh, but it is! You're a loser Joe, an absolute loser. You couldn't make a go of being a decent writer, no one respects you at work, your wife is getting more satisfaction from her lover than you ever gave her, and your kids, Joe, your kids! I'm guessing they pretty much hate you right now sending them away like that. Come on lover boy, admit it, you've given this life game a fair old crack of the whip, isn't it time you just called it quits?'

'What do you mean?'

'Oh, come on Dumbo, don't try and tell me the thought has never crossed your mind. Your life is a mess and it's *never* going to get better. No one would think you were weak if you packed it all in. In fact I think people might say it's the first thing with actual balls that you've ever done.'

'You want me to kill myself?'

'This isn't about my wants, Joe, this is about your needs.' Sliding off the car bonnet she sauntered over to the red metal barriers surrounding the car park and looked over the edge. She turned back to me briefly and beckoned me over. 'Come and take a look. There's nothing wrong with a bit of looking is there? We're just 'trying the idea on for size'.'

I didn't move.

'Oh, come on, Joe, there's nothing wrong with taking a look.'

I still didn't move.

'I promise you, there's nothing to be scared of.'

She waved me towards her again. 'You never know, if you go through with it, you might get lucky and end up with a job like mine. Think about how much fun that would be! We could be work mates!'

Surreal as this all was I had to laugh at that one but then I remembered what it was she was asking me to do. I took a step backwards.

'Fiona, I don't want to die.'

She raised her eyebrows mockingly. 'Now that *really* does surprise me. You've got absolutely nothing going for you.'

'I've got Penny, I've got the kids, I don't need anything more. They might be miles away from me but even the little I have is better than nothing at all.'

Fiona nodded thoughtfully. 'What if I told you I could get you back to them?'

'What? To Harrogate?'

'No, you idiot, to the real world.'

It had to be a trick. This was after all Fiona I was talking to but even so I couldn't help falling for it just a little bit.

'You can get me back to them?'

'I could . . . but you'd have to trust me.'

Here it was, the catch.

'Trust you how exactly?'

'By jumping off this roof.'

My heart sank. For a moment there I'd actually believed she might be telling me the truth.

'And so you should,' said Fiona, doing that listening-to-my-thoughts thing. 'Because this is as honest as I get: this isn't the real world, Joe. I told you that on the day Penny kicked you out and you just wouldn't believe me. I've even shown you your body, lying exactly where it fell when I whacked you, and you still thought I was making it all up. But it's true, Joe, none of this is real. Your real life and everything in it is waiting for you and all you've got to do to get it back is wake up.'

'And to wake up, all I've got to do is throw myself off a building? Now I really know I'm insane.' I pulled out my phone and dialled 999.

The operator answered immediately. 'Emergency, which service do you require?'

'The police,' I replied. They put me through instantly. 'Hi, my name's Joe Clarke, I'm a journalist working for the *Correspondent* and for the past year or so I've been suffering from severe hallucinations. They've become really intense and right now they're telling me to throw myself off the top of Lewisham Shopping Centre car park. I need help fast. Please, hurry, I don't know how long I can resist.'

I ended the call and stared defiantly at Fiona.

'They'll lock you up, you know.'

'To stop me from harming myself.'

'And then you'll be stuck here for good.'

'In the real world where I made a mess of my life? If that's the only option on offer I'll take it.'

'But that's just it. It isn't the only option. You know this world has never made any sense. You were mugged but had no bruises, you think you slept with Bella but can't remember a thing about it. You can see the ghost of your dead ex-girlfriend but you know in your heart of hearts that ghosts don't really exist. You're not mad, Joe, you're dreaming, and you know as well as I do that all the best dreams end with the hero or heroine falling to what feels like their death. Only it isn't. As they fall, they kick out and wake up safe and warm in their own beds.'

It was hard not to believe her. Crazy though it sounded Fiona actually seemed to be making some sort of sense.

'But even if this is remotely true, if this really could all be over that easily, then why didn't you just say so instead of trying to psycho-bitchface me into topping myself?'

Fiona laughed. 'Oh, come Joe, surely you wouldn't deny a girl a little fun?'

I don't quite know what it was that made me believe her but I did. So much so that without thinking I joined her at the railings and together we peered down at the traffic below: cars, lorries, buses and motorcycles all transporting passengers across a London that if Fiona was to be believed didn't actually exist. Was it all part of an elaborate scenario played out by my own mind? If so I really had to wonder at it. This alternate reality my subconscious had supposedly concocted was so detailed and multilayered as to be

369

utterly convincing. The warmth of the metal barriers under my hands emitting the heat they'd absorbed from the early-morning sun. The cool of the breeze against my skin and the constant hum of the traffic beneath us combined with the anthology of smells in the air, everything from the tang of petrol fumes through to the faint scent of decaying refuse. How was it possible that my mind alone had replicated all of these different sensations so authentically? It was awe-inspiring and disturbing all at once.

My thoughts churned around as I looked down at the streets below but the one thing I kept coming back to was how much I wanted to go home.

Without pausing to think any more I climbed over the barrier to the ledge on the other side. As ledges went it wasn't exactly the widest in the world — the fronts of my shoes were hanging over the edge — but with my hands on the barrier to support myself I was sure I wasn't about to go anywhere by accident.

I looked down, trying to gauge where I would land. It was hard to tell from this height. Quite possibly the pavement but if I leaped rather than stepped there was every chance I'd hit the road.

I took a deep breath and counted down:

Five.

Four.

Three.

A noise from behind me. I turned around to see Fiona pulling up the telescopic handle of her suitcase as though she was getting ready to depart. She stopped and looked up at me.

'What's wrong? Why have you stopped counting? Have you forgotten what comes next?'

My gaze shifted from Fiona to the bag and back again.

'What's that about?'

I pointed to the bag.

Fiona looked down. 'Oh, that, it's a suitcase. Why? What did you think it was?'

'I know it's a suitcase. I want to know why you've got it.'

'Why do people normally have suitcases?'

'Because they're going somewhere.'

Fiona clapped her hands slowly. 'Bravo! Brain of Britain! You're not really that dense, are you?'

'But I don't understand. Where are you going?'

'Why would you care where I'm going? You don't like me.'

'Of course I don't . . . it's just that I need to know this isn't a trick. This is my life we're talking about here.'

'Fine, whatever.' She crossed her right hand across her chest. 'Joe Clarke, I do solemnly swear that I am not pulling your plonker; is that good enough?'

In the distance I could hear police sirens. They were coming for me. If I really was going to go through with this I needed to make it happen soon.

I looked at Fiona's bag again. Maybe that was what I was finding so disconcerting. I felt my grip tighten on the railings.

'Where are you going?'

'Why does it matter? Like I said, I'm off.'

'But where?'

'Anywhere that's not here. I'm not a workaholic you know. I deserve a break just like anyone else.'

'Except that you're dead.'

'Says you.'

'Says everybody who was at your funeral.' I looked her up and down. 'And the clothes? Every time I've seen you, you've been wearing the same clothes, only now you're all dressed in black.'

Fiona laughed. 'If only you'd been this observant when we were together! If you really want to know, Joe, I'll tell you: these are my party clothes. I'm letting my hair down, doing a bit of celebrating. Now get on with it before the coppers arrive.'

Suddenly I wasn't so certain about the version of events that had me poised to leap off the top of Lewisham Shopping Centre's car park. Was this the real world after all? Had I lost it completely and been about to commit suicide? Once again Fiona had got inside my head and was messing with my mind for her own amusement.

I began clambering back over the railing with my heart racing at how close I'd come to going through with my crazy plan.

Fiona cried out. 'What are you doing? Get back out there right now, you're spoiling everything!'

I ignored her and didn't stop until I was safely over the other side.

'I can't believe I nearly did it,' I said, gasping with exertion and adrenalin. 'You were going to let me jump weren't you? And then what would've happened once I'd splatted on the pavement? I don't get any of this. Are you back from the dead or have I just conjured you up? Why *are* you here? Whatever you are surely you've punished me enough? I haven't got anything, you've had the lot: Penny, the kids, every single thing that matters to me.'

Fiona laughed, 'And you think *I* did that? What a short memory you have!'

'And I told you I've learned my lesson! Aren't you supposed to be like Jacob Marley? Shouldn't you be returning me to my bed so that I can wake up on Christmas morning a changed man?'

'You're forgetting one thing,' said Fiona.

'And what's that?'

'I hate you. What were the last words I said to you when I dumped you that weekend in Sheffield? I told you that one day you were going to look back at that moment and regret how you'd treated me.' Fiona stopped to grin. 'Well this is that day, Joe. It's been a long time coming but better late than never, eh? So what's it to be? Are you going to jump or not? Because the police are going to be here in' — she checked her watch — 'precisely ninety-two seconds.'

'You think I won't do it,' I replied, studying her face for signs of the truth. 'That's what this whole thing is about. If I don't do it then I'll be stuck here forever without the only woman I've ever loved, living in some coalhole I can barely afford and only getting to see my kids once every month. You know what? You're really clever.' I shook my head in disbelief as I began climbing back over the barrier again. 'You absolutely had me there with your Goth get-up and your daft bag and your 'I'm not telling you to jump' nonsense. I see it now, Fiona, it's crystal clear: you want me to stay here and rot while my family's back at home waiting for me. Well that's not going to happen.'

I looked over the edge again. All I needed was to take one step out and this would all be over.

'What are you waiting for now?' chided Fiona.

She was right. What was I waiting for? A sign? A miracle? A last-minute reprieve?

Heart racing, I turned to face her once more. 'What if I'm wrong? What if you don't exist? What if this is the real world? What if I jump off this building and the only thing that happens is I fall to the ground and spread myself across a very wide area? What if Penny and the kids really are on their way back to Harrogate? I can't have them thinking that I didn't love them enough to carry on living. If this is the only world there is, then a world where I can still see them and talk to them is better than nothing at all.'

Abandoning her suitcase Fiona strode over to the barrier until she was level with me. 'The thing about you, Joe,' she said as I further tightened my grip on the railing, 'is that you've always been too easily led. I was the worst girlfriend in the world and yet instead of growing a spine you just put up with me. All these years later and you haven't changed. That's how you nearly ended up with Slag Face: she turned on the charm and you were just too stupid and spineless to resist. But you're not that man any more are you? Thanks to me you've grown, you've changed, you're nowhere near as weak as you used to be. You're not the finished article quite yet, but with a little nudge in the right direction, you could be.'

Ignoring the screeching of tyres from the fast-approaching police cars Fiona held out her hand to help me back over the barrier but as I let go of the railing she lunged forward suddenly, shoving me in the chest and sending me flying backwards. Time seemed to slow down as I scrambled frantically in the air hoping through sheer force of will that my flailing arms would miraculously restore my balance, but they didn't and so all I could do was accept my fate as Fiona's final words reached my ears. 'It's been fun,' she called. 'We should do this again sometime.'

38

Had it worked after all?

Was I back in the real world?

Or had it been the real world all this time and had I just made an untimely exit?

Of all the options the only one that made sense was the last one — after all how could I still be alive when only a matter of seconds ago I'd been hurtling towards the pavement adjacent to the A21? I'd obviously lost the plot. That's what the inquest into my death would say. The coroner's report would practically write itself. Recently divorced man suffering from undiagnosed depression caused by breakdown of marriage and lack of contact with son and daughter jumps from the top floor of Lewisham Shopping Centre's car park. No one else involved (let's not forget that I made Fiona up!). Verdict: death by suicide.

If I was lucky I'd get a couple of inches in the local gazette and maybe a short piece in the *Correspondent* telling the world what a great person I was to work with. The kids would be devastated obviously. Penny too. She'd blame herself and everyone would wonder why I hadn't left a note.

As for these thoughts of mine they were easily explained. They felt like the fading glow from an old-style valve amplifier, still warm from the power that had once surged through it but no longer connected to the mains. Maybe I had another minute or two left of consciousness, maybe less, after which along with everything I was and everything I'd ever hoped to be I'd fade permanently into the black night of eternity. That was what this was.

Or at least that was what I thought until I heard the voices.

They were indistinct at first. It was impossible to tell one from another let alone pick out individual words — but then I heard Penny's voice. I could hear it as clearly as though she was whispering in my ear. She was saying: 'Joe, please, Joe, please wake up,' in a voice so desperate and heart-broken that I could only conclude she thought I had gone for good.

It was hard to know what to do with this new information. On the one hand I was glad to have been saved from the pain of the injuries the fall had no doubt inflicted on me but on the other it seemed odder by the moment that I should be conscious at all. While mulling over this new conundrum, slowly, very slowly, the other voices I'd heard behind Penny's became more distinct. Now I could hear them as clearly as if I was in the same room as them. 'Look, his eyes are moving,' one of them said. 'I just saw a flicker,' said another. 'Call a nurse,' urged yet another and gradually I worked out that they were talking about me.

Was I alive?

Had I been given a second chance?

Penny's voice again: 'Joe, please, Joe, come back to me.' How long had I waited to hear those words? How long had I dreamed of the moment when she might feel like this about me again? I had to see her. I had to. With all the strength I could muster I tried to open my eyes but it felt as though they were weighted down with lead. I tried again and this time they opened just a fraction. Light. There was light. But where was I? The light was so blinding it was impossible to tell. I struggled on, eyelids parting a fraction at a time, as all the while my irises — sluggish and lazy after their enforced respite — adjusted and focused to reveal more. Gradually the light became less intense, my vision clearer. I could make out a blurred form, a form which after some moments took on the shape and definition of a face, one whose features steadily arranged themselves into those of the only person I wanted to see: Penny.

'It's you,' I said and I couldn't help but smile. 'You came back to me. I thought you were gone for good.'

'I didn't go anywhere,' she said. 'I've been right here all the time. How do you feel?'

It was a good question. I didn't feel much of anything at all. No pain from the fall. I felt groggy but that was about it.

'You're really here aren't you?' I said, my voice slurring slightly.

'I am,' said Penny. 'Yes, I am. You don't need to worry about me. Do you know where you are?'

I looked around the room. A window. No decoration on the white wall. I wasn't at home.

I looked at Penny and smiled. 'I'm not dead am I?'

'You're in hospital, sweetheart,' she said gently. 'The A&E department of the Royal London Hospital. You were mugged in Cambridge Heath. The doctor thinks you were knocked out by a blow to the back of the head. Do you remember anything at all?'

How best to explain? What could I say? That I remembered being mugged but was actually more concerned about the year that followed it and how she had ended up divorcing me?

'It's all a bit of a blur,' I said eventually. 'How did I get here? Did someone find me?'

'The guys from the shoot,' said Penny. 'They found you and called an ambulance.'

'You mean Van, Paul and Stewart? They're good guys you know. The absolute best. I never would have kept it together if it hadn't been for them.'

'I know,' said Penny. 'They acted really swiftly and called an ambulance straight away.'

This wasn't what I meant at all. The Divorced Dads' Club were my friends, they'd been there for me when I'd needed help most, surely I couldn't have imagined everything we'd been through — the nights out to the pub, their help fixing up my house, the camping holiday to Suffolk. 'I've known them . . . I mean, I feel like I've known them forever, Pen. Are they here?'

Penny gestured out of sight and then Van appeared in my line of vision.

'Van mate, how are you?'

'Er . . . I'm fine thanks. More's the point, dude, how are you?'

'I'm OK.' I pointed to his head. 'And your

379

hair's back. Or is that another one of your wigs?'

'My hair hasn't gone anywhere,' said Van, confused. 'It's always been like this. Are you really OK, mate?'

'Sorry, my mistake,' I replied, feeling like every single one of the circuits inside my head was crossed.

'No worries,' said Van. 'When we found you lying there, we thought you were a goner for sure. Didn't we guys?'

Van turned to look to his left. The sound of footsteps across the linoleum flooring then Paul's face loomed into view followed by Stewart's.

'We're just glad you're all right,' said Paul.

'Definitely,' added Stewart. 'The shoot was such a laugh. I'm just sorry it ended like this.'

'We all got on so well that we decided to grab a beer after the shoot,' continued Van. 'We were on the way to the pub near the studio when we found you.'

I looked over at Penny. 'How long have I been here?'

'About three hours.'

'What time is it now?'

Penny checked her watch. 'Just coming up to midnight.'

'That can't be right,' I said. 'It wasn't even midday when I left mine.'

'Left your what?'

'My house.'

'Don't you mean our house? You live with me and the kids, Joe.'

'But I remember you leaving,' I replied. 'You,

and the kids, you left. I thought you were never going to come back.'

Tears formed in the corners of Penny's eyes but she quickly blinked them away. 'The doctors said this might happen, sweetheart,' said Penny. 'It's just the painkillers, they're making you groggy.' She kissed my cheek and I breathed in the wonderful scent of her. 'You don't have to worry,' she continued. 'Everything's going to be fine.'

I felt momentarily soothed even though very little seemed to be making any kind of sense right now. 'It will won't it?' I replied.

'Of course.'

I started to close my eyes. Being conscious even for such a small amount of time seemed draining, but I reopened them as I thought about the kids.

'What about the kids?'

'They're fine, they're with Mum and Tony. They don't know what's happened yet and I didn't know how to tell them.'

'They don't need to know, do they?' I replied.

Penny shook her head. 'No, they don't.'

'They're good kids, aren't they?'

Penny nodded. 'The best.'

'And we love them, don't we?'

'Yes,' said Penny patiently, 'more than anything.'

I tried to squeeze her hand again. 'And you love me, don't you?'

She nodded again and leaned in closer. 'Yes, I do, babe, I love you with my whole heart.' She kissed my forehead. 'Now, you just close your eyes and rest. Don't worry about a thing.'

I didn't manage to get much in the way of sleep because just as I began to doze off the nurse arrived with a doctor in tow and the room was cleared of all visitors including Penny while various checks were made.

'How are you feeling?' asked the doctor, a plumpish, middle-aged man with a beard. 'You gave your wife quite a scare for a while earlier this evening.'

'I feel OK,' I replied. 'A bit groggy though.'

'That's to be expected. The CAT scans we took earlier came back normal but we like to keep an eye on things when they involve head injuries. How would you say your vision is?'

'Fine,' I replied. 'A bit blurry every now and again, but fine.'

The doctor held up his right hand. 'How many fingers am I holding up?'

I counted them all, twice, just to be on the safe side.

'Three?'

'Good.'

He held out his hand and asked me to squeeze it as hard as I could. I doubt that I could have crushed a grape.

'How was that?' I asked.

'Not brilliant, but I'm sure it'll improve with time. Now I need you to follow my finger with your eyes without moving your head.'

I did as requested as he moved his finger from side to side and then up and down in the air. 'That's excellent,' he said. 'You can rest now. I'm done bothering you for the time being.'

'So does that mean I can go home?'

The doctor smiled. 'No, it means we're not worried about there being any lasting damage. You've had quite a nasty blow, Mr Clarke. If your assailant had hit you any harder we'd be looking at a completely different scenario but as it is, thankfully the worst you'll have in the morning is a very sore head. We've had to put in a few stitches to close the wound which will leave a permanent scar, I'm afraid. As I've already said we've scanned you and while there is a small amount of swelling it's nothing to be too worried about but I think it's sensible that you remain under observation for the night at least. How does that sound?'

It didn't sound great. I just wanted to be with Penny and the kids.

'Are you sure there's no way I can go home?'

'Not tonight I'm afraid but we'll definitely talk tomorrow and if everything's looking shipshape you could be discharged by teatime.' He picked up the chart from the end of my bed. 'In the meantime try and get as must rest as you can.' He walked towards the door.

'Doctor, can I ask you a question?'

'By all means.'

'It's a bit of a weird one . . . I was just wondering, is it normal for people knocked unconscious to suffer from hallucinations?'

'Hallucinations?'

'Or maybe really vivid dreams? I mean *really* vivid, with full-on HD detailing, smells, sensations, the lot.'

The doctor came and stood at the side of the bed.

'Is that what you're having now?'

'No,' I replied hurriedly, not wanting to give him a reason to keep me here any longer. 'It's just, while I was unconscious I . . . I mean, I keep remembering things that happened and they feel real, as real as you and I talking right now.'

'It's actually an incredibly interesting field,' replied the doctor. 'In fact only a few weeks ago I was reading a study by some researchers in Belgium who discovered that patients in a minimally conscious state showed sleep patterns very similar to those of a normal healthy subject and also the non-rapid eye movement of slow wave sleep as well as the rapid eye movement of regular sleep.'

I looked at him blankly.

'It means that while not exactly conclusive there's every chance that those patients were dreaming.'

There was a knock at the door and Penny came in. 'Oh, I'm sorry. The nurse told me you were done. I'll come back later.'

'No, that's fine,' said the doctor. 'Your husband and I were just finishing up. I suppose what I'm saying, Mr Clarke, is that given we're still learning so much about the inner workings of the human brain, anything is possible.'

39

Despite assurances that I'd be allowed home the next day it was in fact three days before the doctor finally gave me permission to leave hospital. During this time I received numerous visits from work colleagues including Camilla and even Carl and his assistant who were mortified that they'd been in the pub getting hammered while I'd been lying unconscious less than two hundred metres away. Grateful as I was for their visits, their presence at my bedside only served to remind me that at some point I would have to go back to work, and while work itself wasn't a problem, the fact that Bella was still interning at the paper was a very big problem indeed.

I'd been doing a great deal of thinking about Bella over the past few days, most of which had left me feeling like I'd had my insides sucked out. If, as the doctor had suggested, it was possible to have dreams so real that a year could happen in the space of a few hours then the only conclusion I could come to was that nothing I thought had happened to me from the moment I was mugged through to the moment Fiona pushed me off the edge of the car-park roof had actually occurred. It was all just a dream, the extended Technicolor vision of a troubled mind, and something that I would find extremely difficult to explain to anyone else. But while this news meant that there was a great deal to be happy about — my marriage being intact and my kids still living at home with me being chief amongst them — it also meant that the last contact I'd had with Bella was when I'd agreed by text to meet her in Soho.

I felt sick at the thought of it. If I hadn't been mugged, there was every chance I would have jumped in a cab and met up with this woman. To what end? At the time I'd managed to convince myself that there was nothing in it. I was simply going for a drink. But in the harsh light of day and several hours spent thinking while lying in a hospital bed, not even I bought the idea that our meeting might have remained innocent. I wasn't at all certain now that my resolution to have 'just the one drink' wouldn't have melted instantaneously in the company of that face, those lips and that body. Add into the mix a handful of those 'Oh, you're so talented,'-type comments she'd doled out over coffee on the day I met her and I strongly suspect I'd have had trouble recalling my own name, let alone the fact that I was a married man.

So where did that leave me now? On the one hand I was a man who definitely, one hundred per cent hadn't cheated on his wife, which was clearly a good thing. On the other there had been a time when I had seriously considered it, which obviously wasn't quite so great. Would I have gone through with it had I not been mugged? As much as I had been drunk that night and as low in spirits as I'd felt, I wanted to believe that I still had a conscience but even if I had managed to stay strong that night who was to say I wouldn't have succumbed to temptation on some other occasion?

To complicate matters further, regardless of the fact that my separation and divorce from Penny had been nothing more than a dream, the sense of dread that it had left me with felt very real indeed. It was like a warning: go near Bella and this dream will come true. Not that I wanted it to for a second of course, because having lived through the worst year of my life, even in a dream, had left me a completely changed man. The hopelessness and insecurity I'd felt leading up to that night had vanished without trace. I wasn't the same person any more. I no more felt the need to prop up my ego with the attentions of someone like Bella than I did to get a tattoo or buy a motorcycle. I was cured. Or at least that was what I hoped.

If drug and gambling addicts could relapse after weeks of intensive therapy then surely I could too. How long would the power of the lessons I'd learned in my dream life last? And with Bella's internship not due to finish for another three months, I was terrified that a moment of weakness would lead me to make as big a mess of things in real life as I had in my dreams. If it wasn't going to happen again, I needed to do something daring, something drastic: I needed to come clean to Penny.

★   ★   ★

It was a little after four when Penny arrived to take me home. Despite my protests she refused

387

to let me help pack and so while I sat in the armchair next to the bed feeling completely impotent she emptied get-well cards, toiletries and spare clothes into the hold all she'd brought with her.

'Right, I think that's everything.' She set the bulging bag down on the bed and zipped it up. 'Are you ready to go?'

I looked at Penny and realised that this was my moment to talk things over with her. Apart from anything it would be virtually impossible to have a proper conversation with her when we were back home with the kids and somehow it seemed right that if I was going home — a home which in my dream world at least hadn't existed for over a year — we should start this new chapter of our lives together on a clean page. No secrets, no lies, just the truth.

'Actually, Pen, before we go is there any chance we can talk for a minute?'

'Of course,' she said, looking worried as she sat down on the bed. 'What is it?'

I stood up from the chair and sat next to her. 'I just need to tell you a few things.'

'About what?'

'About that night,' I replied. 'The night I got mugged.'

Penny nodded. Her whole body seemed to tense as though she were bracing herself for a blow. 'OK, go on.'

'It's hard to know where to begin,' I said, taking her hand in mine. 'I think the truth is for a while I'd felt like I was invisible to everyone around me. You were busy getting back into work, the kids missed you so much that they barely noticed me and as for work, well, it seemed like I'd become part of the furniture there. I just couldn't seem to shake the feeling that I didn't matter very much any more to anyone.'

'That's not true, Joe. Things have been crazy since I went back to work but we always knew it would be hard.'

'I know we did. I just never really understood quite how hard.'

Penny nodded. 'I think if I'm honest I knew something was wrong. I haven't felt like you've been yourself for the longest time but between work and the kids there hasn't been any time to talk to you about it. I should've been there for you.'

'It's not your fault,' I said. 'It's just life, isn't it? It gets busy with kids, with work, with a million and one things that constantly need our attention and before you know it everything else gets drowned out by the noise of family life. Anyway, this is going to sound weird but I was coping with everything until Fiona's death sort of tipped me over the edge. She was our age, Pen. She was our age and she thought she had her whole life ahead of her and it wasn't true. It felt like a warning: don't sleepwalk through the only life you're ever going to get.'

Penny withdrew her hand from mine and turned to face me. Her gaze seemed to be trying to penetrate my very soul. 'What is it that you've done, Joe?'

'I didn't *do* anything,' I replied. 'But that's not the point. The point is . . . ' I stopped and corrected myself. 'The point *was* that I nearly did.'

'With who?'

'An intern at work.'

'But nothing happened?'

'No,' I replied, 'but it — '

'Stop,' she said suddenly. 'I don't want to hear any more.' She closed her eyes and drew a long, deep breath. My whole future, our whole future, was riding on whatever came out of Penny's mouth next.

She opened her eyes and looked straight at me.

'Do you love me?' she asked.

'You're everything I've ever wanted,' I replied.

'And you swear that nothing happened.'

'I swear.'

'And you promise that whatever this problem is you'll let me help you get to the bottom of it?'

'I promise you, it's dealt with, it's done. It'll never happen again.'

'And what about this intern? Will she still be working with you?'

I nodded. 'It's difficult. It's sort of out of my hands.'

'But you don't have feelings for her any more?'

'I never did,' I replied.

There was a long silence.

'So what now?' I asked, fearful that the answer would mark the beginning of the end.

'I'm tired, and right now all I want to do is take my husband home and be with the kids who I haven't seen properly in days and forget that any of this ever happened.' She took my hand. 'Come on,' she said, 'let's go home.'

The kids had flung themselves at me before I'd even managed to get properly out of the car but as pleased as they were to see me I was infinitely more pleased to see them safe and happy. Every time I kissed or hugged them I was reminded of that day in my dream life where I'd told them I was moving out and the pain that had caused them. If they had been in the market for new toys, clothes or exotic school trips it would have been the perfect moment to make their requests but as it was all they wanted was a kiss and a cuddle followed by a promise that I would make them their favourite tea of eggs, beans and potato waffles.

'I'm so glad you're back, Daddy,' Jack told me that evening as I tucked him into bed after reading him stories. 'I felt sick yesterday because I missed you so much.'

Rosie was, in her own way, equally effusive. 'I don't like it when you're not here, Dad,' she said when I poked my head into her room to say goodnight. 'Nothing felt right without you.'

'I think that's a good thing,' I replied, kissing her on the forehead. 'It shows that we belong together.'

★ ★ ★

For the next few days I didn't do a great deal of anything at all. Penny insisted that I had to rest and so while she busied herself holding the fort I had no choice but to look on helplessly.

391

Eventually however even she had to agree with my GP that I had fully recovered and was ready to resume my normal duties.

'Are you sure you're going to be OK?' she asked anxiously as we stood on the doorstep on my first morning back at work.

'I'll be fine,' I replied. 'There's absolutely nothing to worry about.'

'I know,' said Penny. 'But to be on the safe side I'll carry on worrying just the same.'

★ ★ ★

As I waved my pass in front of the security barrier I was reminded of the fateful day when I'd first met Bella. I recalled all the tasks I'd had on my mind that morning as I'd squeezed into the lift heading for the sixteenth floor: interviews, meetings, last-minute preparations for the shoot, and how I had been completely oblivious to the existence of the woman who if my dream world was to be believed had the power to completely knock my world off its axis. Today, however, I had only one thought as I edged my way on to the lift: where was Bella and how would I deal with her when we finally came face to face?

She wasn't in the lift and it was all I could do to breathe as I anticipated the doors opening on the *Correspondent*'s floor. Would she be waiting for me? It seemed a crazy thought given that in the real world our relationship so far consisted of an extended coffee break and the exchange of a handful of admittedly flirty text messages. Our affair had never happened. I'd never broken her heart by avoiding her the day we'd slept together. I hadn't waited in the pouring rain months later to try and rekindle what we had between us and I hadn't turned down her advances a second time because I'd discovered that I was still in love with my wife. Everything I felt about her, our entire history together, was imagined, a fiction, and yet the remembrance of the dream was so vivid, it was hard to take comfort in this fact.

Thankfully she wasn't there when the lift doors opened. Neither did she appear at my desk as I fired up my computer and sorted through the mail. Or even when I went to the kitchen to make the first of many cups of coffee. In fact she completely failed to make an appearance during the entire day. It was as though she had gone, or worse still had never actually existed — which really worried me given my tenuous grip on reality of late — but then just as I was about to board the westbound Central Line train at Liverpool Street to take me home I heard someone call out my name and I turned to see Bella standing right in front of me looking undeniably real and as lovely as ever. Before I could say a word she had thrown her arms around my neck and had her body pressed up against mine.

'Joe,' she said, 'it's so good to have you back.'

40

'I've been at a press event at Media City all day with a couple of people from the arts desk,' she explained as, coffees in hand, we sat down at a table outside a café on the concourse of Liverpool Street station. 'I only got into Euston about half an hour ago and Marie, who I'm shadowing at the moment, told me it was OK to go home but of course I'd left a bunch of stuff that I need for tonight on my desk so here I am.' She laughed and tucked a stray strand of hair behind her ear which only served to make her look even more attractive than she already was. 'It's so good to see you. I've been boring everyone in the office to tears asking when you were coming back to work.'

Bella appeared genuinely concerned for my well-being and it seemed churlish in the extreme to be horrible to her on the basis that I'd dreamed we'd slept together after I'd been knocked unconscious. It had proved impossible to find a good reason to turn down her suggestion that she be allowed to buy me a quick coffee so that she could find out how I was. It was, after all, just coffee in one of the busiest stations in the entire world where any one of my colleagues could've walked by and seen me. Nothing was going to happen and while obviously there was still the whole issue of the texts we'd exchanged on the night of the mugging, I reasoned that as long

394

as we avoided that conversation — which I couldn't imagine coming up naturally anyway — everything would be fine.

'We were all so worried about you, Joe,' said Bella. 'And when I heard the news I couldn't help but blame myself.'

'How do you mean?'

'Well, it was only when people at work told me you'd been mugged for your phone that I realised you must have been responding to my texts at the time. I feel terrible. If I hadn't pestered you that night you wouldn't have had your phone out and the mugger might not have targeted you.'

'It doesn't matter,' I said quickly. 'There's no lasting damage and anyway, I'm pretty sure I texted a few other people too so no need to feel guilty.'

She seemed satisfied with my response and at my lead we continued talking for another quarter of an hour covering topics as diverse as plans for her career after the end of her internship right through to the future of print journalism. In fact I was happy to talk about anything so long as it had nothing at all to do with the night I was mugged.

Finally, feeling assured that I had acquitted myself of any accusation of impoliteness or indeed of deliberately putting myself in harm's way, I mumbled something about needing to get home and we both stood up to say our goodbyes.

She kissed me lightly on the cheek. 'I'm so glad I bumped into you, Joe, and I'm glad you're on the mend.'

'Thanks again for the coffee,' I replied, wishing

for all the world that she hadn't come so close to me. 'And I'll no doubt see you around the office sometime.'

'I'm sure you will,' she said, as I prepared to make my getaway. I turned to go but she called after me.

'Joe? A friend of mine's got an exhibition opening tomorrow night and I was just wondering if you'd like to go. It's nothing flash. In fact it's just in a bar in Shoreditch but it should be really good fun. Do you fancy it?'

'I can't,' I replied.

She smiled. 'Galleries not your thing?'

'It's not that,' I said. 'Look, Bella, I'm sorry if I gave you the wrong impression but you do know I'm married, don't you?'

'So?'

'So I can't be going to gallery openings with you.'

She smiled again. 'Well maybe we could grab a bite to eat after work one night instead.'

'It's not the venue that's the problem so much as being anywhere alone with you.'

Bella's face fell and her smile faded. 'I don't understand, why are you being like this?'

'Look, I'm not trying to upset you and I did really enjoy our conversation the other day but whatever this is,' I gestured to the space between us, 'I just can't do it.'

'But we've got unfinished business.' She reached out and took my hand. 'That night, the night you were attacked, I was hoping you were going to come over and meet me, don't you remember?'

'All too clearly.' I pulled my hand away from her.

'So now you're playing the innocent? I saw the way you were looking at me that day in the café. You wanted me like I wanted you. It's just the guilt talking but there's no need to feel guilty. We're both adults here. No one needs to get hurt. And anyway, it's like they say, you only live once.'

You. Only. Live. Once.

There it was again: the blank cheque to absolve us from all our responsibilities.

'You're absolutely right,' I said, looking her straight in the eye. 'You do only live once so you've got to get it right, and this, you and me, isn't right. I have the life I want, it's just taken me a while to realise that.'

Bella laughed. 'Have you any idea how many guys would jump at the chance to be with me? I could have any man I want.'

'No,' I replied. 'You can't.' And without another word I walked away.

★ ★ ★

As I emerged from Lewisham station an hour later and began my walk home I went over the events of the day in my head. Had I been too blunt with Bella? After all I was the one who was married, not her. But I'd had to make it clear that nothing was ever going to happen between us. She was undeniably beautiful but it was the attention she'd paid me I'd really been attracted to. When I'd felt invisible she alone had seen me, and that in turn had made me look at myself in a new light. But it was only ever going to end badly. Penny and the kids were my world, they were all I wanted, and thanks to everything I'd learned, all I needed too. I'd never been so grateful to be me, never been so thankful to come home.

The house was in darkness as I approached, which was odd as Penny and the kids should've been back a couple of hours before but then I wondered whether Penny had had some sort of emergency at work and I'd missed a call from her to collect the kids from the childminder. I checked my phone but there were no messages and so I let myself in and switched on the hallway light. I called out a hello but the house was deadly quiet. I felt a sense of panic rise up within me as I recalled how silent the house had been in the dream world the day the kids had gone missing. I dialled Penny's number but it went straight to voicemail. I headed to the kitchen hoping she might have left a note on the fridge door. As I reached for the kitchen light there was a peal of giggles followed by a roar of 'Surprise!' I flicked the switch and illuminated a room filled not only with balloons, banners and a table groaning with party food but all of my friends and family too.

'I know my memory isn't what it used to be but I'm pretty sure it's not my birthday . . . is it?'

Penny laughed, throwing her arms around me. 'It was all the kids' doing. This morning on the way to school I asked them what they wanted to do tonight and without any kind of prompting they both said that we should throw a party for you.'

'But why?'

'It's like Rosie explained to me this morning after giving me a detailed description of the cake we should buy for you: you shouldn't always have to wait for something big to happen to celebrate. Sometimes you want to throw a party just because you're happy. And we are Joe, aren't we?'

'Yes,' I replied as the kids came to join us in our embrace. 'I couldn't be any happier.'

★ ★ ★

It was late by the time the last of the revellers had gone and having sent the kids upstairs to get ready for bed we managed to get halfway through clearing up the kitchen before I suggested that we leave the rest until morning. Like me, Penny was shattered, and so thankfully she agreed without hesitation and we made our way upstairs.

Jack was fast asleep when we looked in on him. He was sprawled across the bed in his usual style with an arm and a leg poking out from underneath his Spiderman covers. Penny tucked both limbs out of the cold, kissed his head and whispered in his ear, 'Good night, my sweet boy.' I kissed him too and then we left the room careful to position the door just the way he liked it — not so open that monsters could come in and get him but not so closed that we couldn't hear him if he called out in the night.

399

It didn't feel right not to check in with Rosie too and sure enough she was also asleep with a book open on her chest and her hand still clutching the frog she'd owned since she was a baby. I took the book from her hands, tucked the frog under the duvet next to her and then we both kissed our girl goodnight.

'They're still so small,' whispered Penny as we stood in the darkness of the hallway.

'I know,' I murmured. 'They're tiny.'

Climbing into bed I leaned over to kiss a sleepy Penny goodnight when there was a familiar tapping on the bedroom door and silhouetted against the light from the hallway was Jack clutching his favourite teddy.

His voice was tired and fragile. 'I had a bad dream,' he said plaintively. 'Can I get in with you?'

Watching him in the doorway looking so small and thin it was impossible to reject him.

I hadn't finished pulling back the covers before Jack had wriggled into his rightful spot between me and Penny.

'This is the best place in the world to be,' he said, nestling in the crook of my arm, 'I don't ever want to be anywhere else.'

I hoped that Jack might drift off now that he was in our bed but it wasn't much of a surprise when it didn't happen. Instead for the next few minutes it was question after question of the 'Who's your favourite superhero?' and 'Daddy, why does the inside of my head feel itchy sometimes?' variety which only stopped when Rosie knocked at the door and asked to join us too. Once she'd spotted Jack however she didn't even bother to wait for Penny and me to reply. She simply squeezed herself in next to her brother and after a few minutes of bickering both children were soon fast asleep. A few minutes more and Penny was snoring gently too, leaving me lying awake in the darkness, grinning like an idiot. Between all that had happened and everything that I thought had happened I was exhausted and more than a little bewildered but I was home at last, where I belonged. Jack was right: this bed with my family in it really was the best place in the world to be.

One Year Later

'Rosie, you move left a bit . . . Jack, tuck your head in . . . Melody, you're fine where you are and Tom, just straighten your back, mate, so the whole thing doesn't collapse when we put Suzuki on top.'

I picked up a grinning Suzuki still wet from the sea, his wetsuit caked in sand, and placed him on top of the human pyramid Van had spent the past twenty minutes constructing.

A cheer went up from the assembled crowd of parents and partners: Paul and his fiancée were shouting words of encouragement; Van's new girlfriend was furiously snapping away at the scene with her camera phone; and Stewart was hovering around the back of the kids with me ready to steady any wobbling child. In front of this tiny gymnastic formation stood Penny, looking on through eyes half covered by her hands, laughing in spite of herself. A few seconds later, a sneeze from Jack and the whole thing fell apart. There were kids everywhere, but thankfully no tears or major injuries.

Penny came up behind me and put her arms around my waist. 'When you said you wanted to go on holiday with your divorced dad mates I thought you'd lost your mind but this has got to be the best fun I've had in ages!'

I grinned and kissed her hand. 'I always knew it would be.'

The guys and I had been friends for nearly a year now after Van called me out of the blue one day and asked if I wanted to join him and the other guys for a drink. It completely threw him when my reaction to his question was to laugh uncontrollably and agree to meet them without the merest hint of resistance but my biggest reaction came when he named the pub we were to meet in: the Red Lion on Wood Green High Street. I couldn't believe it. What were the chances of Van choosing the same pub as the one in my dream? The only thing I could think was that he must have mentioned it to me in passing on the day of the photoshoot before I was mugged. Spooky coincidences aside however, the guys and I got on like a house on fire that night in part because they were all so easy-going but mostly I suspect because I felt so well disposed towards them thanks to my dream memories. Over the next few months even though the real me had a lot less in common with them than the dream me, we became good friends. In fact it was I who suggested the holiday one wet April evening when we were in the pub celebrating Paul's engagement to his girlfriend, but funnily enough it was Stewart who made it all happen when he turned up at the pub the following week with a plan of where we should go and what we should do. And now we were here it felt odd because very little of it so far was how I remembered it being: Paul and Van both had new partners and Stewart's kids were here on holiday thanks to improving relations with his ex and, of course, I was here with Penny.

Desperate to get back into the sea the kids grabbed Penny by the arm. 'We want you to come in with us, Mum, you'll love it. The water's freezing but you get used to it after a while.'

'Can't wait,' said Penny, pulling a face over her shoulder as she was forcibly manoeuvred to the water's edge. 'If I'm not back in five minutes I'm counting on you to stage a rescue.'

Grinning as I watched them go, I thought to myself how wonderful it was to have Penny count on me for anything. When I remember how close I'd come to taking the wrong path and losing it all it still makes me shudder, especially when I think about Penny falling for Scott and the kids moving to Harrogate even though none of it really happened.

And boy was I grateful that dreams didn't come true. Especially when it came to applying to secondary schools for Rosie. Penny thought I'd lost the plot when I'd insisted that I had a 'gut feeling' Rosie wouldn't get into Watermill Lane, and started looking on RightMove for potential new homes near good schools in Sussex that we either couldn't afford or could at a pinch if we spent our whole lives commuting. On the day we heard the news that Rosie in fact been offered a place at Watermill Lane I could barely believe it and had to read the email three times before the news actually sank in. 'You have the worst 'gut feeling' in the world,' Penny had chided me that evening as we'd celebrated the news with the kids in Nando's.

And as for Penny and me we were better than ever. Yes, we were both still working long hours in the same jobs, and some weeks it felt like we hadn't had five minutes alone to catch up with each other, but despite it all I didn't doubt who we were or what we stood for and when we did get time together we made sure that it counted. And yes, we were still in the middle of our lives and in the middle of our relationship. But none of that mattered now because we were in this together, walking side by side along the same road towards a brighter future.

★ ★ ★

Later that afternoon, having grown tired of acrobatics, the whole group of us went for a stroll along the beach. While the kids walked ahead by the edge of the water we lagged behind talking about how odd it was that we were all friends.

'On paper you wouldn't think it would work,' said Van. 'You know with me being a rock legend and all and you guys being mere mortals.'

Paul laughed. 'As someone who has seen you play live I can only agree.'

'To give him his dues,' added Stewart, 'he does know how to party.'

'Funnily enough,' I said, joining the conversation. 'I've been meaning to take Penny to a Man Halen gig for the longest time.'

'We should make it a date,' said Penny. 'It's years since I've been to a gig. Probably at least twenty.' She nudged me playfully with her elbow.

'If you play your cards right I might even dig out my black woollen tights and eyeliner just for the occasion.'

I stopped and stared at Penny. 'What did you just say?'

She looked at me, concerned. 'I said I might even dig out my black woollen tights and eyeliner just for the occasion. Have I said something wrong? You're looking at me like it's a really big deal.'

How to tell her that it was? Her words were exactly the ones she'd said to me in the dream world when I'd invited her to see Van's band play.

I opened my mouth to speak but before I could say a word the kids started calling us and we went over to see what the commotion was all about.

'Look what someone's done,' said Rosie, pointing. She was standing in front of a huge heart drawn in the sand with an arrow running through it. In the centre it said, 'J.C. 4 P.C. forever.'

Rosie looked at me accusingly. 'J.C. and P.C., that's you and Mum: Joe Clarke and Penny Clarke. When did you do this?'

'I didn't do anything,' I replied. 'I've been with you guys all day.'

Rosie pulled a face. 'Mum, you're always telling me and Jack not to lie, tell Dad to tell the truth.'

'But I am telling you the truth,' I protested.

Penny laughed. 'I wouldn't say Dad's lying exactly, I think he's just pulling our legs, aren't you, Joe?'

409

'I'm not pulling anything. I'm telling you I didn't do that.'

'Well then, maybe it's just a coincidence.'

Rosie stared at me, hands on hips. 'But there's no one else around! Do you honestly think we believe that some random J.C. happened to stop here just before we arrived to draw a big heart in the sand to tell another random P.C. that he loved her? I don't think so!'

'So, what's the alternative?' I replied. 'That I sneaked away from you guys while you weren't looking, ran all the way up here, drew the heart and talked Van into making the suggestion that we should all go for a walk?'

'He's right,' said Van. 'The walk was my and Suzuki's idea, your dad didn't say a word.'

Rosie wasn't convinced. 'He did it,' she said. 'I don't know how, but he was definitely behind it.'

I was about make a joke about how kids love a good conspiracy theory but stopped suddenly as the unmistakable scent of Poison filled the air. I turned to my friends. 'Can you smell that?'

Van took a deep breath. 'You mean the sea air? You should smell the stuff back in New Zealand. It'd knock your socks off.'

'No,' I replied, 'the perfume. It's really intense, you can't miss it.'

Comically everyone, kids included, started sniffing but no one could smell a thing.

'Must be just you,' said Penny, patting my shoulder in a patronising fashion. 'You've not been right since the day you were mugged.'

I looked up and down the beach for any sign of Fiona but there was none; yet mad as it

410

seemed, I had a feeling that she'd been here, that she'd drawn the heart as her way of telling me that I was finally back on track.

'Maybe you're right,' I replied as I took Penny's hand, led her to the point of the heart and stared at the inscription again. 'But I don't think I've ever felt better than I do right now.'

We do hope that you have enjoyed reading this large print book.

Did you know that all of our titles are available for purchase?

We publish a wide range of high quality large print books including:
Romances, Mysteries, Classics
General Fiction
Non Fiction and Westerns

Special interest titles available in large print are:
The Little Oxford Dictionary
Music Book
Song Book
Hymn Book
Service Book

Also available from us courtesy of Oxford University Press:
Young Readers' Dictionary
(large print edition)
Young Readers' Thesaurus
(large print edition)

For further information or a free brochure, please contact us at:
Ulverscroft Large Print Books Ltd.,
The Green, Bradgate Road, Anstey,
Leicester, LE7 7FU, England.
Tel: (00 44) **0116 236 4325**
Fax: (00 44) **0116 234 0205**

THE IMPORTANCE OF BEING A BACHELOR

Mike Gayle

George and Joan Bachelor are the proud (albeit slightly disappointed) parents of three grown-up boys whose lives aren't quite what they had hoped for . . . Adam is addicted to TWKGs (The Wrong Kind of Girls); Luke bears the scars of a savage divorce; and 'baby' Russell's love life contains nothing but heartache. When, months shy of his fortieth wedding anniversary, George Bachelor announces he's leaving the family home to try his hand at the single life, everything is thrown into turmoil. Now as well as sorting out their own love lives, the boys have got to sort out their parents' too . . . or face losing the one thing they could always count on.

THE LIFE & SOUL OF THE PARTY

Mike Gayle

In a year of parties and celebrations, friends get together to have a good time . . . Meet Melissa and Paul: Five years after they split up he's still looking for love in all the wrong places while she wants the one thing she can't have: Paul. Meet Chris and Vicky: They're so in tune they brush their teeth in time with each other. So what is Chris doing risking it all for a meaningless affair? Meet Cooper and Laura: He wants to settle down, she wants to take a grown-up gap year — but can their relationship really survive a year apart?

WISH YOU WERE HERE

Mike Gayle

After ten years together, Charlie Mansell has been dumped by his live-in girlfriend Sarah. All he wants to do is wallow in misery, but mates Andy and Tom have a better idea: a week of sun, sea and souvlaki in Malia — party capital of the Greek islands. But Charlie and his mates aren't eighteen any more. Or even under thirty. And it shows. It isn't the cheap beer, the late nights or even the fast-food that's the problem. It's girls. And life. And most of all . . . each other.

BRAND NEW FRIEND

Mike Gayle

When Rob's girlfriend asks him to leave London and live with her in Manchester, it means leaving behind his best mate in the entire world. Believing that love conquers all and confident that he'll meet new mates, Rob takes the plunge. Six months in, and yet to find even a drinking buddy, Rob realises that making friends in your thirties is not easy, so his girlfriend places an ad in the classifieds. Three excruciatingly embarrassing 'bloke dates' later, he's on the verge of despair . . . until his luck changes. There's just one problem. Apart from knowing less than nothing about football and the vital statistics of supermodels, Rob's new friend has a huge flaw. She's a girl . . .